Other Books by MJ Duncan

Second Chances

Veritas

Spectrum

Atramentum

Symphony in Blue

Heist

one

Parker Ravenscroft glanced over her right shoulder before twisting the throttle on her motorcycle to cut between a scratched and dented cab and a gleaming black Town Car. She smirked at the sound of horns honking behind her as she zipped into the entrance of the parking garage for the ridiculously expensive Upper West Side apartment building where her client lived, and shook her head as she braked in front of the guard booth. The man who came out of the booth looked to be in his mid-forties, with a blossoming dad bod and a more than obvious appreciation for her motorcycle.

"Hey." She flipped up the blackout visor on her matte black helmet that was a perfect match to the paint job on her bike and nodded at the attendant as she fished her wallet from her leather jacket. She flashed him her identification. "Parker Ravenscroft, with Cabot and Carmichael. Wolfgang Zeller is expecting me."

"Oh. Yes." The man nodded, glancing at his clipboard and making a quick note as his attention already shifted back to her motorcycle. "Is that a 2014 Panigale 899?"

She smiled. He must really be a bike guy to be able to recognize the year and model like that. "Yup."

He whistled softly. "Man, that's a pretty bike."

"Thanks. I think so, too." When he continued to just stand there and ogle her motorcycle, she sighed and arched an expectant brow. "Can I get through now? I'm kind of in a hurry, here."

"Oh. Of course." He hurried into his booth and hit the button to drop the spikes in the cement floor and raise the barrier.

She gave him a little wink before she slapped her helmet's visor back down as she revved the engine of the racing bike to give him a bit of a show before she entered the garage. As it was near midday on a Friday, the majority of the assigned spaces were empty, and she steered the bike further down the ramp until she found an open guest spot on the lowest level near the elevator. She tugged off her gloves as she made her way toward the elevator, and had just finished adjusting the straps on her backpack when the Bluetooth speaker in her helmet pinged with an incoming call. Not wanting to look like a total idiot walking around with her helmet on, she tugged it off with her left hand as she retrieved her phone from her leather jacket's inner pocket with her right.

"Ravenscroft," she answered without bothering to glance at the screen to see who was calling.

"Dobrev," the person on the other end retorted.

She grinned as she pinned the phone between her ear and shoulder so she could press the elevator's call button without banging her helmet against the wall. She hadn't been expecting to hear from her brother until later that afternoon. "What's up, Ollie? You get down here early?"

"Nope. I'm still in Boston. Just got a call from Marquis' secretary. She's had a change of plans and won't be flying in until the morning, so she's pushed the meeting back until tomorrow."

Parker huffed an annoyed breath and ran a hand through her hair. "Awesome," she muttered as she watched the way the short pale blond and ice blue strands fluttered through her fingers in the reflection of the gleaming steel elevator doors. Standing a hair under six feet, with long, lean limbs kept in shape by a vigorous five a.m. yoga practice at a popular chain studio near her apartment, she knew she cut an imposing figure. She pursed her lips in frustration as she tugged at the collar of her pale gray button-down shirt that was a perfect match to her eyes. It was one thing to arrive at a client's house on a motorcycle, but it was quite another to walk into a seventy million dollar penthouse looking like she had. "I really hate how people like Marquis think that just because they have a fuckton of money that we have to kowtow to their every whim."

Oliver sighed. *"Do you want me to try to get back into contact with her and tell her thanks but no thanks?"*

The idea was tempting, but she shook her head, sending the longer strands of her hair down into her eyes before she brushed them aside. She'd talked him into declining several meetings like this over the last couple years just because her heart hadn't been in it, but after the last year he'd had, she knew he could really use the money this meeting could possibly bring in. And, her own feelings on the matter aside, she would always do whatever she could to make sure he was taken care of. No matter the cost. "No. It's fine. I know you were looking forward to meeting with her since it's been a while since we've taken a contract like this. We can do the meet tomorrow. I just already cleared my schedule for the night. You still coming down this afternoon?"

"I thought about it, but I've got this project I need to wrap up so I think I'm going to hang low tonight and try and knock it out. I'll hit the road bright and early tomorrow, though, so I'll be there well before we're supposed to meet her."

"We still doing it at Kickshaw?" she asked as she stepped into the elevator and hit the button for the lobby. If she'd had a key, she could have ridden this car all the way to the penthouse, but because she didn't she was forced to take the more pedestrian scenic route.

"Yeah. It seemed like a nice, pretty low-key neutral location. You still cool with that?"

"Not at all. You know how much I hate good food and quality espresso."

Oliver laughed, and she smiled at the sound. They had met in the system back in Seattle when they were in kindergarten, both cast-offs and outcasts, and had formed such a strong friendship that their caseworker had done her damnedest to keep them together as they bounced from foster to foster before finding their final home when they were fifteen. "Yeah, well, I'd love to chat, but I'm actually on my way to meet with a client now, so I'm gonna have to go. Shoot me a text when you hit the road so I have an idea of what time to expect you."

"Will do. See ya later, Parker."

"Bye, Ollie." She slipped her phone into the inner pocket of her leather jacket and pulled her identification credentials from her back pocket as the elevator stopped at the lobby. "Hey," she greeted the security guards sitting at the front desk who were looking far more alert than usual for a building like this. She figured their diligence most likely had something to do with the man and woman waiting at the elevators at the far end of the lobby, whose black suits and stiff posture screamed that they were feds.

"Name?" the shorter, heavier of the two guards whose nameplate read Sullivan asked.

"Ravenscroft." She leaned her elbows on the narrow, chest-height counter that framed their station as she showed him her driver's license so he could check her name on his list. "Here to see Wolfgang Zeller."

Sullivan gave her license only the most perfunctory glance before waving at her that he didn't need it anymore. "Mike called you up already." He tilted his head toward the suits she'd noticed when she stepped off the elevator from the garage. "FBI is headed up there, too."

"Yeah, I kinda figured they'd be showing up sooner or later," she told him with a wry grin. The reported disappearance of a Matisse was pretty much guaranteed to catch the eye of the FBI's Art Crimes Unit. She rapped her knuckles on the black granite counter she'd been leaning against and gave the guards a little wave. "Thanks, guys."

She shoved her free hand into the pocket of her coat as she ambled across the spotless marble lobby, letting her helmet swing lightly as she walked. A car arrived as she neared the bank of elevators, and she lifted her chin in greeting as she edged between the agents to take a spot against the rear wall. She could have very easily gone around them, and she childishly enjoyed the look of disbelief the two shared as she passed. Feds were so easy to mess with, sometimes. The man was shorter than her and looked to have a few years on his partner, with dark hair, blue eyes, and a chiseled jawline that even her gay ass could admit was quite attractive, but it was his partner that caught her attention.

Not because the woman was striking—though she certainly was with her fair complexion, luscious mahogany curls that tickled her upper back, dark blue eyes, and full, pink lips—but because Parker knew her, she just couldn't figure out from where. And, judging by the way the woman's brow wrinkled ever so slightly as she stared back at her, she figured she was not alone in her confusion.

"Where to?" The male agent asked as the doors slid shut.

"All the way up, please," she answered without taking her eyes off the woman, still trying to figure out where the hell she knew her from.

"Holy shit," the woman murmured, a wide, easy smile tugging at her lips as she shook her head. "Parker Ravenscroft?" she asked as the elevator began to rise at a clip.

That sweet, smooth alto was what finally connected the dots for her, and Parker grinned as she nodded. "Sheridan Sloan." *God, how in the world had I not realized it was her?* "Fancy seeing you here."

"Parker and I went to Brown together," Sheridan told her partner before turning her attention back to Parker. "You look great! What are you doing here?"

Parker shrugged. "Same thing as you two, I'm guessing. The Matisse?" When they nodded, she explained, "I'm a recovery investigator with Cabot and Carmichael."

"The insurance firm?" Sheridan's partner asked.

"That's the one," she confirmed with a nod, finally tearing her attention away from Sheridan. She fought back the urge to roll her eyes at the knowing little smirk that tugged at Sheridan's partner's lips, and held out her hand and introduced herself. "Hey. Parker Ravenscroft."

"Kelly Innes." He shook her hand. "So you went to school with this one, huh?"

"I did," Parker replied. "She was a year ahead of me in the program, but we had quite a few seminars together."

"Ah, I see," Kelly murmured, nodding. The elevator stopped at the penthouse, and he whistled softly as the doors slid open to reveal a palatial entryway with twelve foot ceilings and a clear line of sight to the windows on the far side of the unit that overlooked the park. "Damn. Now that's a view."

"Oh good, you've made it," Wolfgang Zeller greeted them as soon as they stepped off the elevator, wringing his hands anxiously. "This way, this way." He waved at them to follow him as he hurried toward the living room.

Parker set her helmet on the floor beside the sofa as she entered the large, square room. She had plenty of questions of her own regarding the missing painting, but she remained quiet as she made her way over to inspect the framed blank space on the wall above the fireplace, content for the time being to listen to Sheridan and her partner question Zeller.

"When did you notice the painting was missing?" Sheridan asked.

"When I returned home from a business trip to Buenos Aires earlier this morning. I called it in right away, of course."

"And how long were you in Buenos Aires?" Kelly asked.

"I flew out last Saturday afternoon. I have copies of my travel papers if you need them. Do you think you'll be able to recover my painting?" Zeller asked, his voice trembling.

"We will do everything we can, sir," Kelly promised in a gentle tone.

Parker hummed softly to herself. Recovering the painting was going to be beyond difficult, but she had a few contacts she could reach out to on the matter. Of course, there was no guarantee that they'd ever hear anything about it—something like this would undoubtedly be traded directly, with probably only one fence working to facilitate the sale between the thief and the person who wanted the painting.

She knew from reviewing her notes from her initial visit to inspect the painting after Zeller had come to the firm about insuring it that it had been wired to the penthouse's monitored alarm system, and she pulled a pair of gloves from her pocket to inspect the empty frame that had been holding one of her favorite paintings the last time she'd seen it. She leaned in closer to look in the three-quarter inch gap between the ornately carved mahogany frame and the wall—the exact depth of the wooden frame the painting had been stretched over—and sighed when she saw that the painting had been sliced from its frame.

"Great. Just great," she muttered.

Not that she could blame the thief, exactly. It was exactly what she would have done if she'd been trying to steal the Matisse since it was the only way to guarantee that no alarms would have been set off, but it meant that she was chasing someone who knew what they were doing. Which sucked because it was so much easier to recover stolen property from thieves who just grabbed something because the opportunity had been too good for them to pass up.

She ran a finger along the side of the narrow mounting frame and shook her head. The canvas had been sliced so precisely that nary a scrap of material was visible, and she immediately began running through her mental list of fences who would be willing to deal with such a valuable, high-profile painting. She pulled her gloves off and shoved them into her pocket. The police had already come through dusting for prints so they'd been completely unnecessary, but she was always careful to never leave her prints behind at any scene she visited.

Parker tuned back into the conversation happening behind her just as Innes said, "We'll need to look at the guards' manifest to see who entered the building this week."

"Duh," she muttered under her breath as Sheridan ambled over to where she stood.

Sheridan chuckled softly and pointed at the frame that was still mounted above the fireplace. "It was hooked to the security system?"

"Well, I mean, it *is* a Matisse," she pointed out with a smile as the vague memory an argument they'd gotten into back in school about the merits of modern art after a lecture by some European artist whose name she couldn't remember flashed across her mind. Sheridan had been a classicist, with little interest in anything newer than the late eighteenth century, whereas she'd always preferred more modern pieces. "He would've been a fool to not have it hardwired to his system."

"And the thief knew about it," Sheridan surmised thoughtfully.

"Apparently so." Parker turned her attention back to the empty frame. "Or, they at least knew enough to check before they tried to pull it off the wall. Our guy here was smart, too—he cut right along the frame. Stretch the canvas just right over a new one and you'd never know anything was different."

"Do you have a picture of the painting?" Kelly asked Zeller.

Parker rolled her eyes. "Seriously?"

"He's a white collar guy who just moved to art six months ago," Sheridan explained quietly, amusement sparkling in her eyes. "Give him a break."

"It's a fucking Matisse," Parker retorted in a low tone. "All he'd have to do is pull out his phone and Google 'Matisse 1938 *La Conversation*' and he'd find a million pictures of it."

"True," Sheridan agreed with a little laugh. "It had been authenticated, then?"

"Yeah. By FreemanArt. I've got copies of the paperwork back at the office. And I inspected it myself when he insured it with us. It's the real deal. It was incredible."

"That's right. You always did love Matisse, didn't you?" Sheridan murmured, a small smile curling her lips. She stiffened slightly when her partner joined them, and waved a hand at the wall. "Cut right out of the frame," she reported in a clipped tone.

"Of course it was," Kelly muttered. "Frame was wired, then?"

Parker nodded. "Yeah."

Kelly rubbed a hand over his jaw. "I've got Zeller putting together a list of everyone who's been inside the apartment for the last month or so, and he's calling down to the front desk to have them print out a copy of the visitor's manifest for us. The police are still running the few prints they found when they dusted the place this morning, but I doubt they're going to find anything useful. There's nothing else we can do here for now," he told Sheridan, "so we can head out whenever you're ready."

Sheridan nodded. "Okay." She turned toward Parker. "You'll let me know if you find anything?"

"Only if you do," Parker quipped, unable to keep from grinning at the way Sheridan arched a disbelieving brow in response. "Hey, I know you alphabet guys only care about catching the thief, but my main concern is retrieving the artwork."

Sheridan shook her head. "I care about the art, too."

"But your job is to catch the bad guys," Parker couldn't resist pointing out.

"True enough," Sheridan conceded with a shrug.

Kelly nudged Sheridan in the side and tilted his head toward the entryway. "I'll meet you at the elevator."

Sheridan nodded and then sighed as she turned back to Parker. "It was nice seeing you again."

"It was," Parker agreed, returning Sheridan's smile with a soft one of her own. They had been friends at Brown, but Sheridan had graduated and joined the Bureau at the end of her junior year and they'd fallen out of touch pretty much immediately. Time, distance, and the realities of life had compounded until Sheridan became little more than a fond memory of her collegiate career, but these few moments they'd had together reminded her just how much she'd enjoyed Sheridan Sloan's company. And since Oliver was staying in Boston until the morning, leaving her calendar for the evening opportunistically clear, she figured there'd be no harm in asking, "What are you doing tonight?"

"I…" Sheridan's brow furrowed adorably as she shook her head. "Nothing. Why?"

"I don't know." Parker shrugged. "I just thought it'd be fun go grab a drink or something and catch up."

Sheridan looked poised to refuse the invitation but, after a few beats, she smiled shyly and nodded. "I think I'd like that."

"Awesome." Parker pulled her wallet out of her jacket pocket and retrieved one of her business cards. "My cell's on there. I know you guys work unpredictable hours, so just give me a call when you're clocking out for the day and we'll figure out where to meet up."

Sheridan glanced at the card before she slipped it into her back pocket. "That sounds great." She smiled and nodded. "I guess I'll talk to you soon, then."

Parker grinned. "Looking forward to it."

"You leaving now?" Sheridan asked, half-turning toward the elevator.

"In a few." Parker shook her head. "I need to speak with my client real quick."

"All right. I'll talk to you later," Sheridan replied, dipping her chin in a quick nod before she turned away.

Parker shoved her hands into her pockets as she watched Sheridan leave. Once Sheridan disappeared from view, she took a deep breath as she turned her attention to Wolfgang Zeller, who was watching her from a few feet away, clearly unsure of what he should be doing. She was going to have to do her due diligence to make sure this reported theft wasn't a case of insurance fraud, but she was willing to bet that the claim was legitimate. In her experience, the guilty tried to hide their nerves behind either overdramatic displays of being distraught or an arrogant confidence that belied their belief that they'd never be caught—but from what she'd observed over the phone earlier and now in person, Wolfgang Zeller was a man who was genuinely upset that he'd been victimized. "Would you mind if I take some pictures?"

"No. Please. By all means." He waved at the spot where the painting had hung. "Do you think you'll be able to find it?"

She had the highest retrieval rate of any of her firm's investigators, but she knew better than to promise anything. Especially on a case like this. "I hope so," she hedged as she pulled her phone from her jacket. When she first started with Cabot and Carmichael, she'd carried a digital camera with her at all times, but the cameras on the new phones were so good that she didn't bother with the extra device anymore. Once she'd taken pictures of the room, paying special attention to the wall where the painting had hung and the sliced frame, she dropped her phone back into her pocket and shrugged her pack off her back. "I've just got some forms I need you to fill out and sign so we can officially begin investigating your claim, and then I'll be out of your hair."

"Yes, of course." Zeller nodded. "In here, or…"

"Wherever you'd prefer," she replied politely.

"Okay." He wandered over to the couch and dropped heavily onto it. He raked his hands through his hair and sighed. "I've never had anything like this happen to me before. What happens next?"

Parker lowered herself to the chair opposite Zeller and pulled out the claim forms she had prepared for the claim back at her office and a pen. "Pretty much what happens in any insurance claim, to be honest. These are the forms for your claim," she began as she slid the papers and a pen across the coffee table for him to look at. "The process will take longer than if you'd been in a car accident or something, of course, given the value of the claim. We at Cabot and Carmichael will first do everything in our power to either recover the painting or else determine that it is irrevocably lost before a reimbursement will be issued, but unless there are extreme circumstances that delay the process, the claim should not be open for more much than a year."

Zeller squeezed his eyes shut as he rubbed a hand over his face. "Okay." He sighed and picked up the pen. "Where do you need me to sign?"

"By the little tabs near the end of the packet." She motioned toward the yellow Post-it tabs that stuck out from the side of the papers. "But you'll want to read through this first to make sure everything is correct. I filled in the details from our phone conversation, but if anything is incorrect, it could be cause for denying the claim as a case of fraud. Which, as I'm sure you're aware—"

"Is a crime," Zeller finished for her, nodding as he began scanning the paperwork. "I appreciate your candor, Ms. Ravenscroft, but I can assure you it is entirely unnecessary in this case. Will you be working with the FBI on this matter?"

"As much as they'll allow me to, yes," she confirmed as she pulled another few pages from her pack. "Their priority is to catch the thief, whereas I couldn't care less about who stole the painting—I just want to get it back. Which is why I'm going to ask you to sign these disclosure forms, as well. The FBI is usually rather amenable to sharing information, but in the case that they aren't this time around, these basically say you allow the other agencies investigating the crime to share information with me. If they don't want to share, they honestly don't have to, but these sometimes help smooth the waters a bit."

Zeller nodded as he scribbled his name across the bottom of the last page of the claim forms before signing the disclosure forms without even looking at them. "I just want my painting back, Ms. Ravenscroft."

She smiled reassuringly and nodded. "I will do my absolute best to find it, sir, I can promise you that." She took the papers and her pen from him and slipped them back into her pack. "I'll be in touch, but please don't hesitate to contact me if you think of anything or just want to check on the progress of the investigation," she said as she zipped the bag shut and got to her feet.

"That sounds great." He offered her his hand. "Thank you so much for your help."

She gave his hand a firm shake. "Have a good day, Mister Zeller."

"You too, Miss Ravenscroft."

She shouldered her backpack before she retrieved her helmet from beside the couch. She wasn't at all surprised when Zeller walked her to the foyer, and she flashed him one last reassuring smile before she stepped into the waiting car.

TWO

"Mhmm," Sheridan hummed into her phone, nodding for good measure to try to convince her partner that she wasn't listening to a dial tone. He'd been a pain in her ass from the moment they had left Zeller's building four hours ago, and she was hoping against hope that if she delayed long enough, he'd give up and go find something useful to do. Instead of leaving, however, Kelly made a show of checking his watch as he leaned against the edge of her desk, clearly more than content to wait her out. She rolled her eyes and set the handset she'd been pretending to use back into its cradle. "What?"

"I can't believe you hung up on Diaz down in the Nineteenth like that." Kelly gave her a playfully horrified look. "That's the absolute worst way to get the LEOs to cooperate with our investigation, you know."

"Right? Guess we better write this one off and just call it a day, then," she retorted, picking up the mess of papers on her desk and tapping them into a uniform stack.

"At four o'clock in the afternoon?" He smirked. "Wow, you must be really excited for your date tonight."

"It's not a date," she insisted for the thirtieth time since they'd left Zeller's apartment. Though, to be fair, part of her had not stopped wondering why in the world she had accepted Parker's invitation from the moment she'd taken her card. They had been friends when they'd been in school, but they almost always had been with a group of some kind when they'd done something outside class or study-groups. Parker had been the golden child of the program from the moment she set foot on campus, brilliant and witty and unabashedly unique and beautiful and the person everyone strived to be noticed by. She, on the other hand, was plain and nerdy and had been far too focused on her studies to compete with such radiance, and she had always felt glaringly inadequate whenever they had spent time together.

"Of course not. Because you don't date," Kelly said, drawing her back to their conversation.

"Exactly."

"One day you'll have to tell me why that is," Kelly mused, though there was no judgment in his tone.

Sheridan lifted her right shoulder in a small shrug and hummed noncommittally. Being partners meant that they'd shared bits of themselves over the last few months, and she was beyond grateful that he never pushed her on the whole dating thing. The last thing she wanted was to drag up memories of coming home from a long day at the office two years ago to an irate girlfriend who was pissed that she had missed yet another dinner reservation because she'd been working a high profile theft from the Philadelphia Museum of Art. Claire hadn't held back that night, telling her that she worked too damn much and that she was a cold, heartless bitch for forgetting their two-year anniversary. Claire seemed to take great joy in telling her that she would end up alone with her precious case files because she was incapable of opening up to anyone, and that there was something about her that was broken and wrong because normal people don't throw themselves into their work to the point that they forget about everything else. That final, scathing remark had been punctuated with an angry sneer followed by the sound of her front door slamming hard enough to rattle the windows a few seconds later, and she'd managed to keep it together long enough to hear Claire's car leave. She'd spent the remainder of the night drinking tequila straight out of the bottle and staring at the engagement ring she'd picked up on her way home until the world blurred and spun and she'd passed out. She woke up on the couch the next morning with a crick in her neck and a splitting headache, and had put in for a transfer to anywhere that wasn't Philadelphia before lunch.

She sighed and shook her head, as if the motion could dispel the ghosts of memories she'd rather just forget. "It's just a drink with an old friend from college. Anyway, the responding officers had nothing for us. The only prints at the scene belonged to Zeller and his cleaning lady who's been working for him for over thirty years, and so far there's nothing popping out as suspicious on the building's guest list, so we've got nothing to go on there. Did you find out anything about a local fence waiting for the Matisse?"

"Nothing." He ran a hand through his hair and shrugged. "I put some feelers out and have Reynolds doing some poking around, but the streets are quiet right now on this one."

She nodded. If anyone could find a whisper of a clue on the streets, it was Lucy Reynolds, the division's Criminal Informant who was working undercover at an exclusive gallery on the Upper East Side.

"Sloan! Innes!" a deep voice boomed from the direction of the glass-walled offices behind them.

"Nothing good ever follows when he yells our names like that," Kelly muttered.

Sheridan looked up at their boss and nodded in agreement with Kelly's statement as she jumped to her feet. Miles Bartz was a living legend in the Bureau, an accounting wizard with such an eye for detail that his closure rate never dropped below eighty percent when he actively worked cases. He was a slight man—the top of his head barely reached her shoulder when they were standing side-by-side—and his once dark hair was now a distinguished blend of gray and white. His obvious age and lack of imposing stature did little to quell the fear of his subordinates whenever they were caught in his laser-like focus, however, and she was no exception. "Better go see what he wants."

"Think he's gonna tell us to just get out of here since it's almost the weekend?" Kelly asked dryly.

"I don't think so." She groaned and shook her head as she fell into step beside him as they made their way toward the short flight of stairs that led to the ranking agents' offices. "What's up, boss?" she asked when they cleared the top step.

Bartz tilted his head toward his office and they obediently filed through the door.

"Take a seat," Bartz said as he shut the door.

She glanced at Kelly as they sat down in the guest chairs opposite Bartz's desk, and bit the inside of her cheek to keep from grinning when he responded to her *what the hell?* look with an arched brow and a shrug.

"Any leads on the Zeller case?" Bartz asked as he rounded his desk to face them.

"Still running through the preliminaries," Sheridan answered. "So far, there's nothing suspicious in the building's guest log."

"I've got Reynolds making some discreet inquiries," Kelly added, "but all of our usual suspects who'd be used as a fence for something like this are quiet. Thief might be lying low before looking to move the piece."

"Or they've already got a buyer lined up," Sheridan added thoughtfully.

Bartz nodded tersely. "Keep me posted on that."

"Of course, sir," she replied, knowing that there had to be something else—some other reason he'd called them into his office like this. A status update on a case that was barely five-hours old certainly didn't warrant this kind of follow-up.

"Right, well, I know that you just got the Zeller case, but while you wait to hear back from those contacts, I need you two to head over to The Met and check out their Valentin de Boulogne exhibit. They've received an anonymous note alerting them to a potential robbery this weekend." Bartz shook of his head. "I know it's getting late on a

Friday, but I need you two to head over there and see what, if any, additional security measures they might be able to implement to ensure the protection of the exhibit."

"No thief is going to announce their plans like that," Kelly scoffed.

"You never know," Sheridan told him in a low tone. "There've been some incredibly ballsy heists in the past, and if somebody is that sure of themselves…" She let her voice trail off.

"Good point," Kelly conceded, rubbing a hand over the designer stubble that darkened his jawline.

Bartz looked at his watch and pursed his lips thoughtfully. "It's going to take you guys close to an hour to make your way uptown, so after you've inspected the exhibition's security, give me a call to let me know what you've found and we'll decide what to do from there. We're going to have to treat this tip as legitimate, which means we need to coordinate expanded security measures with the museum's staff and have a surveillance van on location to keep an eye on things."

Sheridan groaned. She hated the van. And now that she was faced with the prospect of spending the night in an unmarked van and having to cancel on Parker, she was forced to admit that she'd been rather looking forward to meeting her for drinks.

"Plans tonight, Sloan?" Bartz asked.

"No, sir," she answered quickly.

Bartz frowned and studied her carefully. "You're lying."

Sheridan had to force herself to not react. It was beyond creepy how well he could read her.

"Odds are," Bartz continued without missing a beat, "this'll turn out to be a wild goose chase, so there's no reason to ruin your evening. I trust your opinion on their security, but once the assessment is complete and the enhancements to their usual measures are agreed upon, I'll have Moran and Wood take the first shift in the van with Nathan."

"Sir, it's fine—" she started to argue.

"Nope." Bartz waved her off before she could finish. "Unless something comes up on the Zeller case, you two have the eight to four tomorrow. The active case with an actual missing painting is obviously your priority."

"Of course, sir," Kelly agreed with a grin.

"Right. Get out of here, then, and give me a call when you've sorted things out up there. I'll call Moran and Wood and give 'em the good news." He looked practically giddy at the idea.

"He sure seemed happy about sticking the two of them in the van," Kelly observed once they'd gathered their things and were waiting for the elevator. "What'd they ever do to get on his bad side?"

She chuckled. "Nobody knows for sure, but the rumor is that they missed a fleeing suspect on a stakeout a couple months before you transferred in because they were making out in the van. Hence the addition of Nathan to their team for the night."

"You're shitting me!" Kelly whispered.

"I'm not," she assured him with a grin. "Nobody but them and Bartz knows for sure if that rumor is true…but yeah. Assuming the gossip mill is actually right for a change, I'd bet that's why he looked so happy about sticking them in the van tonight. He got raked over the coals from the higher-ups in Washington over the whole thing. No matter what it was that made them miss that collar, though, neither of them got even a hint of a mark on their record for it; so they owe him big-time and won't be putting up much of a fight about the unplanned overtime."

"Goddamn," Kelly murmured, glancing over his shoulder at the women in question. Ivy Moran was leaning against the edge of Rachel Wood's desk that was across the main aisle in the bullpen from her own, her long, long legs stretched out in front of her as she smiled fondly at the redheaded agent. "I didn't even know he realized that they were together…"

Sheridan shook her head. "They hide it well at work. It's probably the only reason they're still partners, honestly. We're not necessarily a high-risk division, but the Bureau doesn't like to flirt with even the idea of romantic loyalties conflicting with the job."

Kelly shrugged, conceding her point. "Why'd Bartz cover for them?"

"Because they are both incredibly good at what they do, and he's a good man," she said as she watched Bartz saunter out of his office and dimly heard him bellow the names of the women in question. She chuckled at the way their heads snapped up in perfect unison to look at Bartz, who was standing on the raised walkway in front of his office and crooking two fingers at them in a come-hither motion, and smiled sympathetically at the way they jumped to their feet.

The elevator doors opened, and Kelly held his hand over the edge of the door for her to go first. "Do you need to let Parker know that you're going to be late tonight?" he asked as he pressed the button for the ground floor.

She pursed her lips and shook her head. "She just told me to call her whenever I got off work tonight, so I don't think it's necessary. If it looks like we'll be super-late I will, but otherwise she seemed to understand that this isn't a nine-to-five kind of job." She shot him a curious look. "Why do you care so much about this?"

He shrugged. "You pretty much never go out after work unless me and Ivy drag you along kicking and screaming, so for you to just run into her after how many years and agree to meet for drinks the same night, it just…" His voice trailed off, and he sighed. "I don't know. Seems like a good thing, I guess?"

She tilted her head and crossed her arms over her chest.

"You like her?" Kelly asked.

"Everybody likes Parker. She's so"—she waved a hand aimlessly in the air—"the opposite of me."

His lips quirked in that half-disbelieving, half-pitying smile he got whenever she made any kind of reference to her social shortcomings, and he shook his head as he rocked sideways to bump her with his arm. "I like you."

She smiled. "I like you too, Innes. Though god knows why, sometimes."

He laughed and, showing why she did like him so much, took the hint her half-assed joke implied and obligingly changed the subject. "So, who's Valentin de Boulogne?"

"How did you end up in Art Crimes again?" she teased with an exaggerated sigh. "He was a follower of Caravaggio."

"Hey! I recognize that name," Kelly pointed out with a grin. "That's good, right?"

"Ten points to Hufflepuff." She chuckled and moved away from the playful elbow he aimed at her. "After Caravaggio died, de Boulogne emerged as pretty much the greatest original realist painter. He passed away when he was only forty-one, so there isn't a huge catalogue of his work out there, which makes it very rare—"

"And very valuable," Kelly interrupted with a nod. "Got it. Do you honestly think we'll be able to suggest any security measures the museum hasn't already taken?"

"Who knows?" She sighed. "Guess we'll find out soon enough, though."

three

The light pouring through the wall of windows at Parker's back and the skylights of her rooftop apartment was cast in hues of red and orange as the sun neared the western horizon, but she paid the view no mind as she frowned at the pages spread across her kitchen table. She combed her hands through her hair as she leaned back in her chair, hoping the shift in perspective would offer some clue as to where the stolen Matisse might end up. None of her usual contacts had anything to offer by way of help, and she couldn't help but wonder if the painting had already left the country. She sighed and shook her head as she scratched out a note on a pink Post-it to reach out to her European contacts Monday morning. There were a handful of collectors on the Continent that she knew weren't above utilizing less-than-legal means if it meant they could acquire a coveted piece.

She looked up at the sound of her washer dinging to announce the end of its cycle, and drained what was left of the water in her glass as she pushed herself to her feet to switch the clothes to the dryer. Normally she'd still be at the office, but since she had cleared her calendar for hers and Oliver's meeting that'd been moved to the next day, she'd decided to take advantage of the break in her schedule to get some of her usual weekend chores done early so she could enjoy her brother's visit without worrying about groceries or laundry or any other grown-up type shit.

She had just returned to the kitchen when her phone blared to life with an incoming call from a blocked number. Her hand hovered over the phone for a few beats because she never took calls from unidentified sources, but she finally answered because she had yet to hear from Sheridan and was hoping that it was her old college friend on the other end of the line. "Hello?"

"Hey, Parker. It's Sheridan Sloan. Am I calling too late?"

Parker smiled and, even though she was alone in her apartment, shook her head. "Not at all. How's it going?"

"Good. Or, well, as good as could be expected, I guess." Sheridan groaned. *"Would you still like to meet up tonight, or is it too late?"*

"It's only seven," Parker pointed out with a little laugh. "So no, it's not even close to being too late. I'm at home, but I can meet you anywhere. Are you at your office?"

"Nowhere even remotely near there, I'm afraid. I'm just wrapping up what was supposed to be a quick meeting at The Met. I have no idea where you live, but is there somewhere between here and your place that would be convenient for you?"

"I'm just on the other side of the park, actually," Parker shared, already running through a mental list of places near the museum where they'd be able to get a table on a Friday night without a reservation. "Why don't I come to you, and we can figure out where we're going to go then?"

"Oh, I couldn't possibly ask you to—" Sheridan started to argue.

"You're not asking, I'm offering." Parker began collecting the pages of the file she'd been working on and slipped them back into their manila folder. "I'm walking out the door now. I'll be there in thirty minutes, tops."

Sheridan chuckled softly, and Parker could just imagine the way she was no doubt shaking her head as she murmured, *"Thirty minutes? On a Friday night? Good luck with that. If I'm not outside, come on in and have the front desk page me."*

"Will do."

"See you soon," Sheridan murmured before hanging up.

Parker grinned as she slipped the phone into her back pocket, and licked her lips as she made her way across the studio apartment to the large, four-by-six foot mirror that was leaning against the wall beside her bed. She ran her hands through her hair before unbuttoning her slacks and tucking her shirt back in, and arched a brow and nodded to herself as she surveyed her reflection. "That's as good as we're gonna get," she decided as she turned to gather her favorite leather jacket from the back of the sofa where she'd left it when she'd gotten home.

She didn't bother locking her door as she pulled it shut behind her before bounding down the stairs, and she smiled at Gregory Ellis when she reached the main floor of the house. She'd been leasing the top floor of his mansion for the last six years at a rate that was criminally below the average price-per-square-foot for the island. He was a kind man with no family to speak of, and it hadn't taken them long to form a bond. He'd quickly become the grandfather she'd never had as a child, and as soon as he met Oliver, he'd taken him under his wing as well. It was something that was impossible to describe to anyone who had no familial ties in the world, but they were all living proof that the blood of the covenant was absolutely thicker than the water of the womb. Both she and Oliver would do anything for Gregory, and she had no doubt that he'd do the same for either of them should they ever need the assistance.

Gregory was sitting in his favorite Queen Anne chair beside the fireplace in the library with a thick book on his lap and his reading glasses perched perilously close to the tip of his nose. His shaved head shone in the lamplight, and he was wearing his usual 501s with a light blue and white striped long sleeve rugby jersey that she knew was older than she was—she'd spent an entire evening not long after she'd moved in being regaled by his stories of his playing days when he was studying at Cambridge in the seventies. A brilliant lawyer with a razor-sharp mind, he'd joined the bench after a brief but highly profitable private career, and he'd stepped away from his judgeship about fifteen years ago to teach at NYU. She'd heard on more than one occasion from random acquaintances that even though he only taught one or two seminars a semester these days, his were always the first classes to be waitlisted at the prestigious law school.

"Well, don't you look excited. Hot date?" Gregory teased as he folded the cover of his book over his right thumb so he wouldn't lose his place.

"I'm afraid not," Parker chuckled. "I ran into an old college friend at work today, and we're going out for a drink to catch up."

"Ah, well, that's always nice too." Gregory smiled. "Have fun."

"I'm sure I will," she assured him. "Oh, hey, before I forget, Ollie's coming down tomorrow for a meeting, but if you've got anything that needs fixing, just leave us a list and I'll make sure we get to it all."

"You two don't need to spend your time together putzing around this old house fixing stuff."

She shook her head. She'd started out doing little things around the house to try to compensate for the ridiculously low rent he charged her, but now she did it just because she liked taking care of him. "Leave us a list, or we'll go hunting for projects ourselves," she warned with a playful smirk.

Gregory guffawed and shook his head. The last time he'd refused to leave them a honey-do list they'd decided to upgrade the home's security system, and it'd taken him a month to figure out how it worked. "Point taken. I'm sure I'll be able to come up with a few things for you guys." He frowned thoughtfully. "The garbage disposal's been sounding off lately—is that something you would know how to fix?"

"I'm sure we'll be able to figure it out. Leave us a list of anything else that you can think of, and we'll do our best to knock through it all tomorrow afternoon."

"Sounds good," Gregory replied kindly. "Thank you, kiddo."

"Of course. Goodnight, Gregory." She smiled and tipped her head in a small bow before she made her way to the marbled foyer and the massive, double front doors that opened onto Riverside Drive.

She glanced only briefly at the handful of joggers on the trails of the park across the street before she turned and hurried down 107th toward Broadway to catch a cab. While she'd prefer to ride her bike over, there was no way in hell she wanted to deal with trying to find a place to park it, and the subway would take too long to jockey down and around the south side of the park to catch the green line up to the museum. Broadway was a predictable disaster of bumper-to-bumper traffic, but she had no problem hailing a cab the moment she stepped up to the curb with her hand in the air, and she checked her watch as she slid into the backseat. "The Met, please."

The driver nodded and zipped away from the curb into a gap in traffic that should have been too small to accommodate the yellow car. He was, somewhat unusually, not the talkative type—although that was probably because of the baseball game that he was listening to on the radio—and she spent the entire ride playing a word game on her phone. She handed him enough cash for the far plus a tip when they pulled to a stop outside the museum, and murmured her thanks as slipped out of the back seat.

The Beaux-Arts facade of the iconic museum was lit perfectly to highlight each arch and column and ornate scrollwork that adorned the roofline, and despite having spent many an afternoon wandering the museum, she still felt a distinctive sense of awe as she jogged up the front steps. There were a few people milling about the grand, domed entry hall, taking advantage of what remained of the museum's later weekend hours, but she didn't see Sheridan amongst them, so she made her way to the front desk.

"May I help you?" a young brunette in a pale blue cardigan greeted her.

"Yeah. Hi. I'm supposed to meet Sheridan Sloan here. Could you page her for me, please?"

"We don't usually—"

"Sloan's with the FBI," the girl's colleague—a bookish-looking man who appeared to be in his mid-forties—interrupted. "I can call up there for you. What's your name, please?"

"Parker."

"Just a moment." He picked up his phone and, after punching a quick extension, murmured, "I have a woman named Parker at the front desk looking for Agent Sloan." He hummed and nodded. "Excellent. I'll let her know." He looked up at her and reported, "They're just finishing up in the smaller exhibition gallery if you'd like to go up to the second floor, or else she said she'd be down in five minutes or so."

Parker nodded. She knew exactly which room he was talking about, and since she hadn't had a chance to check out the latest exhibit, she decided she may as well take a look at it since she didn't know when she might be at the museum next. "I think I'll go on up and see if I can find her."

"Do you need a map?" the man asked helpfully.

"Not necessary," she assured him as she tapped a finger to her temple. "But thank you."

She shoved her hands into her pockets as she made her way toward the grand staircase that led to the second floor. While she could have easily spent hours on end perusing the modern European gallery, she glanced only briefly through the doorways along the main hall that led to her favorite pieces. Her reticence to linger was partly because she was looking forward to seeing Sheridan again, but also because she was intrigued as to what had called the Bureau to the museum in the first place.

She slowed her pace and waved in greeting when Sheridan's eyes found hers. Sheridan was in huddled conversation with her partner, a handful of overweight men in black uniforms that identified them as museum security, a trio of other suits who were clearly Feds, and the museum's director. She watched as Sheridan murmured something as she shook the director's hand before turning to her partner, and Parker chuckled softly as she watched Sheridan roll her eyes at whatever he said before she broke away from the group.

"I can totally kill some time here if you have more work to do," Parker offered when Sheridan was still a few feet away.

Sheridan shook her head. "No, it's fine. We've done all that we can here, I think."

"Can I ask what's going on?"

"You can."

Parker grinned. "Would you answer?"

Sheridan huffed a little laugh and shrugged. "We got an anonymous tip that someone might hit the de Boulogne exhibit, so we're—"

"Fortifying security measures," Parker finished for her with a nod. "I see." She looked around the corridor, her eyes drifting to the numerous security cameras placed around the ceiling and pursed her lips thoughtfully.

"What?" Sheridan asked interestedly.

"Nothing." She shook her head. The last thing she wanted to do was butt-in on their investigation. "Never mind."

"No. Really. If you have any ideas..."

Parker stared at Sheridan for a moment to make sure she was serious, and then shrugged. "May I?" She motioned toward the gallery. When Sheridan nodded and waved for her to go on, she made her way slowly into de Boulogne special exhibit. She didn't stop to actually count, but the walls of the square room looked to hold every one of the painter's forty known pieces, and the center of the gallery was anchored with a quartet of large marble benches pushed together to form a square-shaped seating area.

The museum made no effort to disguise the eight security cameras mounted overhead—overkill, in this case, given that the exhibit contained only paintings and the center of the gallery was wide open, without anything to create a potential blind spot—and she worried her lower lip between her teeth thoughtfully as she spun in a slow circle, taking in as much detail as she could. There was only one entrance to the gallery, which made it a fool's errand to try to rob it, but there was a monitored emergency exit tucked into the southwest corner of the far wall that, she figured, might be useful if one were able to override the museum's security system.

"So?" Sheridan prompted.

Parker shrugged. "If I were going to try to steal something from a second-floor gallery monitored by not just alarms but also a network of cameras, I'd first hack into the security network. Disarm the system, put all the cameras on a loop, that kind of stuff."

"We have our guys looking into that now," Sheridan said with a smile.

"Of course you do."

Sheridan smiled as she crossed her arms over her chest and shifted her weight onto her right leg. "What else would you do?"

"Honestly?" Parker huffed a breath, rather enjoying the mental exercise this problem provided. "I wouldn't try to hit the fucking Met of all places." She grinned when Sheridan chuckled softly in response. "But, if I *were* crazy enough to try, I guess the easiest approach would be to get myself a spot with the cleaning crew and hit the exhibit in the middle of the night when foot security is at a minimum."

"Exit strategy?" Sheridan prompted.

"If cameras are off and the alarms are silent? I'd probably just walk out the back door with it." Parker flashed a wry grin as she waved at the emergency exit. "How'd I do?"

"You would've been caught by the cameras. We've made sure that angle of your plan is adequately covered."

"What if I have a really good hacker on my team?" Parker countered, unwilling to admit defeat just yet.

"You wouldn't have anyone better than us," Sheridan replied smugly.

Parker just lifted her right shoulder in a small shrug. Sheridan was wrong, she knew somebody who could outmaneuver the FBI's Cyber

Division in his sleep, but that was something she wasn't at all interested in cluing the agency into. "Well, I guess we'd better be glad that the only thing I'm looking to take out of here tonight is you." She smiled at the way Sheridan's eyes flicked toward the floor, rather liking the light blush that spread over her cheeks.

She never had been able to resist flirting with a beautiful woman, and there was not a world in any universe where Sheridan Sloan wouldn't be considered drop dead gorgeous.

When Sheridan's eyes remained on the floor after more than a couple beats, she opened her mouth to apologize for making her uncomfortable, but the words died on her tongue when warm blue eyes lifted to land on her own. Parker stared as Sheridan caught her lower lip between her teeth for the briefest of moments, insecurity flickering briefly across her face before she shook her head and let the lip slip free.

Sheridan swallowed thickly and hiked her right shoulder in a small, lopsided shrug. "So, should we get going?"

"Absolutely," Parker agreed in a gentle tone, wary of spooking her again. "I'm guessing you haven't had dinner yet..."

"Not yet, no."

Parker nodded as she ran through the nearby options and settled on the one place she knew they'd be able to get a table without any problems. "I've got just the place, then." She tilted her head toward the exit. "You trust me?"

"For this, sure," Sheridan teased with a smile as they started making their way back toward the stairs. She bumped her with her elbow and added, "For everything else, we'll have to play it by ear."

Parker laughed. "Fair enough, I guess."

Sheridan chuckled softly and jammed her hands into the pockets of her blazer. "So, any leads on the Matisse?"

"Not yet." Parker sighed and shook her head. "How about you guys?"

"We've reached out to our usual contacts and have a C.I. looking into it as well, but so far we've got exactly nothing."

"Reynolds?"

Sheridan arched a surprised brow. "How do you know about Reynolds?"

"We dated, once upon a time, actually." Parker shrugged and smiled. That wasn't the whole truth, of course, but it was all she was willing to divulge. They'd lost touch over the years, but being in the business she was in, she'd heard about Lucy getting paroled early to work as a confidential informant for the FBI.

"You…" Sheridan gaped. "Oh." She shook her head. "Sorry. I didn't know."

"Why would you?" Parker waved her off. That whole mess of a relationship had happened long after Sheridan had left Brown, so there was no reason for her to have any knowledge of it. "It was a quick thing maybe…um, five years ago. We split like two months before she got busted hitting that jewelry store on Fifth."

"Wow. So did you have any idea that she was a thief?"

"I had a feeling there was something going on there, yeah," Parker hedged as she pushed the front door open and waved for Sheridan to go ahead of her. "Anyway, how about you? Any felonious exes in your past?"

"No." Sheridan lips pressed into a tight smile as she shook her head. "No felons."

"Ah, well, I guess you win, then," Parker teased. "Did you drive here, by the way, or are you okay taking a cab?"

"Kelly drove, so I'm good with whatever you'd prefer."

"Cab it is, then." Parker stepped to the curb and lifted her right hand in the air. A yellow sedan pulled out of traffic and up to the curb in front of them almost immediately, and she chuckled softly as she opened the back door for Sheridan. She usually had terrible luck getting a cab, but she'd now hailed two right away without any trouble at all.

"What?"

"Nothing." Parker shook her head. "The gods are just on my side tonight for a change."

"I'm afraid to ask," Sheridan replied softly as she settled into the seat behind the driver.

"Good." Parker grinned. "Second and Seventy-Eighth, please."

The driver nodded and pulled away from the curb.

Parker looked back to Sheridan, who was looking out the window, her lower lip once again caught between her teeth and her hands clasped on her lap. She watched as she took a deep breath and held it for an extended moment before letting it go slowly, and frowned as she turned her eyes back to the road ahead of them, worried that she'd either done or said something to make Sheridan so obviously ill at ease.

The restaurant was less than a mile from the museum, and she glanced at Sheridan as she pulled some cash from her wallet and handed it to the driver. "Keep the change." Parker nodded her thanks as she opened her door and slipped from the car. She offered Sheridan a hand to help her to her feet and was heartened when Sheridan smiled shyly and reached for it.

"Thank you," Sheridan murmured as she took the offered hand to help steady herself as she stepped from the cab.

The feeling of Sheridan's hand wrapping lightly around her own sent a surprising flutter through her stomach, and Parker replied somewhat huskily, "My pleasure."

Sheridan's lips twitched as she let go of her hand, and she looked pointedly at the silver name emblazoned on the black awning that spanned the front of the restaurant. "Stillwater. I've never heard of it."

"Ah, well, you're in for a treat, then," Parker replied, glad that her voice had returned to its normal octave. She crossed the sidewalk to open the door, offering no further explanation for the restaurant as she ushered Sheridan inside. The interior of the restaurant looked like it belonged in a small, northern Italian village instead of the bustling streets of New York's Upper East Side, and she smiled at the look of surprised wonder that spread across Sheridan's face as she took in the rustic, homey atmosphere.

"This is incredible," Sheridan breathed, shaking her head as she looked back at Parker. "How in the world did you find this place?"

Parker shrugged. "I know someone who did some work for the owner's father a few years ago."

"Parker Ravenscroft," a low, familiar voice drawled.

Parker grinned and braced herself for the burly arms that pinned her arms to her sides a split-second later in a crushing hug. "Anthony. I wasn't expecting you to be here."

Anthony dropped her back to her feet with a hearty guffaw and a robust, "It's been ages since you've been by. I was beginning to think you forgot where we were."

"How could I ever forget about you with a greeting like that?" Parker replied as she ran a hand through her hair to smooth any errant strands back into place.

"Excellent point." Anthony tipped his head at Sheridan as he offered her his hand. "Anthony Romano."

Sheridan smiled. "Sheridan Sloan."

"Pleased to meet you." Anthony pressed a gallant kiss to the back of Sheridan's hand before, with a wink at her and a smirk at Parker, he let her hand fall.

Parker rolled her eyes. How could she have forgotten how much of a flirt he was? "So, you got a table for us?" she asked, hoping to speed things along.

"I don't know…" Anthony teased, even going so far as to tap a finger against his chin a few times before he grinned and grabbed a couple menus from the podium. "Sure. Why not?" He waved the menus over his shoulder as he turned and started weaving his way through the restaurant. "How's the best table in the house sound?"

Parker shook her head as she watched Anthony offer Sheridan a small bow as he pulled a chair out for her. "Seriously?" she muttered under her breath as she took the chair opposite Sheridan.

Anthony laughed and winked at her as he handed them their menus. "You ladies have a wonderful evening." He caught Parker's eye and added, "Tell our friend that I say hello."

"I will," she promised. "God, he's such a flirt," she muttered as Anthony walked away.

Sheridan chuckled and shook her head as she opened her menu. "So, what's good here?"

"I always go with the eggplant parmesan. I've also heard that the baked ziti is amazing—apparently the homemade sausage they use in it is incredible—and Anthony will talk your ear off about his chicken parmesan if you give him the chance. If none of that sounds good, I should warn you that I can only give personal suggestions on the vegetarian options."

"Oh, are you a vegetarian?"

"Yep." Parker nodded. "Since my senior year at Brown."

Sheridan hummed. "I've considered it since my metabolism seemed to hit a wall when I turned thirty last year, but I get crabby if I don't get enough protein."

"See, and for me it's carbs."

"Would you care if I ordered something that isn't vegetarian?"

"Not at all. Get whatever you want." Parker looked up as a woman dressed in black slacks, a black button-down, and a blood red tie stopped beside their table.

"Good evening, ladies. My name is Grace, and I'll be your server this evening. Before I ask you about your orders, Anthony sent this out for you, on the house," she said, holding the bottle so they could see the label.

Parker didn't recognize the vineyard, but the colorful grasshopper on the label was certainly eye-catching. "Looks wonderful."

"Excellent." Grace set the bottle on the table and pulled a corkscrew from her apron. She uncorked the bottle and poured a couple fingers of wine into Parker's glass.

Parker obediently picked up her glass and lifted it to her nose—noting hints of blackberry and licorice and the barest suggestion of vanilla—before taking a sip. The wine was outstanding, not that she'd have expected anything less since Anthony picked it out for them, and she nodded as she set her glass back onto the crisp white tablecloth. "Very nice."

Grace smiled and nodded as she promptly poured a generous amount into each of their glasses. When finished, she wiped the neck of the bottle with a small towel she'd had tucked beneath the tie of her apron. "Are you ready to order, or do you need a few more minutes?"

Parker looked to Sheridan, who frowned adorably as her eyes dropped back to her menu. "I think we need a little more time."

Grace nodded. "Of course. I'll check back with you ladies in a bit."

"I'm sorry," Sheridan apologized.

Parker scoffed and shook her head as she waved off the apology. "Why? Take all the time you need. I'm in no hurry."

Sheridan hummed and bobbed her head from side to side before sighing and snapping her menu shut. "I'll go with the ziti you said your friend likes," she decided as she reached for her wine. The flutter of Sheridan's eyelashes as she tilted her head back just far enough to take a sip was utterly hypnotic, and she smiled as she set her glass back onto the table. "Incredible."

"Yeah." Parker looked down at her own glass as she took a long, deep breath and held it for a moment before letting it go, reminding herself that this was just dinner with an old friend, and not a date. She swallowed thickly as she lifted her eyes back to Sheridan, and did her best to appear relaxed as she leaned back in her chair and asked, "So, Sheridan Sloan, besides becoming an FBI agent—what else has changed since I saw you last?"

Sheridan smiled a full, eye-crinkling smile, and shook her head. "Nothing much, honestly. Just work."

"Bullshit," Parker muttered.

Sheridan laughed. "I don't know what you want me to say. I honestly work pretty much all the time."

"Shame." The light blush that tinted Sheridan's cheeks was the most enchanting thing Parker had seen in a while, and she bit the inside of her cheek to keep from smiling too widely at the sight. "Okay, so you're a workaholic. Then what about that? What was your absolute coolest take-down?"

"Well, there was this one case where we ended up chasing the thief down to the Keys. It was close, but with the help of the Coast Guard we caught him just before he crossed into international waters."

"Sounds like a hell of a story. Do I get to hear the rest of it?"

Sheridan looked up at her through her eyelashes. "You really want to?"

"Of course."

Sheridan shook her head. "I don't want to bore you."

"You could never bore me, Sheridan." Parker paused, knowing that she shouldn't say anything too flirty, but also hating the flash of insecurity that dampened Sheridan's smile. It didn't take much mental gymnastics to figure out that someone she cared about had hurt her in the past by commenting on her dedication to her job, and if sharing even a little bit of what she thought about Sheridan helped put a sparkle back in those beautiful blue eyes, she was only too willing to oblige. "I thought you were the most interesting woman at Brown when we were in school, and I've seen nothing from you today that makes that any less true. So, come on. Tell me your story, Agent Sloan, and maybe I'll tell you one of mine."

FOUR

Sheridan was not a morning person. She knew this and accepted it and compensated by drinking unhealthy amounts of coffee, so when her cell began blaring Kelly's personalized tone—the *White Collar* television show theme song he had demanded she download for his contact information not even two weeks after they'd been made partners—barely five hours after she'd gotten home from her night out with Parker and fallen asleep, she swore loudly into her pillow as she reached blindly for the phone. She rolled onto her back as she swiped her thumb across the bottom of the screen, and squeezed her eyes shut against the sun that was just beginning to stream through the east-facing windows of her third-floor loft. "You better have a good goddamn reason for calling me before seven on a Saturday morning, Innes."

"Late night?" Kelly teased. *"You didn't forget that we're supposed to relieve Wood and Moran in the van at The Met in like an hour, did you?"* When Sheridan growled in response, he laughed and continued in a somewhat gentler tone, *"I'm kidding. We've been called into the office. Bartz got a call from one of his contacts at Teterboro. Evie Marquis' plane landed in Jersey at just after six this morning."*

"Holy shit. You're kidding me." Sheridan sat up slowly, instantly regretting the second bottle of wine that'd seemed like such a good idea seven hours before. She wasn't hung over, exactly, but she also didn't feel like she was at her best, either. She pressed her hand to her forehead as if to push what remained of what had been a pleasant wine-induced haze from her skull as she asked, "The Antiquarian is in New York?"

"Indeed she is. I'm on my way into the office now."

"Can you swing by and pick me up?"

"You at home?"

"Yeah." She frowned. "Where else would I be?"

Kelly chuckled suggestively and murmured, *"No idea."* And then, before she could respond to the insinuations so evident in his tone, he signed off with a quick, *"Be there in thirty."*

Sheridan swore softly under her breath as she tossed her phone onto the comforter piled at the foot of her bed, and sighed as she swung her legs free of the sheets. She scrubbed her hands over her face, and smiled in spite of herself at her partner's wake-up call as memories from the night before flitted through her mind. She'd had no idea what to expect when she'd left The Met with Parker the night before. Part of her had expected them to just go for a quick drink somewhere with passable appetizers that would hold her over until she could grab a proper meal, and she'd been pleasantly surprised when Parker took her to Stillwater instead. The food had been outstanding, but even better than that had been their conversation. Parker was just as witty and charming as she remembered, and she honestly could not recall an evening where she'd had so much fun sitting and talking with someone.

They had even made vague plans to meet up again soon—something she was quite looking forward to—but for now she needed to focus. Evie Marquis, the reclusive billionaire collector with a reputation for hiring the best and the brightest to procure that which she could not attain through legal channels, was wandering the streets of New York.

Sheridan showered and dressed at a sprint, and was just slipping her government-issued Glock into her shoulder holster when her phone buzzed with a text from Kelly telling her that he was in front of her building. She grabbed the blazer she'd worn the day before from the coat hooks beside the front door, and held her keys in her teeth as she slipped her arms into the soft, satin-lined sleeves.

After making sure both the deadbolts on her front door were locked, she hurried down the hall to the elevator. Kelly was idling at the curb when she walked out the front door of her building, and she smiled at the white paper coffee cup he offered her as she slipped inside. "Thank you."

"Peace offering for waking you up." Kelly chuckled as she grabbed the cup before she'd even closed the passenger door behind her. "So," he drawled as he pulled away from the curb, "how was your night?"

Sheridan rolled her eyes. "My evening was fine, thanks. How was yours?"

"Excellent. I ordered in a pizza and spent some quality time playing *Call of Duty*."

"How exciting," she drawled.

"Hey, we can't all have non-dates with hot women. Some of us have to make do with what we got."

"You're ridiculous," she laughed.

He smirked. "So you admit Parker's hot."

Sheridan tipped her head, not bothering to argue the point. Gay, straight, or anywhere in-between, a person would have to be blind to not see that Parker Ravenscroft was an incredibly beautiful woman, so there was no reason for her to even try to deny it. "Parker is very good-looking, yes."

"Where'd you go? What'd you do?" Kelly questioned her in a sing-song voice as he turned off Broadway and onto Worth.

She smiled and shook her head. She should've just walked the three blocks from her apartment to the office. "We ended up going to a little Italian place by the museum that she knew of. I honestly don't know what you're expecting here, Kel, but it was just dinner."

"But you had fun?" Kelly pressed as he turned into the underground parking garage beneath Federal Plaza.

There was an unmistakable brotherly edge to his tone that squashed whatever ire she might have directed his way at being pushed. She sighed as she nodded and confirmed softly, "I did."

He smiled. "Good."

She was grateful that he let things drop after that, and she sipped at her coffee as they circled through the underground garage looking for a parking spot. Her phone buzzed as they got on the elevator, and she frowned as she pulled it from her pocket, wondering who in the world would be texting her this early on a Saturday morning.

She couldn't keep from smiling when she saw that it was Parker. *Hey. Just wanted to let you know that I had a lot of fun last night and can't wait to do it again. Hope you have a good weekend.*

She turned her phone to hide the screen as she typed out a quick reply that basically echoed Parker's sentiments, and she rolled her eyes when she saw that Kelly was smirking at her. "What?" she demanded as she shoved the phone back into her pocket.

He shook his head. "Nothing."

"Damn right, nothing," she muttered.

He laughed, his amusement fading into a groan as the elevator doors opened to reveal utter chaos in the bullpen of the Art Crimes Unit. "Happy Saturday," he muttered as he waved at her to go first.

"Sloan! Innes!" Bartz hollered as soon as they stepped through the doors to the unit. He pointed at the conference room at the top of the stairs and, once they nodded their understanding, spun on his heel and marched purposefully into the room.

"On the bright side, maybe this'll get us out of van-duty," she murmured as they hurried past their colleagues to the stairs.

"I don't know. Staring at a museum might've been easier," he pointed out as they jogged up the stairs.

Bartz was standing at the head of the long conference table that anchored the room, his palms flat against the dark wood as he surveyed a dossier that was open in front of him. The remainder of their team—minus Moran, Wood, and Nathan, who were still in the van at The Met—sat at the far end of the table, wary of their boss' wrath. He had been chasing Evie Marquis for close to twenty years, and every time he'd gotten close, the scant evidence he had tying her to the crime of the moment disappeared. Warrants that'd been served had been laughably ineffective—never once had any agency found any hint of illegal property during a raid—and Marquis had threatened on more than one occasion to sue the Bureau, among other agencies, for harassment.

"Marquis, huh?" Sheridan lowered herself into the chair to Bartz's right, which put her back to the wall of windows that overlooked Broadway. She waited until Kelly dropped into the chair opposite her to ask, "Do you think she's here for the Matisse?"

"The timing is certainly suspicious," Bartz conceded, his brow furrowing with what she recognized as thoughtful frustration.

"I thought The Antiquarian was all about rare books?" Kelly asked as he picked up his copy of the dossier and began flipping through it.

"She usually is," Sheridan confirmed. Her phone buzzed in her pocket, and she reached into her pocket to silence the alert. Whatever it was would have to wait. "But she's suspected of having financed the heist of a Degas from a private residence in Boston two years ago, and has bid on a number of high-value pieces of art at various auctions. Books are her passion, but she's a collector at heart. If it's rare and valuable, she wants it. Do we know what items she's been interested in lately?"

"A little bit of everything from what I can tell," Brett Cornell, an agent who'd been working Art Crimes for not much longer than she had, answered. He tapped the tip of his pen on his open file and shook his head. "A few paintings, sculptures, stuff along those lines. Believe it or not, she hasn't been very active in the rare book market lately."

"Which makes you think she's here for the Matisse," Sheridan guessed, looking to Bartz for confirmation.

Bartz nodded in agreement and turned his attention to the group clustered around the far end of the table. "Are we any closer to figuring out where she went after she left the airport?"

Holly Chang, who was sitting to Cornell's right, answered, "No, sir. The plane taxied from the runway to a private hangar, and three SUVs left the hangar a few minutes later. We have no way of knowing which car she was in, so we're using traffic cams to track each vehicle. Two have made quick stops in different private parking garages, the third has been driving in what appear to be completely random paths through the city. There's no way for us to know who is in each of the cars, or if they got out at either of those stops. We're working on warrants now to access the security footage."

Bartz blew out a frustrated breath. "Oh, she was in one of those two cars that stopped, but she's in the wind, now. We're just going to have to keep eyes and ears out to hopefully get a clue of where she's headed." He pointed at Cornell's group. "Cornell, Hall, keep working on the warrants. Chang, Coffey, and Patel, keep an eye on what those SUVs are doing." He looked at Sheridan and Kelly. "Sloan, Innes, go talk to Reynolds again—see if she's got anything new for us that might help. I want to know if Marquis has any connection to our missing Matisse, or if we've got a whole different problem forming. I'll borrow a team from White Collar to man the van at The Met to give our team a break for now, and I'll decide how we're going to handle that one later today after we've looked more fully into Marquis."

"Yes, sir," Sheridan murmured, cocking her head at the door as she got to her feet. She tossed her empty coffee cup into the trash as they started for the stairs, and pursed her lips as she and Kelly made their way to the main floor of the bullpen. Cornell and their other colleagues were bouncing ideas off each other as they followed in their wake, and she rubbed a hand over the back of her neck as she pushed the large, solid glass door open with the other.

"What?" Kelly asked.

"I don't know," Sheridan admitted. Marquis being in town for the Matisse just didn't *feel* right, but she'd also been in the field long enough to know that a gut feeling wasn't enough to dismiss an angle of investigation. "I don't think Marquis is here for the painting, but maybe Reynolds will have heard something about what she is in town for."

"Not quite the lazy, bored out of our minds in the van Saturday you were thinking we'd have, huh?"

She groaned and nodded as the doors of the elevator they'd ridden up in opened to carry them back down to their car. "I need more coffee."

"Me too," Kelly agreed as he pushed the buttons for the main floor and the third level of the parking garage. "You go hit Starbucks and I'll swing by and pick you up."

She nudged him with her elbow. "And this is why we're such a good team."

He grinned and rocked onto his right leg to bump their shoulders together. When the elevator stopped at the main lobby, he said, "Make mine a double."

She snapped off a playful salute. "Coming right up."

The din of traffic was a white-noise soundtrack to her thoughts as she strode along the front of the FBI's building, hurrying to a quick jog as the light changed so she could cross with traffic. She jammed her hands into the pockets of her blazer as she hopped up onto the curb opposite the office, and when her fingers brushed against her phone, remembered that she'd missed a message while she'd been in the meeting. She scanned the sidewalk ahead as she pulled the phone from her pocket, and smiled when she saw Parker's name on her lock screen.

You doing anything tomorrow night?

The idea of spending the evening with Parker was a million-times more appealing than what she had on her calendar, but she knew better than to cancel on the Ambassador. *Unfortunately, yes. I've got a dinner appointment that I can't get out of. Rain check?*

Parker's response was immediate. *Of course. Tell whoever it is that they're damn lucky to have your company for the evening.*

She smiled. She had a feeling her mother was approaching their dinner with the same mindset as she was—as an obligation and nothing more—but it was nice to know that Parker thought so highly of her company. A guy in his early twenties held the door open for her as she neared the Starbucks on the corner of Worth and Lafayette, and she nodded her thanks as she stepped inside. The coffee shop was less crowded than it would have been during the week at this time, but there were still five people ahead of her when she took her spot at the back of the line.

She didn't mind the wait, however, because it gave her time to continue her conversation with Parker without Kelly teasing her for it. *Damn lucky, huh?*

Clearly, Parker's friendly banter from the night before had rubbed off on her, and she smiled wider when her phone buzzed with Parker's response.

Yes. I'm quite jealous, tbh. :) What are you up to today? Surveillance at The Met?

Sheridan chuckled softly and shuffled forward with the line. *No need to be jealous—I'm meeting my mother for dinner. It's going to be awful, but she leaves for London on Monday so I can't cancel on her.* She hit send and then continued. *And, I wish. Kel and I are heading over to meet with Lucy Reynolds about something. Depending on how that goes, we may or may not be able to avoid the van later*

A few minutes passed, and she was beginning to wonder if she'd said something wrong when Parker finally responded. *I'm sorry. Hope Luce has some information that can help you out, then. I'm actually heading off to a meeting of my own here in a few so, if it makes you feel better, you're not the only one wasting a beautiful Saturday working. You gonna be around this week?*

"Ma'am?"

Sheridan looked up and smiled apologetically. It was her turn to order, and she was holding up the line because she'd been staring at her phone. "Yes. I'm so sorry." She locked her phone and dropped it into her pocket, trading the device for the slim wallet she carried that had just enough room for her IDs and a few credit cards. "Can I get a large mocha with a double-shot of espresso, and a large caramel macchiato to-go, please."

"Name?"

"Sheridan."

The barista scribbled her name onto a couple paper cups and set them in line for the girls who were actually preparing the drinks.

Once she'd paid, she wandered to the far end of the coffee bar to wait. She perched on the edge of a barstool at a raised café table and pulled her phone back out of her pocket. A soft smile tugged at her lips as she re-read Parker's message, and she sighed as she replied, *Good to know it's not just me. I should be around, unless something comes up and I'm ordered elsewhere.*

She hit send and held her breath when her screen immediately showed a gray bubble with flashing ellipses.

I will talk to you later, then. Hope you have a good day... Go catch some bad-guys. ;)

She huffed a laugh and then looked up to make sure nobody was paying attention to her. Once she was assured that she was as invisible as ever, she replied, *I shall do my best. Hope you have a good day, too. Good luck with your meeting. Talk soon...*

"Sheridan!"

She lifted her free hand in the air to signal the barista that she'd heard them as she slipped off her stool, and dropped her phone back into her pocket so she could carry their drinks. A glance out the window showed Kelly parked at the curb, bobbing his head to whatever song was on the radio, and she sighed as she grabbed their cups and headed to the door.

She schooled her expression as she handed Kelly his drink through the open passenger window—she'd already endured his teasing about

Parker and had exactly zero desire to revisit that topic of conversation. "Did you get ahold of Lucy? Is she working this morning?"

He nodded. "Yeah. Gallery doesn't open until ten, but she's going to come in early to meet us. Said to wait by the back door if we get there before she does."

"Okay." She set her drink between her legs as she buckled her seatbelt and then held it on her knee as he pulled away from the curb. "Let's go see if we can't figure out what The Antiquarian is doing in New York."

five

It was normally beyond difficult to get a table at Kickshaw on a Saturday morning—the café had a killer menu, great coffee, and easily made the top-ten eateries list of anyone who'd ever been—but Parker and Oliver had arrived just late enough in the morning to take advantage of the semi-lull between breakfast and lunch, which meant that they'd had to wait less than twenty minutes before they were shown to a private table at the rear of the narrow restaurant.

"So, did you finish your project?" Parker asked as their server left them to their food that she'd just delivered.

Oliver nodded and raked a hand through his dirty blond hair that was a near-identical match to her natural color before she'd decided to take a walk on the colorful side. "Yeah. Sent everything over this morning before I left to come down here."

"That's good," she murmured through a yawn. She shook her head and blinked. "Sorry."

"Did you not get enough sleep last night?" he teased as he picked up the absolutely massive breakfast burrito he'd ordered.

"Apparently not." She took a slow, deep breath as she pulled her bowl of yogurt closer and picked up a spoon to mix it with the homemade granola piled on top of it.

"Did you actually go out last night?" Oliver's dark brown eyes twinkled with amusement as he took a bite of his burrito.

"I did." When he just arched a brow and motioned with his right hand for her to continue, she sighed and asked, "Do you remember Sheridan Sloan?"

It was a stupid question because Oliver remembered everything. It was how he'd been able to fly through his undergrad and grad work in five years without ever having to really study. So, had she not been preparing herself for the reaction she was sure she was about to receive, she would have laughed at the way his eyes widened as he hurried to swallow. "Sheridan oh-my-god-Ollie-she's-so-hot-I-think-I-might-be-gay Sloan? From Brown?"

She rolled her eyes, but didn't even try to deny that she had crushed hard on Sheridan back in the day. "Yeah."

He laughed. "That's nuts. When did you see her?"

"Not five minutes after I got off the phone with you yesterday morning, actually. She's with Art Crimes at the FBI now, and I ran into her in an elevator on the way to meet with a client who's missing a Matisse."

"Wait. What Matisse?"

"The 1938 *La Conversation*. Sliced right off its frame. You haven't heard anything about that, have you?"

"Nope. I can make some calls for you later if you want, though." He waggled his eyebrows suggestively as he shifted their conversation back to what he thought was much more intriguing. "So you went out with Sheridan Sloan last night?"

"It was just dinner. To catch up." She pointed her yogurt and granola coated spoon at him. "So don't even go there."

"Go where?" He countered playfully. "How late were you girls up last night?"

"Oh my god," she muttered.

"I don't know, Park, you're yawning like you barely slept a wink. I've heard those FBI agents have some crazy stamina..." His voice trailed off into an amused chuckle.

"Shut up. Sculpt was brutal this morning, okay?" Of course, hitting the class on only a few hours of sleep didn't make it any easier, either.

"I seriously don't know how you do that shit six days a week. I'd rather pull a double at CrossFit than do that again."

Parker smiled. Vinyasa yoga with the added difficulty of free weights and some cardio thrown in just to keep things interesting certainly wasn't for everybody, but she loved it. Oliver had gone with her exactly once, and she'd had to practically carry him back to her apartment afterward. "Tomorrow's my skip day, but there's a nine o'clock we could go to before you head home if you'd like," she teased.

"Fuck no." He grimaced. "Now, stop trying to distract me. I want to hear all about your date with Sheridan Sloan."

"One, it wasn't a date. And two, why do you keep calling her by her full name?"

He shrugged. "I don't know. It's just fun to say. Rolls off the tongue nice and smooth, you know? Though I'm sure you'd prefer to know how she rolls on your tongue..."

Parker laughed in spite of herself and shook her head. "Please shut up."

"Okay, fine," he chuckled. "I'm done teasing. Though I would like it noted that I did notice you didn't exactly deny that one."

She rolled her eyes and tipped her head to acknowledge the fact that he wasn't necessarily wrong. Sheridan was beautiful, smart, and as enchanting as she remembered, and just thinking about her now made her realize that she wasn't nearly as over her old crush as she'd thought she was.

"But for real, where did you guys go?" Oliver asked as he adjusted his grip on his burrito. "Is she still as gorgeous as you thought when she pretty much single-handedly heralded-in your big gay awakening?"

"Honestly, Ollie, she's even prettier. I'd forgotten how *blue* her eyes are, but they're so..." She sighed and shook her head. "Anyway, she was working late at The Met so I took her over to Stillwater. Anthony says hi, by the way."

Oliver almost choked on his food, and he dropped his burrito as he reached for his glass of water to take a healthy chug to help clear his throat. "You took Sheridan Sloan to meet Anthony Romano? Did you not learn anything from that time you took what's-her-name there for a first date and he totally seduced her away from you?"

"Can you please just call her Sheridan?" Parker muttered. "And, yeah. You would think that'd be kind of hard to forget, but I actually did right up until he started being all flirty with Sheridan. Now that he's married he's definitely toned it down, but yeah. Same old Anthony. Anyway, it was getting late when I met her at the museum and she was hungry and, let's be honest, Tony's place has the best food on that side of town."

He set his water back onto the table and began trying to figure out how to pick his burrito back up. "No wonder you haven't had a serious girlfriend since Lucy."

She shook her head. "Thanks for the support, bro. Love you too."

He laughed, and then sighed as his expression became more neutral and he tilted his head toward the front door. "Marquis just got here."

"Yeah. See that," she murmured. Even if she hadn't been keeping half an eye out for Marquis, the billionaire patron of the talented, less-than-honorable few who had the skills to help her acquire what she desired, there was no way she'd have missed the woman herself. Parker dragged her eyes over ridiculously sexy black heels, toned calves, and taught thighs that were hugged oh-so-deliciously by a beige pencil skirt that, she noticed, had a daring slit up the right side. Her white silk blouse with thin cranberry-colored stripes fluttered open at her neck, revealing the sharp line of her collarbones and drawing attention to the delicate line of her neck. Her full, pink lips were quirked in a challenging smirk, her dusty-blonde hair curled in gentle waves that bounced seductively with each step she took, and she arched a haughty brow as she wrapped her long fingers around the back of the chair opposite them.

"Mr. Dobrev and Ms. Ravenscroft?" Marquis greeted them as a man who could only be described as a polished thug in a black-on-black designer suit stopped two steps behind her.

Parker couldn't blame Marquis for being careful—even in her heels she was positively tiny, and Parker doubted she weighed much over a hundred pounds—but the sight of an ever so slight bulge beneath the man's coat for what she guessed was a concealed firearm made her nervous.

She hated guns.

Oliver nudged her foot with his, telling her that he saw it too as he flashed Marquis a polite smile and tipped his head in a small nod. He pushed himself to his feet and extended his hand. There was a reason they had a reputation as being among the last of the gentlemen thieves, after all. "It's an honor to meet you, Ms. Marquis."

Marquis' smirk widened at the overt flattery, and she made a small gesture with her left hand to her bodyguard as she shook Oliver's hand with her right.

The bodyguard nodded once in unspoken understanding and drifted back a few steps to take a seat at the very end of the bar. He flagged down a server and murmured something that had the boyish twenty-something nodding, before he angled his body in a way that allowed him to keep an eye on their table as well as anyone who might dare try to approach them.

Parker stood to greet their company properly as well. "Ms. Marquis."

"Ms. Ravenscroft," Marquis murmured, staring intently at her.

Parker held her breath and bit the inside of her cheek as she straightened beneath the heavy weight of Marquis' gaze. There was no mistaking the fact that she was being judged, and she wondered what would happen if Marquis found her to be lacking.

And then she saw it—the slightest quirk of at the corner of Marquis' lips, the faintest hint of a crinkle at the corner of her eye, and she let out the breath she'd been holding as Marquis' hand tightened briefly around her own before letting it drop.

Marquis pulled one of the chairs across from them out and regally took a seat. She motioned for them to do the same, adding, "Please, don't let me keep you from your breakfast."

Parker and Oliver shared a glance as they retook their seats. Before the reason for their meeting could be broached, however, the pretty male server Marquis' bodyguard had spoken to approached their table with a steaming cappuccino. He set the oversized cup and saucer onto the table and, with a curt nod, hurriedly backed away.

Marquis hummed appreciatively as she picked up the mug and leaned back in her chair, cradling the simple white porcelain cup between her hands. She tilted her head ever so slightly to right as she crossed her legs, her keen gaze appraising as she studied them over the rim of her mug. "Shall we dispense with formalities and get down to business?"

"Of course," Oliver agreed with an amenable smile.

Marquis sipped at her cappuccino. "There are some rare books that I would like to add to my collection that have been, shall we say, rather difficult to acquire as none of the owners seem at all inclined to part ways with them. After some discreet inquiries, it came to my attention that you were exactly the team I needed to assist me in this endeavor. You have quite the reputation," she added in a low, impressed tone.

"We do try our best," Oliver confirmed with a small nod.

Parker stirred absently at her yogurt, her appetite gone for the moment as she focused on the conversation at hand. "How many titles are you looking to acquire?"

"Six."

"We don't do museums," Oliver informed her.

"Yes, I was made well aware of that fact by the people who recommended you," Marquis assured him with a smile. "Each volume is privately held. And none of them are insured by Cabot and Carmichael," she added, looking at Parker.

"Very good," Parker murmured, not at all surprised that Marquis had done her due diligence in researching them. Hell, if Marquis lived up to even half of her reputation, she probably knew their blood types and college GPAs.

Marquis tilted her head and sipped at her coffee. There was obviously more to her offer, and she seemed to be enjoying the slow reveal. "However, the books are spread across New York, Seattle, Paris, and London."

Oliver made a small sound of interest that wasn't at all hard for Parker to decipher. Something on that kind of scale would have to pay incredibly well, and she was willing to bet that he was calculating how much he still owed on his medical bills from his car accident the year before that had left him hospitalized for two weeks with two broken legs. Because he'd been young, healthy, and self-employed, he'd opted for the bare minimum for insurance coverage so that he wouldn't get fined, and it came back to bite him in the ass when the couple-hundred thousand dollar bill came due. The therapy bills that dwarfed the one from the hospital only added to his debt, none of which was helped by the fact that he'd been unable to work due to his injuries and the effort it took to recover from it all. She'd offered to chip in to help settle the debts but he'd refused, which was pretty much why she'd agreed to let him take this meeting in the first place.

He wouldn't take her money, but he would accept her help.

Marquis smirked, clearly convinced that she already had them on the hook, and continued, "The finder's fee is one million per title, to be paid upon receipt on a book-by-book basis. If you agree to take the contract, I will not seek further assistance in this matter unless you become unable or unwilling to complete it. If you decide at any point that you're no longer interested in pursuing our agreement, we will part ways, no harm, no foul. I will, of course, expect your discretion in all aspects of this matter regardless of when we part ways."

Parker cleared her throat softly and asked, "Is there a timeline for this job?"

Marquis uncrossed her legs as she leaned forward to set her mug back onto its saucer, and shook her head as she sat back and re-crossed them, folding her hands over her stomach. "No timeline, per se, but I am willing to offer another million dollars as a bonus if all the books are delivered to me by the first of October."

Parker swallowed thickly and tried her best to not look completely gobsmacked by the idea of a seven million dollar payday. Even if they only got two books from Marquis' list, Oliver would be able to pay off the bills from his accident completely and still be able to bank a little something to rebuild the savings he'd wiped out covering his expenses while he'd been unable to work.

Although there had been a time when she'd absolutely gotten off on the thrill of the heist and had more than enjoyed the payoff, she got a similar thrill when she recovered an especially valuable piece of art and she really didn't want to go back to doing shit like this. But Oliver could hack any security system ever created, and with him watching her back, she had no doubt that she'd be able to get in and out with the desired items. It'd be child's play compared to some of the stuff they'd done in the past, something they could pull off with probably very little trouble, but there was still one problem.

Sheridan Sloan.

Rare books, while not what most people might first think of when they heard the word "art," absolutely fell under the purview of Sheridan's unit. Doing this meant that, at the very least, she would have to have to lie to her. And she didn't even want to think about what she might be forced to do if things went sideways...

Oliver nudged her with his foot under the table, and she almost sighed when she looked over at him. He wanted this one. It was clear as day on his face, and she bit the inside of her lip as she weighed her options that, in reality, weren't really options at all.

This was her brother. He needed this and he needed her to pull it off, and she wasn't going to let him down.

She nodded, a leaden feeling settling in her chest as his eyes lit up. She'd tell him later that she was done with this life for good once they'd wrapped up this job, but for now they had to finish hammering out the details for it all with Marquis.

Oliver grinned and turned his attention to the woman opposite them. "Do you have a list?"

Evie Marquis cocked her head and held out her right, a please smile quirking her lips when her bodyguard laid a folded sheet of paper onto it. "Of course." She handed the paper to him as her bodyguard took his position just off her right shoulder, his hands folded in front of himself as he did his best impression of a statue. "These are the titles, along with their current owners. Let me know when you have any of these volumes in your possession, and we'll set up an exchange at that time. You still have the number to contact me?"

Oliver nodded and tapped his temple. "Right here."

"Excellent." Marquis blew out a soft breath and got to her feet. "I look forward to doing business with you. Good day, Mr. Dobrev. Ms. Ravenscroft." Parker and Oliver stood as well, murmuring their own goodbyes, and Marquis smiled as she drawled, "Oh, and, Ms. Ravenscroft, about that Matisse you're investigating…"

Parker arched a brow in surprise. "Yes?"

"I suggest you give Hugo Lecomte a call—he might be able to help you in your search."

Parker's eyebrows about shot off her head at that. "I see. Thank you." After a beat, she added, "Might I ask why you're telling me this?"

Marquis winked. "Let's just say I'd rather Lois Smythe not add a crown jewel to her collection."

And with that, she sauntered toward the front door with her bodyguard on her heels.

"So do you think Marquis is on the level with that Lecomte tip?" Oliver asked as he unfolded the paper from Marquis and spread it out on the table between them.

"I…" Parker pursed her lips thoughtfully and glanced around the restaurant that was beginning to fill with the lunch crowd. She'd been wondering the same thing, honestly, but there was a mischievousness in her smile right before she'd brought up the Matisse that suggested she'd been telling the truth. "What do you know about that Smythe woman?" she asked as she scooped a generous spoonful of yogurt and granola onto her spoon.

"Um, she's the CEO and founder of *Metropolitan* magazine in London. I read somewhere that she's trying to expand the brand to Paris, which puts her newly established *Metropolitan Paris* in direct competition with Marquis' media company. Granted, *Metropolitan* is a monthly magazine and *Avant* is a quarterly publication, but still." He picked up his breakfast burrito and shrugged. "On the surface, at least, I'd wager that that's what's driving Marquis' decision to help you out."

"And since Marquis notoriously hates to lose at anything, I'm willing to bet that her tip is legit. Remember that whole thing with the *Tribune*?"

Marquis' reputation as a collector was well-known, but they had done a little more digging into her background after they'd agreed to take this meeting. Most of what they'd discovered wasn't particularly unexpected, but one anecdote that stood out from the rest was the time she had gone out of her way a few years ago to buy a small, local electric company outside Nice. No one could figure out why she would bother at first since utilities weren't exactly her thing, but her plan became clear when she used the company to literally shut down a small gossip rag that'd had the gall to publish a story about her going on holiday in Barcelona with her son and female assistant at the time, who was now her wife.

Oliver nodded as he finished chewing. "Yeah, pissing her off is definitely a bad idea," he muttered. "Anyway, assuming the Lecomte tip pans out and the Matisse is actually in Paris, it looks like two of the books on her list—a first-edition of *Don Quixote* and a 1865 printing of

Alice in Wonderland—are both owned by a guy named Andre Dumas who lives in *Saint Germain-des-Prés*."

Parker nodded. "Okay. I agreed to do this and I will but, and I'm being dead serious here, Olls, I'm out for good after we're done with these books. All right?"

"All right," he agreed. "Thanks, though, for saying yes. After last year I just really…"

"I know," she murmured, shaking her head. "We gotta look out for each other, right?"

"Yeah." He smiled.

She blew out a soft breath and looked at Marquis' list. "I haven't been to *Saint Germain-des-Prés* since the last time we had a job there. I wonder how much it's changed…"

"I had a meeting with a client there last summer. It's pretty much the same. So, if you have to go to Paris to retrieve the Matisse anyway, I could fly out there to meet you and we should be able to knock this one off quick."

Parker bobbed her head from side-to-side thoughtfully and took a small bite of yogurt. If they really were going to do this, she did like the idea of not having to take a few days off work to make an extra trip to Paris if she didn't have to. "Yeah, but depending on what Lecomte says, I might be flying out there as early as this week, next week at the latest, I'm sure, to retrieve the Matisse. That's not a lot of time for us to sketch out a plan."

"Yeah, but it's do-able. I don't have any immediate projects in the pipeline right now with my company, so I can start building profiles for each target right away. I'll start with Dumas and branch out from there."

"Probably want to save Seattle and here for the end," Parker mused. "We don't need to bring the FBI into it any sooner than absolutely necessary."

"Worried your girlfriend will catch us?" Oliver teased, looking entirely nonplussed about the idea as he took another huge bite of his burrito. They'd avoided the Art Crimes Unit in the past, and it was clear that he didn't see the addition of Sheridan to their team as a genuine threat.

She rolled her eyes at his continued insistence on calling Sheridan her girlfriend. "One, she's not my girlfriend. And two, it's just smarter. The only common law enforcement between London and Paris is Interpol, and since they only coordinate the various international agencies, it'd require the local investigators to go to them for help. I mean, anything we hit will be eventually entered into the Art Loss Register, but there's significantly less risk of us drawing attention to ourselves in Europe."

"Yeah," he conceded. "But, I'm looking at it like this—we can bounce around a bit so we're always moving. Keep them guessing by mixing it up, you know? Paris, New York, London, Seattle, New York... Something like that to avoid drawing too much attention to it all. One heist with a month or more before the next one will significantly turn the heat down on the investigation because they won't seem connected."

"That's a good point, I just..."

"Hmm?"

"I don't know." Parker shook her head. There was no point bothering him with her worries about how this little walk on the dark side might impact her life. "Let's just start with you looking into Dumas when you get home, and we can sketch out a rough plan for that in case the Matisse actually is in Paris. We can figure the rest of this shit out later. We've got time, there's no reason to rush anything."

SIX

After a weekend of running down dead-end leads and sitting in a surveillance van long enough that her ass had fallen asleep too many times to count, Sheridan was sorely tempted to cancel on her mother, pick up some Chinese food from the little place by her apartment, and call it a night. If she did, however, her mother would passive-aggressively pretend that everything was fine, and she *really* didn't have the energy to deal with that on top of everything else. So, instead of picking up an order of garlic chicken, slipping into her comfiest sweats, and eating dinner in front of the television, she found herself walking into Trattoria Dell'Arte in her nicest slacks and blouse, the blazer her mother had given her for her birthday the year before, and a pair of heels she'd carried around all day just for this occasion.

She flashed a tight, tired smile to the hostess as she stopped in front of her podium, and murmured, "I'm meeting Phyllis Sloan. Is she here yet?"

"She just arrived," the hostess reported with a poorly concealed grimace that told Sheridan her mother was already in rare form. Great. The girl waved a hand toward the back of the restaurant and added, "If you'll just follow me, please."

Sheridan tipped her head in a small nod and fell into step behind the girl, following her down the narrow aisle that ran the length of the restaurant. Every table was full, and yet she was not at all surprised to find her mother seated imperiously at a discreet corner table that was, no doubt, the best in the house.

"Sheridan, darling, you made it," Phyllis Sloan murmured, half-rising from her chair in a show of manners that ended the moment Sheridan waved at her to stay seated. There was a glass of Chardonnay in front of her, and she gathered the goblet in her left hand as she retook her seat.

"Of course I did, Mother."

"Enjoy your meal," the hostess excused herself with a small bow.

Sheridan watched her go with no small amount of envy and shook her head as she pulled out the chair opposite her mother and sat down, placing her purse between her feet. She picked up her menu and looked up at her mother as she opened it. "I hope I didn't keep you waiting."

"Not at all. I just got here, myself," Phyllis replied smoothly, her mask of a politician's smile firmly in place.

Sheridan nodded and steeled herself for whatever it was her mother had up her sleeve. She hadn't been expecting warmth and genuine conversation—that wasn't her mother's way—but the fake smile told her that there was a reason her mother requested this dinner beyond the guise of maintaining the appearance of a healthy mother-daughter relationship. "Good," she murmured, knowing that her mother would expect some kind of response as she dropped her gaze to her menu.

The faster they finished dinner, the better.

She had just decided on the first thing she saw that sounded vaguely appetizing when her mother spoke again.

"I ran into Marcia Petersen this morning," Phyllis began in what anyone else might think of as a conversational tone.

She, however, knew that what the tone actually meant was that her mother was going to spend the next however many minutes she was stuck in this godforsaken restaurant making snide comments about her life choices and belittling any accomplishments she dared let slip. She wished she'd had to wait longer to be proven correct.

"Michelle is being made a junior partner at her firm next month."

"That's impressive." And, truly, it was. Michelle was a year younger than she was, which meant that she'd made partner at her prestigious D.C. litigation firm by the age of thirty—a near-impossible task. "Next time you see Marcia, please give her my congratulations."

"Oh, I doubt I'll be seeing much of her," Phyllis drawled airily. "Michelle and David are getting married at the end of the year, so she's going to be busy planning the wedding."

Ah, there it was. So this was going to be an attack-Sheridan's-relationship-status type of evening. How fun. And entirely unoriginal. It'd only been something like two months since the last time her mother had decided to focus on that particular shortcoming of hers. "I didn't realize they'd gotten engaged," Sheridan replied, eyes still on her menu as she pretended to survey her options. Their waitress arrived just then, and she looked up at her gratefully. "Can I get a Macallan, neat, please? And, um, make it a double."

The woman nodded and turned to her mother. "Another glass of wine for you, ma'am?"

Phyllis shook her head. "I'm fine for now. Sheridan, are you ready to order?"

"Sure." She looked up and, when her mother arched an expectant brow at her, sighed and offered their server a tired smile. "Could I get the *tagliolini del forno*, please?"

"Of course. Would you like to start with some soup or salad?"

Sheridan shook her head. A starter would only draw out the evening, which was already feeling interminable. "No, thank you." She closed her menu while her mother ordered, and almost regretfully handed it back to the server. Without the menu to serve as a distraction, she'd have to face the brunt of her mother's scathing commentary on her life head-on.

"How's work going?" Phyllis asked once their server had left their table.

The change in conversation threw her for a moment, and she blinked as she quickly shifted gears. "Quite well, actually. Our closure rate is just under ninety percent, and Director Bartz is giving us plenty of latitude in how we approach the majority of our cases."

"And how's that handsome partner of yours?"

Sheridan schooled her expression, knowing what was coming next. "Kelly is fine."

"Have you reconsidered dating him?"

"No, mother," Sheridan murmured, barely resisting the urge to roll her eyes. Granted, she'd been later than some in the whole self-awareness process and hadn't realized she was queer until she was a recruit at Quantico, but she'd been out for close to six years now and her mother still refused to give up the idea that she just hadn't found the right man yet. "I'm still not at all interested in dating men."

"Is it because of the woman Marcia saw you leaving The Met with the other night?"

"Parker?" Sheridan asked, too surprised by the question to evade it. She shook her head. "No, Mother. Parker and I went to Brown together, and we met up on a case this past week. It was just an evening out with an old friend."

"Pity. Marcia said the woman—Parker, you said?—was quite striking, even with her unusual hair color. If you absolutely must date women, it'd be nice if you could find somebody who makes such a strong first impression. Goodness knows that woman Claire was a walking stereotype of a dowdy librarian. The only thing anyone ever noticed about her was the horrid color of her cardigans."

"Please leave Claire out of this," Sheridan muttered, barely resisting the urge to pinch the bridge of her nose to try to ward off the headache she could feel beginning to build.

"Honestly, Sheridan. It's been two years, for god's sake. You need to get over it already," Phyllis brushed her off with a dismissive wave of her hand.

Sheridan looked up as a crystal tumbler was set in front of her. "Thank you," she breathed as she reached for the glass. It took more self-control than she'd thought she possessed to restrict herself to only taking a long sip of the alcohol instead of downing it in one go.

"You're drinking again." It was a statement, not a question, and there was no mistaking the judgment in her mother's tone.

And, okay, maybe she had spent more time in the bottle than was necessarily healthy those first couple weeks after Claire had left, but she had never let the drinking get in the way of her job and she'd gotten it back under control the moment she realized it could be becoming a problem.

"I'm having a drink, yes," she replied tightly. "As are you, Mother."

Phyllis tutted under her breath and shook her head as she pulled her hand away from the stem of her wine glass. "So what does your friend Parker do?"

Sheridan knew this angle of conversation would only fuel her mother's unwanted interest in her lack of a love life, but she also knew that if she tried to avoid talking about Parker that her mother would pick up on it and things for her would be worse than if she played along. "She's with Cabot and Carmichael."

"The insurance firm?"

Sheridan nodded. "She's in their recovery division."

"Is she single?"

"I honestly have no idea, Mother." Her fingers twitched against the side of her glass, but she resisted the urge to pick it up. "Are you ready to return to London?"

"I am," her mother, thankfully, rolled with the change of topic. "Eleanor called earlier today to let me know that everything is ready there, so I should be able to jump right back into my duties without too much delay. It's been nice being home for a bit, but I am quite looking forward to getting back to work."

"Anything interesting on the agenda?" The more the conversation focused on her mother, the less time she'd be stuck trying to defend her life choices.

"Oh yes." Phyllis picked up her wine glass and smiled to herself as she lifted it to her lips. She took a small sip and set the goblet back onto the table as she launched into describing all the meetings with top diplomats she had scheduled for the following month, as well as the state functions she was looking forward to attending.

When she was young, she used to resent her mother's single-minded dedication to her job because it meant that she was left in the shadows, but as she grew older, she grew to appreciate not being the focus of her mother's scathing scrutiny. She'd long since mastered the art of encouraging her mother's rambling with only a few words here and there, and it wasn't until their dinner plates had been cleared away that Phyllis saw fit to return their conversation to her.

"When are you seeing your friend Parker again?"

"I'm not sure. We may meet for dinner one night this week if our schedules allow it."

"Surely she doesn't work the same insane hours you do."

"I have no idea what her hours are, Mother. But seeing as most recovery agents only get paid on commission for items recovered, I would assume she doesn't hold to your standard nine-to-five."

"That'd be good for you." Phyllis took the leather folder with the bill for their meal, slipped her credit card inside, and handed it back to their server without looking at the total.

"I'm sorry?"

"Dating a woman who had her own busy career." Her mother leaned back in her chair and crossed her legs. "So she wouldn't be staring at the clock, waiting for you to come home."

Sheridan sighed. "While I'll admit that you may have a point there, I quite like my life the way it is now."

"All you do is work."

Sheridan arched a brow in silent challenge, but wisely didn't say anything on that topic. As far as she was concerned, her mother had no right to comment on how much time she devoted to her job. Not when she'd grown up with a string of nannies that changed every time her mother accepted a different post and they'd had to move. The only constant from her childhood had been Andrew Talbot, the man who'd been assigned to her personal security detail from the moment her mother assumed her first Ambassadorship in Brussels until she entered Brown her freshman year.

"Have you heard any rumors about possible advancement opportunities?" Phyllis asked.

"Nope." Of course, she hadn't looked into it at all, either. All she'd ever wanted from the moment she became an agent was to work Art Crimes, and she would be perfectly fine spending the rest of her career right where she was. Which, she recognized, was part of her mother's issue with her. If she were a Unit Chief or something, her mother could brag to her friends about her, but as far as the Ambassador was concerned, there was no glory to be had in her current position.

Phyllis shook her head and looked poised to pick up some thread of her tired arguments about how she just didn't understand how Sheridan could lack any real drive to move up the ladder when their server returned with the bill for her to sign.

Sheridan's phone buzzed in the pocket of her blazer just as her mother scribbled her name across the bottom of the tab. "Sorry," she murmured as she pulled the phone from her pocket, half-praying for it to be something from work that absolutely had to be taken care of right that moment. Instead, it was something better—a message from Parker.

How's dinner with your mother? Do you need me to cook up an emergency so you can escape?

She bit her lip as she reread the text three more times, touched beyond words that Parker cared enough to even think to offer her a way out.

"Well, that's quite the smile," Phyllis drawled. "I'm guessing that's not a work-related message."

"I…" Sheridan schooled her expression as she turned her phone face-down on her lap. "No. It wasn't work."

"Good." Phyllis smiled and pushed herself to her feet. "I'm aware that it's still early, dear, but I really do need to finish packing. I'll call and check in with you once I'm settled back in London?"

"Of course." Sheridan nodded as she gathered her purse and stood as well. She forced a tight smile as she accepted the light, one-armed hug her mother pulled her into, before she fell into step behind her as they left the restaurant. A black Town Car with blackout windows was waiting at the curb, and she wasn't at all surprised when the suited man standing sentry by the rear door tipped his head in greeting and opened the door for her mother. Protective details were supposed to blend in, but the Ambassador liked hers to stand out just enough to make her look important to people passing by.

"I'll talk to you soon," Phyllis said, offering her a small wave before she ducked her head and slipped into the back seat. The door shut behind her a moment later, and Sheridan blew out a soft breath as the driver doffed his cap in her direction with a sympathetic smile before he hustled around the front of the car and climbed behind the wheel.

Once the car had disappeared into the flow of traffic, Sheridan pulled out her phone and, after a split-second's hesitation, pulled up Parker's number.

"Hey, you," Parker answered on the second ring, sounding a little surprised, making her wonder if calling Parker instead of just texting had been a mistake. *"Is everything okay?"*

She closed her eyes and nodded. "Yeah. It's fine. Thankfully, my mother wasn't interested in drawing the evening out any longer than strictly necessary, so I'm leaving the restaurant now. I just wanted to call and thank you for offering to try to save me. I appreciate it."

Parker cleared her throat softly. *"Yeah, well, that's what friends are for, right?"*

She smiled. "I guess so."

"How'd it go? Yesterday you kinda sounded like you'd rather have a root canal…"

"It was predictably awful, but survivable," she answered honestly.

"Wow." Parker blew out a soft breath. *"What a glowing report. You want to meet up somewhere for a drink or a coffee or something?"*

Sheridan ran a hand through her hair and looked around the busy intersection in front of her. She'd been looking forward to heading home all day, but she found herself absolutely grinning at the idea of seeing Parker instead. "I could go for a drink. What do you have in mind?"

Parker chuckled. *"Well, I'm in joggers and a tank right now, so I'll just need to change real quick before I head out. Where are you?"*

"South side of the park. Near Columbus."

The line was quiet for a moment before Parker suggested, *"What about The Poet? It's about halfway between there and my place. Or, if you have somewhere else you'd rather go…"*

"That sounds great," Sheridan assured her even though she'd never heard of the place before. "Can you give me the cross streets so I know where I'm going?"

"Eighty-First and Amsterdam. You heading over there now?"

"That's what I was thinking, yeah…"

"Okay," Parker replied with what sounded like a smile in her voice. *"I'll be there as soon as I can. See you soon."*

"Yeah," Sheridan whispered, her heart fluttering lightly in her chest. "See you soon."

seven

Parker checked her watch as she jogged up the stairs from the 79th Street station. About half an hour had passed since she'd hung up with Sheridan, and she blew out a loud breath as she started to make her way back up Broadway toward 81st. The Poet was only three-and-a-half blocks or so from the subway station, tucked into a quiet corner not far from the Museum of Natural History, so before she could worry too much about keeping Sheridan waiting, she was standing in front of the familiar black wood and glass facade of the bar that was a little slice of Ireland tucked away in the heart of Manhattan.

It didn't take her long at all to spot Sheridan at a booth near the front window, staring into the tumbler of ocher alcohol clasped lightly in her right hand. The top three buttons of her emerald green blouse were left open, causing the soft fabric to billow enticingly around the point of her collarbones and cling to the subtle curve of exposed cleavage, and Parker caught a flash of black lace as Sheridan shifted back in her seat, her shoulders rolling back as she sipped at her drink. She looked absolutely beautiful, and Parker gave herself a good mental thrashing for not changing into something nicer than her favorite pair of jeans and a hoodie leftover from her days at Brown.

It was too late to do anything about that now, however, so she squared her shoulders as she made her way across the narrow bar toward the table where Sheridan was sitting. And as she studied

Sheridan's expression, she couldn't help but wonder what had happened during her dinner with her mother to make her look so tired. Sheridan's normally vibrant eyes were dulled and her lips were tugged down at the corners with what could only be weariness, but her expression shifted the moment her gaze landed on her, a spark of warmth blossoming in her blue, blue eyes as a breathtaking smile lit her entire face.

Parker's step faltered for a moment as her stomach flip-flopped under the warmth of that enchanting smile, and she had to remind herself to breathe as she did her best to appear unaffected by the way Sheridan was looking at her. She shouldn't have even texted Sheridan in the first place, but Oliver had messaged to let her know he'd gotten home okay and then her thumb somehow found its way to Sheridan's name in her recent messages list. Probably because she'd been thinking about her all afternoon, lamenting the fact that it was in everyone's best interest—not just hers and Oliver's, but also Sheridan's—if they didn't see each other again until everything with Marquis was settled.

She had read through their messages with a surprisingly bitter feeling of regret considering they'd only just reconnected, and then she saw the one about Sheridan's dinner with her mother. Sheridan had seemed to be dreading it, and she figured that, even though she was going to have to keep her distance, it couldn't hurt to send her a text that could give her a way out if she needed it. And that was all she'd meant to do, but then Sheridan had called instead of texting back, sounding so worn-down that she heard herself suggesting they meet up somewhere before she even realized what she was doing. She'd almost apologized and taken the offer back, but then Sheridan had accepted with a clear smile in her voice and she was a goner.

God, she was such a mess.

"Hey," Sheridan said as she slipped into the booth opposite her.

"Sorry it took me so long to get here," Parker apologized. "I hope you weren't waiting too long."

Sheridan's smile softened. "You're fine, Parker. Really. Honestly, it's probably better that I had a few minutes to brood on my own."

Not knowing how to respond, Parker bit the inside of her cheek and looked around the bar. Being that it was closing in on nine o'clock on a Sunday, there were less than a dozen other people in the place besides them and only one person working, and she sighed as she realized she'd have to go up and order her drink. She flashed Sheridan a small smile and motioned vaguely toward the bar. "It looks like there's just the one bartender working now, so I'm going to go get a drink real quick. Can I get you another?" she asked, hiking her chin toward Sheridan's nearly empty glass.

Sheridan looked tempted, but she hesitated for a few beats before nodding. "Okay. Yeah. Sure. Why not?" She reached into her purse that was sitting on the bench beside her.

Parker shook her head and waved her off. "I got it. What are you drinking?" She eyed Sheridan's glass and guessed, "Scotch?"

Sheridan shrugged. "I'm not picky. Just not vodka—it goes right to my head and is basically an instant hangover."

"You know I can just ask the bartender what you're drinking, right?" Parker said as she pushed to her feet.

"You don't need to get me another of this," Sheridan said quickly, placing a hand over the top of her glass. "Honestly. I'm fine with whatever you're going to get."

"I'll be right back," Parker assured her with a wink, already set on getting Sheridan another round of whatever it was she had bought for herself before she'd arrived.

The bartender greeted her with a smile. "Hiya, Parker. What can I get ya?"

"How's it going, Colin?" Parker grinned as she leaned against the bar and shook his hand. Colin O'Donahue was a Dublin transplant who'd been tending bar at The Poet for the last two years as he worked his way through law school at NYU, and they'd spent many an evening discussing everything from his coursework to sports to both of their horrendous dating lives. "Can you tell me what my friend over there is drinking?"

Colin looked over at Sheridan, his smile turning sly as he answered, "Aye. That'd be a twenty-one-year-old Macallan, neat. She ordered a double. So, I don't know what you did to drive a pretty lady like that to drink expensive scotch, but if I were you I'd be apologizing for it post-haste."

"We're not dating." Parker rolled her eyes at the way Colin smirked in response. "She had a rough dinner with her mother and I offered to meet her for a drink to help her forget about it. So how about you get me two doubles of that expensive scotch she's drinking so I can get on with that?"

"She must be a keeper if you're drinking scotch for her," Colin teased.

"Shut up," Parker sassed as she handed over her credit card. She glanced over her shoulder at Sheridan who was watching her with an inscrutable expression and sighed as she turned back to Colin, who was smiling his most annoying *I know something you don't know* smile. "What?"

"Nothin'," he replied as he tapped at the screen above the register and swiped her card. "You're a good woman, Parker Ravenscroft. And she'd be lucky to have ya."

"You're a sap," Parker muttered, making Colin laugh as he handed her back her card.

"Aye," he confirmed with a tight nod. "Be right back with those drinks." He knocked on the bar and ambled toward the middle of the sleek mahogany slab to pull a bottle from the glass shelves that spanned the side wall of the bar to pour their drinks.

A handful of guys in Columbia University hoodies sauntered into the bar just as Colin was returning with the two glasses of Macallan, which meant he could do little more than murmur a quick, "Good luck," as he handed them over before he had to pay attention to his new customers.

Parker chuckled under her breath as she picked up the drinks and turned back toward the booth where Sheridan was still watching her with that same inscrutable look on her face. Her dark eyes simmered with something Parker wished she could identify, but she forced herself to ignore the way it made her pulse stumble over itself as she slipped onto the bench across from her. "Milady," she drawled as she slid a glass across the table to her.

"Thanks." Sheridan tilted her head toward the bar where Colin was pulling pints for the guys who'd just come in. "You come here a lot?"

"Enough," Parker admitted with a small shrug. "I'll stop in on my way home from work after a particularly long day. Colin's a 3L over at NYU, and on slower nights we'll sit and chat."

"Is that why he keeps looking over here?"

Parker turned to glare at Colin who was, indeed, looking in their direction, and she huffed a laugh when his expression turned into a classic *oh shit* look when he saw that he was busted before he hurriedly turned away. "Who knows?" She shook her head and turned back to Sheridan. "So…" She drawled as she picked up her tumbler and took a cautious sip of her drink. She was more of a beer and wine type of girl, and she was pleasantly surprised by how smooth the scotch was. "This is actually pretty good."

"Not a scotch drinker?" Sheridan asked, her lips curving in an amused smirk.

"Not usually, no."

Sheridan laughed and shook her head. "You didn't have to get it. I told you I was fine with whatever."

"Yeah, well, I wanted to make sure you got something you liked, so I had Colin give me two of what you ordered yourself before I got here."

Sheridan's eyes went wide. "Parker, you didn't have to—"

"I wanted to, okay?" Parker interrupted with a soft smile. "You sounded like you had a shitty day, and I wanted to do something to try to make it a little bit better."

The slow slide of Sheridan's tongue over her lips as she shook her head was hypnotic, so much so that Parker was still staring at her lips when Sheridan breathed, "You are too much. You know that, right?"

Parker swallowed thickly as her eyes dropped to her glass. "Yeah, well..." she murmured, hoping that was enough to let Sheridan drop it. Because if Sheridan kept looking at her like that, she would probably do something incredibly stupid—like begin to believe this one-sided crush of hers that was raging back to life might actually be reciprocated. Or that she could even do anything about it right now, anyway.

Bad timing was one thing, but she'd watched Sheridan date enough preppy, trust fund frat boys back in the day to know that letting herself hope that Sheridan might feel something for her too would not end well.

"So..." Parker cleared her throat and took a deep breath as she forced her eyes back to Sheridan's. "I haven't talked to you since yesterday morning—what's happening at The Met?"

"Nothing." Sheridan shook her head. "There has been exactly no suspicious activity in the Valentin de Boulogne exhibit. And if it continues to stay that way for too much longer, I have a feeling Bartz is going to pull us out of there so we can focus on the Matisse and figuring out why the hell Evie Marquis came into town yesterday morning..."

Parker choked on the sip she was in the middle of swallowing at the mention of Marquis, and she coughed into her elbow as she tried to recover. "Sorry."

"You've heard of Marquis?"

"Who in our line of work hasn't?" Parker countered, her heart beating in her throat.

"Good point."

"How'd you guys even know she was here?"

"My boss, Miles Bartz, was the lead investigator on a Degas heist a few years ago, and even though he couldn't prove it, he was convinced she was involved somehow,. He's kept a flag on her passport and jets and whatever with customs so that we get a head's up every time she flies into the country."

"Damn," Parker muttered. She wanted to ask if they knew why Marquis was in town, but she wasn't going to put Sheridan in any kind of situation where it might come back and bite her in the ass later. Them being out together was bad enough.

Sheridan laughed. "What?"

"Nothing. I just didn't realize that was something you guys could actually do. I mean, yeah, she's been suspected of a bunch of stuff, but nothing has ever actually been proven."

"Yes, well…" Sheridan shrugged. "There's a first time for everything," she murmured as she lifted her glass to her lips. "How was your meeting yesterday?"

"Oh." Parker blinked. She'd honestly forgotten she'd said anything about that to Sheridan. "It wasn't exactly a meeting, per se," she lied, hating the way her stomach tightened as the words left her lips. She wasn't a bad liar, but she didn't like doing it. She much preferred to work in partial-truths. But if the FBI was already aware of the fact that Evie Marquis had been in town, she didn't want to hint at anything that might suggest a connection between her and the billionaire—no matter how many hypothetical hoops one would have to jump through to make that connection. "But it was good. My brother came down from Boston for the day because it's been a while since we've seen each other, and after we replaced Gregory's garbage disposal, we took advantage of the weather and spent the day in the park." That much, at least, was entirely true. It'd taken them an hour or so to replace the garbage disposal, and then they'd spent the rest of the afternoon wandering the walking paths in Central Park, brainstorming different approaches for how they might go about acquiring the items on Marquis' wish list.

"I didn't know you had a brother. Older? Younger?"

"Younger, but only by about five months. He does love to lord that over me though. Especially since I turned thirty in March and his birthday isn't until the end of August." Parker chuckled at Sheridan's look of confusion and explained, "We're not related by blood. We met in kindergarten and, partly because we were both being shuttled through the system in Seattle so we got each other in a way nobody else really could, we quickly became best friends."

Sheridan's mouth fell open, and she closed it quickly. "I'm sorry. I had no idea."

"Why would you? It's not like it's something that comes up in everyday conversation," Parker pointed out in what she hoped was an understanding tone. "I'm not going to say it was easy—god knows bouncing from foster to foster with everything we owned in a trash bag was anything but—but we were lucky enough to be taken-in by the Johanns when we were fifteen."

"Wow…"

Parker smiled. "Yeah. So, long story short, we finished high school in an upper-middle-class suburb of Seattle, and after we graduated we both moved East—me on scholarship to Brown, and him on a full-ride to MIT."

"That's…I had no idea…" Sheridan shook her head. "Do you still see your foster parents?"

"I do my best to remember to call once a month to check in and say hi and whatever. But Ollie and I try to go back once a year for a long weekend. Brett and Tina have a new set of kids they took in like five years ago—Jenny and Vivienne are freshmen in high school now—so even though they like when we come back to visit, it kinda feels like we're invading the kids' space. We had our turn, you know? We had the Johanns when we needed them most, but Jen and Viv deserve to have all their turn now. They deserve a chance to feel loved and supported while they figure out where they fit in the world that, until the Johanns found them, didn't want them."

"I…"

"And that got way heavier than I'd meant it to," Parker added with a wry grin and a small shake of her head as compassion shone in Sheridan's eyes. She wasn't ashamed of her past, she'd done what she'd had to do to survive and get herself to where she was now, but she hated being pitied for it. And god knows that if she told Sheridan about how she'd never had a brand new pair of shoes or clothes that weren't from Goodwill until the Johanns took her in that the compassion in Sheridan's eyes would quickly become pity. "Sorry about that."

"No. Don't be. I mean, yeah, it was a little heavy, but I…" Sheridan sighed. "Thank you for sharing all that with me."

"Thank you for actually caring," Parker whispered, feeling suddenly vulnerable under Sheridan's warm gaze. She looked away and took a healthy swallow of scotch. "Anyway," she stressed the second syllable hard as she set her glass back onto the table, "enough sob stories. Pick something lighter…"

Sheridan pursed her lips thoughtfully for a long moment before settling on, "Who's Gregory?"

"My landlord." Parker smiled, glad to have something less fraught with painful memories to talk about. "He was in the same fraternity as my boss when they were undergrads at Harvard, and now he's a semi-retired law professor at NYU. Colin's actually taking one of his seminars this semester." She waved a hand toward the bar. "Anyway, he's brilliant with the law but completely helpless when it comes to tools and stuff, so I like to do little things around the house to help him out a bit."

"That's nice of you."

"Not really." Parker shrugged. "He's…it's hard to explain, but something clicked between us that day I showed up on his doorstep. It was like we'd been destined to cross paths or something, I don't know. But he's part of my found-family now, and he's pretty much adopted Ollie too, so we like helping him out when he'll let us."

"I'm impressed you can do all that home-maintenance kind of stuff. I'll have to call you next time something breaks at my loft—it always takes me forever and a lifetime to get anyone out to fix anything."

Parker knew she should leave that one alone, but the smile curling Sheridan's lips pulled the flirtatious quip she'd intended to keep to herself from her own before she could swallow it. "Got a thing for girls in tool belts, do you?" She bit the inside of her cheek as soon as she said it, and that proved especially fortunate as it kept her from grinning at the furious blush that spread across Sheridan's cheeks.

"I...you're..." Sheridan cleared her throat and took a long drink of her scotch. She licked her lips as she set the glass down and chuckled softly as she replied, "I plead the fifth."

At that, Parker let the laugh she'd be holding back spill free, and she shook her head as she picked up her glass and threw a flirty wink at Sheridan. "I'll have to go buy one tomorrow, then, just to be ready." The way Sheridan's mouth and eyes widened in shock only made her laugh harder.

"You...you..." Sheridan stammered, her blush spreading so that her ears were now on fire, too. She dropped her head to the table and muttered, "Oh my god. Please tell me you're kidding."

Parker wished she knew why Sheridan was so flustered. Was if it was because of the whole women in tool belts comment, or because she was embarrassed by her teasing? Although, Parker had a feeling it was the latter, rather than the former. Sheridan always had hated being the butt of any joke no matter how playful or well-intended, but she couldn't stop the way the little spark of hope inside her bloomed at the turn their conversation had taken. Still laughing softly, she reached across the table to cover Sheridan's hand with her own. "I'm sorry. Yes, I was kidding."

Forehead still pressed to the tabletop, Sheridan shook her head. "You're fine. I'm just..."

"Adorable," Parker finished for her in a soft voice. She smiled when hesitant blue eyes lifted to look at her, and dragged her thumb over the back of Sheridan's knuckles as she tilted her head to the side and whispered, "I was just messing around, and I apparently took it too far. I didn't mean to make you uncomfortable."

Sheridan shook her head as she flipped her hand under Parker's, curling her long fingers around the edge of Parker's palm and giving it a light squeeze. "I'm sorry," she stressed, leaning forward slightly. "I'm just...my mother takes great joy in pointing out all my shortcomings, so I guess I'm just a little overly sensitive to jokes on my behalf right now. But I do know that you really were just teasing me," she hastened to add when Parker's eyes widened at her confession. "And I'll admit that my response to what you'd said more than warranted it, but I just need you to understand that this"—she waved a hand at her still slightly-flushed cheeks—"is not because I didn't like the turn our conversation had taken. I'm just..."

Parker looked down at their hands and sighed. She stroked her thumb slowly over the path between Sheridan's wrist and thumb in a silent show of understanding because if anyone could understand feeling like they weren't enough, it was her—the former foster-kid who'd grown up hearing and thinking that something must be wrong with her because nobody wanted her.

"That feels nice," Sheridan whispered.

"Yeah?" Parker blinked back her surprise as she looked up at Sheridan.

Sheridan nodded, the look in her eyes as soft as her smile. She tightened her grip on Parker's hand as she asked, "Can we just...try and find that lighter conversation again?"

"Of course."

They stared at each other for a few heartbeats, each trying to find an appropriate avenue of conversation, and the silence was finally broken when Parker ventured, "I was chased by an angry Iranian this morning who screamed at me that I was the devil."

Sheridan huffed a laugh. "You're serious?"

"Yes!" Parker grinned, pleased to see Sheridan smiling again. "He called me, me!, the devil! All because I recovered the Maserati he stole from his ex-wife after it'd been given to her in their divorce settlement. Can you believe it?"

"Not at all," Sheridan admitted with a small shake of her head. "Do I get the rest of the story?"

"Do you want the rest of the story?"

"Of course!" Sheridan's brow wrinkled and added quickly, "Unless it'd make me have to arrest you. I don't want to have to arrest you."

"Fear not, brave law-abiding federal agent, my reacquisition of the vehicle was perfectly legal. Ish. It's not like he's going to call it in since he stole it in the first place, right?" When Sheridan nodded, she added, "And I would much rather you not arrest me, either."

"Good to know."

Parker nodded. There was a joke about there being times where she wouldn't mind being handcuffed, however, that was on the tip of her tongue, but she instead just launched into her story of that morning's excitement. "So, Ollie and I were walking back to my place after getting coffee because he needed to head home, and we're passing by this stupid-expensive bistro that does an incredible Sunday brunch when the valet comes rolling up to in front of the restaurant in a cherry red GranTurismo MC that I'd been keeping tabs on for the last week waiting for the right time to slip in and grab it."

"You're kidding."

"Not at all. I mean, I could've totally talked my way into the parking garage at his firm and broken into the car to get it back, but where's the challenge in that—right?"

"Of course…" Sheridan drawled, the right side of her mouth lifting in a small smile.

"So, anyway, there we are, just walking down the sidewalk, enjoying our coffee, and the car I've been tracking is left at the curb, door wide open, with the key in the ignition."

Sheridan sipped at her scotch as she waved her free hand in a motion for her to continue.

"I murmured to Ollie what was going on, and on the fly he came up with the idea to 'accidentally' crash into the guy and spill his coffee all over his pimpalicious, white linen suit."

"Oh my god," Sheridan chuckled.

"Exactly. So while he's standing in the middle of the sidewalk, distracted by the coffee that is literally dripping off his suit, I yell at him that Cabot and Carmichael appreciates his assistance in recovering their lost property, Ollie and I jump into the car, and we peel off as he's shaking his fist at me cartoon-villain style and screaming that I'm the devil."

"Wow. Do all your recoveries go like that?"

"No. Unfortunately. I mean, usually I have to work with the police and get warrants and all that bullshit, this was like a gift—a beautiful, Sunday morning gift from the gods."

Sheridan whistled softly. "You definitely had a better morning than I did, that's for sure."

"Why? What'd you do?"

"Sat in the van outside The Met. Did a few laps through the museum just to stretch my legs, but it was mostly just a lot of sitting around."

"Exciting."

"I can assure you that it absolutely was not."

Parker smiled. "Makes me glad I didn't follow in your footsteps and join the Bureau, then."

"Did you really consider it?" Sheridan asked, her eyebrows lifting in surprise.

"Briefly. Very briefly," Parker admitted. "But then Professor Wells—you remember her?" When Sheridan nodded, she continued, "Professor Wells put me in touch with a friend of hers at Cabot and Carmichael, and two percent of the insured value per recovery sounded a lot more appealing than a government salary."

"I'll give you that." Sheridan yawned and glanced at her watch. "And I bet your hours are a lot more flexible than mine, too." She smiled sheepishly. "It's getting late, and my apartment's down in Tribeca near the office—would you mind if we call it a night?"

"Of course I don't mind." Parker downed the rest of her drink. "Are you going to cab it, or…"

"Subway, probably."

Parker nodded and slid out of the booth. "I'll walk with you, then." She waited while Sheridan scooted out of the booth and slipped on a black blazer that matched her tailored slacks. "Ready?" she asked when Sheridan finished shouldering her purse.

Sheridan smiled. "I am."

An easy silence engulfed them as they made their way out of the bar—Parker pointedly ignored the sly grin Colin threw her way as she held the door for Sheridan—and toward the subway station. The night was cool but comfortable, a sure sign that the humid days of summer would be upon them soon enough, and she couldn't resist stealing little glances at Sheridan as they walked. The streets were nearly empty, and the subway station was equally quiet as they made their way toward the center of the platform.

The distinctive rumble of an incoming train from the north side of the tunnel announced the imminent arrival of Sheridan's train. "I think your ride is here," Parker murmured.

"Yeah," Sheridan agreed, her right hand lightly grasping Parker's forearm as she turned toward her. "Thank you for meeting me tonight."

"It wasn't a problem at all. I had a good time."

"I did, too," Sheridan sighed as the clatter of the train became louder, warning them that they were running out of time. She smiled shyly and, slowly, as if she were preparing herself to be turned down, held out her left arm as she took a small step into Parker's space.

Parker smiled and pulled Sheridan into the hug she was offering. And, oh, it was, without a doubt, the stupidest thing she could have done, because there was no way for her to pretend that she didn't notice how perfectly Sheridan fit in her arms. "Text me when you get home?" she asked as she gave her a light squeeze to prepare herself to let go. "Just so I know you made it back safe?"

"You haven't had enough of me yet?" Sheridan asked, her voice a low purr next to Parker's ear that was barely loud enough to be heard over the screech of the train stopping beside them.

"I honestly don't think that's possible," Parker admitted softly, squeezing her eyes shut as she remembered why she shouldn't be doing this.

"I'll text you when I get home," Sheridan promised as her arms fell back to her sides and she pulled away.

"Good." Parker smiled, trying to hide the fact that her heart had beat its way up into her throat. "Talk to you soon, then."

Sheridan's answering smile was soft as she echoed, "Talk to you soon."

Parker nodded as she watched Sheridan step onto the train just before the doors whooshed shut. She waved as the train began to move, her stomach fluttering with happiness as she saw Sheridan do the same, and she blew out a soft breath once the train had disappeared into the dark tunnel. She shook her head as the sound of her train approaching reached her ears, and huffed a sardonic laugh as she ran a hand through her hair.

"Wow. I am so fucked."

EIGHT

"You look like shit, my friend."

"Thanks. Love you too," Sheridan muttered as she slipped into the passenger's seat of Kelly's car for the short ride to the office.

"Rough dinner with your mom?"

Sheridan closed her eyes and leaned her head back against the headrest. She didn't have a hangover, surprisingly, considering how much scotch she'd had the night before, but she definitely wasn't feeling one hundred percent, either. "No worse than usual, but yeah. Everybody else's kids are preparing to take over the world and I'm a flaming disappointment in a menial government job." Her lips quirked in a small smile at the sound of disdain that Kelly made. "Oh, and she wanted to know if I'd considered dating my 'handsome partner.'"

"Well, I am very pretty."

"Yes, you are. If I had to pick a dude, you'd be near the top of the list," she agreed with a little laugh that trailed off into a yawn. "Ugh. Sorry."

"Geez, how late did your dinner go?"

"We were done by eight thirty or so, but I ended up meeting Parker for a drink afterwards."

"Oh you did, did you?" Kelly shot her a playful smirk. "And how did that go? Did you get a sweet kiss goodnight?"

"Don't be ridiculous." She looked out the side window as a light blush warmed her neck.

A kiss would have been nice, but the hug they'd shared on that grimy subway platform had been perfect. She'd been unable to stop the constant replay of last night's events from the moment she'd watched Parker disappear from sight as her train rattled away from the station. She hadn't known what to expect when she'd accepted her invitation for a drink; all she'd known at the time was that she wasn't ready to be alone.

She'd replayed their conversation over and over again in her mind in the time that'd passed since, worrying that she'd confessed too much and that Parker would realize what a mess she was and run away. But more than that—more than her insecurities and the doubt that bloomed inside her as she picked apart every word spoken and every look directed her way—she could not stop thinking about the way Parker had felt in her arms. Could not stop remembering the details of that blissful moment: the intoxicating scent of rosewood and spice of Parker's perfume, the soft press of her breasts above her own, the strength of her arms as they wrapped around her waist, pulling her close, and the warmth of Parker's cheek against her own.

"Why is that ridiculous? You're beautiful, she's beautiful, you guys would make a beautiful couple..."

"Do you know any words besides beautiful?" Sheridan teased, hoping it'd keep him from pressing. It was one thing for her to realize that she was beginning to develop something of a crush on Parker, but it was quite another for her to let him in on it. She'd never hear the end of it. "And, besides that, no, I'm not. She absolutely is, but—"

"While I am usually more than happy to bow to your opinion," Kelly interrupted, "on this I must disagree."

"Kelly..."

"Hush. I'm a man with eyes, and you know I can't lie for shit, so just shut up and accept it."

Sheridan sighed. "Okay. Fine. Thank you."

"You want to know what else I've noticed?"

"Do I have a choice?"

Kelly chuckled and shook his head as they turned into the underground garage beneath Federal Plaza. "You like her."

"We've been over this, Kel. Everybody likes her. She's Parker freaking Ravenscroft. What's not to like?"

"Yeah, but you like her, like her. You've been out with her twice in three days. Twice!"

"It doesn't matter," Sheridan murmured, shaking her head.

"And why, exactly, doesn't it matter?"

"Because she's Parker freaking Ravenscroft," she replied, as if Parker's name, in and of itself, was answer enough.

"And you are Sheridan fucking Sloan," he retorted as he whipped the car into a parking space at a speed that had her bracing a hand on the dashboard. "Badass FBI agent extraordinaire. Holder of every one of Quantico's shooting records." He killed the ignition and grinned. "Speaker of four languages and the worst cook I've ever met. You know everything there is to know about art, and," he stretched the single syllable out until he ran out of breath, "sometimes you look like a giraffe trying to Rollerblade when you run."

"I…" Sheridan laughed. "Wow. Okay. You do realize that not all of those were compliments, right?"

He winked at her as he opened his door. "Eh, gotta keep you humble. I don't want to work with an egomaniac or anything."

"Right," she muttered as she slid out of the car and they started toward the elevator.

She took advantage of the fact that Kelly was flipping through his phone as they waited for the elevator to make its way down from the lobby to pull out her own. She glanced at him as she opened her messages, and sighed when she looked back at her phone and her eyes locked onto Parker's name and the final message she'd received from her the night before.

Glad you made it home safely. Sweet dreams, Sheridan.

Her heart swooped and dove in her chest as she reread that message again, and she shook her head. She was being ridiculous. Kelly was wrong and, even if he wasn't, she wasn't interested in getting her heart broken again. That's what she told herself, at least, as she sent Parker a quick little note to thank her again for meeting her the night before.

A gray bubble with ellipses appeared almost immediately, and she bit the inside of her cheek as she waited for Parker's reply. It was a good thing, too, because it kept her from ginning like a fool when Parker's message came through a moment later.

It was my pleasure. I hope you're feeling better today?

"Tell Parker I say hey," Kelly quipped as the doors in front of them opened.

"How do you know I'm looking at anything having to do with Parker?" Sheridan asked as she walked to the back of the car and leaned against the wall. She rolled her eyes at the way he grinned and tapped his temple. "I'm already starting to rue the day you two properly meet," she mumbled as she typed out a quick reply. *I am. How about you? Oh, Kelly's looking over my shoulder as I type this—he says 'hey' btw.*

Kelly bumped their shoulders together. "That was so smooth, Sloan, I feel like I should be over here taking notes."

Sheridan gave him a light jab with her elbow. "I'm not trying to be smooth."

"Well, that's good. Because you suck at it."

"You—" Sheridan's answering insult was stopped in its tracks by a new message popping up on her screen.

Hello, Sheridan's partner. Do you have a warrant to be reading our private messages?

Kelly chuckled and held Sheridan's gaze as he took a long step to the side so he couldn't see the phone anymore. "I like her. And tell her that I'm working on it."

"He says he's working on that one, and then proceeded to pointedly move away," Sheridan recited as she typed. She hit send and added, *I had fun last night.*

Her smile was untamable when Parker replied after a few seconds, *Me too.*

"Oh my god, just tell her you love her already," Kelly teased from the far side of the elevator.

"You're lucky I can't reach that far to kick you," Sheridan retorted.

"Why do you think I moved over here before I said it?" Kelly shot her a knowing smirk as the elevator stopped at their floor. "Now, say goodbye to your little friend, it's time to go catch bad guys."

Sheridan sighed dramatically as she stepped out of the elevator. He was right, however, so she sent Parker one last note. *Talk more later? Just got to work.*

She set her purse and phone on her desk, and was in the middle of taking off her coat when her phone buzzed. *Of course. I guess I should be paying better attention to this interminable staff meeting, anyway. ;)*

"What's got your partner so happy, Innes?"

Sheridan barely resisted the urge to pinch the bridge of her nose at Ivy's teasing tone, and sighed as she looked up at the leggy, six-foot-tall agent who was standing beside Kelly's desk with a manila file in her hands.

"She met a girl," he told her.

"Really?" Ivy replied, her smile widening. "Our Sheridan?"

"She's just growing up so fast," Kelly replied with a mock sob.

"Oh my god, just knock it off, you two." Sheridan shook her head. "She's just a friend, okay?"

Ivy smirked. "Yep. I totally smile like that when I'm thinking about my friends, too."

Sheridan huffed a breath and dropped into her chair. And, even though she'd already effectively ended her conversation, picked up her phone. *Forget what I said. My partner and colleague are being idiots. What's your meeting about?*

"Is she texting the girl?" Ivy asked in a mock whisper.

Kelly laughed as Sheridan flipped them both off. "Looks like it."

New insurance regulations and how they impact our existing policies and how new policies will have to be drafted to compensate for them. I don't know why they need the recovery division here since it has nothing to do with us, but at least there are bagels. A new text bubble appeared and then disappeared, and she was about to put her phone away when it appeared again. And then, after what seemed like forever of staring at the flashing ellipses, a new message appeared. *Why are your partner and colleague being idiots?*

Sheridan pursed her lips, realizing that she couldn't tell Parker why they were teasing her without giving anything away. *They just like teasing me.*

"Why's Sheridan smiling like that?" Rachel asked as she sidled up next to Ivy.

"She met a girl," Ivy shared.

"Should we get everyone over here?" Sheridan sighed as she arched a brow at the small group watching her.

"If you'd really like us to," Kelly shot back with a grin.

Sheridan groaned. "Oh my god."

Rachel smiled. "Leave her alone, you two. Besides, Bartz wants us in the conference room in five for the Monday morning meeting to review where we stand on our open cases."

"Ugh," Ivy groaned. "He's going to send us back into the van, I just know it…"

Sheridan tuned out the conversation happening around her as she read the message that popped up on her screen. *Oh. Well, I can't blame them for that. You are pretty cute when you're embarrassed. However, while we covered last night that I'd rather not get arrested, if you need me to come down there and knock some heads to get them to ease up on you, I can…*

"Better you than us," Kelly replied, which earned him a light smack upside the head from the folder Ivy was holding. "Damn. Rach, get your woman under control."

"Like that's possible," Rachel laughed.

"I am under control, thank you. See?" Ivy smacked him again. "Perfect control."

Sheridan was glad they were distracted by tormenting each other, because she could feel her cheeks coloring. Parker had called her adorable the night before, and now cute? What the hell did all that mean? It was ridiculous to think that Parker was flirting with her, and yet... She pursed her lips as she reread the message.

"Damn it, Ivy!" Kelly swore.

"What? You want me to do it again?" Ivy taunted.

Their bickering was the perfect excuse for her to just tap out a response and stop overthinking, and she shook her head as she typed—*My hero. :) We've just been summoned to a meeting of our own, however, so your head-knocking skills aren't needed at this time.*

"You want to go down to the training room and settle this?" Kelly challenged.

Sheridan could hear the smirk in Ivy's voice when she replied, "I don't think that'd be fair. For you, I mean."

"I can handle you," Kelly insisted as her phone buzzed with Parker's response.

Damn. I was in the middle of looking up where I could find a cape between here and there so I'd look the part when I came to rescue you.

Sheridan shook her head. *You're too much.* She hit send and looked up at her partner as she got to her feet. "Kelly, she's got an E3 patch in Krav Maga. You've got a high school letter in wrestling. From what, like fifteen years ago? It's not a fair fight."

"You're supposed to be on my side," Kelly told her, much to Ivy's amusement as she blew on her nails and buffed them on her shoulder.

"I am. I'm trying to keep you from getting killed." Sheridan gave him a pointed look. "And, if we're talking about being on each other's side..."

Kelly snapped his fingers twice and pointed at her. "Trying to get you a date *is* being on your side, so there!"

"I have no interest in dating," Sheridan said, though the words held less weight than usual. She sighed, knowing exactly who was behind this softening of her defenses, and shook her head.

"You keep telling yourself that," Kelly retorted, though his tone was light, like he knew it was only a matter of time before she caved. "And, for the record, I graduated high school seventeen years ago."

"Oh, because that makes your argument so much better," Rachel teased.

"You're just sassy because you're dating the Krav Maga expert," Kelly retorted as they started making their way toward the stairs that led to the conference room.

"Can you blame me?" Rachel asked.

"No," Kelly admitted with a huff.

Sheridan laughed softly as they filtered into the conference room, and was unable to keep her smile from softening as her phone buzzed with Parker's final reply, *It seems I just can't help myself when it comes to you, Sheridan Sloan.*

Her smile was replaced a moment later by her most professional neutral expression as Bartz strode into the conference room, looking like he was two seconds from turning the place upside down. He scowled at his team assembled around the table and asked, "Do we have anything on anything?"

"No, sir," Ivy answered, taking one for the team. "There's been no movement on the de Boulogne exhibit."

"And we've yet to catch a break on the Matisse," Sheridan added.

"May have something on the Balloon Dog," Cornell offered. "I'm in the middle of running down the lead now."

"I still don't see how that thing sold for almost fifty-eight and a half million," Brandon Nathan muttered.

"Ditto," Kelly agreed.

Sheridan shared a smile with Ivy. The sculpture in question really was awful.

"It's not our job to rate the artwork, it's our job to catch the guys who stole it and get it back," Bartz intoned.

"Yes, sir," Kelly and Nathan chorused.

Bartz rolled his eyes in a way that would make his seventeen-year-old daughter proud. "Okay. Moran, Wood, Nathan—work The Met. We'll give it the week to see if anything pans out, and then we'll pull out. I'm starting to think the whole thing was a hoax, but I'm not going to risk our reputation by having one of the most prestigious museums in the world robbed on our watch."

The three agents' shoulders dropped as they nodded, clearly resigned to their fate. "Yes, sir."

"Sloan, Innes. Find me something on the Matisse. Reach out to Interpol, see if they have anything working that might give you some ideas. Cornell, Coffee—you're on the ugly dog sculpture." He sighed and shook his head. "What are you all waiting for? Go!"

"Yes, sir," the group answered, their blended voices mingling with the rustle of movement as they all jumped to their feet.

"Another exciting week at the ol' Federal Bureau of Investigation, eh?" Kelly murmured as they joined into the line making its way out of the room.

Ivy turned and caught Kelly's eye. "I'm gonna need to work out after sitting in the van all day. You want to spar after work?"

"Fuck yeah, I do." Kelly grinned. "You're on."

nine

Parker waved goodbye to the two Boston PD officers who had helped her in serving a search warrant that ended in the successful recovery of an eggplant-sized lioness-woman statue carved out of limestone. It'd taken her over a year to nail down the statue's location, and the recovery had gone more smoothly than she could have hoped. "Thanks, guys."

"Our pleasure," the bigger of the two replied with a smirk as he and his partner rather forcefully guided the man who'd been in possession of the statue toward their cruiser.

Parker grinned and snapped off a quick salute before turning toward her car. She would have preferred her bike for the trip since the weather was gorgeous and there was something indescribable about roaring down the interstate with the wind curling around her body, but the fifty-seven million dollar statue she now carried meant that she needed a more responsible mode of transportation.

She popped the trunk of her rented Civic coupe and pulled the custom-made, foam-filled, energy-absorbing thermoplastic case that she'd brought with her to transport the piece. She carefully laid the statue on the carpet of the trunk before flipping the lid open, and she held her breath as she picked it back up to transfer it to its new, temporary, cushioned home. The foam interior was state-of-the-art, designed to depress and mold itself to any shape pressed into it, making it the absolute safest way to transport statuary and other three-dimensional pieces that were especially fragile.

Parker blew out the breath she'd been holding once the statue was secured and she was able to slowly lower the lid until the foam inside it, too, molded around the statue and she was able to close it completely. State-of-the-art technology or not, there was no way she was going to travel with such a valuable artifact in a crumple zone, and she carefully lifted the case from the trunk and moved it to the floor behind her seat. She checked her watch as she slipped behind the wheel, and briefly considered trying to make it home that night even though it was already pushing five o'clock, but decided against it almost as quickly. Hugo Lecomte had finally returned her call while she'd been making the trek up to Boston from Manhattan, and Marquis' tip had been spot-on. Lecomte gave her everything she needed to be able to recover the Matisse, which meant that she and Oliver needed to sit down and figure out what they were going to do.

She pulled out her phone as she started her car and set it in the cup holder between the front seats as it began to ring through the Bluetooth. Her brother picked up on the third ring. "Hey, Ollie. Please tell me you're not busy."

"Nope, just doing some research on the Marquis stuff. What's up?"

"I'm in town. Just recovered a statue near Harvard Square, and we need to talk. I finally heard from Lecomte."

"You want Thai or pizza?"

"It's Thursday."

"Right, so Thai-Thursday it is."

Parker grinned. "Go ahead and order me my usual."

"See you in a few," Oliver replied with a hint of a smile in his voice before disconnecting the call.

She'd spent enough time in Boston over the years visiting Oliver that she knew all the little back streets that let her avoid most of the end-of-workday traffic that clogged the roads, and it ended up taking her only five minutes longer than usual to make the trip from Beacon Hill to Oliver's place in East Cambridge.

"What's with the case?" Oliver asked as he opened his front door and waved her inside.

Parker dropped her duffle against the wall in the condo's tiny foyer and smirked. "A statue that'll net me a nice little million-dollar payday."

He grinned and gave her a high five. "Can I see it?"

"Sure." She laid the case on his dining room table, flipped the latches, and slowly lifted the lid.

Oliver made a face when the statue was finally revealed. "How is that thing worth so much? That might be the ugliest statue I've ever seen."

"There's no accounting for taste," Parker chuckled, shaking her head as she studied the piece. It was odd, for sure, but there was something about the statue that she found rather beautiful. She had no idea where the lioness ended and the woman began, but the figure was strong, with carefully carved muscles, and she definitely appreciated a culture that portrayed women as being fierce. "And there are certainly far uglier pieces floating around. Honestly though, it's a one-of-a-kind artifact from Sumer. Ergo, it's valuable not because of its aesthetics— which I actually like—but because of its rarity. I mean, it *is* over five thousand years old."

"Yeah, that'd have to be it," Oliver agreed with a small shake of his head. "You art people are weird. Anyway," he continued as she closed the lid of the case and flipped the latches shut, "food should be here in maybe ten, fifteen minutes."

"Sounds good."

"What'd Lecomte have to say about the Matisse?"

"First of all, never do business with that guy," she told him as she moved the case with the statue onto one of the chairs so they'd have room to eat. "I don't know if Marquis has something on him or what, but he was way too helpful. On the other hand, he was incredibly helpful so, in this case, I'm willing to overlook the fact that he apparently has no problem selling out the fence who is handling the transaction or confirming the fact that from everything he's found out about the piece that it is, in fact, headed to Lois Smythe."

"Damn." Oliver whistled softly. "If he's that loose with information, I'm surprised he's still in business. It's good for you, though."

Parker nodded and pulled out the chair next to the statue. "We do have a problem, though."

"With what?" Oliver asked as he took the seat opposite her.

"The FBI is keeping tabs on Marquis. They knew she was in town over the weekend."

"You're shitting me. How the hell did they know that?"

She shrugged and draped her left arm over the back of the chair beside her as she slumped in her seat. "Apparently Sheridan's boss was the lead investigator on a Degas heist who knows how many years ago that he swears she was involved with even though he couldn't prove it. But since she has enough ties to unsavory characters, the rumors of her being possibly involved in whatever case she's linked to is enough cause for the FBI to put a flag on her passport so they can keep tabs on her whenever she enters the country."

"Well, fuck," Oliver muttered and ran a hand through his hair.

"Exactly."

"I'm guessing Sheridan told you this?"

"Yeah, I ended up meeting her for drinks Sunday night and she was talking about work and it just kinda came up."

"You ended up meeting her for drinks," he repeated with a smirk. "Really?"

"Shut up," Parker muttered. "She'd had a rough dinner with her mother, and we met at The Poet for a drink to help her forget about it."

"Did you get a goodnight kiss?" he teased.

"No. We're just friends, Ollie, okay?" *Though that hug was pretty damn spectacular*, she couldn't help adding silently. She shook her head at how dreamy her inner voice sounded, and sighed. "Anyway, her mentioning how the FBI watches Marquis has me second-guessing this whole thing. I mean, I know you could use the money and all, but…"

Oliver pursed his lips and sighed. "I get what you're saying, but we're talking seven million bucks, here. We wouldn't have to worry about anything ever again."

"It's pretty much a white whale," Parker agreed softly, shaking her head.

"Exactly."

"I just really don't like the idea of working with somebody the Bureau is keeping such close tabs on, though. Minus that first job we pulled," she said, referring to the small-scale heist they'd pulled to settle an ill-advised College World Series bet Oliver had made with the worst possible bookie his junior year at MIT, "we've always avoided doing anything that put us on the radar of the FBI. And this isn't just on their radar, Ollie, it's right in their fucking crosshairs."

"So we don't deal with Marquis on US soil," he reasoned with a shrug.

"Two of the titles on her list are in the US."

Oliver tipped his head in a small nod. "True. However, acquiring those titles doesn't mean that we have to deliver them here. I have no problem flying to wherever in Europe to deliver them. My job is, after all, a lot more flexible than yours. I'll set up a shell account in Switzerland to take her payments, and then I'll route the money through numbered accounts in the Caymans, Panama, and the Seychelles that I've used in the past for jobs before depositing it into a numbered account in Luxembourg."

"Ollie…"

The doorbell rang before he could respond, and he knocked on the table as he got to his feet. "Hold that thought…"

She closed her eyes and slouched further in her seat so she could lean her head against the back of the chair as she waited for him to return. She wasn't surprised that he'd jumped from her concerns to trying to find a way around them, it was just…

"Are you honestly that concerned about the FBI being onto Marquis?" Oliver asked, pulling her from her thoughts as he set three bags of food onto the table. "Beer?"

"Sure." She dug into the bags and began sorting their food, raising her voice so he would hear her as he disappeared into the kitchen to fetch a couple beers. "Yes and no? I mean, I'd prefer they weren't, because I'm not a fucking idiot, but I trust you to get us in and out of each job before the FBI can crash the party. I know we're good, I just also know…" Her voice trailed off as he reentered the dining room with two bottles of Grey Lady Ale, his right eyebrow arched questioningly.

"What?"

She sighed and slid the container of veggie spring rolls between their plates so they could share. She offered Oliver a weak smile as she took the beer he handed her and pursed her lips thoughtfully as she took her seat.

"Parker, just say it," Oliver cajoled as he pulled two packages of disposable silverware from the bag and tossed one toward her.

"I told you that day at Kickshaw that I was done after this, but I don't know if I really want to even do it anymore," she admitted softly. "I'm sorry, Ollie, I am, but I like my life the way it is, and I really don't want to fuck it up."

Oliver hummed and leaned back in his chair, studying her silently for a moment. "I get it. I do. And, yeah, I like my life the way it is now too, it's just…" He sighed and shook his head. "Seven million dollars, ya know?"

"I know." Parker opened her container of vegetable pad Thai and stirred the noodles and veggies around with her fork as she waited for her thoughts to settle. "It's a shitton of money."

"Yeah," Oliver agreed as he dug into his chicken pad Thai. "Are you honestly saying that you could walk away from a payday like that? Because I can't…"

"Ollie," Parker sighed.

"Just, hear me out," he murmured, standing his fork up in the middle of his noodles. "I hear what you're saying. I do, Parker, okay? But this is a stupid amount of money on the table for what are honestly a handful of really fucking easy jobs. I looked into Dumas, the guy in Paris who has two of the books on Marquis' list. He's running a five-year-old security system that I could've hacked in junior high, and the entire job would maybe take us hour from start-to-finish—probably less, depending on how quickly we locate the book. I've got blueprints and entry/exit routes already mapped because it's that fucking simple. The others are all the same. Filthy rich people who think they have the best security in the world and who are in all actuality begging to be ripped off. We can do this."

"I know we can do it, Ollie." She dropped her fork and reached for a spring roll. "What I'm questioning is if we *should.*"

"Do you want me to see if I can get someone else to take the job with me? I can see if Rick is available…"

"Fuck no. Rick is an idiot." Parker barely suppressed a shudder at the memory of the one job Oliver had brought Rick Frasier in on because they'd needed a third man to pull it off. He'd set off a trip alarm thirty-seconds after they'd gotten into the building, had the gall to try to blame her for it when everybody fucking knew it was his fault, and then proceeded to try to yank the wrong goddamn painting from the wall despite hers and Oliver's orders that the only thing they needed him to do was keep an eye out for anyone coming near the building and let them handle it. "I don't want either of us to end up in jail, Ollie."

Oliver chuckled. "He's not an idiot."

She stared at him and arched a brow in silent challenge.

"Fine, he's kind of an idiot," Oliver admitted. "But you only gotta be able to read the spine of a book on this one, Parker," he pointed out. "It's not like trying to pick out a forgery in a stack of originals or anything."

"He's sloppy and I don't trust him."

"Then who do you suggest I call?" Oliver asked, holding his hands out to his sides imploringly. "I mean, I'd call Lucy, but she's on a fucking anklet and working for the FBI so she's out. Sven is underground somewhere ever since he pulled that da Vinci job in Italy last summer. Neal is working a long con in Brussels that he's not going to abandon, and…"

She closed her eyes and blew out a soft breath. "You're serious about this one, aren't you?"

"It's seven million dollars, Parker."

Parker puffed her cheeks out and shook her head. She didn't trust many people to watch Oliver's back, and those few she did—Sven, Lucy, and Neal—had just been crossed off the list of potential partners on this job. And for as much as she didn't want to go through with it, she couldn't let him try this on his own. Or, god forbid, with fucking Rick. "Okay. Fine. I'll do the jobs with you, but this is the last time, Ollie. I swear to god, I'm done after this."

"Me too," Oliver agreed quickly. "I wasn't kidding when I said I like my life, Park. I'd just like it a hell of a lot more without a mountain of bills hanging over my head and a nice little cushion in a numbered offshore account."

She nodded. "Okay. So what's the plan? Have you worked anything out besides Dumas' place?"

He grinned. "Sit tight." He jumped up and ran down the hall to, she guessed, his office, and returned a moment later with a blue spiral notebook that had random loose-leaf sheets fitted between the pages. "So, Dumas is easy because he's in Paris and you're going to Paris soon, I'd guess, given the intel from Lecomte?"

"Next week, probably." She nodded. "Lecomte said the Matisse is going through authentication in Barcelona and will be in Paris by next Thursday at the latest. Smythe is in Hong Kong on a business trip until that Sunday, so we'd have Friday and Saturday to recover the painting from the fence before she returns."

"You don't want to try to nab her too?"

"While I'm sure Marquis would love that, it'd be easier to swoop in and grab it from the fence before he can deliver it. If he gives Smythe up to *Gendarmerie*, that's on him. I don't get paid any extra for arrests, and I'd rather not deal with a high-powered law firm trying to claim the piece belongs to their client and dragging this shit out."

"Good point."

"Thanks. Anyway…" She rolled her hand in a circle as she picked up her fork. "Plan?"

"It's fluid," he insisted. "I mean, we'll pull the Dumas job next weekend when you're in Paris for work because that's too good an opportunity to pass up. I think we'd be better off to space the US jobs between the ones in Europe because it'd hopefully slow Sheridan's unit down in their investigation. If you want to save the two in New York until the end, we can do that too. Ideally, we'd work around the target's schedules—hit them when they're out of town on business or whatever—but all the jobs would be easy enough to pull when the target is out to dinner or something. Books are small and easy to move and private residences don't take long, you know that as well as I do, so it's just a matter of making sure we have a solid game of misdirection happening to keep Sheridan Sloan and company off our ass."

"If it doesn't feel right…"

"We will pull out," he agreed. "But I honestly don't think we'll need to. We'll finish this one last job and ride it into the sunset. You'll see. It'll be a walk in the park."

She pointed her fork at him. "It better be."

"It will," he insisted. He shook his head and traded his fork for his beer. "You're not going to tell Sheridan about the Matisse lead, are you?"

"Why?"

"Besides the fact that you seem pretty hell-bent on avoiding landing on her unit's radar?" When Parker tipped her head and lifted her right shoulder in a *well yeah, besides that* type gesture, he took a long drink of his beer and shrugged. "That was pretty much my whole point."

"It's a good point," she allowed. "However, as I'm going to need to enlist the help of the *Gendarmerie Nationale* because I can't legally just waltz into France and recover the painting without letting local law enforcement know what I'm doing, bringing her into the loop on the location of the Matisse would make my life a hell of a lot easier. She can pull strings I'd have to try like hell to avoid tripping over."

Oliver shook his head and lifted his beer to his lips.

"If you can't get us around an investigative unit whose jurisdiction we technically won't be in, just call the whole damn thing off, Ollie," she sighed.

"I can do it, no problem."

"Good."

Oliver smirked, looking far too pleased with himself as he replied, "Good."

TEN

Sheridan brushed her hair out of her eyes as she sidestepped a tourist who was busy looking anywhere other than where they were going and reached for the door of the upscale art gallery on the Upper East Side.

"Do you think this'll work?" Kelly asked as he took the door from her and motioned for her to go on ahead of him.

Sheridan sighed. She'd discovered when she'd been combing through sales at the Sotheby's here on the island that Matisse's *The Young Sailor I* had been up for auction the year before. It was unusual for a Matisse to end up on the open market, and the discovery had yielded a goldmine of information because it gave them a recent list of people who were interested in acquiring the late artist's work. And since it wasn't unheard of for people with means to occasionally find alternative ways to acquire the pieces they desired, she and Kelly had spent the last five days looking into the people who had bid on the piece. Background checks and phone interviews had cleared every individual on the list, except one.

The person who had won the auction.

They had done everything they could to unearth the name of the buyer, but the person had hidden their true identity behind a series of impenetrable shell corporations. A warrant would have been enough to unearth the buyer's identity, but they didn't have nearly enough to convince a judge to sign one and so they'd decided to take a trip to visit the woman who had facilitated the purchase to see if she had any information that might help them divine where Zeller's Matisse might be headed.

"Who knows," Sheridan murmured as she glanced around the large, open space. The walls were a predictable soft white—all the better to not influence the colors of the artwork—and the floor was a light maple that added to the brightness of the room. There was nothing particularly noteworthy about the gallery itself, it fit into the accepted aesthetic for the type, and she couldn't help but wonder if this idea of theirs was going to pan out.

The art on display was more diverse than she had expected from the outside. There were plenty of rather pedestrian, simple yet gorgeous landscapes and cityscapes spread along the walls, interspersed by gauzy, impressionist-inspired works that, while interesting, fell short of the masters the artists were undoubtedly trying to imitate. Those styles filled the majority of the walls, though there were a handful of thoroughly modern, obnoxious Pollock-inspired canvases that disjointedly bleated their faux-greatness to the world pieces littered amongst them.

She would never understand people who thought that paint flung haphazardly at a canvas constituted "art."

"Pretty sure a monkey finger-painted that one," Kelly whispered, motioning toward an especially awful piece.

She huffed a laugh. "I'm pretty sure that monkeys around the world would be offended that you'd dare suggest that they would ever create something so hideous."

"Good point," he chuckled. "I know I'm not trained in art like you or anything, but these don't look anything like Matisse's stuff," he observed, waving at the paintings around them.

"They don't," she agreed with a small nod.

"Can I help you?" a new voice interrupted them.

Sheridan forced a tight smile as she looked up at the woman who'd appeared from the back of the gallery. The woman was tall and thin, with dark brown hair and even darker eyes, and everything from the gigantic diamond on her left hand to her designer dress and the designer heels she was wearing screamed money. "I hope so. Are you, by any chance, Amelie Tyrell?"

"I am." Tyrell frowned and crossed her arms over her stomach, instantly defensive. "And you are?"

Sheridan nudged Kelly with her left elbow as she reached into her pocket with her right hand for her badge. "Agents Sloan and Innes with the FBI."

Tyrell's posture stiffened almost imperceptibly for the briefest of moments before her shoulders dropped and her hands fluttered to her sides in what Sheridan was sure was supposed to pass as nonchalance. It was not usual for people become defensive in their presence, it was a natural reaction when faced with a so-called authority figure, but Tyrell's sudden, unconvincing reversal was interesting. Sheridan made a mental note to look into the woman more when they were back at the office.

"I see," Tyrell replied slowly. "What can I do for you, Agents?"

"While looking through old auction paperwork, we noticed that you represented the buyer of a Matisse at Sotheby's last year, is that correct?" Sheridan asked.

"I did…" Tyrell shook her head. "Though, I can assure you that, to the best of my knowledge, everything regarding that transaction was legal."

"I'm sure it was, Ms. Tyrell," Kelly assured her with a smile. Sheridan groaned inwardly. He always took the 'good-cop' half the equation. "We're looking into a missing painting here in the city, and are just trying to figure out who might be interested in art like that."

"A Matisse has been stolen?" Tyrell asked, suddenly much more alert.

"We're not at liberty to discuss an open investigation," Kelly replied smoothly, sidestepping her question while still getting across the fact that something of incredible value had been stolen, "but we were hoping you could share the name of the buyer you represented with us. Or if there is anyone else you're aware of who might be interested in acquiring a rare piece of art?"

"I'm afraid that I don't know the name of the buyer I represented." Tyrell shook her head, looking genuinely sorry to not be of help. Maybe Kelly flirting with her was a good thing, after all. "I was hired by a gentleman in Paris who represented the buyer to facilitate the purchase here. They thought it'd increase their odds of securing the painting to have a local on the ground, or something like that. I don't know. It worked, I guess, because we won the auction."

"Do you have any notes on the purchase?" Sheridan asked.

Tyrell frowned. "I might. Wait here, please," she instructed as she turned on her heel and strode into the back where her office was undoubtedly tucked away.

"Fingers crossed," Kelly muttered once she was out of earshot. "Do we know the big art dealers in Paris?"

"No, but the *Gendarmerie Nationale* would. If she doesn't have the name of the guy, we can always call over to Paris and see if they've heard anything or would have anything that might help us out," Sheridan mused.

"Marquis is based out of Paris, right?" Kelly double-checked.

Sheridan bobbed her head from side-to-side. "Her businesses are in Paris and she stays in the city during the week but, last I heard, she still calls her estate in Nice home."

"Would she have bid on the Matisse that was auctioned?"

"With The Antiquarian, it's anyone's guess," Sheridan confirmed with a sigh. "Her representatives are always quite active on the auction scene and she's always finding new ones so we certainly can't rule her out, that's for sure." She stood straighter when Tyrell strutted out of the back room with a triumphant smile on her face and a manila folder in her hands.

"I could only find a few notes from that purchase," Tyrell announced as she stood in front of them. She offered Kelly the file. "I made copies of them all and put them in there for you. The gentleman who'd contacted me was named Phillip Vasseur. His phone number and the address of his antique shop in Paris are in there—" she motioned toward the file "—but that's it, I'm afraid."

"We'll definitely look into Vasseur," Sheridan said. "If he doesn't end up having anything that might help us, is there anyone else you could think of who'd be willing to purchase a stolen Matisse?"

"Not really, no. I'm sorry. Everyone I've ever worked with has been completely above board."

"We just always have to ask," Kelly assured her with a roguish smile that made Tyrell flush. "This is great, thanks."

Sheridan barely resisted the urge to roll her eyes at his antics. "Yes, thank you, Ms. Tyrell. We'll be back in touch if we can think of any further questions."

Tyrell smiled at Kelly. "I look forward to it."

Sheridan groaned quietly and bumped Kelly with her elbow as she turned. "Let's go, Innes."

He smiled at Tyrell one last time before he fell into step beside her. "Well," he declared once they were back on the sidewalk. "That wasn't a total bust, huh? Think the *Gendarmerie* have dealt with this Vasseur guy before?"

"Only one way to find out," Sheridan said as she opened the passenger door of their car. "Let's get back to the office and give them a call."

"You gonna call Parker and tell her what we found?" Kelly asked as he slipped behind the wheel. "Maybe she's heard of this Vasseur guy."

Sheridan hummed thoughtfully as her hand drifted toward the jacket pocket where her phone was. "We don't really know anything yet, though."

"You just don't want to call her with me close enough to listen-in, is that it?" Kelly teased.

She tipped her head in a small nod. She'd traded a few texts with Parker over the last five days, but they hadn't actually *talked*, and she'd much rather wait until Kelly wasn't sitting two feet away from her to give her a call. "I don't want to bug her about this until we have something more concrete to go on." He frowned and gave her a disappointed little pout. "Fine," she sighed. "I'll send her a text to tell her a little bit of what we just found out, and that I'll call her later. Better?"

He smiled and shrugged, clearly pleased with himself for forcing her hand. "Sure thing, Sloan. If you think that's best."

"God, you're annoying," she muttered as she pulled her phone out of her pocket and fired off a quick message to Parker. *Might have a lead on the Matisse. Will call later after we chase this lead down.* "There. Sent. Happy?"

"Incredibly," he sassed.

Before she could respond, her phone rang, and she had to glance out her window to hide her smile when she spotted Parker's name on the screen. "Hey, you. What's up?"

"Besides that smile?" Kelly teased in a hushed whisper.

She punched him in the shoulder and turned further toward the side window as Parker replied, *"Nothing much. Am just driving home from Boston. I scanned your text but can't really reply right now, so I thought I'd give you a call to see what you found because I'm pretty sure that I found something too."*

"Why were you in Boston?" Sheridan asked.

"Oh. I finally recovered the Guennol Lioness *that I've been tracking for over a year,"* Parker shared with a smile clear in her voice.

"Holy shit. Seriously?" Sheridan's eyebrows lifted in surprise.

"Seriously," Parker laughed.

"Damn. We've been stuck at a dead-end on that thing forever! How in the world did you track it down?"

"Blind luck. It honestly just took a lot of digging through mountains of false information before I finally found the lead that pointed me in the right direction. But, back to your message about the Matisse. You guys might have a lead?"

"Yeah," Sheridan confirmed. "We were running down buyers of Matisse's *The Young Sailor I* that was sold at Sotheby's last year, and a local dealer who represented an anonymous buyer was hired by an antiques dealer in Paris named Phillip Vasseur. That in and of itself isn't illegal, but it is odd. There's no reason a European intermediary couldn't bid remotely on an item. It happens all the time on big auctions like that. Have you heard of Vasseur before?"

Parker hummed. *"I have. And, you're gonna love this, I have a source in Paris who's told me that he's the guy working as the fence for our missing Matisse. I was actually going to call you when I got back to my office later this afternoon to ask if you could reach out to the* Gendarmerie Nationale *to see if they could help me in trying to recover the painting."*

Now it was Sheridan's turn to laugh. "They're actually who I'll be calling as soon as we get back to the office. How much do you trust your source?"

"In this case, I'm pretty confident in what he's given me. And, before you ask, no, I can't tell you who it is. Confidentiality is currency in my job, I'm afraid, and I can't afford to burn bridges I might need in the future."

"I understand," Sheridan assured her with a small shake of her head. "But, just to be safe, I'll still ask the *Gendarmerie Nationale* if they know anything about Vasseur. They'll probably want to do a little investigating themselves but, provided it all looks good, we could possibly be in Paris next week recovering your painting."

"I like the sound of that," Parker murmured.

"I'll bet you do." Sheridan smiled at the sound of Parker's soft laughter. "How's your schedule looking? Would you have time to meet for dinner or something this weekend?"

"Now that was smooth," Kelly murmured approvingly. "Good job."

She shot him a glare that had him immediately looking back out the windshield like he'd never said anything in the first place, and held her breath as seconds ticked by without Parker answering. She knew it was stupid to care so much because Parker was just a friend, but that did nothing to make her feel less nervous as she waited for Parker to respond.

Finally, after what seemed like forever, Parker cleared her throat and said, *"I'm so sorry, but I don't think I'm going to have time this weekend. Between this recovery I'm going to have to do all the paperwork for before I can return it to the museum it'd been stolen from in Dallas, and then everything with the Matisse…"*

"No. That's fine. I totally get it," Sheridan muttered, feeling her cheeks flush.

Parker sighed. *"I really do want to,"* she insisted gently. *"I just… Work. You know?"*

"Yeah. I know. Maybe some other time." Sheridan licked her lips and shifted in her seat so the cool air blowing out of the vent hit her square in the face to hopefully help chase her embarrassed blush away.

"I'm so sorry," Parker apologized.

Sheridan closed her eyes. If she responded to Parker's apology, she'd sound even more pathetic to Kelly, and after a week of quietly looking forward to the time she'd get to see Parker again, the last thing she wanted was to deal with his teasing. "I'll call you after I've talked to the *Gendarmerie*, and we can figure out where we're at on the Matisse. Sound good?"

"Sounds wonderful," Parker murmured. *"Again, Sheridan, I'm so sor—"*

"I'm sorry," Sheridan cut her off, "but I've got another call coming through. Talk to you later?"

"Yeah, of course. Hope you have a good rest of your day," Parker replied softly.

"You too," Sheridan muttered as kindly as her wounded ego allowed before she disconnected the call. She blew out a harsh breath and shook her head as she warned her partner, "Not a word."

"No idea what you're talking about," Kelly lied smoothly.

"Good."

"She's an idiot, though."

"Kelly…" she sighed.

"Just sayin'," he insisted. "You're a catch, Sheridan Sloan. And she's a fool if she doesn't see that."

She glanced over at him, and was glad to see he was staring dutifully at the traffic in front of them. "She just recovered the *Guennol Lioness*. So between closing out that recovery and returning it to the museum it'd been stolen from, and then everything with the Matisse…"

"She's got a lot on her plate right now." Kelly glanced at her and grinned. "Okay, so maybe she's not a total idiot. On the bright side, assuming Vasseur is our guy, maybe you'll get to go out with her when we're in Paris…"

She waved a hand at the signal in front of them that'd just turned green. "Just drive, Innes," she muttered, beyond grateful that her voice didn't betray the hopeful way her stomach fluttered at the idea.

eleven

Parker dropped her suitcase beside her bed and flopped face-down onto the mattress with a groan, too worn out from traveling to appreciate being in her own apartment for the first time since before dawn Saturday morning.

Authenticating statuary was more difficult than paintings because one couldn't simply chip off a piece of the stone to carbon date it or anything, and so she'd spent the weekend in Washington DC while the Smithsonian's resident expert in Sumerian art inspected the *Guennol Lioness*. She spent her days alternating between hovering along the perimeter of the basement labs watching the historian work and taking brief excursions beyond the museum's castle-like walls to give herself—and the historian who didn't seem to appreciate having an audience—a break from it all.

And on any other weekend, it wouldn't have been a bad deal. She loved meandering the museums and pathways of Washington DC, but it'd been impossible for her to find any real enjoyment in the trip this time around because her phone was constantly buzzing with texts from Oliver about the Dumas job and Sheridan about the Matisse recovery. Add to that the guilt she still felt about the rejection she'd heard in Sheridan's voice when she'd forced herself to decline her dinner invitation, and it'd been, perhaps, the longest weekend of her life.

She knew that the best thing she could do was keep her distance from Sheridan, but no matter how many times she told herself that she'd done the right thing, she couldn't stop thinking about her. Couldn't stop hearing that little hitch in Sheridan's breath when she'd turned her down, or keep from wishing that there was a way for her to go back in time and say yes, she'd love to go to dinner.

Her heart was waging a full-scale war on her better judgment, and it was winning. Oh, how it was winning. Every time she'd begin to find something other than Sheridan to focus on, she'd get a text or a phone call from her as the pieces of the Matisse case began to fall into place, and she'd lose any ground she'd made.

And then there was Saturday night, when the conversation about the case had been exhausted for the evening, but then her phone rang and she saw Sheridan's name on the screen. She'd answered immediately, because it'd been a long day and the sky was dark and her self-restraint was gone, and they'd spent *hours* on the phone, talking about everything and nothing, and all the stuff in-between.

Keeping her distance from Sheridan Sloan, she was coming to accept, was a nearly impossible task. And it was also becoming one that she was increasingly reticent to even attempt.

For all her failings on remaining emotionally distant, though, her job did a pretty good job at forcing a geographic distance. After close to two days of studying the *Guennol Lioness,* the Smithsonian's expert had declared the statue to be authentic late Sunday afternoon, and she was off to Dallas before the crack of dawn the next day.

Returning the statue to the Dallas Museum of Art should have taken only a few hours, just enough time to present the museum's director with the Smithsonian expert's analysis and wait for them to accept it before, with a few handshakes, she bid her farewell and retreated to her hotel for the evening. Instead, the director and the president of the board had insisted on taking her to dinner to celebrate the return of their statue. And, since there was no way she could decline their invitation without damaging Cabot and Carmichael's reputation, she'd accepted with all the grace she wished she could have shown Sheridan the Friday before.

The five-star restaurant they had taken her to had been packed, and they'd both seemed to delight in introducing her to what seemed like everyone in the place as they boasted about how she'd found their missing statue, and it had been after eleven o'clock by the time she'd managed to convince them that she really did need to get back to her hotel.

She'd rolled out of bed roughly six hours later in order to make it to the airport for her flight home, and then spent the majority of the morning on her phone while she waited for her plane to be discharged from whatever emergency maintenance it'd had to undergo. While she lamented the loss of the sleep she could have gotten had she known the plane wouldn't be leaving until a good seven hours after its scheduled departure, she had been able to find a quiet corner in a cafe where she had been able to return the call she had missed from Sheridan the night before. Even though they had mostly discussed the recovery they would be attempting in a couple days' time, she had felt calmer and more rested after talking to Sheridan for those fifty-four minutes than she imagined she would have been even if she'd managed to take a nap.

And, oh, how she could have used that nap, because once a plane had finally arrived at their gate and they'd been allowed to board, she had spent the entire trip from Dallas to JFK trapped between the window and a disproportionally overconfident sleazeball of a businessman in a cheap suit who had tried to chat her up the entire time.

It'd been a hell of a trip and she was going to have to do it all the next day, and she took a deep breath as she picked her head up enough to look at the clock on her bedside table. Eight forty-five. She let her head fall back to the bed with a groan.

"Fuck me," she muttered into the soft down of her comforter as she placed her hands under her shoulders and pushed herself up off the bed and back onto her feet.

She had less than eighteen hours to sleep, unpack and repack her bag, and get over to her office to finalize the claim paperwork for the *Guennol Lioness* and gather what she needed for the Matisse recovery before she had to be back at JFK for her flight to Paris.

Work and packing would have to wait though, because what she needed to do now was to get some food and charge her phone. It was undoubtedly full to bursting with messages and alerts by now, and she knew that she'd have to deal with at least some of them before she would be able to go to bed.

She knew from having run her phone all the way down too many times to count that it would take at least ten minutes for the phone to get enough charge to turn on, so once she had plugged it into the charger on her kitchen island, she set about digging through her fridge for food. Nothing really looked good, and she was too tired to put much effort into making anything that required more than a couple steps. After what seemed like forever staring into the fridge, she decided to just toss a couple pieces of whole grain bread into the toaster and then slather them in peanut butter.

She glanced at her phone as she took a bite of her toast, and hummed around the peanut butter sticking to the roof of her mouth when she saw that the red battery had turned green. The phone would have to stay plugged-in for her to use it, but at least she could check her messages now.

Her lock screen loaded with a screen full of alerts, and although her eyes immediately landed on Sheridan's name amongst the banners, she forced herself to open her email instead. Work first, Sheridan second, she told herself as she one-handed a message to her boss to let him know that she'd be in the office by seven the next morning to finalize the paperwork for the *Guennol Lioness* before she left for Paris. There were a few other work-related emails she was able to clear out of her inbox without too much effort, and she shoved the last bit of her toast into her mouth as she closed out her email app and switched to her messages.

Both Oliver and Sheridan had sent a few messages while her phone had been dead and, although she would have much rather ignored her brother for now, she knew that she couldn't. He'd arrived in Paris Sunday morning to begin the legwork for the Dumas job, and if he needed something from her or had come across a problem, she'd need to take care of that before she could let herself get distracted by Sheridan.

She took a swig of water from the refillable bottle she always kept on the counter as she read Oliver's message. *Ran a test of the security system tonight. No problems. Will monitor security company to see if they notice anything, but everything is looking good for this weekend. Give me a call once you land here and we'll figure out where to meet up.*

Since everything sounded like it was going according to his plan and that he didn't need a response from her on it all, she just replied with two thumbs up emojis and a quick, *Should land around 0730 Thursday. Will call once I'm on the ground.*

That gave her a little over twenty-four hours to finish coming to terms with the fact that she was once again going to venture into a world she thought she'd left behind. Once upon a time, nothing beat the thrill that she'd gotten out of their heists. But as she became more and more proficient in her career, the heady defiance of outwitting the authorities had given way to the deeper satisfaction of besting outright swindlers and thieves. In the past few years, she had discovered that she liked not having to look over her shoulder or the constant moving that kept her under the radar.

It helped, too, of course, that she regularly brought home a more than decent paycheck.

Then there were the times when she met people who, like her, genuinely appreciated art for far more than its dollar value. She wouldn't soon forget her first major recovery, an O'Keeffe cityscape.

To her surprise, the silver-haired, grizzled owner had stood there for a long moment with tears in his eyes when she returned the painting. "Thank you," he'd said gruffly. "This was my mother's favorite. My father gave it to her after they married…"

He trailed off, embarrassed, and to her further astonishment, Parker found herself saying, "She was one of the first artists whose work I could recognize—on sight, I mean—without looking at the signature. Her flowers are gorgeous, of course, but even with her New York skyscrapers you couldn't help but fall in love with her vibrant use of color. Georgia was a bold artist from the start."

The elderly man smiled. "That's what my mother liked about this one, too. They were staunch New Yorkers, and one day they stepped into a gallery, and the way my father tells it, my mother was captivated on sight. He wasn't so sure about it himself, it was only 1929 after all, and here was this modernist canvas, and by a woman no less. But my mother loved it, and when my father was assigned abroad, she made sure it had a place in every home we went. She said it felt like we'd brought a piece of home with us. The thought that I'd lost my mother's painting…" He cleared his throat, and the conversation reverted to formalities and paperwork soon after.

The O'Keeffe recovery was memorable also because it had been not only her first significant commission, but also the one that got her a fully credited position in the recovery division at Cabot and Carmichael. That paved the way for her to move from a closet of a studio apartment in New Jersey into Manhattan itself, and that was when she'd been introduced to Gregory.

The life she had now was everything she'd once wanted. She was putting down roots in a vibrant city, and there were people in her life that she considered family, as well as friends.

And now there was Sheridan.

She took a deep breath as she switched over to Sheridan's thread, and let it go slowly when she saw that she'd missed a handful of messages from her. The first four were about their case, mostly rehashing and confirming things they'd already discussed, but it was the last one in the thread that had her staring at her phone as if entranced.

Are you ignoring me?

The message was followed by a winking emoji—which suggested the question was playful and not accusatory—but her stomach still sank as she reread the message. She really *should* be ignoring her. If she was smart, as soon as she had the Matisse back in her hands, she knew that she should delete Sheridan's contact information from her phone and try to forget her.

She pressed her thumb to Sheridan's name at the top of the message thread to bring up her contact information. Her throat tightened and a hollow feeling settled in her chest as she imagined deleting Sheridan's information from her phone. It'd been a long, long time since anyone had made her feel like Sheridan did and, though she was completely aware of the fact that there was nothing right about the timing of all of this, she didn't want to give that up.

Didn't want to give her up.

Even though it would be the best way to protect everybody in case the Marquis job went sideways.

She blew out a rough breath as she looked up at the skylights overhead. A text explaining what had happened would more than suffice, but the sky was dark and her self-restraint was once again all but gone, and all she really wanted was to hear Sheridan's voice.

She was being stupid, she told herself as she pressed her thumb to the call button. Reaching out to Sheridan like this was the worst possible thing she could do, but she was too tired to fight against herself.

Sheridan answered on the third ring, and Parker closed her eyes at the way her heart swooped up into her throat at the sound of her voice.

"So you're not ignoring me?"

"Yeah, sorry about that," Parker apologized as she blinked her eyes back open. "I had the travel day from hell and my phone died, and…"

Sheridan laughed. *"I was just teasing you. I'm sorry your day sucked. Did you at least get everything squared away with the statue?"*

Parker nodded as she pushed herself to her feet and unplugged her phone as she wandered across her open apartment to her bedroom area. "Still have some paperwork to finish up in the morning," she shared as she plugged the phone into the charger beside her bed and toed off her shoes, "but everything in Texas is handled, yeah." She groaned softly as she laid down on her bed. "From the messages I missed, it looks like you've finalized everything with the *Gendarmerie* for Friday. Do I need to do anything there?"

"Nope. I've got it covered. You just have to show up."

"I can do that."

"I'm so very glad to hear it," Sheridan teased, her voice low and smooth with just enough of a husk that it sent a pleasant flutter through Parker's stomach.

Parker smiled. "Are you, now?"

"I am," Sheridan murmured. She cleared her throat softly and added in a fragile whisper, *"I'm really looking forward to seeing you again."*

Parker closed her eyes and swallowed thickly. She was playing with fire and she knew it, but if the risk of being burned meant that Sheridan would whisper words like that in her ear, she would gladly welcome the flames. "Me too," she breathed. The little sound of a pleased hum from the other end of the line made her smile in spite of herself, and she licked her lips as she rolled onto her side, cradling her phone against her ear as she pulled her knees up toward her chest. "When do you guys land in Paris?"

"Friday morning. So I'll have a whole six hours to try to recover from my jet lag before we gotta be at the precinct. Oh, you never said, or, well, I mean, you didn't respond to my text because you phone was dead and whatever, but—"

Parker smiled. "Breathe, Sloan."

Sheridan blew a little raspberry that made her smile even wider. *"Shut up. Anyway, would you want to meet up somewhere near the* Gendarmerie Nationale *so we can all get there at the same time?"*

"That sounds wonderful. Text me the time and the place, and I'll be there."

"With bells on?"

"Pretty sure they wouldn't go with my outfit, but if you'd really like that, I'll see what I can do."

Sheridan laughed. *"All right. No bells, then. I'm assuming you're going to be pretty busy tomorrow since you fly out at night, so I guess I'll talk to you Friday?"*

"I can't wait."

"Me neither," Sheridan replied softly, a smile evident in her tone. *"Goodnight, Parker."*

Parker stifled a yawn and whispered, "Goodnight, Sheridan."

She let the yawn she'd held back rip free as she opened the app that allowed her to remotely control the lights in her apartment, and shook her head as she flipped the digital switches to kill them all. She set her phone onto the bedside table to charge while she slept, and then shucked her pants and shirt that were wrinkled and dirty from traveling. Once she was down to just her underwear, she slipped beneath the duvet, and she sighed as she snuggled deeper beneath its weight, the memory of Sheridan's voice whispering in her ear the perfect lullaby to send her off to sleep.

TWELVE

It was all Sheridan could do to stifle the yawn that desperately wanted to break free as she waited to place her coffee order at Sparrows, a cute little coffee shop not far from the Paris branch of the *Gendarmerie Nationale*. A string of what felt like never-ending days spent fine-tuning the details of their upcoming raid on Lecomte's shop had left her utterly exhausted even before their red-eye to Paris that'd touched down an hour after sunrise that morning, and she was running on fumes. She was in desperate need of a cup of coffee—or three, or four—and she silently cursed the handful of people in front of her who were keeping her from her caffeine.

She'd honestly thought that the coffee shop would be deserted at twelve-thirty on a Friday afternoon.

A yawn slipped free before she could reign in it, and she shook her head as she willed the line ahead of her to just fucking move already. They needed to be at the station in an hour, which meant that she had sixty precious minutes to shake off her jet lag, and if she could just get a goddamn cup of coffee…

Her inner rant was interrupted by the soft brush of a body against her side, and she stiffened at the unexpected contact. She relaxed a split-second later when a familiar voice drawled in her ear, "Your partner just offered me twenty bucks to grab your ass."

Sheridan's heart fluttered into her throat as she turned to look at Parker, who was dressed similarly to herself in a white oxford and black slacks, and her lips curled to match Parker's gentle smile as their eyes locked. She had known that she'd missed Parker, but she hadn't realized exactly how much she'd missed her until this very moment. "Oh, he did, did he?"

Parker nodded. "He absolutely did."

Sheridan chuckled and rolled her eyes. She wished she could say she was surprised by it, but the offer was so perfectly Kelly that she knew Parker was telling the truth. "And what did you say?"

"I told him he was selling you short. An ass like yours is worth at least a Benjamin." Parker waggled her eyebrows comically and grinned when she laughed. "And then I told him that I never put my hands on a lady without her permission, so both you and his money were safe."

"What a gentleman," Sheridan chuckled.

Parker shoved her hands into her pockets, looking entirely pleased with herself, and rocked back onto her heels. "I do try. Your partner, on the other hand…"

Sheridan groaned. "What'd he do?"

Parker glanced back at Kelly, and then shook her head as she turned back to her. "He said that if I got your permission, he'd give me two hundred bucks."

"Of course he did." Sheridan shot a glare over her shoulder at Kelly, who grinned at her and gave her two thumbs up. She rolled her eyes as she looked back at Parker, and smiled in spite of her annoyance with her partner. "He thinks he's so damn funny." She shook her head. "You know what? Just go ahead and do it, Parker."

"I…" Parker cleared her throat and blinked twice in a most adorable way. "I'm sorry. What?"

"He's been driving me nuts all week," Sheridan explained vaguely. She would die before she told Parker about the way he'd gleefully teased her about having a *thing* for her, if only because, if she did, she'd be forced to do something about it. And she was not at all ready to even think about that yet. "Take his money."

He'd have a field day teasing her about it later, but his wallet would be two hundred dollars lighter, and that was a fair trade so far as she was concerned.

"You want me to grab your ass?" Parker clarified, her brow furrowing with confusion.

Sheridan's hand twitched with the urge to reach up and smooth the crease with her thumb, and she bit her lip as she tilted her head in a small nod. "We're friends, Parker. I trust you."

"Well, that's…" Parker blew out a soft breath. "Can't I at least buy you dinner first or something?"

Sheridan laughed. "You really are a gentleman, aren't you?" She grinned at the sheepish smile that tugged at Parker's lips and the faint blush that spread across her cheeks as she ducked her head. Parker was usually so confident and suave that she'd honestly expected her to just roll with all of this without this utterly charming display of chivalry. "How about you grab my ass now"—she shook her head at the ridiculousness of that statement because who says something like that?—"and you can buy me dinner later if you still think it's necessary?"

"Okay. Yeah. That sounds good." Parker nodded slowly. She ran a hand through her hair as she turned to look either at Kelly or the street beyond the shop's front windows. It was clear that she was searching for something, though Sheridan had no idea what that might be, but she must have found it, because when she looked back at her, the right side of her mouth was quirked in a small smile. "What about tonight? After we recover my painting and you guys do whatever it is you do after stuff like this?"

"That sounds wonderful," Sheridan agreed softly.

"Okay." Parker nodded. "So, um…" She rubbed a hand over the back of her neck, clearly still hesitant to go through with the whole thing despite the fact that she had told her it was okay. "I'm going to grab your ass, now, I guess." Her forehead wrinkled. "How do you want to do this, exactly?"

"God, you're adorable," Sheridan murmured, enjoying the way Parker blushed in response, and turned back toward the counter to see that the line in front of her had shorted to one lone soul who was staring at their phone. She took a few steps forward to close the gap that'd developed while they'd been talking, and held her breath as Parker's fingertips pressed lightly against the small of her back.

She had suggested this only to make Kelly pay for daring to use Parker to push her buttons, had honestly expected to feel nothing more than the platonic touch of a friend, but as those soft, almost hesitant fingers drifted lower, she realized how wrong she was. The gentle bump of Parker's fingers on her belt beneath the tail of her blazer made her breath catch, and her heart fluttered into her throat at the feeling of Parker's hand sliding slowly over her left cheek. She licked her lips at the way Parker hesitated for the briefest of moments before her hand curled around her behind, and her eyes fluttered shut when Parker's grip tightened in a light squeeze.

"Is this okay?" Parker whispered.

Sheridan nodded, not trusting herself to speak because her heart had yet to leave her throat. *Okay* was a bit of an understatement, because Parker's touch was wonderful, but it was also the last possible adjective she'd use to describe the situation because she was not at all prepared to deal with anything like this. The feeling of Parker's arms around her on the train platform had been heavenly—strong and sure and comforting and just what she'd needed after those awful couple hours with her mother—but she'd never anticipated something as innocent as a quick ass-grab to make her feel so utterly, embarrassingly aroused.

Or so utterly, embarrassingly disappointed when Parker's grip loosened and her hand fell away.

A playful wolf-whistle drew her back to the present, and Sheridan blew out a shaky breath as she did her best to glare at Kelly, who was grinning and clapping his hands as he rocked back in his chair.

"I don't know how you put up with him," Parker muttered, her voice just a touch huskier than usual.

Before Sheridan could respond, however, Kelly's eyes widened in horror as his chair tipped past the point of no return, and she laughed as he landed flat-backed on the Art Deco patterned tiled floor. He groaned loudly and rubbed the back of his head as he rolled to his side, and she sighed as she looked back at Parker. There was a glimmer of something in Parker's eyes that suggested she was not alone in her reaction to what'd just happened between them, but she didn't have time to worry about what she thought about that right now. They were here to work. Her mess of a life and whatever all this was, would have to wait.

"Well, stuff like that helps," she murmured as she tilted her head toward her partner, who was now climbing gingerly to his feet.

Parker chuckled and nodded in agreement. She cleared her throat softly and tilted her head toward the counter. "We're up. What would you like?"

Sheridan shook her head. "I'm getting our lunch and stuff, not just coffee. Neither of us have really eaten since last night, New York time."

"That's fine. It's not my money," Parker replied with a grin, hiking a thumb over her shoulder at Kelly. "I just won two hundred bucks."

Parker looked like she meant it, so Sheridan nodded. "Thank you." She stepped up to the counter and quickly scanned the board behind the bar. Neither her or Kelly were particularly picky when it came to food, and she decided on the first thing she saw that looked good. "Hello," she smiled at the barista and, though she knew her accent needed a little work, rattled off hers and Kelly's orders in French. "Could I please have two ham and brie croissants, and two double-shot cappuccinos. And my friend, here…" She turned to get Parker's order in case she didn't speak the language.

Parker winked at her and, in an accent that sounded like she'd been born and raised on the streets of Paris itself, said, "I guess it's my turn. Could I get a veggie croissant sandwich and a cappuccino, please?"

"Of course," the barista replied in lightly accented English. He smirked at their surprised smiles and added, "We'll bring your food to your table once it's ready. Would you prefer to wait for your drinks or have us bring those over as well?"

Sheridan shrugged when Parker looked to see what she wanted to do. Honestly, she'd rather have a few minutes more away from Kelly and whatever little remarks he had up his sleeve, but she'd bow to whatever Parker would prefer.

"We'll wait for the coffee," Parker replied with a tip of her head. She pulled a credit card from her back pocket and offered it to the barista with a grin as his partner behind the counter began working on their sandwiches. Once he ran the card and handed it back, they retreated to a small, raised table on the other end of the counter to wait for their drinks. "You didn't think I spoke French, did you?" she asked in a low, teasing tone as she perched on the edge of a raised barstool.

"I didn't know either way," Sheridan replied honestly as she slid onto the empty stool across from Parker. "Do you speak any other languages?"

"A few. How about you?"

"Not counting English and French? Just Italian and Spanish. And I guess I could also include Latin, but only for reading. You?"

"Not counting English and French?" Parker smirked, her old confidence and swagger settling attractively back onto the playful curve of her lips. "I'm fluent in German, Italian, Spanish, Polish, and Russian. I also do a passable job at Latin—though my reading comprehension is much better than my verbal fluency. Not a lot of opportunities to practice that one, ya know?"

"Showoff," Sheridan muttered, chuckling softly when Parker laughed at the teasing jab. "Why Polish?"

Parker shrugged. "I've had a few recoveries there over the years. I already knew Russian, and even though there are grammatical differences between the two, they're close enough that I didn't have much trouble picking it up."

"That makes sense. I guess with the both of them being Slavic…"

"Exactly." Parker smiled. "So, how was your flight? Did you manage to get any sleep?"

"I dozed," Sheridan shared with a rueful sigh. "Kel snored the whole flight over, though, so at least one of us is rested. It would have been nice if we flew-in yesterday like you did, just so we'd have had a chance to adjust to the time change, but by the time the travel request got pushed through, last night's flight was our only option."

"The guy next to me on my flight snored the whole time too, so I understand how you must be feeling. I'm sorry."

"Why? It's not like you had anything to do with the bureaucracy that held the whole thing up."

"Well, yeah. But I'm still sorry you are having to do this on basically no sleep. We don't have to go to dinner tonight if you'd rather call it an early night. I'd totally understand."

"No. It's fine." Sheridan shook her head. "I'll grab a power nap after we wrap things up this afternoon and I'll be more than rested enough to go out tonight."

"Do you have anywhere in particular you'd like to go?"

"Not really." Sheridan shrugged. "Surprise me."

"I can do that," Parker murmured with a slow smile.

"I'm sure you can."

"Your drinks," the barista announced as he slid three large white cups onto the raised counter at the end of the bar.

"Thank you," Sheridan and Parker replied as they went to collect their drinks.

"You owe me two hundred bucks," Parker told Kelly with a smug smile as she used the toe of her boot to pull a chair away from the table for Sheridan before taking the one beside it for herself.

"Best money I've spent in a while," Kelly retorted. He smiled at Sheridan as she set his coffee on the table in front of him and pulled his wallet from his back pocket.

Parker arched a brow in surprise, clearly not expecting him to have the money on him at the moment, and winked at Sheridan as she slipped the bills into her back pocket. "It's a pleasure doing business with you, Agent Innes."

Sheridan shook her head at him. "I can't believe you did that."

"Please. Sure you can," he retorted with a laugh. "Besides, if one of us has any reason to be surprised by any of what just happened, it'd sure as hell be me."

"Why?" Parker asked, looking between them with an amused smile.

"Because she doesn't date," Kelly answered.

"Kelly," Sheridan warned.

"What?" he asked, looking perfectly innocent. And, yeah, okay, she didn't mind the jokes when it was just the two of them, or even when Ivy and Rachel were around, but the last thing she wanted was for Parker hear it all.

God, she was going to kill him later.

"That wasn't a date," Parker came to her defense. "That was an ass-grab. There's a difference."

"She gave you permission to grab her ass," Kelly pointed out. "That's huge."

Sheridan didn't miss the pleased little smile that tugged at Parker's lips before she shot back with a challenging look, "Jealous?"

"Oh my god, can you two just stop already?" Sheridan groaned. "You were not supposed to get along."

Parker laughed. "Sorry."

"I'm not," Kelly said. "This is the most fun I've had all week."

"Whatever fight you got into that gave you that shiner wasn't fun?" Parker teased, waving a finger at the fading purple and gray circle beneath his right eye.

"You should've seen the bruise he had on his arm last week," Sheridan shared with a smirk. "He and another one of the agents in our unit have been sparring."

"Jesus. What'd you do to piss them off?"

Kelly rolled his eyes. "Nothing. It was a bet."

"This time, anyway," Sheridan added, glad that she was no longer the focus of their conversation.

"You guys are fond of those over at the Bureau, huh?" Parker asked.

"He thought he could take down a Krav Maga expert," Sheridan explained.

"I got her down twice this week," Kelly protested, frowning as he sipped at his coffee.

Parker laughed, and Sheridan could have kissed her for it because it made Kelly blush as he stared into the depths of his coffee.

"Whatever. I'd like to see you do better," Kelly grumbled. He took another sip and then set his mug back onto the table. "Anyway, Bartz said to call and let him know how the raid this afternoon goes and that we can do our reports when we're back in the office Monday."

"How kind of him," Sheridan drawled, though, really, it was. It left them whatever remained of the day after the raid and all of the next to wrap everything up, and whatever time was left was theirs to enjoy.

"Still flying back tomorrow evening?" Parker asked.

Kelly nodded and rocked back in his chair as a young woman in a faded black tee approached the table with their sandwiches. "Assuming everything this afternoon goes to plan."

They all murmured their thanks before she left, and Sheridan groaned as she picked up a half of her croissant sandwich. "Food."

"Tell me about it," Kelly agreed around a mouthful of pastry and cheese and ham. He'd wasted exactly zero time tucking into his lunch. "What about you? Are you staying until Sunday?"

"Nah, I'm heading home tomorrow evening, too. We're on the same flight, actually. What time do we need to be at the station again this afternoon?" Parker asked as she carefully picked up half of her sandwich so the sprouts hanging over the sides didn't fall out.

Kelly glanced at his watch as he finished chewing. "We've got like half an hour until the briefing is supposed to start. Ze French," he added, in a purposefully awful imitation of a French accent with a dramatic swish of his hand, "zey are ver-y pre-cise like zat."

Parker laughed, and Sheridan smiled at her partner as she kicked him playfully under the table. "That was terrible."

Kelly grinned. "Yeah, well, we can't all speak four languages."

Sheridan laughed. "Yeah, I guess you're right. Parker only speaks eight."

"Geek," Kelly teased.

Parker smirked. "I could totally make a quip about being good with tongues, but it'd just be too easy of a joke for a lesbian to make, ya know?"

Kelly barked out a laugh and held out his fist for Parker to bump. "I like you, Parker Ravenscroft."

Sheridan shook her head as she watched Parker reach across the table to give him a light fist bump.

"Thanks, man," Parker replied with a laugh. "You're not too bad, yourself."

Sheridan didn't miss the way Parker's eyes slid to her to as she pulled her hand back to make sure that she was comfortable with the direction their banter had taken, and she smiled as she dipped her chin in a slight nod to assure her that she was fine.

Parker smiled shyly at her before turning back to Kelly to add, "Your partner is still my favorite FBI agent though."

"Yeah, well, I can't blame you there. She's got the whole package going for her. She's impossible to resist."

Sheridan blushed as Parker looked back at her and nodded.

"Yes, she certainly is," Parker agreed softly, smiling at the way Sheridan's blush deepened.

Kelly, thankfully, didn't push the issue further, and a comfortable silence settled over their table as they tucked into their lunches, all too aware of the fact that they did not have very much time to waste.

thirteen

Parker struggled to keep from visibly yawning as the image on the screen at the front of the briefing room changed from a map of their target's street to a blueprint of the building. They'd been over these details three times already but Bellet, the agent from the French Art Crimes Unit agent leading the briefing, continued to drone needlessly on in what was clearly an attempt to prove his department superior to the visiting FBI.

If it weren't for the fact that Sheridan, Kelly, and the handful of French agents in the briefing looked equally annoyed by his antics, Parker would have wished that she'd just broken into Vasseur's apartment and taken the stolen painting back herself.

"Any questions?" Bellet asked, looking imperiously toward the trio of Americans in the back row.

"Pretty sure we had it all the first time," Kelly answered for the group with a tight smirk.

Bellet stiffened as a ripple of laughter spread through the room. "Fine. Let's go, then." He glowered at Kelly for what was probably supposed to be an imposing few seconds before he practically stomped out the door, but it mostly made him look constipated.

"Wow," Parker chuckled. She shook her head and let the yawn she'd held back earlier rip free.

"Stop," Sheridan mumbled as she yawned too.

"Sorry." Parker smiled sheepishly. She might have landed in Paris the day before, but she'd caught only a quick nap after getting to her hotel before she'd had to head out to meet Oliver at a café near Andre Dumas' apartment to do a little reconnaissance and run through the details he had dug up during his research. She had stumbled back to her hotel not long after daybreak for some much needed rest, but the six hours of sleep she had managed before her alarm went off again were hardly enough to make up for all the sleep she'd missed over the last week.

"After you, ladies," Kelly declared with a small bow and a gracious sweep of his arm toward the door the French team had begun filtering through.

"Thanks," Sheridan drawled. "Did you forget that we're supposed to be playing nice this weekend?"

Parker chuckled as she fell into step beside Sheridan and reached out to stop the door from closing on them.

"That was playing nice," Kelly argued as he slid an arm across the door over Parker's shoulder to take it from her. "If I wanted to be an asshole, I wouldn't have waited for him to ask."

Parker tilted her head toward Sheridan as they strolled into the hall and murmured, "He has a point."

Sheridan sighed and lifted her eyes heavenward as if praying for strength. "Please don't encourage him."

Parker smiled. This was the first time she had spent any time at all with Sheridan and Kelly as a pair, but their back-and-forth reminded her a lot of herself and Oliver. "Only because you asked so nicely, Agent Sloan," she teased. She didn't miss the small shiver that made the muscles in Sheridan's neck tense, and she found her thoughts drifting once again back to the café.

Really, she'd only told Sheridan what Kelly had said to her because she thought it would make her laugh and roll her eyes and maybe take some of the edge off the exhaustion she could see weighing heavily on her shoulders. The absolute last thing she had ever expected was for Sheridan to tell her to go for it.

"You two are so sweet I'm getting a cavity back here," Kelly teased, effectively snapping Parker's thoughts back to the present.

"Fuck off, Innes," Sheridan threw over her shoulder.

"Rude," Kelly retorted in his best valley-girl impersonation.

"It's astonishing that you actually made it through Quantico," Sheridan told him in a playfully aggrieved tone.

"I know, right?" Kelly grinned.

Parker laughed and shook her head as they turned the corner and walked out into the parking lot tucked in the middle of the square-shaped building that housed the *Gendarmerie*. She didn't miss the way Sheridan and Kelly's posture shifted, all playfulness discarded as they made their way to the back of the first of two black Range Rovers lined up near the exit of the parking lot where Bellet waited for them.

"Here." Bellet tossed a bulletproof vest at Kelly with more force than was strictly necessary, and he scowled when Kelly snatched it out of the air with his left hand and swung it over his head without missing a beat. "Vasseur doesn't have a reputation for being armed, but better safe than sorry," he explained as he tossed vests at Sheridan and Parker.

Parker blew out a loud breath as she yanked the vest's Velcro side straps free and slipped the body armor over her head. She'd donned a bulletproof vest while working with law enforcement officers plenty of times in the past, and she shot Sheridan a small smile as she looked over to see her doing the same thing. "You FBI guys sure know how to show a girl a good time."

"Yeah, we're pretty awesome like that," Sheridan quipped without missing a beat as she tugged the vest over her head.

Parker had been surprised when Sheridan and Kelly had shrugged off their blazers earlier to reveal matching shoulder holsters, and she'd been even more surprised when Kelly had pulled a couple of thigh holsters from his computer pack and tossed one to Sheridan. Her surprise must have been obvious, because Sheridan had explained in a voice low enough that nobody else in the room could hear that federal agents operated under diplomatic immunity while traveling beyond their home borders, so they had no trouble carrying their own firearms onto foreign soil.

Parker was still fussing with the straps on her right side when Sheridan finished fitting her own vest, and she startled when Sheridan's hand wrapped lightly around her wrist.

"Do you need help with that?" Sheridan asked softly.

"I..." Parker shook her head, somehow not at all surprised that Sheridan Sloan looked just as good in a pair of black slacks and a tactical vest as she did in anything else. The fact that she knew she shouldn't find the sight of Sheridan in body armor with a gun strapped to her leg alluring did nothing to reverse the fact that her throat suddenly felt like the Sahara, and she cleared her throat as she forced herself to focus on the task at hand. "I got it. But thanks," she muttered, biting her lip as she looked down at herself to make sure the vest was positioned where she wanted it.

The weight of Sheridan's gaze sent a warm shiver down her spine, and she grit her teeth as she willed herself to ignore it. *She's just making sure I know what I'm doing,* she lectured herself as she adjusted the shoulder straps to give the body of the vest a little more length.

"You know, it's a little disconcerting how good you are at that," Sheridan observed.

Parker shrugged and flashed Sheridan a small, wry smile. "Yeah, well, this isn't my first rodeo."

"Innes, Coan, and Marchon will ride with me in the first car," Bellet snapped. Clearly he'd had enough of their dawdling, even though a quick glance at the group huddled between the SUVs donning protective gear showed that there was still a French agent still adjusting his vest. "Sloan, Raven, you're with Guillard and Herault in the second car."

"Ravenscroft," Sheridan muttered.

Parker looked down at her feet to hide her grin at the annoyance in Sheridan's tone, and gave her a little shoulder bump to show her thanks. With how quickly he'd moved away after she had introduced herself earlier, she was honestly surprised he'd gotten that much of her name correct.

The French agents disbanded with curt nods, scattering to their individual vehicles, and Parker fell into step beside Sheridan as they followed the agent who had motioned at them toward a black Range Rover that was identical to the one Kelly had climbed into. Thankfully for Kelly, Bellet was too focused on being superior to everyone that he didn't notice the face Kelly pulled behind his back as he slipped into the back seat.

Parker followed Sheridan's lead and climbed into the back seat of the SUV as their French cohorts for the next few hours took the front, and she pursed her lips to keep from laughing when Kelly's car rolled past them.

Innes had his palms pressed flat to the window, his expression playfully frantic as he mouthed, *Help me!*

Sheridan was less successful, though her soft laughter was nothing compared to the bark of amusement the agent behind the wheel of their car let out.

"I love your partner," the French agent in the passenger seat declared in heavily accented English.

"He is certainly one of a kind," Sheridan agreed in the agent's native tongue, her expression an adorable blend of mirth and disbelief.

"You speak French?" The driver, Anne Guillard, asked as her gaze darted between Sheridan and Parker in the rearview mirror. Guillard was the agent Sheridan had worked with to arrange everything for the raid, but when Sheridan had introduced her and Kelly to her when they'd arrived at the station, she'd done it in English and, judging by the surprise evident in Guillard's expression, Parker was willing to guess that all of their conversations finalizing the details of the raid had been conducted in English as well.

"Quite well," Parker piped up with a grin.

"Why am I not surprised that all that back there was Bellet coming down from his glass tower to grab control and show off again," Guillard muttered. She waved at the woman beside her and added, "And this is Eve Herault."

Parker's eyebrows lifted in surprise at the open hostility Guillard showed for her superior. Interdepartmental tension was pretty much a given in this line of work, but it was unusual for an agent to vent about it to veritable strangers from a visiting agency. "So, I take it he doesn't usually work with your unit?"

"No. He spent a total of eight months in the field before he moved to admin. He only cares about getting his face on television and working his way up the ladder. He's too important to be worried about getting his hands dirty."

"Unfortunately, I know the type all too well," Sheridan commiserated. "Though, to be fair, Agent Innes doesn't speak a word of French that would be appropriate outside a bar, so it's probably a good thing he was trying to show off a bit."

"First, last, and only time," Eve chuckled wryly. She turned in her seat to face Parker. "How do you find the insurance recovery business?"

Parker shrugged. "Depends on the day. It's definitely a hot-and-cold type business where you can go weeks or months between recoveries, but it's been a good couple of weeks for me recently."

"Because we're going to recover the Matisse?" Eve asked with an interested smile.

Parker nodded. "That will certainly add to it, yeah."

"She recovered a Sumerian statue last week that'd been missing for over a year," Sheridan piped up.

Parker looked at Sheridan, surprised by the edge of jealousy in her tone. It was certainly new, and she bit her lip to try to keep from outright grinning at the thought that Sheridan Sloan might actually be jealous of another woman flirting with her. Of course, Kelly had said something earlier about Sheridan not dating, so that brought up a whole other avenue of questions about all of this, and she found it suddenly much easier to keep a straight face.

"I see," Eve drawled as she looked between Parker and Sheridan.

Parker hated the way Sheridan stiffened ever so slightly beside her, as if uncomfortable with the idea that someone might think they were anything other than occasional colleagues, but she was forced to push that stomach-clenching thought aside when Eve spoke again.

"So it'd been missing for a year? That had to have been quite the exciting grab, then. What statue was it, if you don't mind my asking?"

Parker smiled. Finding the statue after thirteen months of running down dead-end leads before coming across one that wasn't and then rushing to Boston to recover it had certainly been quite the high. "The *Guennol Lioness.*"

Guillard whistled. "Damn. How did you find it?"

"Good old fashioned legwork," Parker replied vaguely, not about to give up any hint of her less-than-honorable sources when surrounded by a trio of agents from two different agencies whose job it was to catch those who are considered less-than-honorable.

"Fair enough," Eve chuckled.

Guillard tapped at the in-dash GPS screen and nodded to herself. "Gear up, ladies. ETA, two minutes. Local police is on site and waiting for us, so we're going to hit the ground running."

Parker looked out the window at the city beyond for the first time since they'd left the station. The street was calm, quiet, a picturesque upper-class enclave in the heart of Paris. The café on the corner had striped blue and white awnings, and a handful of the storefronts along the boulevard had window boxes overflowing with colorful flowers. Doors along the street were propped open to take advantage of the temperate springtime weather, and the windows of the apartments on the upper levels of the buildings were thrown open as well, their curtains billowing lightly in the breeze.

While Guillard focused on the SUV in front of them, Eve and Sheridan pulled their weapons from their holsters to check their lethality. Parker would have much preferred to do this without the guns, but there was something reassuring about the almost robotic way Sheridan's lips pressed into a hard line as she popped her clip to check that it was full before using the heel of her hand to slam it back into place. No matter what happened in the next few minutes, the set of Sheridan's jaw and the sudden steeliness in her gaze made it clear that she was more than prepared to handle it.

The car in front of them stopped, and Parker felt as she always did in these moments—like she was in a slow-motion action sequence in a movie. Guillard steered their car to the curb about thirty yards from their target and threw it into park as she killed the engine, and Parker followed Sheridan's lead as she threw her door open and jumped out. Her orders had been clear: she was to stay out of the way until the agents had secured the scene before making her way inside to search for the painting. She was more than fine with that directive given her lack of tactical training, but she'd be lying if she said she didn't feel the rush of adrenaline the raid elicited inside her.

But while her role was to hang back and wait for the all-clear, Sheridan's was to join the agents descending on the front door to the antiques shop Vasseur used to host both his legal and illegal businesses, and she was surprised when she rounded the back of the SUV to find Sheridan waiting for her just off the corner of the rear bumper. They only had a few moments before Kelly and the other agents assigned to the back of the building got into position, and it was clear from the chatter on her earpiece that that time was nearly gone.

Sheridan's expression was serious, her hold firm as she grabbed Parker's wrist, her fingertips pressing pleadingly into sensitive skin. "Don't be a hero, Parker. Okay? Just stay behind me."

A raid that, moments before, had been routine and nothing to worry about became suddenly serious as she stared into Sheridan's unblinking gaze. Every scrap of intel gathered for the retrieval indicated that Vasseur would be in his shop, unarmed and alone since the woman who worked for him took every Friday off to visit her aging, ill mother in nearby Aubervilliers. There was, on paper, exactly nothing to worry about beyond finding the painting.

But there was no mistaking the concern in Sheridan's eyes, no possible ambiguity to the firm press of fingertips against her inner wrist, silently begging her to comply. Sheridan clearly needed this from her, and so she nodded, her throat thick with something that wasn't quite fear, and whispered, "Okay."

Relief flashed across Sheridan's face the moment those two syllables hit the air, and she sucked her lower lip between her teeth as she ducked her head in a small nod. Her hold on Parker's wrist loosened, the pressure of her fingertips relaxing into a gentle hold while still not letting go. "Thank you," she murmured.

Before Parker could respond, a gruff accented voice announced through their comms, "We are in position. Ready to go on your mark, Bellet."

Sheridan's grip on her wrist disappeared in an instant, her expression a mask of callous-professionalism. She blinked once as if to shutter what was left of her emotions behind whatever wall she'd just erected in record time, and then, with a quick tip of her head, spun on her heel to take her position toward the front of the group, just behind Guillard and Bellet.

The worry that had caused Sheridan to beg her to stay out of the way while the agents secured the building settled uncomfortably in Parker's stomach as she stood by and watched them all disappear into the building. She grit her teeth as the hushed chatter of the team began filtering through her earpiece, listening for any suggestion that Sheridan's sudden worry wasn't a premonition of chaos.

Sheridan's group at the front of the store reported their all-clear first, and she let out a sigh of relief as she took a step toward the antique shop's front door.

"Backroom's clear," Innes reported in a clipped, professional tone that sounded more robotic than human.

"I've got Vasseur," Bellet reported, sounding gratingly smug. "Sloan, Guillard, Marchon, check the second floor apartment."

A jumble of voices clattered their understanding, and Parker could have sworn that Sheridan's was one of them. She fisted her hands at her sides, listening intently as she waited for the final *all-clear* to be given.

And waited.

It should not take this long to clear a rather small shop and the two-bedroom apartment above it.

Her earpiece went silent, and she looked up at the open windows above the store, trying to see inside, wanting nothing more in that moment than to hear Sheridan's voice. She was too focused on what was happening beyond her field of vision to worry about why her pulse was pounding with dread. Just when she was about to tap on the line and *ask* Sheridan if she was okay, her earpiece came alive.

"Second floor is secure," Guillard reported.

"Nicely done, team," Bellet drawled.

Clear.

Everything was fine.

Parker's feet began to move before her thoughts caught up to them, and she was halfway to the door to Vasseur's shop when Sheridan sauntered out, her smile positively blinding as she beckoned her forward with a wave. "You can come in now."

The way Parker's stomach fluttered with relief at the sight of Sheridan was enough to make her falter, and she shook her head as she stopped in front of Sheridan and gave her a quick once-over. Sheridan looked perfectly put-together except for an errant curl that had slipped out of her braid, and Parker grit her teeth as she just barely resisted the urge to reach out and tuck it behind her ear for her. "You're okay?"

"I'm perfectly fine." Sheridan gave Parker's wrist a light, reassuring squeeze. "Vasseur looked like he might have been tempted to run out the back door there for a minute, but then that guy that looks like he could be a starting tight end for the Giants that was leading Kelly's unit blocked the doorway and he, quite wisely, surrendered."

Parker's thoughts were a jumbled mess of what she wanted to say and what she should, so instead she just nodded and murmured, "Okay."

Sheridan smiled and tilted her head toward the shop. "Let's go find your painting."

Parker whistled softly as she followed Sheridan into the antique shop. Vasseur clearly favored the organized clutter approach to display his wares, as there was just enough room to walk through the clusters of antiques. The place was, simply put, a disaster. Though, judging by the handful of pieces she around the room that she was able to identify at a glance, an incredibly valuable one.

She shook her head as she looked at what appeared to be an eighteenth-century Duplessis vase sitting atop a perfectly ordinary mahogany side table that had definitely seen better days. "That vase should be in a museum," she muttered under her breath to Sheridan.

Sheridan hummed softly in agreement. "I'd say. Where do you think he'll have stashed the Matisse?"

Parker shrugged and let her eyes drift over the crowded space. "Out here would be way too Edgar Allan Poe-y," she thought aloud. "If I had to guess, I'd say he's probably got a safe somewhere. Where's his office?"

"Upstairs," Kelly answered from the back of the shop. He cocked his head at the hall behind him. "I'll show you."

"Yes. You three do that. Let me know if you find anything," Bellet instructed them as he marched a small, impeccably dressed man in tailored slacks and a crisp pink sport shirt past the cash register counter. Parker recognized Vasseur immediately from the file she'd compiled on him during the last few days. He looked smaller than the five-foot-seven noted in his dossier, and his skin was noticeably ruddier than the most recent picture she'd found online. Even though she'd never dealt with him in the past, she turned and feigned interest in the vase she'd noticed earlier to hide her face just in case he recognized her from somewhere.

The last thing she needed was for him to identify her to the assembled group of agents.

"He isn't talking," Bellet continued barking at them all, leading by volume instead of competence. "And he has asked for his lawyer. Coan!"

"Sir?" The agent who had to be the one Sheridan had described as a tight end prospect stepped forward.

"Help me get this guy outside," Bellet instructed as he gave Vasseur a shove in Coan's direction. "I want you and Herault to take him back to the station and get him into an interrogation room. I want him ready to go when I get back to the station."

"Yes, sir."

Vasseur was so busy being offended by the fact that he had a new set of connected bracelets on his wrists that he didn't give her so much as a second glance, and a moment later he was gone. When Parker looked back up, she saw Eve stopping to say something to Guillard before following the men out the front of the store. While Parker could understand wanting an agent the size of Coan to be present in case Vasseur decided to become uncooperative, it was clear from the look on both Guillard and Eve's faces that they didn't appreciate being split up.

"Guillard, Marchon, I want every item in this shop catalogued," Bellet ordered as he spun around to stare down his remaining agents. "We've been looking for an excuse to get in here for months, let them"—he waved a dismissive hand at Parker, Sheridan, and Kelly— "worry about their painting."

"Great guy," Sheridan muttered, shaking her head. "No wonder he has their undivided loyalty." She shook her head and waved a hand toward the stairs. "Do you want to go on up and see if we can't find a safe?"

"Yeah. Let's go find my painting," Parker said as she followed Sheridan through a narrow path through Vasseur's treasures to the stairwell, and was surprised when Kelly stepped aside to allow her to go first. She tipped her head in thanks as she started for the second floor apartment, noting the way the narrow treads she climbed were worn in the middle from years of use. The apartment at the top of the stairs was comfortable, the living room small and just as crowded as the store below, and Parker pursed her lips thoughtfully as she scanned the room. Two hallways led off the space, which she knew from the briefing earlier led to the two bedrooms—one on either end of the apartment.

She turned to look at Sheridan and Kelly. "Which way to his office?"

"That way." Sheridan pointed toward the front of the apartment. Which made sense. The back bedroom would be much quieter for sleeping.

Parker pulled a pair of gloves from her pocket and pulled them on as she made her way down the hall. The office was just as much of a disaster as everything else—random artifacts scattered atop available surfaces and tucked into corners—and she blew out a soft breath as she gave the room a thorough once-over. The closet seemed the best bet for a safe the size she expected Vasseur to have, and she glanced only briefly over her shoulder at Sheridan as she crossed the room and pulled the slatted accordion doors open.

Bingo.

She'd figured Vasseur would have a large safe given his profession, and he certainly didn't disappoint. Her best guess put the safe at six feet tall, five feet wide, and probably close to four feet deep. It would've been a Herculean feat to haul this monster up to the second floor, and the prep work it would've taken to strengthen the joists beneath the closet wouldn't have been an easy task, either. Vasseur wasn't messing around when it came to his security, but she couldn't contain her smile as she read the name of the safe on the top left corner of the door. She certainly couldn't blame Vasseur for wanting to go old school—electronic safes were too easily hacked by somebody with the right tools and skillset—and the Tresorx9 was certainly a high-security safe.

Unluckily for him, however, it was also one she had come across before and she knew, despite the manufacturer's claims to the contrary, that it was breakable.

It'd been years since she'd taken on a lock like this and her fingers itched to reach for the dial and see if she still had it in her to crack it, but she knew that she couldn't. If she'd been alone, she absolutely would have given it a shot, but there was no way she could do it with Sheridan and Kelly standing over her shoulder.

Grabbing Sheridan's ass earlier and then asking her to dinner was reckless enough for one day.

Not to mention the fact that she was going to have to meet Oliver after that to help him pull the Dumas job.

Parker closed her eyes and took a deep breath. She had gotten used to her life being stable and predictable these last few years, and she just hoped that, after she and Oliver managed to wrap things up with Marquis, she'd be able to find a way to slip back into that life again.

And that, maybe, just maybe, she'd be able to keep Sheridan a part of it.

She cleared her throat softly and flashed what she hoped passed as a playful smile over her shoulder at Sheridan. "Anyone got the number of a locksmith?"

"What, can't you just break into it yourself?" Kelly teased.

"Unfortunately"—Parker shook her head—"my lock-breaking skills top out at the Master Lock you probably use to secure your stuff at the gym."

"You're kidding," Kelly laughed.

Parker shrugged. If she'd had a halfway-decent sound magnifier, she was pretty sure she could still crack the Tresorex9 in front of her. "Am I?" she challenged with a devious smirk.

Kelly crossed his arms over his chest and studied her carefully for a moment. "If I found a lock like that could you prove it?"

"Kelly," Sheridan sighed, though there was an edge of amusement in her tone. "Could you just go ask Bellet if he's got a locksmith he can bring in to drill this thing, please?"

"Fine," Kelly agreed with a dramatic sigh. "But I'm only doing this because you two"—he waved a finger between them—"look like you're just dying to score some alone time." He laughed and danced away from the elbow Sheridan aimed at his side. "Be good. Don't do anything I would do," he sing-songed as he walked out of the office.

"I'm so sorry about him," Sheridan apologized once he'd gone. She shook her head as she sat down on the floor and leaned back against the wall. "He's—"

"Just doing it because he knows it'll annoy you," Parker interjected as she took a similar position, but with the safe at her back so she was facing Sheridan.

"Probably," Sheridan agreed with a little laugh as she straightened her legs out in front of her.

"Oh, there's no 'probably' about it. But, you know, he also wasn't totally wrong, either." Parker stretched her legs out and nudged Sheridan's foot with her own. The way Sheridan's right eyebrow lifted as a small, almost worried smile that tugged at the right side of her lips begged her to explain, and she swallowed thickly as she stared into Sheridan's eyes. She knew that she should make a joke about being glad he was off bugging somebody else for a bit, but the truth slipped free first. "I've missed you."

"I've missed you too," Sheridan whispered.

Parker's heart seemed to seize in her chest as Sheridan's smile slowly blossomed to light her entire face, gentle and radiant and so goddamn lovely that—if she wasn't already sitting down—it would have brought her to her knees. The very idea that she might somehow manage to still keep her distance from Sheridan became an impossibility in that moment, and she held her breath as she looked down at where their feet rested lightly against each other.

This was stupid. Monumentally, impossibly stupid, but she was only human, and Sheridan Sloan was a force she wasn't strong enough to resist.

She lifted her eyes back to Sheridan's, and blew out a shaky breath as the air between them seemed to crackle with electricity. Part of her hoped that this thing she felt for Sheridan was completely one-sided, because then things would be at least a little less complicated, but the rest of her prayed that it wasn't.

Some of her inner turmoil must have shown in her expression, because Sheridan's smile softened and she tipped her head toward the door. "How long do you think he'll be gone?"

Parker cleared her throat softly and shook her head. "No idea," she husked, beyond grateful for the line Sheridan was throwing her. "I wouldn't put it past Bellet to make him try to run down a locksmith himself, though."

"Me neither." Sheridan took a deep breath as her gaze shifted to the safe over Parker's shoulder. "Do you really know how to crack a Master Lock?"

"Doesn't everybody?" Parker smiled at the way Sheridan chuckled and shook her head. "That actually is a skill in my bag of tricks, yes."

"How in the world did you learn to do that?"

Parker bit her lip and glanced toward the door to make sure they were still alone. She didn't have a problem sharing the story with Sheridan, but she also didn't want it making the rounds, either. "I was placed with a family when I was in fifth grade that was much more interested in the money they got for fostering me than they were in actually taking care of me." She shrugged off the flash of anger that pinched Sheridan's brow. "It was actually better than the house I'd been at before because they kept their hands to themselves, but it meant that I had to get a little, shall we say, creative to take care of myself. But they really weren't that bad. They got me new clothes from

Goodwill when the ones I had got too small or worn out, and even though I knew that it was just so that it was so they'd look like they were taking care of me and they could keep getting their checks, it was still better than before."

"Parker…" Sheridan murmured.

Parker forced a small smile and shook her head at the pity she could see beginning to swell in Sheridan's eyes. "Really, I was cool with all of that. The problem was that they didn't want to spend the money they got for me on extra groceries, so I only got a cheese sandwich for dinner every night. Which, I swear, wasn't that bad because I'd get breakfast and lunch at school so it wasn't like I was going to bed really hungry or anything."

"But what about when you didn't have school?" Sheridan asked, her voice dark with anger, like she already knew the answer.

"That's when it got a little rough. They kept the fridge and pantry locked up with your standard Master Lock so I couldn't just sneak a few extra pieces of bread and cheese or anything when they weren't around, so…" Parker shrugged. "At first, Oliver tried to bring me food from his foster's house, but they didn't like feeding a kid they weren't getting paid for, so we had to figure something else out.

"One day when we were at the park we found a five dollar bill buried in the sand. Ollie thought we should take it to McDonald's to get me a happy meal or something, but we wouldn't have had enough money for two of them, so I talked him into going to the 7-Eleven so we could both get a treat instead. The teenager working the counter was so used to kids coming in and out during the summer for Slurpees and whatever that he didn't pay any attention to us, so while I was paying for whatever junk we picked out, Ollie stole a Master Lock like the one my fosters had locking up the food."

"And you figured out how to break it," Sheridan surmised with an almost proud smile curling her lips.

"Eventually, yeah. Took me a couple weeks to figure it out, but once I did, I was able to get just enough food to supplement my cheese sandwich so I wasn't starving."

"Did they ever find out?"

Parker shook her head. They had been so sure that their system was impenetrable that they'd never noticed that the loaf of bread was shrinking faster than it should, or that any other groceries had gone missing. "Anyway, I made it through the summer, and then the next year I was placed with a different family. They didn't lock up the food or anything, but I still practiced with that damn lock every night so that if me or Ollie ever found ourselves in a position where we'd need it, I'd be able to do it."

"Did you ever need to do it again?"

"A couple times," Parker admitted softly. "But eventually the Johanns found us. They took care of us like we were their own—which is kind of hilarious because they're like only fifteen years older than us—and I didn't need to crack a lock to get food or break Ollie out of his room or find us a garden shed to sleep in anymore."

Sheridan took a deep breath and let it go slowly. The pity that Parker had glimpsed earlier was now replaced with pride, and she shook her head as she murmured, "I'm glad the Johanns found you."

"Yeah. We are, too."

"Yeah, I'll bet," Sheridan agreed with a smile. She took a deep breath and let it go slowly. "You made it sound like you could still do it earlier. Can you?"

"It's a fun party-trick." Parker shrugged. That much was true, at least.

"What's a fun party-trick?" Kelly asked as he ambled back into the office, spinning a closed combination lock on his finger. He arched a challenging brow at Parker and offered her the lock. "Fifty bucks says you can't open this."

Parker grinned and winked at Sheridan as she held out her hand. "I mean, I hate to take more of your money, but if you really want to just give it away like that…" She gave the dial a couple spins to get a feel for its tension. It was nice and loose, which would make it easier for her to pick up the soft spots.

Kelly laughed and shoved his hands into his pockets. "Go on, then…"

"Innes…" Sheridan groaned.

"Quiet in the peanut gallery," Parker drawled as she focused her attention on the lock. She smiled at the way Sheridan and Kelly fell quiet at her command, and began working at the lock. It was child's play compared to the safe at her back, and she made sure to hold Kelly's gaze when, only a few minutes later, she yanked it open and handed it back to him. "There you go, sir."

"Dude!" Kelly cheered as he took the lock. "How in the hell did you do it?"

"I've just got the magic touch," Parker quipped.

Kelly smirked. "I bet you do…"

"Oh my god," Sheridan muttered.

All three of them looked at the door at the sound of heavy boot steps coming their way, and Parker scrambled to her feet as a wiry man in jeans and a polo entered the office with a large toolbox.

"Where's the safe?" he asked in French.

Parker waved a hand toward the closet. "Right there."

"Ah, a Tresorex9. I've always wanted to drill into one of these," the man muttered as he reached into his bag. He pulled out an absolutely massive electric drill and a pair of safety goggles, and nodded at the outlet next to the closet as he handed Parker the cord for his drill. "It's going to be very loud," he warned as he dug in his toolbox. He pulled out a plastic container of foam earplugs and tossed it to Kelly. "You'll want these."

It took him close to an hour to drill through the lock to open the safe, and he grinned when he finally shut his drill down and pushed himself back to his feet. "That should do it. Who wants the honors?"

"Go for it, Parker," Sheridan said.

Parker glanced at the door. Bellet had come up a few times while the locksmith had been working to check the progress, and she had a feeling he'd be back soon now that the drill had been turned off. "You sure?"

"It's your recovery," Kelly agreed.

"All right," Parker muttered as she nodded her thanks to the locksmith, who was winding up the power cord to his drill while the tool cooled down a bit, and reached for the handle of the safe. "Here we go," she announced as she gave the handle a twist and the door swung open.

Kelly and Sheridan moved behind her to survey the safe's contents. The top shelf inside the safe had a velvet covered compartmented tray that held loose gemstones and jewelry, and a medium-sized Ming Dynasty vase on the second shelf. A long, heavy-duty black telescoping tube was angled across the taller bottom section of the safe, and Parker was willing to bet that her painting was inside it.

"Fucking hell," she muttered as she pulled the tube from the safe and began unscrewing the top.

She'd hoped that the thieves would have transported the painting flat because anything else risked the paint being damaged. She carefully tipped the contents of the tube into her hand, and held her breath as she pulled the length of canvas free. Her heart raced as she carefully hooked the side of her thumb over the edge of the canvas, and her throat tightened as she began to unroll it.

Please be the Matisse.

A quiet laugh slipped past her lips when she finished unrolling the painting, and she grinned as she turned to show it to the small collection of agents that'd gathered in the room behind her. "Ladies and gentlemen, may I present to you, Henri Matisse's 1938 masterpiece, *La Conversation.*"

FOURTEEN

Sheridan jumped when her phone began to vibrate on the vanity beside her, sending a cascade of evocative notes from a symphony she had fallen in love with the year before on a visit to Los Angeles through her hotel room's tiny bathroom. The tile made the acoustics of the piece even more striking, but she was too frazzled to appreciate the way the reedy oboe tones bounced off the porcelain. The quick nap she'd meant to grab upon returning to her hotel from the *Gendarmerie* had turned into a marathon, and she'd jolted awake a scant thirty minutes before she was supposed to meet Parker in the lobby of her hotel to find her hair looking like a rodent had made a nest out of it and dried drool caked to her cheek.

She knew that Parker wouldn't have minded if she'd called to postpone their dinner to a night where she wasn't so tired, but she didn't *want* to cancel. She'd had more fun working with Parker that afternoon than she had all week—witty texts and late-night phone conversations paled in comparison to actually talking face-to-face—and she hated the idea of forfeiting an opportunity to spend more time with her when she had no idea when they would manage to both be free next.

So, no, she couldn't possibly cancel, but that left her rushing through a shower to make herself presentable, and now she was standing at the vanity in her bathroom, makeup half done, wearing nothing but a towel. The only thing she had going in her favor was that she'd already dried and tamed her usually unruly curls.

She answered the phone on speaker so she could talk and continue to try to hurry through the rest of her routine, and leaned closer to the mirror as she lifted the wand to her right eye. The last thing she needed was to blind herself in her rush to get done. "Parker, hi."

"Hey. Everything okay?"

Sheridan rolled her eyes at her reflection. Of course Parker picked up on the edge of distraction in her tone. "Fine," she lied. "Are you here?" Her hotel was apparently closer to wherever they were having dinner, and Parker had insisted on picking her up.

"Nearly. I ended up sleeping a little longer when I got back to my hotel this afternoon than I'd intended, so I'm probably ten minutes away. I just wanted to call and let you know that I'm running late so you didn't think I was standing you up or anything."

"I wouldn't have thought that but, now that you've brought it up, do I need to be worried about you standing me up in the future?" Sheridan smiled at her own joke as she swiped the mascara wand over her lashes.

"No. Absolutely not."

Sheridan bit her lip as her heart gave a hopeful little flutter at the warmth in Parker's tone. "That's...um, good to know," she whispered. She cleared her throat softly and continued in what she was relieved sounded like a much stronger voice, "Anyway, you aren't the only one who accidentally overslept when they got back to their hotel this afternoon—I'm still getting ready."

"Oh. So I should probably let you go, huh?"

"That would probably be a good idea," Sheridan agreed as she screwed the mascara wand back into its tube. "God knows wherever we're going probably wouldn't appreciate me showing up in a towel," she added wryly

"I... You're... Oh." Parker coughed. *"Okay. I guess I'll...um, see you soon, then."*

Sheridan frowned as the line went dead before she could respond. It wasn't like Parker to not wait for some kind of reply, but she was thankfully saved from worrying about it by the fact that she only had ten minutes to finish getting ready.

She had just finished slipping on her shoes when her phone rang again, and she closed her eyes in relief that she had actually pulled-off getting done in time when she saw Parker's name on the screen. "I'm walking out the door now," she answered by way of a greeting as she grabbed her purse from the dresser.

"Okay. Should I wait down here in the lobby?"

"Yeah. I'll be right there." Sheridan paused in front of the full-length mirror hung on the wall beside the bathroom and gave herself one last once-over. She was wearing the charcoal slacks and pale pink blouse she'd packed for the following day because she hadn't brought anything for a night out, and she crossed her fingers that her work clothes would be appropriate for the restaurant Parker had chosen.

"Can't wait."

Sheridan hummed and nodded once at herself in the mirror before she reached for the door. "Me neither."

The elevator had taken forever to climb the three floors to her room earlier, so she decided to avoid the lift altogether and instead pushed her way through the door to the emergency stairway opposite her room. The dimly lit stairwell was vaguely ominous in a way that made her rethink leaving her gun in the safe hidden in the closet of her room, but she brushed the thought aside as she hurried down the steps. Tonight she wasn't an agent, she was just a woman going to dinner with a friend. And if push came to shove, Ivy had shown her enough Krav Maga over the last year and a half that she'd be more than able to defend herself.

She exited into an empty hallway on the first floor and adjusted the strap of her purse on her shoulder as she made her way toward the lobby. A small smile tugged at her lips when she saw Parker standing near the cozy seating area across from the front desk, her attention clearly focused on the elevators in front of her. It wasn't often that she had the opportunity to look at Parker without being noticed, and she couldn't resist slowing her pace to give herself a few moments to appreciate the woman in front of her.

Parker looked lean and fit in a pair of tailored, light gray pinstripe slacks and a perfectly fitted waistcoat whose silky silver back contrasted beautifully with her light blue button down, and she swallowed thickly as her eyes drifted over the narrow plane of Parker's body. She might have stumbled into her sexuality a little later than most, but she had always had a thing for beautiful women in suits, and there was no denying the fact that Parker was the most beautiful woman she'd ever laid eyes on.

But more than the clothes or the shape of Parker's body, it was the subtle confidence that showed in her posture even when she was standing still that drew the majority of her attention. The way her shoulders rolled back leaving her heart wide open and the slight cock of her hip were both sexy as hell, and even her hair that seemed to glow silver and ice blue beneath the warm bulbs that lit the lobby shouted confidence. A person had to be incredibly secure in themselves to do something so wholly unconventional—lord knows she'd never in a million years be bold enough to even think of doing anything like that.

Parker turned in her direction when she was still a few feet away from being able to reach out to touch her arm, her smile pleased and warm and inviting, and Sheridan held her breath as her heart did that hopeful fluttery thing again. "Hey."

"Hey yourself, Agent Sloan," Parker murmured. Her weight shifted onto the balls of her feet for the briefest of moments as if she was going to lean in for a hug, but she gave her head the smallest of shakes and took a step back instead as she swept her arm toward the street. "Ready?"

"Of course." Sheridan smiled and tipped her head in thanks when Parker held the front door for her. The lightest brush of Parker's fingertips against her back as she passed sent a pleasant shiver tumbling down her spine, and she glanced shyly at Parker when she joined her on the sidewalk. "So, now will you tell me where we're going?"

"It's a surprise," Parker replied with a Cheshire Cat grin. She steered her toward the curb where a black sedan idled at the curb with a gentle touch on her back. "I had to work some magic to get a reservation on such short notice since it is a Friday night," she elaborated as the driver of the car jumped out and opened the rear driver's-side door, "but I'm pretty sure you're going to love it."

"And if I don't?" Sheridan couldn't help teasing as Parker gestured for her to climb in first.

Parker shook her head. "It's impossible to not love this place."

Sheridan laughed as she slid across the seat to make room for Parker, who followed right after her. As soon as they were inside, the driver nodded once and closed the door after them. The limo wasn't large enough to warrant an opaque partition between the driver and the back seat, but she'd spent enough time being chauffeured around over the years with her mother to recognize a highly competent, professional driver when she saw one. The driver's eyes remained squarely on the road—he didn't even glance at them in the rearview mirror—and without a word to Parker he steered the car smoothly away from the curb.

Clearly, Parker had already discussed their ultimate destination with him.

Sheridan smiled shyly at Parker, touched by the effort she'd put into their impromptu night on the town. "Well, if that's the case, I can't wait." She looked out the window at the streetlights that were only just beginning to flicker on despite the fact that the clock on the dash said that it was a quarter to nine. "Were you able to secure the painting okay?"

"Oh yeah. One of the many perks of staying at the Plaza is that their hotel safe is more secure than the majority of banks'."

Sheridan gaped. She knew the Plaza quite well—it was the hotel her mother favored whenever she visited Paris, so she'd spent many a night as a child alone in a suite with her nanny of the moment and Andrew, her protective detail—and there was no way the Bureau would ever splurge on accommodations like that. "Damn."

"It's pretty nice," Parker agreed with a small shrug. "The only reason the firm okays the expense of the place, though, is because of the safe. The Plaza is more than used to dealing with high-value guests who roll in with millions in jewelry that needs to be protected, and their security staff is all ex-military. Honestly, the painting is probably safer at the hotel than it'd be in lockup at the *Gendarmerie*, which makes the expense of two nights there more than worth it to my bosses."

"I think I'm in the wrong business," Sheridan murmured.

"Well, we are always looking for new talent at Cabot and Carmichael." Parker smiled and nudged her with a playful elbow. "I'm sure you'd be hired in a snap if you ever decided to submit a resume. Of course, the Bureau would probably offer you the Director role if you ever tried to leave, so…"

"Yeah, right," Sheridan laughed. She looked out the window, and her brow furrowed as she connected what she'd just learned about Parker's hotel and the direction their cab was heading. "Parker," she murmured as she turned to look at her, "you said my hotel was closer to the restaurant and that you wouldn't be going out of your way to pick me up, but I'm pretty sure we're heading toward the seventh arrondissement. Where your hotel is," she added for emphasis.

Parker made a show of looking out the window as if to confirm that Sheridan was right, and smiled sheepishly, her eyes shining with playful amusement as she turned back toward her. "It would appear you're correct, Agent Sloan."

"Don't you 'Agent Sloan' me, Parker," Sheridan laughed. "Seriously, why didn't you let me meet you at your hotel?"

"Because I wanted to pick you up," Parker replied with a little shrug. "I didn't want you to have to come all the way to my hotel by yourself."

Sheridan shook her head and murmured, "You're too sweet."

A flicker of a shadow darkened Parker's gaze before she looked down at the seat between them and muttered something that Sheridan couldn't quite make out.

Sheridan smiled and dared to reach out and hook a gentle finger beneath Parker's chin to lift her eyes. It was a wholly presumptive move to demand Parker's attention like this, but there was an undercurrent of *something* in the air that she desperately wanted to understand. "What are you thinking about, right now?"

"Honestly?" Parker asked softly.

Sheridan hummed and nodded as she let her hand drop. "Yeah."

"I..." Parker quirked her lips in what was probably supposed to be a wry grin but came off looking more like a grimace. "I mean, I know that this isn't...that we're not..." She sighed and shook her head. "Honestly? I don't even know if you're into women, but sometimes it feels like we're flirting—which I'm cool with, don't get me wrong—but Kelly said something earlier today about you not being interested in dating, and I guess I'm just...confused? By what the dynamic here is..." She waved a hand weakly between them. "And I don't want to do anything that would make you uncomfortable."

"Oh..." Sheridan nodded slowly as she processed everything Parker had said. She glanced at the back of their driver's head, knowing that even if he wasn't listening, he could still hear them, but she figured she'd never see him again after tonight, so if he heard something she'd rather not share with the world, oh well. "I'm gonna kill him," she muttered.

"I'm sorry," Parker apologized quickly.

"Don't be. You have nothing to be sorry about," Sheridan assured her. She sighed and decided that she may as well start at the beginning. "I am interested in women. Exclusively, it turns out. I figured it out not long after I got to Quantico. And I've also noticed that we seem to be flirting quite a bit, but I just chalked it up to you being the outgoing, confident woman that I remembered from when we were at Brown and that I was misinterpreting things."

"Oh…" Parker breathed.

"And if I'm going to be honest, part of me hoped that I was misinterpreting it all." She reached for Parker's hand as she watched her expression fall. "Not because of anything you've done, but because of the whole 'not dating' thing that Kelly so helpfully blabbed about earlier…" She took a deep breath and let it go slowly. "I love my job. I've worked incredibly hard to get where I am, and it is very demanding. When the phone rings I need to answer it, and sometimes I don't come home for a couple days because I'm working a lead and can't take two minutes to breathe. I had a girlfriend in Philly who I thought was 'the one'"—she shrugged, trying to play it off as if the memory of that night didn't still haunt her—"but it turned out she wasn't. And when she left, she said some…things…that really…" She shook her head. She wasn't going to go down that road right now. "It wasn't good. And so I decided that instead of putting myself in a position where I could be hurt like that again, that I'd just focus on my job and not worry about trying to find someone since I apparently suck at the whole relationship thing."

Parker sucked her lower lip between her teeth and nodded slowly as she let it slip free. "Right. Okay."

The little wrinkle between Parker's brows was utterly adorable, and it was all Sheridan could do to not reach out and smooth it away with the pad of her thumb. She hadn't been looking for a relationship, but there was no way she could ignore the fact that, when it came to Parker, she wasn't as opposed to the idea as she'd been in the past. "Even though we've mostly just been talking on the phone, I swear I've smiled more in the last two weeks than I have in the last year combined, and I… I *like* when you flirt with me. I like the way you smile when I flirt with you. I just don't know…"

Parker's lips quirked in a small, shy smile. "I like all that, too. And I don't know either, to be honest. Because neither of us have a typical nine-to-five and…" Her voice trailed off as the car pulled to the side of the road and the driver killed the engine and climbed out of the car without a word. "We're here. Let's finish this outside?"

"Sure."

Parker nodded and reached for her door. As soon as she had cracked it open, the driver—who'd made his way around to the sidewalk side of the car—pulled it open the rest of the way and offered Parker a hand to help her out. Once Parker was on her feet, she murmured her thanks as she dismissed him with a nod, and turned to offer Sheridan a hand out of the car.

There was no missing the iconic landmark that loomed over Parker's shoulder as Sheridan took her hand, and she smiled as she gazed across the river at the Eiffel Tower. It looked like something from a postcard, tall and dark and distinctive against the colorful backdrop of the evening sky, and she was struck as she always was when she returned to Paris by its beauty.

Of course, for as striking as the Eiffel Tower was, it paled in comparison to the woman in front of her, and she swallowed thickly as she finally registered the way Parker's long fingers curled around her hand. There was a lightness in the touch that kept it from being necessarily confident, but she liked it. A lot. A moment later that gentle touch disappeared, however, and she curled her fingers into a fist at her side to keep from reaching for Parker's hand again as she had a quiet conversation with the driver about calling when they were ready to be picked up.

Arrangements made, Parker smiled and tilted her head toward the edge of the plaza that overlooked the *Jardins du Trocadéro* and the Seine and the Eiffel Tower beyond, and she nodded. The *Palais de Chaillot* was as much of a national landmark as the tower across the river, and the esplanade was predictably crowded with Parisians and tourists alike as they enjoyed the beautiful evening. They found a measure of privacy near the corner of the balcony overlooking the fountain, and Parker sighed as she turned her back to the view to look at her.

"I didn't mean for the evening to turn into this," Parker apologized as she leaned her back against the railing. "I thought we'd just go to dinner, have a drink or two, and hang out for a bit."

"Honestly, this conversation wasn't one I thought we'd be having tonight either," Sheridan admitted with a smile as she rested her forearms on the barrier next to Parker's elbow. "Or ever, possibly. But I think it's good that we did." She leaned into Parker so their shoulders touched and, with her heart in her throat, whispered, "I like you, Parker."

"I like you too, Sheridan," Parker murmured. Her lips pinched thoughtfully, and she nodded slowly, her jaw working from side to side in a way that suggested she was having a silent argument with herself about what she should say next.

Sheridan was touched by the thought Parker was putting into this when it was her issues making things so complicated. She sighed as she wished she was strong enough to say fuck-all to the what-ifs and go for it, but she wasn't. She didn't have it in her to take a chance and lean in and kiss the doubt from Parker's lips.

Yet.

But the idea that she might someday get there was enough for now. In the grand scheme of things, considering taking that risk and putting herself in a position where she was so completely vulnerable was an absolutely huge step forward for her. "How about…we just roll with whatever this is?" she offered hesitantly.

Parker closed her eyes and swallowed thickly. "You mean, just keep being ass-grabbing friends who occasionally flirt with each other?"

"Something like that, yeah," Sheridan agreed with a quiet laugh. "Though I meant something more along the lines of just taking things slow. Maybe not rule out the idea of someday but, for now, to just…"

"Keep doing what we're doing," Parker finished for her. "And if someday it becomes something more…"

Sheridan nodded, relieved that Parker seemed to understand. "Is that okay?"

"Yeah." Parker smiled and ducked her head. "I do like the idea of someday, though," she whispered.

And, god, the way her stomach flipped at that left little room for doubt in Sheridan's mind that she quite liked it too. "Me too."

"Good." Parker nodded and glanced at her watch. "Do you still want to go to dinner? Because our reservation is in five minutes. Or did all of this ruin the night for you and would you rather just go back to your hotel?"

"Nothing's ruined, Parker. And I absolutely want to still go to dinner." Sheridan looked around the *Esplanade du Trocadéro*. While she was familiar with the area, she wasn't familiar enough to be able to pinpoint which restaurants were nearby. "Where...?"

"You'll see." Parker shoved herself off the balcony and offered Sheridan her arm. "Shall we?"

"And people say chivalry is dead," Sheridan teased as she slipped her hand over the crook of Parker's elbow and allowed herself to be steered back toward the street.

Parker laughed and flexed her bicep. "I'm glad you approve."

It was impossible not to, really, but Sheridan kept that comment to herself as they ambled across the esplanade toward the building that framed the left side of the courtyard. She ducked her head in thanks when Parker stepped up to hold the door for her, and arched a brow in surprise when she recognized the name beside the elevator button for the top-most floor of the building. She had never eaten at *Café de l'Homme* before, but she'd certainly heard of it, and she wondered how in the world Parker had managed to secure a reservation on such short notice.

Working some magic was one thing, pulling off the impossible was quite another.

She kept her questions to herself until they were seated at an intimate table in front of one of the floor-to-ceiling windows that overlooked the Seine and the Eiffel Tower beyond, but couldn't hold back once they were alone. "How in the world did you get a reservation here?"

"The owner of the restaurant has quite a few pieces insured through the firm," Parker explained as she draped her napkin over her lap. She shrugged and glanced out the window for a moment before turning back on Sheridan, her lips curled in a soft smile. "I actually recovered a statue of his that'd been stolen a few years ago, and he was so grateful to have it back that he will give anyone from the firm a table on a moment's notice. So when you said I could take you out tonight, I knew I had to bring you here because it's the most amazing place I know of in the city."

"But when...?" Sheridan shook her head.

"I ducked into a cubicle at the *Gendarmerie* when you and Kelly were talking to Bellet's boss and called to get us a table." Parker shrugged as if it wasn't a big deal.

But it was a big deal. Because she'd grown up being passively ignored and had never been with anyone who put this kind of consideration into doing anything for her. And the fact that Parker had put this much thought into where they should go for dinner when a corner café would have more than sufficed sent a pleasant warmth through her chest. "You are too much, Parker Ravenscroft."

Parker smiled and winked playfully. "Just for you, Sheridan Sloan."

The gentleness in Parker's tone made her blush, and she cleared her throat softly as she reached for her menu.

"So, Ms. Sloan..." Parker drawled as she opened the leather-bound wine list that was almost as thick as a short novel. "Do you prefer red or white?"

"Red, usually. But I'm good with either," Sheridan replied as she began scanning the menu.

"So helpful." Parker heaved a dramatic sigh. "Fine, I guess I'll just have to decide on my own and surprise you."

Sheridan grinned at Parker over the top of her menu. "Well, you've done pretty good so far, so I'm sure you'll do just fine." The answering smile that curled Parker's lips was utterly charmed, and her stomach fluttered as she dropped her eyes to her menu.

It was fun to flirt without expectations, to be able to just go with the banter that came so naturally when she was with Parker without having to think about something being taken in a way she wasn't comfortable.

A pleasant lull settled between them as they perused their menus, and when she'd finally made up her mind on what to order, she couldn't resist peeking over the top of her menu at Parker, who was gazing softly out the window at the view. It was bizarre to think that it had only been two weeks since they'd reconnected, and now they were sharing an intimate table for two overlooking one of the world's most famous landmarks in what was arguably the most romantic city in the world.

This kind of thing didn't happen to her, and yet…

Somehow, it had.

She licked her lips as her eyes traced the curve of Parker's cheek and the dimple at the corner of her lips. She lingered on that hint of a smile, that proof that Parker was enjoying herself despite everything for a few heartbeats before her gaze drifted over Parker's jaw and danced along the plane of her throat.

God, she's beautiful.

She shook her head. She had no idea if their decision to take things slow and see if anything developed would work out for them but, as soft gray eyes turned to capture her own, making her breath catch in her throat, she prayed that it would.

fifteen

The streets of *Saint-Germain-des-Prés* in Paris' sixth arrondissement were deserted as Parker made her way from the metro station to the two-bedroom apartment Oliver had rented through Airbnb. The online rental site was a godsend for people in their illegitimate line of work, as it made it ridiculously easy for them to blend into a neighborhood to do reconnaissance on potential targets. Strangers seen lingering on a particular street would raise attention, but if there was a constant stream of new faces, the sight of someone a local didn't recognize perched for hours a day at a café overlooking a particular area wouldn't raise too many eyebrows.

She blew out a soft breath as she skipped up the stairs to the main entrance of Oliver's building and kept her eyes toward the ground so the security camera wouldn't pick up her face as she quickly punched in the code that would unlock the door. The building was clean, the marble tile in the foyer immaculate, but she paid the decor little attention as she headed for the stairs. She'd learned first-hand the night before that the mechanicals for the small lift that had been shoehorned into the back curve of the graceful, arcing staircase—while beautiful with its gold and silver finishes—hadn't been upgraded since it'd been first installed in the thirties. It was loud and slow and honestly a menace; and the last thing they needed was for the neighbors to be aware of the fact that they were out and about when the clock had passed midnight over half an hour earlier.

She knocked softly on the door at the very top of the stairs, and glanced behind herself at the deserted stairwell as she waited for Oliver to let her in.

"You're late," Oliver greeted her as he opened the door.

She absolutely was, and she didn't regret it in the least. Not when it was because she'd been too lost in Sheridan's company to bother looking at the time. She'd been a little worried that taking Sheridan to *Café de l'Homme* might have been a little too much, but the evening had been wonderful. After their unexpected heart-to-heart on the ride to the restaurant, she'd been worried that things would be awkward, their conversation stilted and self-conscious as they became accustomed to the shift in their relationship, but it hadn't been. The evening had been perfect, their conversation easy and light and playful in a way that it'd never been before. So when Sheridan suggested they take a stroll across the *Pont d'Iéna* after dinner to enjoy a walk around the *Champ de Mars*, she'd immediately agreed, too eager to spend as much time with Sheridan as possible to worry about the time and the other commitments she had to honor later that night.

Despite the fact that they'd agreed to take things slow, the entire evening had, without a doubt, been the most romantic night of her life. The soft curve of Sheridan's lips and the joy that sparkled in her eyes as they wandered beneath the belly of the tower was an image that would be forever burned into her memory, a breathtaking moment of utter perfection that she still couldn't believe she'd been blessed enough to witness.

Which made being here, now, on the precipice of jumping back into a world she had thought she'd never enter again, all the more difficult to wrap her head around. The two halves of her night couldn't have been more different, and she rolled her eyes at the sly smirk that tugged at Oliver's lips as he waited for her to respond.

"Shut up," she muttered as she shouldered her way past him into the apartment.

Oliver laughed and made a show of rubbing his arm where she'd bumped him as he closed the door. "What? Did your date not go well?"

"It wasn't a date," she insisted as she flipped her hood off and wandered toward the living room. "And it went great, thank you. You should be thankful that I'm here instead of enjoying her company instead," she informed him as she slipped her backpack from her shoulders and dropped it over the back of the couch.

"I am," he replied sincerely. "Really."

Parker sighed. "It's fine. She was pretty tired by the time we got back to her hotel, anyway." *And I promised you I'd help with this, so let's just get it done,* she added silently. "What's the status on Dumas?"

"He left around five o'clock for his business trip to Berlin, his wife and son not long after for their weeklong vacation in San Sebastian."

"It is pretty creepy that you know all this, by the way."

Oliver shrugged. "Not really. It didn't even take any hacking on my part to figure it out. His firm was bragging all over their website about sending him to this conference in Germany to be a keynote speaker and receive some investing award, and his wife and son were telling everybody around here about their trip. His son seemed especially happy to be missing a week of school to go on holiday."

"Still..." She looked over at the dining room table that was covered with maps and blueprints and random notes on colored Post-its.

"Yeah. People need to be more careful about announcing when they're going to be going out of town. Makes them an easy target."

Parker huffed a laugh and nodded. "Right. You're so kind, thinking of others like that." She waved a hand at the evidence of their planning. "So, we're good to go with what we walked through last night?"

"Yeah." He nodded. "I'll stick the security cameras on the roof between here and Dumas' place on a loop before we leave, and then I'll be able to disarm the penthouse's alarms with my laptop from that spot on the roof overlooking the street while you're inside. I also hacked the police scanner for this part of town, so I'll know immediately if we fuck something up, but it should be fine."

"It better be." Parker took off her hoodie and reached for her pack. She had swung by her hotel for a quick wardrobe change after she'd dropped off Sheridan, so she was already dressed for the job in a pair of black cargo pants and black long sleeve compression shirt, and all she had left to do was to cover her hair—which was her most easily identifiable feature, anyway.

"Ah, you're going with the Alice wig," Oliver observed as she pulled a dark wig out of her bag.

"God, I wish I looked like Milla Jovovich when I wore this thing," she retorted as she made her way to the nearby powder room to put it on. "Or, you know, ever." She pursed her lips at her reflection as she combed her hair away from her face, and sighed as she slipped the dark wig on over her hair.

"I'm sure Sheridan likes you just the way you are," Oliver called from the other room.

Parker couldn't help but smile at that because, yeah, that was what she got out of their little talk earlier.

"Now that's a smile," Oliver noted in a light, teasing voice from the doorway.

She flipped him off and then tugged at the ends of her wig. "So, how do I look?"

Oliver smiled and nodded. "Like Milla freaking Jovovich."

"You're a liar. But I love you for it." She brushed a light kiss over his cheek. "Let's go make some money, huh?"

"Right behind ya, sis," he replied with a laugh as they turned toward the French doors at the back of the apartment that overlooked a lush, tree-filled private garden.

Parker grabbed her thin black backpack and pulled it on as she made her way through the open doors, and she took a deep breath as she climbed onto the wrought iron railing that framed the narrow porch. From there, it was a quick hop and a push to get onto the roof. She took a moment to enjoy the view of the Louvre just across the river as she pulled on a pair of leather gloves, and she smiled when, as she turned to watch Oliver muscle himself over the ledge, she spied the Eiffel Tower in the distance, its lights flickering and dancing for the last time of the night.

Once Oliver had clambered on the roof in a move that was more muscle than grace, they set off across the rooftops, keeping to the back side of the pitch so they were hidden from the street. Dumas' penthouse was at the opposite corner of the block from the one they'd just left, with sweeping views of the Seine and the city beyond. The windows were predictably dark, but she still waited at the edge of the roof as Oliver perched himself next to the jut of the firebreak wall on the western side of the unit that gave him an unimpeded view of the street below. She kept her eyes on him as she listened to the wind and the hum of traffic, keeping her eyes trained for a sound that seemed like it was out of place as he powered up his laptop.

She was committed to this course of action, but she also had no problem delaying the job if something seemed off.

Nothing did, however, and a few minutes later Oliver flashed her two thumbs up and nodded.

Time to go.

Parker took a deep breath and slipped over the edge of the roof, her fingertips wrapping around the edge of the limestone facade to lever herself onto the balcony outside the kitchen. She crouched low as she pulled a slim wallet of lock pick tools from the side pocket of her pants, her ears trained for anything suspicious as she slid the narrow tools into the lock and quickly popped it open.

The rush of adrenaline that flooded her veins after she pocketed the tools and wrapped her hand around the door handle was neither unexpected nor unpleasant, and she took a deep breath as she tightened her fingers around the lever.

"Here we go," she murmured as she pressed down and pushed the door slowly open, tensed and ready to bolt at the first sound of an alarm.

"You're good, Park," Oliver's voice assured her through her earpiece as she edged inside. The kitchen was large for a city apartment, with rich hardwood floors, sparkling marble countertops, and professional-grade appliances.

"I'm in."

"Good. After you go through the kitchen, you'll be in the dining room. Beyond that is a hallway that opens to the foyer. Sitting room is on the left, the library is on the right."

"Got it," Parker murmured as she made her way into the dining room. She walked so softly that her footsteps were silent even on the hardwood, and a moment later she was standing in the doorway of the library. She took a moment to gather her bearings, letting her gaze drift over the shadows in the room before she crossed to the lone window and pulled the curtains shut.

She turned on her flashlight as the room was plunged into darkness, and whistled softly as she looked at the absolutely gorgeous mahogany bookshelves that surrounded her. Every available expanse of wall was covered in shelves that stretched from the floor to the twelve-foot ceiling overhead, and there was a comfortable-looking armchair and ottoman angled into each corner of the room for reading. It was a book-lover's paradise, and she whistled softly. "This library is insane."

"Any sign of the books?"

"Not yet," she reported. "We still good?"

"Yup."

"I'll be as quick as I can, then," she signed off. She set her flashlight on a small reading table beside the armchair to the left of the window, slipped her pack from her shoulders, and laid the backpack on the chair. Since the last thing she needed was to damage the books on Marquis' list, she traded her leather gloves for a pair of white cotton inspection gloves that she retrieved from the small front pocket.

Properly gloved, she picked up her flashlight and began running it over the shelves encircling the room, looking for a clue that would tell her where Dumas kept the books she needed. Going over every title in the library would take too damn long, but a true collector would either store their rare books in boxes to protect them from the elements or opt to display them in a glass case away from direct sunlight. Anything else would be reckless, and she hummed when her light landed on a section of glass doors three shelves high by three sections wide.

"Guy is a pretty serious collector," she observed softly as she made her way over to the left-most display case. "He has to have close to a hundred rare books here," she elaborated for Oliver since he couldn't see what she could.

"Doesn't surprise me. He's old money, and that usually translates to old heirlooms."

"Or maybe he just has a thing for collecting rare books," she replied as she squinted against the reflection of her light in the glass doors. The shelves beneath the volumes were also glass, and she smiled at the thought he showed in caring for his collection. Somehow, she wouldn't be surprised if, when she finally opened a door, a rush of cool air would greet her. Dumas had taken every other precaution in tending to his collection, adding climate control to the displays would be of little added expense to a man who could afford a collection like the one she was looking at now.

It was impossible to not be awed by the names on the books in front of her—Whitman, Keats, Hugo, Camus, and others that regularly graced the syllabi of literature courses at universities around the world—and she eventually found one of the two books on her list on the top enclosed shelf in the middle section of the display.

While Oliver had been in charge of researching elements for the heist itself, she'd done her share of legwork looking into the books themselves. The last time a first edition of *Don Quixote* had traded hands on public record had been in 1989, at an auction where it had sold a hefty one-and-a-half million. The buyer had been anonymous, so she had no idea if this was that copy of the book, but she figured that an authentic first-edition would easily go for at least three times that amount now.

She held her breath as she opened the cabinet door and carefully, oh so carefully eased the novel from its shelf. The book had aged well over the centuries, she noted as she ran her fingers over the dark brown leather cover that showed only slight hints of weathering, and she held her breath as she carefully opened the book. The inside of the front and back covers were covered in an ornate gold and black patterned design that glinted under the light, and beneath the bound pages on the inside of the spine showed a dark green and gold striped fabric. It was exactly what she'd been expecting to see, and she let out the breath she'd been holding as she moved from the structure of the book itself to its pages. The paper was appropriately aged considering the book she was looking for had been printed in 1605, and she nodded to herself as she tested the flexibility of the parchment.

Perfect.

The title page would be easy enough to forge, so she gave it only a brief enough look to confirm that it held all the necessary details to be considered authentic. She flipped through the book, checking the signature and interior artwork that one would put less effort into forging if the novel had been a fake, but it all checked out.

It was the real deal.

"Got *Don Quixote*," she reported as she turned and carefully set it on the small side-table beside the reading chair on her left where she'd set her bag.

"*Nice.*"

She hummed in agreement as she reached for her backpack. Even though she hadn't had much time to herself over the last week, she'd gotten lucky to find books that were—in size and appearance—perfect matches for the ones she'd be leaving with in a little shop not far from the Smithsonian.

She couldn't help but chuckle as she pulled a collector's edition of *The Count of Monte Cristo* from the bag, and nodded to herself as she held it up to the Cervantes. The color of the leather cover was her biggest concern since she'd only had pictures to compare to, but she was pleased to see that, while not identical, they were close enough that the replacement wasn't going to stand out as being something that didn't belong. She set the Cervantes novel back onto the table and slipped *The Count of Monte Cristo* into its spot on the shelf. Once the book was lined up perfectly with the others, she took a step back to assess her attempt at deception.

It was as good as she was going to get, and she shook her head as she began scanning the books behind the glass for the 1865 copy of *Alice in Wonderland* that she was still missing.

She eventually found it tucked away behind the last cabinet door, its dark red leather cover a stark contrast to the soft faded browns on either side of it, and she couldn't keep from grinning as she opened the door to pull it from the shelf. While researching the job, she'd learned that only two thousand copies of this particular edition had been printed because the illustrator had been displeased with the print quality, and she'd committed to memory some of the most discernible issues with that original run.

Even though she knew it was the illustrations that would tell her if the book was a forgery or not, she still went through the same field authentication steps as she had with *Don Quixote*. The gold embossed frame around the edge of the cover checked out, as did the image of Alice holding her book in the center of the front cover. Interior, signature, and most importantly the illustrations all matched what she was expecting to see, and she grinned as she moved to place it atop the copy of *Don Quixote* on the side table.

"Got Alice. Replacing it with the copy of *The Time Machine* from my bag now. We still good out there?"

"*Still good,*" Oliver confirmed.

Once *The Time Machine* was snugly ensconced on the shelf, she closed the glass door and turned back to her ill begotten treasures and her backpack. The case she'd brought to transport the books wasn't as high-tech as the one she used for statuary, but it was still much more sophisticated than an average person would ever even dream might exist. She'd bought it from a fence in Vancouver who dealt almost exclusively in rare books, and he'd claimed that the carbon fiber shell could be run over by a tank and still wouldn't crack. But it wasn't just the outside of the case that was special. Inside, the top and bottom of the case were lined with inch-thick foam, and there was an inflatable cushion along each edge that could be adjusted to the exact dimensions of whatever rectangular object was inside.

She pulled a couple polyethylene bags from the case and slid each book into one to protect the covers, and then carefully arranged them in the center of the base before using the little hand pump that fit into the handle of the case to inflate the side bumpers. Once the books were secure and the case was back in her pack, she switched her gloves again and then re-opened the curtains, making sure to leave everything as she'd found it. The more time that passed without the books being reported, the better.

Her heart raced as she made her way through the apartment to her entry point, and she couldn't keep from grinning as she stepped out onto the balcony and closed the door behind herself.

"I'm out." She pulled her picks from her pocket and set about re-engaging the lock. "And, the door's locked. We're good to go."

"*Gotcha.*"

She tightened the straps of her backpack and took a deep breath as she climbed onto the balcony railing. She tested her grip on the edge of the limestone facade twice before she gave a little hop and pulled herself up onto the roof.

Oliver was just finishing repacking his laptop in his backpack when she reached the firewall where he'd been hidden, and thirty seconds later they were moving at a clip across the rooftops toward his rented apartment.

Recovering stolen property was a rush, but it had nothing on the high that hit after completing a job. It didn't matter that she was only doing this for her brother, or that she didn't want anything to do with this life, that old adrenaline rush, potent and intoxicating, still hit her like a freight train. She laughed as she ran across the rooftops, her legs pumping so fast that she felt like she was flying with Oliver at her side, his grin as wide as her own. They slipped over the edge of the roof onto his balcony like a couple of shadowed ghosts, floating through the air and landing lightly on their feet before spilling into the apartment.

"God, that was fun," Oliver declared as he closed the doors behind them and turned on the lights.

"It's certainly a rush," she agreed as she slipped her bag from her back and set it on the floor beside the couch before she flopped onto it.

"Piece of cake, right? Just like I said it'd be?"

"Pretty much, yeah." She stretched her arms up over her head and arched her back. "So, when can we hand them off to Marquis? I'd rather not be in possession of stolen property any longer than strictly necessary."

Oliver turned his wrist to look at his watch and shook his head. "It's close to two. She's probably asleep right now and I don't see a reason to wake her up for this. I'll send her a text on the burner I picked up for this job first thing in the morning and set it up. You want to be there for it?"

"If it'll happen sometime in the next twelve hours, sure. My flight leaves at four and Sheridan's on it, so I can't try and catch a different one. I don't want to do anything that'd make her suspicious since these books will eventually be getting reported stolen."

"That makes sense. I'll see what I can do. You want to crash here, or were you planning on going back to your hotel?"

The offer was tempting, but she shook her head. Not that it mattered, because the Matisse was locked up tight in the safe back at the Plaza, but she'd sleep better knowing she was in the same building as it. And she figured it'd be better for her to be where she was supposed to be in case her firm or Sheridan tried to reach her through the front desk for some reason.

Speaking of...

She pulled her phone out of her backpack and turned it on. No messages. Good. Though, if she was being honest with herself, she wouldn't have minded a goodnight text from Sheridan.

"I better head back to the hotel." Parker pulled the case with their two million dollar payday out of the bag and handed it to Oliver. "In case something can't be arranged for later this morning, here are the books for the exchange."

He nodded and set the case on the coffee table. "Sounds good. I'll let you know as soon as I get it all sorted with Marquis."

"Okay." She pulled of her wig, folded it inside out, and set it in her bag. She combed her fingers through her hair and shook her head to try to get it looking back to normal, and then blew out a loud breath as she pulled her hoodie back on and pushed herself to her feet. "Hopefully I'll talk to you soon. But, you know, feel free to make it after eight. I'm fucking exhausted."

He laughed and offered a little salute. "Yes, ma'am." He yawned as he followed her to the front door, and pulled her into a light hug when they stopped in the foyer. "Love you, sis."

She smiled as she sank into his embrace and gave him a big squeeze. "Love you too, Ollie," she murmured.

The street was even quieter than it'd been when she arrived a little over an hour ago, and she kept her head down as she made her way back the way she came, her footsteps silent on the pavement as she drifted along in the shadows.

SIXTEEN

"So glad I woke up for this," Sheridan muttered as she and Kelly made their way out of the observation suite attached to the interrogation room where Vasseur was still refusing to talk. Watching Bellet try to hide how much it pissed him off was amusing, but she desperately needed another cup of coffee if she was going to pull off pretending to be properly awake.

"Tell me about it," Kelly replied through a massive yawn.

Sheridan shot him a curious look. Out of the two of them, he should have been more rested, and yet the circles under his eyes were darker than her own. "Why are you so tired?"

Kelly rubbed a hand over his jaw and smirked. "I went to that little bar down the street from our hotel for dinner last night and ended up not getting back to my room until after dawn."

"Should have guessed," she chuckled. For as much as he teased her about the whole not dating thing, he claimed to be just as opposed to the prospect of a long-term relationship, preferring to scratch that particular itch whenever he was in the mood and a willing partner was around. "Do you even remember their name?"

Kelly hummed and nodded as he muffled another yawn. "Marie." He waggled his eyebrows. "Want me to describe her for you? Because good god was she hot."

"I'll take your word for it, thanks," she assured with a laugh. "You were safe?"

"Yes, mom. We were safe," he grumbled playfully.

"Well, then I'm glad you had fun."

"I did. So," he drawled, stretching that single vowel out until he needed to take a breath, "how was your big non-date with Ms. Ravenscroft?"

She rolled her eyes at his phrasing, but was also glad that she didn't have to correct him about the nature of their evening. "It was wonderful, thank you."

"Nice. Where'd you go?"

"*Café de l'Homme.*" At his blank look, she huffed a laugh and explained, "A restaurant over by the Eiffel Tower."

Kelly whistled softly. "Damn. So on a scale from one to ten on the oh-my-god-it-was-so-romantic scale, how was it?"

"At least a thirteen," Sheridan said as she led them into the unit's break room. The coffee was terrible, but she didn't feel like it'd be good for them to head out for a better cup until some kind of consensus had been reached on what to do with Vasseur. Technically it wasn't their case anymore, but Bartz would want any information they could get on who had been using him as a fence and she didn't trust Bellet to share the information if he got it.

"Oh, really?"

She rolled her eyes. "When the restaurant overlooks the Eiffel Tower, there's literally no way for it to be anything but romantic, Kel. Anyway, we talked."

"Well, I would hope so." Kelly pulled a paper cup from the stack beside the machine and handed it to her. "Would have been a rather boring night out if you just sat and stared at each other the whole time."

The playfulness in his tone told her that he was messing with her and wasn't going to push for details she might not be comfortable sharing, but she was surprised by how much she suddenly *wanted* to talk about it all. She'd replayed their conversation more times than she could count and, while she was pleased with what had happened, she didn't know what to do next. And Kelly, annoying as he sometimes was, had a much better handle on the whole relationship thing than she did. "I meant we talked about this…thing, with us."

"And?" Kelly asked, his expression carefully concerned.

For as much as he loved to tease her, he also understood when to knock it off and listen, and she wasn't surprised he'd picked up on the shift in her tone. Part of her wanted to go off on him for forcing her into the situation in the first place with his little "Sheridan doesn't date" comment the day before, but she knew they would've eventually gotten to the point where the elephant in the room with them couldn't be ignored any longer. "I don't know. We pretty much established that we like flirting with each other, but we're not… She seems as hesitant as I am to do more than that, right now, so we're just…" She blew out a loud breath and shrugged. Maybe she wasn't ready to talk about it after all.

"That's good though, right? I mean, if she said she likes flirting with you?"

Sheridan nodded and set her cup on the counter beside the machine. "Yeah."

"And you like flirting with her?" When she nodded, he asked gently, "So you're just gonna hang out and flirt for now?"

"I think so, yeah." She rubbed a hand over the back of her neck. "Is that weird?"

Kelly smiled and shook his head. "No. I think it's exactly what you need right now." He wrapped a brotherly arm over her shoulders and pulled her into his side. "Slow is good, Sloan."

"I…" She closed her eyes as she let herself sink into his side. "I like her."

"I know." He squeezed her shoulders. "And, from watching you guys yesterday, I can tell you that I'm pretty sure she feels the same way. So go ahead and take things slow. Hang out. Flirt. Have fun, for fuck's sake. God knows you can use it."

Sheridan choked out a laugh and shook her head as she wiped at her eyes. "Thank you."

"My pleasure, partner," Kelly murmured. He gave her shoulders one last squeeze before he let his arm drop. "So, which shitty-ass coffee would you like?"

"The one that hasn't been sitting out all night," Sheridan replied as she eyed the stained carafes warily.

"Sorry, that's all we've got." Kelly picked up the fuller of the two carafes and filled each of their cups, leaving more room than usual at the top for them to add sugar and creamer and whatever else they could find to try to make the coffee palatable.

Doctoring the coffee did pretty much nothing to make it taste any less awful, and she winced as she choked down the burned, bitter brew. "Ugh. We should've gone out."

Kelly took a sip of his coffee, spit it into the sink, and threw the paper cup into the trash. "Yep."

She stared at her cup for a long moment before she tossed it into the trash as well. No caffeine was better than *that* caffeine. And, coming from her, that was definitely saying something.

A roar of laughter from the squad room drew their attention, and Kelly arched a curious brow before he made his way toward the noise with her hot on his heels. A small group of agents were clustered around a desk in the middle of the bullpen. And at the center of the group was Guillard, who had a small combination padlock in her hands that looked like the kind she used to secure her gear at the gym.

"What's going on?" Sheridan asked as they joined the group.

Guillard swore and tossed the lock onto the desk. "Trying to crack a stupid lock. It isn't going well."

Sheridan grinned. The story of Parker cracking the lock while they waited for the locksmith at Vasseur's place the day before had spread like wildfire through the unit. Not that she was all that surprised, it was exactly the kind of story that would have had everyone talking back home, but never in a million years would she have imagined the French agents would try to replicate her result.

"You want to have a try?" Guillard asked.

Kelly turned to her with a grin.

Sheridan waved a hand for him go for it. "Go knock yourself out, Innes."

Kelly took the lock from Guillard and looked over at Sheridan. "I wish I knew how she learned to do it."

Sheridan hummed and shrugged noncommittally.

"Think she'll tell me if I ask?" Kelly asked as his eyes dropped to the lock in his hand.

Sheridan chuckled and shook her head. "Nope." She had no doubt that Parker would weave a tall tale that didn't even hint at the truth of why she'd been forced to learn how to do it. But, while it would have been amusing to hear what she came up with, she also hated the idea of seeing that shadow that had clouded Parker's eyes when she spoke about the darker parts of her childhood.

"Did she tell you?"

She nodded. "And trust me, you don't want to know the story, okay?"

"Bad?"

"Yeah."

It was clear from the frown that wrinkled Kelly's forehead that he was curious, but the way he tipped his head in a small nod assured her that he'd never ask her about it. He sighed and looked down at the padlock in his hand. "It was still pretty damn impressive."

"It was," Sheridan agreed.

A door slammed down the hall, and they all looked up to see Bellet storming through the bullpen toward the stairs that led to the administrative floor above.

"Think the interrogation is going well?" Guillard chuckled.

"Oh yeah," Sheridan laughed.

"Is it bad that for as much as I'd love to know who was using Vasseur as a fence, I'm honestly fine staying in the dark about it all if it pisses him off like that?" Kelly asked.

Guillard barked out a laugh and shook her head. "Not at all, Agent Innes. Not at all."

seventeen

Parker looked out the windshield at the private airfield where they were meeting Evie Marquis to deliver the books in the case cradled between her feet. The airfield was small, with only one runway and a row of a half-dozen hangars spanning the length along either side of the asphalt, set in a picturesque valley surrounded by forests and farmland. She would have rather done this in Paris where she was at least moderately familiar with the territory, but neither side had been willing to try to make the trade at Marquis' office, and knowing that the FBI was in town made her hesitant to find another location in the city limits. So when Marquis suggested the private airport, it had seemed the best available option. And, as she counted four Ford Explorers circling the perimeter of the airfield, just inside the imposing eight-foot tall, barbed wire-topped fence that framed the property, while a fifth SUV was cruising the tarmac, she had to admit that the security was impressive—if not borderline excessive.

The guard booth that anchored the gap in the fence was made of concrete and looked like it could double as a fallout shelter, and the traffic drop arm that spanned the one-lane road in and out of the airfield that was massive enough that it could probably go head-to-head with a tank and put up a decent enough fight. Two security guards dressed in all black exited the booth as they coasted toward it, their expressions as serious as the semi-automatic rifles they carried.

One guard made his way to the other side of the barrier and, while he didn't aim the weapon at them, there was no ignoring the way he stood at the ready, clearly prepared to shoot in an instant if needed.

"The fuck kind of airport is this?" Oliver muttered, pressing the button for his window as he eased to a stop.

Parker hummed in agreement, not wanting to say anything more since Oliver's window had started to open. The last thing she wanted to do was provoke the guys outside the car who looked like they'd be just as comfortable running a black-ops mission somewhere awful as they were guarding the airfield.

Oliver tipped his glasses up on his head and addressed the guard standing outside his window with a clipboard. "Oliver Dobrev and Parker Ravenscroft. Here to meet with Evie Marquis."

The guard nodded and peered into the car. "Identification, please?"

Oliver fished his wallet out of his back pocket to retrieve his driver's license, and she pulled hers from the back pocket of her slacks where she'd slipped it and a credit card before leaving her hotel room that morning. They shared a *what the fuck have we gotten ourselves into* look as she handed him her ID, and she did her best to look completely non-threatening as Oliver handed the licenses to the guard.

The guard leaned down to triple-check that they matched the pictures on the licenses before he handed them back to Oliver. "Just a moment," he instructed as he nodded at his partner before disappearing into the building. He emerged a moment later with his gun slung over his shoulder and a clipboard, looking slightly more relaxed but just as deadly. "Hangar four, sir." He pointed to a hangar toward the end of the line. "This side of the tarmac. You can park in front of the building. The front entrance is unlocked, as per Ms. Marquis' instructions." His expression was appropriately aloof, no doubt working at a facility like this he saw more than his fair share of powerful people, but there was a tightness in his posture that suggested Marquis' name carried more weight than most.

"Thanks." Oliver gave him a little salute.

Parker's phone buzzed with a text alert as they waited for the drop arm to lift out of their way, and she smiled when she saw that the message was from Sheridan. *Thought you'd like to know there's a bullpen full of French federal agents over here trying to crack a Master Lock thanks to you.*

"Everything okay?" Oliver asked as they rolled through the gate under the watchful eye of security guard number two.

"Yeah. It was from Sheridan. She says a bunch of the agents over at the *Gendarmerie* are trying to crack a padlock." The laugh that bubbled in her throat died as she noticed the way the guard's trigger finger did not move from its ready position as he watched them drive past. She blew out a soft breath and shook her head as she directed her attention back on the road in front of them.

"Do I want to know why they're trying to do that?" Olive asked with a little laugh.

She smirked as she typed out a quick, *That's awesome. Has Vasseur given you guys anything?*, before she turned her attention back to her brother. "Before Sheridan's partner went to find a locksmith yesterday afternoon he made a joke about me not being about to just open the safe myself, so I lied and said that my skills topped out at a Master Lock."

"At least you didn't try and crack the damn safe just to show off."

"Right?" She ran her hands through her hair and shrugged as if the idea hadn't crossed her mind. "Anyway, he came back with a gym lock that he found god knows where, betting me that I couldn't crack it, so I did. And apparently word of that has made its way through the *Gendarmerie*..."

"So they're trying to do it, too." Even though he had sunglasses on, Parker could still tell that he punctuated that little comment with a rather epic eye roll. "Way to lay low, Park."

"It's not like I cracked the Tresorex in Vasseur's office," she pointed out. "Which we both know I could have."

"Good point," he conceded with a smile. "Did Sheridan ask about how you learned to do it?"

"Yeah. When her partner went to go find the locksmith, before he came back with the lock."

"What'd you tell her?" Oliver asked as he turned into a parking space outside hangar four.

"The truth." She pursed her lips and lifted her right shoulder in a little shrug. "I'd told her before about growing up in the system, and I'm not ashamed of what I had to do to survive."

"How'd she take it?"

"Good, I guess." Parker nodded slowly and stared blankly at the corrugated metal wall in front of them. "She seemed almost more angry on my behalf than anything, which…"

"Is a million times better than pity," he finished for her with a slight tilt of his head. "Yeah."

Her phone buzzed again, and she blinked as she refocused her gaze enough to read the screen. *Not yet. Bellet stormed out of the interrogation room a few minutes ago looking pissed. Morale in the bullpen went up a few notches at that.*

"Exactly," Parker agreed as she typed out a quick reply. *Lol. I'll bet. What time are you planning on getting to CDG?*

Sheridan's response came almost immediately. *Two-ish? Maybe earlier depending on how things pan out here. Why?*

"God, smile a little harder, why don't you," Oliver teased as he reached for his door handle. "I'm gonna check things out real quick while you wrap shit up with Agent Sloan." He checked his watch. "I'm willing to bet Marquis is already inside, though, so make it quick. Okay?"

"Yeah." She turned her attention back to her phone as he climbed out of the car. She pursed her lips thoughtfully and then tapped out, *I just wanted to know when I get to see you again.*

She hit send and shook her head as she opened her door. For as much as she'd rather sit and flirt with Sheridan, they had a job to do. And the sooner they got that job done, the sooner she could stop worrying about how in the world she was going to keep these two opposite sides of her life from intersecting. Her phone buzzed in her hand as she leaned back into the car to retrieve the carbon fiber briefcase that held the books, and she prayed Sheridan wouldn't be offended that she wasn't going to be able to continue their conversation right now. Even though she didn't have time to respond, however, she couldn't resist looking at the phone to see what Sheridan had said.

Whenever you want, Parker. All you have to do is ask.

Her smile was untamable as she slipped the phone into the back pocket of her slacks.

"How's Sheridan?" Oliver teased as she reached his side.

"She's good."

Oliver laughed. "I bet she is." He cleared his throat and tilted his head toward the hangar. "You ready?"

Not at all, but she nodded anyway. The sooner they made the exchange, the sooner they could get out of here. "Let's get this over with."

"I hear ya," Oliver muttered.

It was always nerve-wracking walking into somewhere new completely blind, and she looked around cautiously as she stepped through the pedestrian access door. The large door at the back of the building the plane had come through was shut, blocking them from any prying eyes that might be on the airfield beyond. The interior of the hangar was clean and well-lit, unlike those often shown in the movies, the windows to the office on their right were dark and the machinery that was arranged along the left side of the building looked equally deserted.

Parker didn't know a lot about private jets, but even in her utter ignorance she recognized that the one parked in the middle of the cavernous hangar—with its sleek body and distinctive upturn at the end of its wings—had to have cost a mint, and she whistled softly as she imagined what the inside of it must look like. The door just behind the cockpit that doubled as the plane's stairs was open, but there was nobody in sight, and she arched a brow at Oliver.

Surely they weren't supposed to just go on up?

He shrugged and stopped a few feet from the foot of the plane's stairs.

"Mr. Dobrev. Ms. Ravenscroft," a deep voice with a polished English lilt called out from behind them.

Parker tensed and, beside her, she felt Oliver do the same. Heart in her throat, she tightened her grip on the handle of the briefcase in case she needed to use it as a weapon as she turned to see who had addressed them. She didn't relax her grip even when she recognized the man as the bodyguard who'd accompanied Marquis to their meeting at Kickshaw. His suit and tie did little to detract from the air of lethality that surrounded him, and the hint of a gun on his left side only reinforced that impression.

"I apologize if I startled you." He smiled and held his hands up to show he wasn't a threat.

Parker blew out a soft breath as her heart began sinking back where it belonged, and did her best to not show exactly how startled she had been by his unexpected appearance as she leveled what she prayed passed as an inquisitive expression on the man.

"I was making sure you weren't followed," the bodyguard explained as he looked at the case clasped in Parker's fist. "Are the items in there?"

She turned the case so it was flat, and flipped the latches to show him the books nestled safely inside. "Yeah."

He looked in the case and nodded as he took a step back and waved a hand at the plane. "Very good. She'll see you in the lounge."

Parker glanced at Oliver as she snapped the case shut and nodded when he tilted his head for her to go first. The leather soles of her shoes scraped softly against the rough texture of the stairs, and she focused on taking deep, slow breaths as her pulse picked up its tempo with every step. She hated not knowing what she was walking into, had learned too long ago that crossing her fingers and blindly hoping for the best didn't always work, but she didn't let any of her apprehension show as she stepped through the doorway of the plane.

The entryway was tight, just a narrow vestibule that forced those entering the plane to choose a direction. The cockpit was through the open door on her left, with two seats and a confusing array of buttons and switches and displays. Only the left yoke had a pair of headphones draped over it, however, which suggested that Marquis had flown with only one pilot that morning. Which made sense as the flight from Nice to Paris was hardly a long one and, provided Marquis returned home right after this, the pilot should be excused well before lunch.

She turned to the right, and her eyebrows lifted as she took in the sleek gray and white patterned carpet, varnished teak accents, and supple cream-colored leather seating options. Evie Marquis smiled and slipped elegantly from her seat at the second of two tables that spanned the left side of the plane, each surrounded on either side by a couple of seats that put the ones in first class on the fanciest airliner to shame, and smiled warmly.

"Ms. Ravenscroft. I must say, I'm impressed," Marquis drawled as she pulled her glasses from her face and twirled them by the earpiece. She was dressed casually, though her jeans and linen blouse no doubt had some haute couture designer's name sewn on the tag, but she was all-business as she set her glasses on top of a pile of papers on the table. "I didn't expect to hear from you so soon. Were you able to recover the Matisse?"

"I was. Thank you for the tip," Parker said, ducking her head in a small nod.

"You're most welcome. Hello, Mr. Dobrev."

"Ms. Marquis," Oliver replied with a small bow.

"So…" Marquis' attention dropped to the case in Parker's hand. "The books?"

Parker set the case on the table nearest the door as it wasn't covered with Marquis' paperwork. She thumbed the latches open and lifted the lid, and grabbed a pair of white cotton inspection gloves from inside it before she spun the case toward Marquis. She held out the gloves. "Do you need…?"

"I have my own," Marquis brushed her off with a little wave as she leaned over the side of the seat to her right and retrieved a set that was identical to the ones in Parker's hand.

"Very good." Parker nodded as she slipped the gloves she'd offered Marquis onto her own hands and waited to be asked about the books.

The 1865 copy of *Alice in Wonderland* was on top, and Marquis hummed softly under her breath as she lifted the novel from the case and slipped it from the polyethylene bag Parker had secured it in. She flipped through the book carefully, inspecting the illustrations, and looked up at Parker with a small smile. "You inspected each title for authenticity?"

"As much as I am able, yes. Books aren't my specialty, as I'm sure you're aware, but I've learned enough over the years to be able to confidently say that this is the real deal." Parker held a hand out toward the book. "May I?"

Marquis nodded and handed it to her.

"You'll notice here"—she opened the book to its middle and then flipped to find the page she wanted before handing it back to Marquis—"that the image is not quite blurred, but that the line along Alice's back here varies in thickness, like too much ink slipped into one third of it while another was just right and the last didn't get enough. It was the quality of the illustrations that made them pull this run of books, for issues just like the one you're looking at now. That, coupled with the weight and blend of the pages, the aging of the leather cover, and the actual printing itself is enough for me to confidently say that this is one of the 1865s."

"Excellent," Marquis murmured. She slipped the book back into its polyethylene bag and set it on the table so she could inspect the *Don Quixote*. "And this one?"

Parker nodded and moved half-a-step closer to walk Marquis through the details of the book and how she went about confirming that it was the first-edition Marquis was looking for. She pointed out certain pages that highlighted specific aspects original to the first-edition, and also walked her through the more technical aspects with regard to the binding that were authentic for the era the book was produced.

"For this not being your area of expertise, you have an admirable eye for the finer details," Marquis complimented as she closed the book and returned it to its polyethylene bag. She then retrieved her own briefcase from the chair beside the window opposite the one she'd been sitting at when they arrived and set it on the seat beside her.

"Thank you." Parker took off her white cotton gloves and tossed them in her case before she closed the lid and lifted it from the table. She let it dangle from her fingertips as she watched Marquis carefully place her new treasures inside a leather briefcase that looked every bit like an executive's daily accessory.

"So, I guess that's all that's left now is to discuss payment," Marquis surmised as she snapped her briefcase shut. "I'm assuming you would prefer an electronic transfer to an old fashioned cheque?"

Oliver chuckled. "We would."

Marquis hummed. "Very well." She grabbed her phone from the table she'd been working at earlier and looked expectantly at Oliver. "Do you have the account number?"

Oliver nodded and pulled his phone from his pocket to confirm that the money landed in the account before they parted ways. "Ready?"

"When you are, Mr. Dobrev," Marquis confirmed with a smirk.

Oliver returned her smirk with one of his own as he rattled off the International Bank Account Number from memory.

"Switzerland. How pedestrian," Marquis noted as she entered the code into her banking app.

Parker looked away to hide her smile as Oliver sighed softly in her ear. She shouldn't have been surprised that Marquis knew which country the account was in by the number alone, but it was still impressive that she did.

Marquis tapped at the screen and then turned it so they could see. "There you go. Two million US."

Oliver looked at his phone and nodded as he saw the transfer come through. He tapped at the screen, redirecting the funds to a different Swiss account that Marquis didn't have the number of, and then smiled as he slipped the phone back into his pocket. "It was a pleasure doing business with you, Ms. Marquis."

"I bet it was," Marquis murmured with a playful smirk. "Until next time?"

Parker looked at Oliver and nodded. "Oh," she breathed as she thought of something new.

Marquis lifted a brow and waited for her to elaborate.

Parker felt like she shouldn't share the information because she'd be betraying Sheridan's confidence, but in the essence of keeping her own ass out of jail, she figured it'd be best for Marquis to be aware of the situation back in the US. "I'm not sure if you're aware or not, but I thought you would like to know that your passport has been flagged by the FBI so they are alerted every time you enter the country."

"I had a feeling that was the case, yes, but thank you for confirming it for me," Marquis replied kindly. "I'm assuming then that you would prefer the remainder of our exchanges not occur on US soil?"

"We would," Parker confirmed. Even though they'd only briefly discussed it, she knew that Oliver would go along with it if it made her feel safer about going through with this.

"Not a problem at all. It'll take a little planning so we won't be able to meet as quickly as we did this time, but I don't see it being too much of an issue. Is there anything else?"

Parker looked at Oliver and shrugged. She didn't have anything else she wanted covered.

"I think that's it," Oliver said, offering Marquis his hand. "We'll let you get on your way, then."

"And you, I'm sure." Marquis shook his hand, and then turned to Parker to shake hers as well. "When you pass James outside, would you tell him that we're done here?"

"Of course," Parker murmured, assuming that Marquis meant the bodyguard they'd yet to be formally introduced to.

"I look forward to hearing from you again soon, then," Marquis dismissed them with a small nod.

Parker followed Oliver out of the plane and immediately spotted James, the bodyguard, standing at parade rest with his gun in his hand facing the door they'd come through earlier. He turned at the sound of their approach, and she forced herself to not stare at the gun as she passed along his boss' message. "She said to tell you that we're done here."

He nodded. "Very good. I will notify the guards at the front gate that you are on your way."

"And if you didn't call them...?" Oliver asked.

Parker grit her teeth, somehow knowing that they really didn't want to know the answer to that one.

James shook his head. "It's better that I make that call, Mr. Dobrev. Believe me."

"Right. Okay, then," Oliver drawled, nodding slowly. His lips curled in that sly, smart-ass smile he'd had since kindergarten, and Parker was about to mutter a warning to not say anything stupid when Oliver barreled on, "Hey, any chance you guys could be a little less terrifying next time?"

Parker's huff of disbelief was drowned out by the deep rumble of laughter from Marquis' bodyguard. "I don't think that's possible, Mr. Dobrev. We have reputations to uphold, you know..."

"Eh, it was worth a shot," Oliver chuckled and shrugged. "See you when we see you, James."

James snapped off a crisp salute that told more of his background than anything else they'd seen from him so far, and stepped out of the way to let them pass.

Parker rolled her eyes as they stepped out of the hangar into the bright, late-morning sun and muttered, "You just couldn't help yourself, could you?"

Oliver grinned and pulled the car keys from his pocket. "Nope."

"Tell me again why I'm helping you with this?"

"Because I'm the best brother in the world and I look awful in orange?"

She laughed as she climbed into the car. "Pretty much."

"Whatever," he grumbled, swinging a playful slap at her thigh as he slipped behind the wheel. "You want to grab a bite before we head back to your hotel, or is there someone else you'd rather meet up with?"

There absolutely was, but it was still before noon and Sheridan had said she wouldn't be at the airport until two, so there was no reason to rush. "Sure. You're buying, though."

"Of course I am." Oliver muttered and pressed his thumb to the ignition button. "I mean, if you're going to go out with me instead of Agent Oh-So-Sexy-Sloan, it's the least I can do—right?"

Parker smirked. "Yep."

EIGHTEEN

The international departures terminal at Charles de Gaulle was a bustling hub of people and luggage and *noise*, and Sheridan bit back a groan as she wound her way through the crowd, careful to not accidentally whack anyone with the carry-on she dragged behind her. Crowds and this seemingly impenetrable wall of noise weren't her favorite things anyway, but after having spent the morning essentially twiddling her thumbs, she had even less patience for it all than usual. She glanced over her shoulder to make sure Kelly was still following her as they neared the entrance for the security checkpoint, and chuckled in spite of her annoyance at their situation when he shot her an exaggerated grin.

"Ready to get grilled by the French TSA?" Kelly asked, sounding way too excited about the hoops they were going to have to jump through before they'd be allowed past the checkpoint with their guns.

"Not at all," she drawled as she turned her attention on the concourse ahead of her just in time to avoid running over an old lady who'd stopped to check on her Chihuahua that was yipping angrily in its carrying-case. She murmured an apology in French and smiled politely even as the woman glared at her, and then put her head down as she hurried past her.

"I thought granny was gonna sic her little rat dog on you," Kelly laughed.

Sheridan rolled her eyes. She had too, there for a second. Before she could respond properly, however, a familiar voice caught her attention even over the overwhelming noise. Her eyes immediately sought and found a familiar lean frame with a shock of silver-blue hair at the little side table behind the metal detectors where privacy was routinely violated in the name of the greater good.

"Please be careful!" Parker's hands twitched at her sides as the transport police officer roughly dropped the hard plastic telescoping case on the inspection table, and Sheridan knew it was killing her to not be able to reach out and do it herself.

Sheridan looked over at Kelly and sighed. "I'm…"

"Dude, go." Kelly gave her a little shove toward Parker. "Before she flips out on that idiot and gets arrested."

"Yeah, but how?" Sheridan asked seriously. This wasn't America, where she could flash her badge and waltz through the line.

"Sloan! Innes!" a new voice called out.

Sheridan's brow wrinkled as she turned to see Anne Guillard hurrying through the terminal toward them with her partner Eve hot on her heels. "The hell?"

The French agents grinned when they slid to a stop in front of their American counterparts. "Sorry, didn't get your cells earlier, so we thought this would be the best way to get ahold of you quickly. Vasseur finally cracked and gave us a name. Michael March. Have you heard of him?"

Sheridan arched an interested brow at the name. "Yeah, we've come across him before." They'd suspected March had been involved in a string of robberies at upscale art galleries the year before, but had never been able to get anything concrete enough to tie him to the thefts. Vasseur dropping March's name would be enough for them to bring him in for questioning, and maybe they'd finally get something on him that would stick. "We will look into him as soon as we get back to the office." She pulled out her phone. "Can I get your contact info—"

"Seriously, please be careful!" Parker's panicked voice interrupted them.

"Ravenscroft?" Eve arched a brow in surprise.

Sheridan looked over her shoulder and sighed. Parker looked about ready to vault over the table and rip the telescoping case right out of the security officer's hands. "Can you...?" she asked, eyes pleading as she turned back to the French agents.

"I'll go save your girl," Guillard assured with a laugh as she jogged up to the front of the line and flashed her badge. After a brief conversation she was waved through, and Sheridan held her breath as she watched her make her way toward Parker, who was looking more and more like she was going to lose it.

"It'll be fine," Eve murmured, placing a gentle hand on her shoulder.

"I sure hope so," she sighed. She bit her lip as Guillard slid a hand over Parker's shoulder when she got to the inspection point, and was relieved when she saw Parker relax, her body language becoming less adversarial as Guillard took over the conversation.

"She'll take care of it," Eve assured her. "You want me to put Anne's and my information in your contacts?" she asked, motioning to her phone.

"Please." She handed her the phone, her attention still focused on the scene playing out on the other side of the security checkpoint. Guillard's hands were waving like she was conducting a symphony as she pleaded Parker's case with the officer, and a moment later Parker motioned to her backpack that was on the table beside the telescoping case. Guillard opened the front pocket, pulled out a pair of cotton inspection gloves, and handed them to Parker, who put them on before carefully easing the Matisse from its protective case.

The look on the security officer's face when Parker slowly unrolled the canvas was comical—a hilarious blend of *oh shit!* and wide-eyed awe—and the smug smirk Guillard shot their way when Parker began oh-so-carefully re-rolling the canvas so it'd fit in the tube assured her that the issue had been resolved satisfactorily.

"See. No problem." Eve grinned and handed Sheridan her phone. "Now, let's get you two through the line, huh?"

"I like the sound of that," Kelly agreed.

Sheridan nodded as she slipped the phone back into her purse, more interested in the way Parker was now smiling in her direction than the conversation happening around her. Her heart fluttered as her lips curled in an answering smile, and she sighed as she lifted her right hand in a little wave. Parker pointed toward the spot where travelers exited the security checkpoint, her eyebrows lifting as she mouthed something that looked like, *Do you want me to wait for you?*

"You are so fucked," Kelly whispered loudly.

Eve laughed, but did her best to try to hide it with a cough, and Sheridan just barely resisted the urge to roll her eyes at them because the last thing she wanted was for Parker to think she was the cause of her annoyance. She shook her head and motioned for Parker to go on ahead, and when Parker nodded and turned on her heel, she turned her attention back to her sniggering companions. "Funny, Innes."

"He isn't wrong," Eve pointed out softly in French, her kind smile and gentle tone assuring Sheridan that, while she agreed with his assessment, she understood and sympathized with her situation. "For what it's worth," she continued in French—much to Kelly's annoyance, given the way he threw his hands in the air and turned around, "she looks at you the same way."

Sheridan shook her head, embarrassed that she'd been so unprofessional that veritable strangers could pick up on it all. "I'm sorry."

"Why?" Eve asked, sticking to the language Kelly couldn't follow as her gaze drifting to where Guillard stood at the checkpoint beckoning them over. "Sometimes there's no point trying to fight it."

The half-smile she flashed at Guillard and the way Guillard returned it told Sheridan that she had completely misread the relationship between the two agents, but before she could say anything, Eve nudged her with a playful elbow.

"Anyway," Eve said, slipping back to English now that their little heart-to-heart moment was over, "let Anne and I speed this whole process up for you two so you can catch your flight home. God knows it's a headache trying to get on a flight armed, credentials be damned." She smiled when both Sheridan and Kelly nodded in agreement. "We'll touch base soon to see if we can't figure out who this March guy is and if he was involved in the Matisse heist."

"Sounds good," Sheridan agreed. "Thank you for your help with this."

"Thank you for helping us get a fence off the streets," Eve replied good-naturedly as they started toward the gate where Guillard waited for them.

The combination of four badges from two different federal organizations was enough to make the security screening process moderately bearable, and once the requisite hoops had been jumped through, she and Kelly were cleared for their flight.

"Thanks for your help," she told the French agents.

"Yeah," Kelly echoed.

"You can return the favor if we're ever sent your way, huh?" Guillard teased. "It was a pleasure working with you." She shook their hands in turn. "Have a safe flight."

"We will." Sheridan nodded as she and Kelly shook hands with Eve as well.

They went their separate ways with a wave and a promise to be in touch the following week, and Kelly sighed as he bumped her with his shoulder. "Not a bad trip, huh? Parker got her painting back, we got a name to run down..."

"No, not a bad trip at all," she agreed as they wound their way through the crowded terminal.

Kelly pointed at a restaurant about halfway down the concourse. "I know we had lunch a couple hours ago, but I'm gonna grab a sandwich for the plane. You want anything?"

"Yeah. That's probably a good idea." She nodded.

"If you want to go find Parker, I'll pick something up for you," Kelly offered.

"I…" She was about to decline the offer, sure that he'd tease her mercilessly for being in a rush to see Parker again, but there was something in his smile that told her he was giving them space before he joined them. "Sure. That'd be great, thanks. If there's a vegetarian sandwich or wrap or something, could you grab one for Parker?"

"I can absolutely do that." Kelly gave her a playful shove toward their gate. "Get out of here, Sloan."

She laughed. "Okay, okay. Geez, Innes." She adjusted her purse because the added weight of her iPad in the bag was making the strap dig into her shoulder, and shook her head as she took a pointed step away from him. "I'm going. Chill."

"Good." Kelly winked and changed his course so he was headed toward the little airport café that had a line out the door despite the fact that it was early afternoon.

Airports were perfect for people-watching, but she kept her eyes on the traffic swirling around her as she made her way toward their gate, the little wheels of her carry on suitcase humming quietly on the tile floor behind her. The line at the café meant that it would be a while before Kelly found them, and she was looking forward to spending a few minutes alone with Parker before he came back.

Parker was sitting at the end of a row of chairs facing the large windows that overlooked the tarmac, and Sheridan was helpless to contain the smile that tugged at her lips when she spotted her. Parker was oblivious to her approach, her attention focused on the phone she'd propped on the end of the storage tube that she held between her legs instead of the crowd, and Sheridan placed a light hand on her shoulder as she stopped at her side. "Is that seat taken?"

"For anyone who isn't you, yes." Parker smiled as she looked up at her. She then looked past her and added, "Where's your partner?"

"Getting food," Sheridan shared as she maneuvered around Parker. She slid her purse from her shoulder and set it on the ground between her feet as she sank into the passably comfortable seat on Parker's left.

"That's not a bad idea, actually…"

"I asked him to pick something up for the both of us, too."

"You are too good to me, Sheridan Sloan," Parker murmured.

The softness in Parker's gaze made Sheridan's stomach flip, and she cleared her throat softly as she replied, "Says the woman who took me to the most perfect five-star restaurant last night."

"Tell me you didn't like it."

"I can't." She shook her head and smiled. "The entire evening was wonderful."

"I thought so too." Parker tilted her head and whispered, "We'll have to do it again sometime soon."

"I…" Sheridan's eyes darted to the line where the red carpet met the glass, overwhelmed by the way her body responded to the suggestion in Parker's tone. It was ridiculous, she knew, because they'd talked about this the night before and Parker had confessed to being interested in something more than friendship, but knowing that did very little to slow the suddenly frantic beat of her heart or still the butterflies that swooped in her stomach. She took a deep breath and let it go slowly as she forced herself to meet Parker's gentle, understanding gaze, and nodded. "I would like that."

Parker smiled and reached over to give her hand a light squeeze. "I'm glad."

The feeling of Parker's long fingers curling around the side of her hand made her throat tight, and she swallowed thickly as she curled her hand beneath Parker's just enough that she was able to curve her fingers around Parker's. The way Parker just hummed softly and relaxed in her seat, leaving their hands resting together on her leg her smile, and she stared down at their hands for a handful of heartbeats before shifting her gaze up to look at Parker, who was staring out the windows in front of them with a serene smile tugging at her lips.

"Is this okay?" Parker whispered, glancing at her from the corner of her eye. Her smile widened when she saw she was being watched, and turned toward her, the tiniest of creases forming between her pinched brows as she waited for her reply.

Sheridan squeezed Parker's hand. "Yes."

"Good," Parker breathed. She crossed her legs as she sank back in her chair, her butt sliding to the front of the seat as her back curved into the red leather that was a near-match to the carpet of the gate area, and sighed as her fingers flexed around Sheridan's hand.

Sheridan nodded. It was better than good—sitting here with Parker like this was perfect—and she shifted to mirror Parker's posture as she dragged the pad of her thumb over Parker's fingers. She smiled at the way Parker's eyes fluttered shut and the softest of sighs spilled from her lips at the touch, and felt the chaos of her thoughts and worries about work and Parker and life in general become quieter and quieter with every brush of her thumb. How long they sat there like that was anyone's guess, and she jumped in surprise when a light hand ghosted over her shoulder for the briefest of moments before falling away.

Kelly's smile was pleased and just a little mischievous as he glanced at their hands on her lap, but he nodded in understanding at the glare she shot him as he set a bag beside her feet. "Food, miladies."

Sheridan tensed as she waited for Parker to pull away, and was surprised when the hand atop her own tightened for the briefest of moments before relaxing enough to allow her to decide what she wanted to do. The problem was, she didn't know what she wanted to do. It was one thing for them to do, well, this, when it was just the two of them, but it was different when they had an audience.

"Thanks, Innes," Parker drawled, interrupting her spiraling panic. She watched the way Parker lazily blinked her eyes open, seemingly nonplussed by the fact that he'd caught them holding hands, and wished she could be so cool and calm and collected. "So," Parker glanced at Kelly before her eyes flicked back to Sheridan, "a little bird told me a bunch of agents were trying to break a Master Lock at the station this morning. Were you one of them?"

Kelly gasped in mock-outrage. "You told her!"

Sheridan stared at Parker, who was watching her with a gentle smile, and the subtle flex of Parker's fingers told her that she was okay with whatever she decided to do about their current situation. And, while she wanted to be as unflappable and collected as Parker, the truth was that she wasn't. She was scared of how acutely Parker affected her and entirely unsure if she was willing to open herself up to be potentially devastated again, and she prayed that Parker understood the apology she tried to let shine in her eyes as she pulled her hand free. She breathed just that little bit easier when Parker's lips curled in a soft, reassuring smile as she moved her hand back to her own leg.

"Well," Parker challenged him with a smirk, and Sheridan could have kissed her for the way she so effortlessly took the weight of Kelly's attention off of her. "Could you do it?"

"No," Kelly admitted with a huff. He brightened and added, "Will you teach me?"

Parker laughed and shook her head. "I don't know, man. Sheridan might kick my ass if I do."

"She is pretty scary like that," Kelly agreed, shooting Sheridan a playful wink.

Sheridan smiled in spite of the tightness that still squeezed her chest and shook her head. "Shut up, Innes."

"Whatever. You love me," he retorted.

"Just keep telling yourself that," she shot back.

Parker laughed and looked at the counter where two flight attendants in navy blue skirt suits were beginning to shuffle paperwork around. "While you two sort that all out, I need to go talk to them real quick about the painting." She stood and looped the strap of the case over her shoulder. "Can I leave my backpack here?"

Sheridan nodded. "Sure."

"Thanks," Parker murmured, her smile so soft and warm that she was helpless but to return it. "I'll be right back."

Sheridan nodded again, her heart beating into her throat as she watched Parker glide through the crowd to the desk where she ran a hand through her hair as she leaned in to talk to the attendants. When the weight of Kelly's eyes on her became too much to bear, she turned her attention to her partner and arched a single brow for emphasis as she said, "Don't go there."

"Go where?" Kelly asked, shrugging as if he had no idea what she was talking about. He grinned and pulled a king size Snickers from his bag. "Snickers? I hear they satisfy."

She laughed in spite of herself and rolled her eyes. "Shut up."

MJ Duncan

nineteen

Experience had taught Parker to not let clients know about a recovery until she could deliver the piece, since there were a plethora of hoops to jump through before she could return the item in question to its rightful owner. She'd known on sight that the painting she recovered in Paris was the missing Matisse, but her word meant pretty much nothing in the long run and the painting had spent the last three days being thoroughly authenticated with a combination of Morellian Analysis and materials dating. The authentication lab had called her just before lunch to report that the painting had passed with flying colors, and she'd spent the next few hours pushing through the required paperwork to finalize the claim.

Once she'd dotted all her i's and crossed all her t's, she was able to pick up her phone and place the call she'd been itching to make ever since she landed at La Guardia Saturday night. She spun her chair to look out the window as she listened to the call ring through, and smiled when it was answered on the second ring by a professionally chipper woman.

"Thank you for calling Zeller and Ezekiel Law Firm. How may I help you?"

"I need to speak with Mr. Zeller, please."

Without missing a beat, the woman replied, *"May I ask who's calling?"*

"Of course. You can tell him that it's Parker Ravenscroft with Cabot and Carmichael. I have an update for him on the claim he filed with us roughly three weeks ago."

"Please hold."

Parker took a deep breath and crossed her right leg over her left as she leaned back in her chair. She bounced her foot to the beat of the contemporary classical music coming through the phone, and wasn't at all surprised when she heard the distinctive click of the line being picked up not even a minute later.

"Ms. Ravenscroft?"

Zeller's voice held a distinctive tremble of what she guessed was a combination of hope that she had some news for him and fear that she didn't, and she smiled as she skipped formalities and got straight to the point. "Good news, Mr. Zeller. I've got your painting." A quiet thud on the other end of the line made her sit up straighter in her chair. "Sir?"

"You really found it?"

"I really did." Parker smiled. "Is there a time that would be good for you to meet so I can return it?"

"I can leave my office now and be back home in twenty minutes."

Parker chuckled. "It might take me a little longer to get over there, Mr. Zeller, but I can absolutely head out now as well."

Zeller blew out a long sigh, and it wasn't hard to hear the smile in his voice when he replied, *"I look forward to seeing you soon, then."*

She looked up at the sound of knuckles rapping quietly on the frame of her door, and smiled when she turned and saw Jess Klick, the more proficient of the recovery division's two assistants, hovering in her doorway. Jess was also, despite the fact that she technically worked for her, her best friend at the firm. Parker held up a finger to let her know she was almost done and pushed herself to her feet as she turned her attention back to Zeller. "Perfect. I will see you soon, Mr. Zeller."

Parker shook her head as she dropped the phone back into its cradle on her desk. "What's up, Jess?"

"Nothing. You taking the painting back to Zeller?"

"I am," Parker confirmed as she rounded the corner of her desk. "I can't wait to clear this one out—it'll make two huge recoveries in a month."

"Yeah it will," Jess agreed as Parker slipped her phone into the front pocket of her backpack that was sitting atop her lateral filing cabinet. "Whatcha gonna do to celebrate?"

Parker smiled as she zipped the bag shut and slung it over her left shoulder. She hadn't seen Sheridan since they'd said goodbye at the airport Saturday night, had wasted more time than she would ever admit to thinking about her over the last five days, and she could think of no better way to celebrate than to spend a few hours in her company. "I'll figure something out."

"Oh you will, huh? What's her name?" Jess teased.

"Who said there's a 'her' in these plans?"

Jess *tsked* and wagged a knowing finger at her. "You've been spinning your phone in your hands all week with a faraway look in your eyes."

"You're insane," Parker scoffed.

"Maybe." Jess shrugged, taking the playful jibe in stride. "However, I am not wrong. Am I?"

Parker sighed and shook her head. "No, you're not." She rolled her eyes at the shit-ass grin Jess shot her. "Shut up."

"Of course, Ms. Ravenscroft," Jess drawled.

"Keep it up and I'll fire your ass, Klint," she chuckled.

"Uh huh. Yeah. Sure you will."

Parker huffed a quiet laugh at Jess' teasing as she grabbed the handle of the flat portfolio case the authentication team had delivered the un-stretched canvas in a few hours earlier that was leaning against the file cabinet. "I'm calling it a day after I visit Zeller, so feel free to get out of here early whenever you're done with whatever you've got left to do."

"And that's why you're my favorite." Jess stepped out of the way with a small bow. "Have a good night, Parker."

"You too, Oh Annoying One," Parker grumbled playfully as she slipped past her.

"I'll pick up your dry cleaning on my way home in case you need a change of clothes here in the morning," Jess assured her in a mock whisper as she stopped at her desk.

Parker laughed and flipped Jess off over her shoulder as she continued toward the elevators without breaking stride. She had only ever shown up at the office in the same clothes from the day before once, and she'd much rather Jess think it was because she had gotten lucky with a girl than what had actually happened—that she had spent the night and wee hours of the morning frantically trying to find a way to get Lucy out of a room-sized safe tucked in the basement of an Irish mobster's townhouse in Brooklyn. She had succeeded, eventually, but that had been the straw that broke the camel's back for her in that relationship, and two months later Lucy was picked up by the Feds trying to brazenly rob a jewelry store on Fifth Avenue. "Goodnight, Jess," she called to Jess' amused laughter ringing out behind her.

As she made her way down to the street, she was glad she'd been too tired after yoga that morning to bother trying to find the energy to drive herself to work, because at least that meant she wouldn't have to come back to the office for her bike. She managed to hail a cab fairly quickly, and she carefully maneuvered the portfolio case into the back seat with her as she rattled off Wolfgang Zeller's address.

The driver, thankfully, got the hint that she wasn't interested in conversation after she only replied to his questions with noncommittal hums, which left her free to mull over what she wanted to say when she texted Sheridan.

The liminality of their situation was both a blessing and a curse, but they both had very good reasons to be cautious. The problem was that whenever she was with Sheridan, she forgot all the incredibly valid reasons there were for her to not fall for her. Which wouldn't be an issue if she could just stay away from her, but she'd accepted the fact that that particular task was impossible. So she was stuck in this unsettled existence where she was trying to find some kind of equilibrium as the two sides of her life—her obligation to her brother, and her desire to explore this thing that was happening between her and Sheridan—tugged her in very different directions.

And, as if to emphasize how truly fucked she was, her phone buzzed right then with a text from Sheridan. *Hey, you. Might actually get out of here at a reasonable time for a change. Want to meet somewhere for dinner?*

She chuckled wryly. Yeah, she didn't stand a chance. *Sounds great. The Matisse finally got released from authentication this morning, so I'm delivering it to Zeller now and I'll be calling it a day after that.*

Her phone buzzed with Sheridan's reply almost immediately. *So we're celebrating! Is there somewhere between his apartment and my office where you'd like to meet?*

Parker shook her head as she typed back, *I don't really care where we go. I just really want to see you again.* It was perhaps a little too honest of a confession, but she didn't regret it. Not when she'd been thinking about reaching out to Sheridan with some variation of that sentiment all week. She stared at her phone as a conversation bubble with ellipses appeared on her screen not two seconds after she'd hit send, and she tapped her thumb on the side of her phone as she waited for Sheridan's response.

Eventually two words appeared on her screen. *Me too.* Not exactly the verbose reply she'd been expecting given how long it'd taken for the message to come through, but it still made her smile. A new conversation bubble appeared, and a moment later she read, *Would you want to just come down here when you're done?*

Parker took a deep breath and let it go slowly. She wasn't particularly keen on the idea of brazenly walking into the FBI given her current association with Evie Marquis, never mind the fact that if her and Oliver ever ended up on the agency's radar for some reason, it could really come back to bite Sheridan in the ass.

She was wracking her brain to come up with a decent restaurant down Sheridan's way she could suggest they meet up at instead, when another message from Sheridan popped up on her screen. *I know it'd be a trek for you, but this way you wouldn't be stuck waiting for me somewhere in case something happens and I can't get out of here as quickly as I thought.*

Parker sighed. Sheridan's reasoning was sound, and she couldn't think of a way to counter it that wouldn't seem suspicious or make her sound like an ass. *I can do that.* She hit send and looked out the window as she waited for Sheridan's reply. The cabbie had opted to take the route to the West Side through the park, and the blur of trees beyond her window was a perfect, indistinct scene to stare at without having to think.

Sheridan's answer came through as they passed the carousel. *Great! If you text me when you're done with Zeller, I can try and start wrapping things up here so I can be done when you get here.*

Try as she might, there was no ignoring the happy flutter in her chest that she felt when she saw that, and she sighed as she typed out, *Will do. See you soon.*

I can't wait.

Parker shook her head as she slid the phone back into her pack, resigned to the fact that she was pretty much well and truly screwed when it came to everything related to Ms. Sheridan Sloan. Not that she minded, she just hoped that she would be able to keep juggling the two halves of her life in a way that didn't end with her screwing everything up.

A bike messenger rolled past them doing a pretty epic wheelie, and Parker sighed as she sank back into her seat. All told, traffic was flying given the fact that it was nearing the end of the workday, and she sighed with relief when the cab pulled to a stop in front of Zeller's building a little less than half an hour later.

Zeller must have told them he was expecting her and to send her right up, because the guard at the front desk who looked only vaguely familiar smiled at got to his feet the moment she walked through the front doors. He nodded and offered her an elevator card to get her to the penthouse as she neared the desk. "Here you go, Ms. Ravenscroft. He's waiting for you."

She smiled her thanks as she took the card, and as she stepped into the elevator, she couldn't help but recall the last time she'd been there. It was bizarre to think that it'd been only three short weeks since she'd run into Sheridan again, and part of her wanted to thank whoever was responsible for stealing the Matisse because without that, who knows if they would have ever have reconnected.

And what a shame that would be.

She tightened her grip on the portfolio case as the elevator stopped at the top floor and chuckled softly when she saw Wolfgang Zeller waiting for her in the foyer of his home. "Mr. Zeller."

He smiled and motioned at the case. "Is that it?"

"It is. The canvas is still loose, however, because while we can recommend people you could call to have it re-stretched, it is a liability the firm isn't willing to take. Is there somewhere we can lay this case down flat so you can see it?"

"Yes, yes." He turned and motioned for her to follow him into the living room. He cleared a blown glass bowl and a handful of magazines from the coffee table and waved a hand at it. "How's this?"

"Perfect." She laid the case down on the table and turned it so that the lid, once opened, wouldn't tip the entire thing onto the floor. "Would you like to do the honors, Mr. Zeller?"

He smiled and nodded, looking every bit like a little kid on Christmas who knows they're about to open the one present they wanted the most. She took a step back and watched as he reached with trembling fingers for the zipper, and couldn't help but grin with him when he flipped the lid to reveal the painting.

"You are amazing. Thank you."

Parker tipped her head in a small bow. "It's my pleasure. I'm glad it's back where it belongs."

He nodded and looked back at the painting. "You said you have names of people you recommend to fix this?"

"I do." She slid her bag from her shoulder and opened the biggest pocket. The list he was asking for was paper-clipped to the top of the file for the claim, and she pulled it from the stack and handed it to him. "Here you go." Inside the file were a few different things left to go over, and she sighed as she asked, "I just need to go through a little paperwork with you to finish out the claim."

"Come into the kitchen." He waved at the sunny eating area just off the living room. "Can I offer you a drink?"

"I'm good, thanks." She sat down at the small, four-person round table in a nook that overlooked Central Park, and smiled as she laid the folder with all the necessary copies of documents for the claim from her bag. "These are for you," she began as she handed him a navy blue pocket folder. "I know we did this before, but here is a copy of the report from the authentication firm that confirmed the painting in the case out there is really your missing Matisse."

"I will add it to my files, thank you."

She nodded. "And these are the documents from Cabot and Carmichael that you need to sign. This page is to indicate that you have received the authentication report for the retrieved property and are satisfied that it is exactly what you filed a claim for." She pointed at the tabbed signature line and waited for him to read the page and sign before moving onto the next page. "This is to indicate that you've taken possession of the property." She grinned at how energetically he just scribbled his name across the line at the bottom of the page without reading the legalese above it. "And this"—she flipped to the last tab—"is to finish out the claim. By signing here, you are hereby forfeiting your right to any further action on this claim, thus absolving Cabot and Carmichael of any further responsibilities in this matter."

He nodded as he scanned the page. "Everything looks in order," he declared as he signed.

She took the signed pages from him to put back in her bag. "I will send copies of these over via courier tomorrow. Would you prefer I have them sent here or to your office?"

"My office is fine," Zeller said as he straightened the documents she'd given him, giving her time to repack her bag. Once she was done, he smiled and offered her his hand as he pushed himself to his feet. "Thank you so much, Ms. Ravenscroft."

"The pleasure is mine, sir," she assured him as she shook his hand. "I'll leave the case the canvas is in with you to protect it, if you'd like? Once you get it re-stretched, you can give me a call and I'll send somebody to pick it up from you."

"That would be wonderful, thank you."

Parker smiled and, in what was an almost anticlimactic conclusion to everything she'd gone through to recover the painting, she shouldered her backpack and followed him back to the elevator in the foyer. The doors opened the moment she pressed the button, and she glanced at him as she stepped inside. "Have a good evening, Mr. Zeller."

"Thank you." He tipped his head in a small bow. "You, as well."

"I will do my best," she replied with a smile as she pressed her thumb to the button for the lobby.

She pulled her phone from her backpack as the elevator started its measured descent and pulled up Jess' direct line. "Docs are signed on the Zeller case. We're officially off the book on it."

"Nice!" Jess cheered. "So, you figure out how you're gonna celebrate?"

"I did."

"Do I get to know what you're doing?"

"Absolutely not," she chuckled. "I'll see you in the morning, Jess." She disconnected the call with a grin, having no trouble picturing the way Jess was no doubt glaring at her phone at being brushed off, and shook her head as she opened her messages.

The app opened to her conversation with Sheridan, and she glanced at the descending numbers above the door as she typed out— *Leaving Zeller's now. Still good to come down?*

She palmed the phone as the elevator slowed at the main floor, and nodded at the security guards who stood to receive her. "Here ya go, fellas. Thanks." She slid the elevator card across the counter toward them. Her phone buzzed with Sheridan's reply, which was a million times more interesting to her than playing nice, and she waved at them as she veered quickly toward the front doors, throwing a light, "Have a good night," over her shoulder at them.

She looked at her phone as she stepped onto the sidewalk and smiled when she saw Sheridan's message. *Absolutely. We're finishing up a couple things now, so I should be done right around the time you get here. Just come on up when you get here so that way if I'm still not quite done, you're not stuck hanging out in the lobby. They kind of frown upon that around here. ;)*

Less than half an hour had passed since she'd arrived at Zeller's building, but there was no mistaking the uptick in traffic along Central Park West, and she sighed as she let loose a sharp whistle lifted her hand in the air. Taking the subway down would be a hell of a lot cheaper, but she wasn't in the mood to deal with the crowds of people trying to get home from work. She winced as a cab jumped three lanes of traffic to get to her, and offered a silent prayer to the transportation gods that she would arrive safely as she slipped into the backseat. "Federal Plaza."

"You got it," the cabbie drawled, taking off at warp speed as soon as her door was shut.

Relieved to have something to focus on instead of her potentially imminent death, she texted back—*I can do that. What floor?*

She smiled when the telltale ellipses appeared and Sheridan's response popped up on her screen almost immediately. *27th. After you get through security, just go to the first bank of elevators and they'll take you right up. Our division is to the right of the elevators.*

She nodded as she replied, *Will do. See you soon, Agent Sloan...* She glanced out the windshield of the cab at the sea of brake lights as she hit send, and sighed as she pulled the zipper case from her backpack that held her wireless headphones. She took a deep breath and leaned her head back against the headrest as the first beats of her favorite flow playlist began to play, and focused on her breathing in an attempt to ease some of her anxiousness about walking into Sheridan's office as the car began inching its way down the island.

By the time her cab swerved out of traffic to stop in front of Sheridan's office, she'd made it through close to two-thirds of the hour and fifteen minute playlist, and she muttered her thanks as she swiped her credit card to pay. She repacked her headphones as she made her way past the row of cement pylons, and slipped them and her phone into her backpack as she entered the building. She pulled her driver's license from her wallet as she approached the security guards at the line of metal detectors, and took a deep breath as she offered the identification to the uniformed cop at the front of her line and set her backpack on the table beside it.

"Destination?" The officer asked as she inspected the I.D. while her partner, a scrawny guy with a sharp widow's peak and coke-bottle glasses, rifled through Parker's bag to make sure she wasn't bringing in any weapons.

"Twenty-seventh floor. Meeting Sheridan Sloan."

"Agent Sloan called down to let us know she was expecting you. You're clear to go up," the officer confirmed with a polite nod as she handed Parker both her I.D. and a visitor's badge. "Clip the badge where it can be seen and return it to the front desk here when you leave."

"Bag is clear," Officer Widow's Peak announced as he pushed it to the far side of the table so she could pick it up after she'd gone through the scanner.

"Will do, thanks," Parker assured her as she stepped through the metal detector. She shouldered her bag as she made her way to the elevators Sheridan had told her about and shoved her hands into her pockets as she waited.

When an elevator did arrive, she had to rush inside before the doors closed after waiting for the crush of dark-suited federal employees who'd ridden it down to exit, and she blew out a soft sigh as she pressed the button for the twenty-seventh floor.

She smiled politely as she edged her way through the crowd waiting to leave for the night when the elevator doors opened at Sheridan's floor, and held her breath as she made her way through the glass doors to the unit's bullpen. The unease that sat heavily in her stomach was a million times worse than the trepidation she'd felt in the moment she pushed the balcony door at Dumas' penthouse open, and her heart beat heavily in her throat as she looked around the bustling bullpen. Part of her couldn't help but think that she'd have felt less intimidated walking completely unarmed into a lion's den.

She was pulled from her thoughts when Kelly Innes shouted, "Hey! Sloan! Parker's here!"

Parker shook her head when he caught her eye and smirked, and blew out a loud breath as she made her way across the bullpen to shake his hand. "It's nice to see you again, Agent Innes."

"Ooh! Is this Sloan's girl?" A tall woman with Asian features and short black hair asked with a grin as she rounded the corner with a coffee mug.

Parker covered her smile with her hand as she heard Sheridan groan from somewhere unseen, "Kill me now."

"I don't know about that, but I'm Sheridan's friend, yes," Parker demurred as she offered the woman her hand. "Parker Ravenscroft."

"Yeah, you are," the dark-haired agent practically purred. She shot Kelly a sly smirk and added in a mock whisper, "I see why Sloan's so—"

"That's enough, Ivy," Sheridan interrupted as she dropped a stack of files on what Parker assumed was her desk.

"Sorry. I just couldn't resist." Ivy winked at Parker. "Have a nice dinner."

"I'm so sorry about that," Sheridan apologized as she grabbed Parker by the arm and pulled her toward her desk. "It's been a long week, and they like to blow off stress by acting like they're back in high school or something."

"It's fine," Parker assured her.

"It's really not," Sheridan argued with a tired smile. "Anyway, you ready to go?"

"When you are. Anywhere in particular sounding good?" She turned to see what Sheridan was rolling her eyes at, and huffed a quiet laugh at the way Ivy and Kelly were making goo-goo eyes at each other.

"Anywhere that isn't here," Sheridan muttered as she grabbed her blazer from the back of her chair and slipped it on. She pulled her purse from the bottom drawer of the desk and glared pointedly at her colleagues. "I will see you idiots in the morning."

"Hey! Is that Sheridan's girl?" a new voice piped up.

Parker caught only the briefest of glimpses of a pretty redhead rounding the corner with a curious look on her face before Sheridan practically dragged her out the door. Even though she'd found the entire all-too-brief round of introductions rather amusing, it was clear that Sheridan was mortified by it all. She sighed when she noticed the way Sheridan was biting her lip and staring at the floor as if, with enough concentration on an inanimate object, she'd be able to force the blush currently spreading over her cheeks and neck to disappear.

Thankfully the other agents in her unit stayed in the bullpen and the elevator arrived quickly, and once they were safe from prying eyes, she slid a careful arm over the back of Sheridan's shoulders in a light embrace. "Want me to go back in there and knock some heads? I never did get that cape, but Edna says they're bad anyway, so…"

"I… Who?"

Parker smiled, pleased that Sheridan was at least looking at her. "You haven't seen *The Incredibles*?" When Sheridan shook her head, she said, "It's a Pixar movie about superheroes. Remind me to show it to you sometime."

"Okay," Sheridan breathed, the smallest hint of a smile tugging at her lips. "And, for as much as I appreciate your gallant offer to defend my honor, Ivy's the Krav Maga expert that delights in kicking Kelly's ass, so I don't think head-knocking would be a good idea."

Parker sighed dramatically. "Fine." She gave Sheridan's shoulders a light squeeze and let her arm fall back to her side. "If it makes you feel better, my assistant will probably be just as bad if you ever come by my office."

"Neutral meeting locations it is, then," Sheridan muttered. She smiled shyly and glanced up her lashes as she added, "For a while, anyway."

And if there had been any doubt in Parker's mind about just how totally screwed she was when it came to Sheridan Sloan—which there wasn't, but still—the sudden tightness in her throat and the pleasant dip of her stomach pretty much confirmed the fact that she would do pretty much anything to make Sheridan smile at her like that again. "For a while," she agreed softly.

Parker cleared her throat when the elevator stopped at the main floor, and braced her left arm over the doors so Sheridan could exit the car safely.

"Goodnight, Joan," Sheridan said as Parker pulled the visitor's badge from the collar of her shirt and dropped it into a little plastic basket by the security exit.

"Goodnight, Sheridan," the woman who had checked Parker in replied with a polite smile and a nod.

"Is there anything you're in the mood for?" Sheridan asked as they made their way out onto the sidewalk along Broadway.

Parker shook her head. Honestly, there was nothing more she wanted in this moment than Sheridan's company and that gentle smile turned her way, but she knew better than to dare say that aloud. Especially given the way Sheridan reacted upstairs, to what was fairly benign teasing. "I'm good with pretty much anything as long as there's a vegetarian option."

"My turn to surprise you, huh?" Sheridan teased as she turned toward the south and offered Parker her hand. "Come on, then. I've got just the place."

Parker arched a brow at the sudden disappearance of all the nerves and embarrassment Sheridan had been suffering from pretty much the moment they saw each other, but did not hesitate to take her hand. "So...do I get a hint of where you're taking me?"

"Do you trust me?" Sheridan asked. Her tone was playful, but there was a shadow of seriousness in her eyes that prompted Parker to answer as earnestly as she could.

"Absolutely." It was the truth, of course, but it was also clearly the right answer, judging by the way Sheridan's grip on her hand tightened and the way of her smile brightened, and she swallowed thickly as she squeezed her hand back and shared, "I've missed you this week."

Sheridan's smile turned shy and hopeful and so beautiful that it was all Parker could do to not lean in and taste it, and she sighed as she whispered, "Me too."

TWENTY

Sheridan pointed a warning finger at Kelly as she made her way to her desk at six minutes after nine the next morning. "Shut up."

"What?" Kelly laughed and folded his hands behind his head as he rocked back in his chair. "I didn't say anything!"

She dumped her purse on her desk and glared at him. "Good."

"Although…"

"How did I know you were going to ruin it?" Sheridan grumbled.

"Because you're never late?" Kelly offered unhelpfully. "Good dinner last night?"

"Yes." She picked up her coffee mug and sighed as she turned toward the break room to go in search of caffeine.

Once she had gotten over her embarrassment of the way everyone had over-enthusiastically greeted Parker, the evening had been as perfect as every other time they'd spent together. Because Parker had left the decision on where to go up to her, they had ended up at a local upscale bar that had all the ambiance of a five-star restaurant and none of the obstacles such establishments presented. She didn't go to Maxwell's often, simply because she preferred a quiet night a home if she was able to leave the office at a reasonable hour, but she'd been there enough times with Kelly, Ivy, and Rachel after work to know that it was perfect for what she wanted. She and Parker had spent hours at their little table in the back corner of the main room, just talking as they worked their way through a good portion of the small plates menu, and by the time they agreed to call it a night, it was nearly ten o'clock. Which, granted, wasn't terribly late, but she needed her sleep and, she was horrified to learn, Parker had a five o'clock yoga class she attended every morning.

"She's insane," Sheridan muttered to herself as she set her coffee mug on the counter beside the machine and went in search of the creamer and sugar that would make the bargain beans halfway palatable.

"Who's insane?" Ivy asked. She set her mug on the counter beside Sheridan's and smirked. "How was your date?"

"It wasn't a date," Sheridan grumbled as she tilted the container of dried coffee creamer over her cup. "Oh, fuck me," she swore when the lid came off and half the bottle poured into her mug.

"Well, if it'd been a date, maybe you would've had that taken care of already," Ivy teased with a laugh as she slid her mug over to Sheridan's. "Go ahead and pour some of that into mine. We'll just dump the rest."

Sheridan chose to ignore that little jab and tilted her mug over Ivy's. "Tell me when." She poured until Ivy signaled for her to stop, and then tapped the powder she didn't want from her mug into the trash can as Ivy filled her mug with coffee from the carafe.

"Sloan," Ivy drawled as she set the glass carafe back onto the hot plate.

Sheridan sighed and looked up at her. "Hmm?"

Ivy smiled. "For what it's worth, you two looked good together." She held up a hand when Sheridan opened her mouth to protest. "I'm not teasing right now. Okay? Even though I don't know what, exactly, they are, I know you have your reasons for taking things slow. And that's honestly commendable in this day and age. But any girl who would pretty much cross the fucking island at rush hour to come to your office to pick you up for dinner is a keeper."

"I know she is," Sheridan admitted softly. She slid her mug over to Ivy and smiled her thanks when she filled it up for her.

Ivy nodded. "And I know we can be asshats around here when it comes to this kind of shit. I'm not sure about everybody else but, in my case, I like to joke around because it's an easier way to relieve stress than kicking your partner's ass. I mean, don't get me wrong, that's still my favorite, but I gotta give his ego time to recharge between beatings." She grinned when Sheridan chuckled softly. "But, from now on, I'll keep everyone in line whenever she stops by, okay?"

"I...thanks?"

"You're welcome." Ivy sipped at her drink and grimaced. She shook her head as she reached for the large sugar dispenser beside the machine and poured way too much into her cup. She offered Sheridan the sugar and rolled her eyes when the offer was waved off. "Your funeral. This shit is worse than usual. And we both know that's saying something."

"Okay, give it here, then." Sheridan reached for the sugar. As she poured an unhealthy amount into her already over-creamered coffee, she asked, "Can I ask why?"

"Why I'm gonna keep the crew in line?"

Sheridan nodded. "I mean, it's not that I don't appreciate it, because I do, it's just not the way things usually go around here."

"Honestly?" Ivy ran a hand through her hair and shrugged. "Because the way you smile when you talk about her is the way I smile when I think about Rachel. And maybe that means something, and maybe it doesn't," she hastened to add when Sheridan's eyes widened, "but if it *does*, I don't want our juvenile assholery to be the reason you don't go for it."

Even though the idea of her colleagues being able to read even some small measure of what she was feeling when it came to Parker in her expression was mildly off-putting, she couldn't keep from offering Ivy a small, shy smile. "Thank you."

"Don't mention it," Ivy murmured, bumping her shoulder lightly with her own.

"Um, guys," Kelly interrupted, looking genuinely apologetic as he rapped his knuckles on the frame of the open break room door. "Sorry to interrupt. Sheridan, Guillard is on the phone for you."

Sheridan frowned. "Why? What's up?"

"Don't know." He shrugged. "Said something big has been called in over there and she wanted to pick our brains about it."

"What happened?" Sheridan asked.

"No idea. She said she'd to wait to explain until we were both on the line."

"Who's Guillard?"

"One of the French agents we worked with last weekend," Sheridan explained with a shrug. "You want to listen in?"

"May as well," Ivy muttered. "Do you mind if I grab Rach?"

"Go for it. We'll take the conference room," Sheridan decided. She shot Kelly a look and added, "Want to see if Bartz wants to sit in on it?"

"Probably a good idea if we're hijacking part the team," Kelly agreed. "I'll patch the call through to the speaker up there and then I'll poke my head in his office and see."

Sheridan nodded and, with her cup of terrible coffee in her hand, made her way toward the corner conference room where they held all their team meetings. She watched Kelly through the glass wall, and when she saw him finish flash her a thumbs up, she pressed the button on the speaker and greeted the French agent in her native tongue. "Hey, Guillard. Kelly made it sound like this was important, so I asked a few other members of my team sit in on this call if you don't mind."

The more the merrier, Guillard replied. *Eve is here with me too.*

"Figured that might be the case," Sheridan said as Ivy entered the conference room with Rachel. "Hello again, Eve."

Hey, Eve drawled.

"You two okay doing this in English?"

"Of course," Guillard replied.

Kelly entered the room next, followed almost immediately by Bartz, who nodded at her to get things rolling.

"Okay, Anne Guillard, Eve Herault," Sheridan switched to English. "I'm here with Kelly, Miles Bartz, the Director of our unit, and two of our colleagues, Ivy Moran and Rachel Wood."

"Good morning," Guillard began. *"So, we got a call yesterday morning from a couple detectives in the sixth arrondissement precinct. They'd taken a report for a theft of a couple of rare books and called us in to investigate. There was no sign of forced entry, there were no unexpected prints or anything in the apartment, and the thieves replaced the two rare first-edition titles with other volumes that were similar enough in appearance as to not draw attention to them. The only reason Monsieur Dumas realized that the books were missing was he'd been at a conference for work since last weekend and apparently told a colleague who's also a collector of rare books, that he'd send him a picture of the internal binding of a first edition* Don Quixote.

"Anyway, I'm waiting on the administrator of the Art Loss Register to see if anything like this has been reported recently because if this is a one-off, it's going to be pretty hard to find the thieves unless they make a mistake selling the books, so I thought that since we just worked together on that Matisse case that I'd see if you guys have had anything similar to this over there?"

"Nothing recently," Sheridan thought aloud as she scanned the group assembled. "The last rare book theft I can remember here was, hmm, maybe a year ago?"

"The Copernicus. That's right," Ivy supplied. "A copy of *De Revolutionibus Orbium Coelestium* was stolen from a collector in Arizona."

"Was it ever recovered?" Guillard asked.

"Not that I remember," Rachel piped up with a frown. "Everything was quiet here about the heist itself, and since it never showed up on the black market anywhere the case just kind of stalled."

"Did you guys ever hear anything about that one?" Kelly asked.

"Nothing," Eve answered. *"Was the copy of Copernicus replaced with a doppelgänger?"*

"No. That's actually quite a smart way to go about it, though," Sheridan said.

"Yeah. I mean, if this Dumas guy hadn't been looking for something specific, who knows how long the theft could've gone unnoticed," Kelly added.

"This is Director Miles Bartz. You said two books were stolen?" Bartz prompted. "What was the second title?"

"Good morning, sir," Guillard said with a more formal edge in her voice. *"It was an 1865 edition of* Alice in Wonderland."

"What were the books replaced with?" Sheridan asked. Not that it mattered, but sometimes little details like that were a clue that might help find the person responsible for the theft.

"The Don Quixote *was replaced with a nice but not especially valuable collector's edition version of* The Count of Monte Cristo…"

Rachel sniggered. "Okay, I kinda love them for that one." When she was met with nothing but silence and blank stares, she explained, "The thief slipped a book written by Alexandre Dumas into the bookshelf of a guy named Dumas that they were robbing. That's kinda awesome."

"In an entirely illegal kind of way," Kelly agreed with a nod.

"And the second book?" Bartz prompted with a sigh, though the slight tug at the right corner of his lips suggested he found the thieves' choice amusing as well.

"The Time Machine *by H. G. Wells. Another beautiful edition that's pretty identical in appearance to the stolen novel, but it's basically worthless in the grand scheme of things,"* Eve supplied.

"What about the street cameras? Anything there?" Sheridan asked.

"Nothing out of the ordinary. No suspicious looking cars on the street, no unusual movement in the garden behind the building. We did a canvass of the building this morning but nobody reported noticing anything irregular."

"I'm assuming the apartment has an alarm system?"

"It does. It's not the newest on the market, but it's certainly more than your average-grade home security system. The alarm was active when Dumas returned

home from his business trip Wednesday night. A call to the firm that monitors the security feed gave us nothing—they're showing that the system was working perfectly the entire time Dumas was gone. It was only disarmed once, the day before Dumas returned from his trip, and it was the housekeeper's code. She said she didn't notice anything suspicious when she cleaned the flat, and building security confirmed that she came and went according to her usual schedule. We brought her in for questioning, but she's clean. She's been working for Andre Dumas' family for close to forty years, and it was pretty obvious that she didn't do it."

"Damn," Kelly murmured.

"Yeah," Ivy agreed softly as Rachel nodded in agreement.

"Do you think Evie Marquis was involved?" Bartz asked.

"Given the items in question, we're not ruling her out, but she's also had her lawyers file enough harassment claims against us to force us to take things very slowly where she's involved," Eve replied. *"I honestly think you all have a wider birth to look into her dealings than we do."*

"Would you want us to look into her for you?" Sheridan offered.

"We might take you up on that if we find anything that makes us think she was involved. Given her reach within the system here, I'd rather not tip our hand until absolutely necessary," Guillard replied.

"Just let us know and we'll see what we can do, then," Sheridan said.

"Thank you," Guillard murmured. *"Anyway, I guess that's all we've got for now. Will you keep an ear out and let me know if you hear anything on this?"*

"Absolutely," Sheridan agreed. "Hey, since you're on the phone, have you guys found anything on that March guy that Vasseur said gave him the Matisse?"

"Nothing. You?"

"Same," Sheridan admitted with a sigh. They'd had no trouble pulling him in for questioning in the past, but he had all but disappeared from the face of the earth recently. She arched a brow at the rest of the room and, when nobody seemed to have anything new to offer, said, "So, I guess we'll keep in touch?"

"That sounds perfect. Thanks for letting us pick your brains on this one," Guillard signed off as Eve echoed the sentiment in the background.

"No problem," Sheridan spoke for the group. When nothing but the flat hum of a dial tone came from the speaker, she turned it off and looked at her boss. "So?"

Bartz shook his head. "There's nothing we can do unless we pick up a similar case here or the books make an appearance in our jurisdiction. Let's just hope that the crew that pulled that job stays on the other side of the Atlantic. God knows we've got enough of our own shit to try to keep track of."

twenty-one

"I brought pizza," Oliver announced as he barged through Parker's front door, carrying two cardboard boxes from the boutique pizzeria down the street that she loved and a six-pack of Allagash White. "Also, Gregory says his water heater is having issues—have you noticed anything?"

Parker shook her head as she watched her brother storm her apartment like he owned the place. Granted, the pizza smelled delicious, and she was actually starving, but leave it to her brother to arrive on only a few hours' notice running at Mach six. "Hello, Oliver," she drawled as she rolled off the couch she'd been lounging on while she read and onto her feet. "It's nice to see you. Please, come on in."

He set the food onto the workstation island that separated the kitchen from the dining area and turned to grin at her as he slipped his backpack from his shoulders and set it on the floor at the side of the island. "Sup, sis?"

"Oh you know, not much." She tossed Maeve Dylan's latest offering onto the coffee table and made her way into the kitchen where she pulled two plates from the cabinet over the sink. "And, no, I haven't noticed any hot water issues," she told him as she set the plates on the counter beside the pizza boxes. "But I have my own tankless unit up here, so I wouldn't have any idea if his was having any problems. Do you think it's something you could fix?"

"Depends on what the problem is. If it's something simple, probably yeah, but if it's an older unit that's on its way to crashing, he'll have to call a plumber out to replace it." He flipped open the lids of the pizza boxes. "Anyway, since you didn't answer when I called from the pizza place, so I got you the spinach and artichoke one you had last time I was down."

"Eh, I've been kinda craving it lately anyway, so that's probably what I would have asked you to get me." She retrieved the bottle opener from the drawer closest to the living room in the island and slipped it into her pocket. "And I didn't answer your call because I was on the phone with Sheridan and I figured that if whatever you needed was important, you'd text."

"On the phone with Sheridan, huh?" He smirked. "How is Agent Super-fine? You guys boning yet?"

"Classy, Ollie…" Parker rolled her eyes as she flipped the lids on the pizza boxes and pulled two pieces of her spinach and artichoke pie onto her plate. "No, we're not boning. We're barely hugging, if you want the gory details." She laughed when he stuck his lip out in a pout. "You're ridiculous. But, since you asked, she's doing great. We went out to dinner at a little place by her office last week, and she came over for a bit Sunday afternoon to hang out."

He leaned across the counter to slide half the pepperoni, sausage, and mushrooms concoction he'd ordered onto his plate. Or, more accurately, he slid the points of those six slices onto his plate—the crust was hanging all over the sides.

"Christ, Ollie. Why even bother with the plate at that point?"

"Because I'm not a heathen," he shot back as he carefully picked up the plate, using his forearms to balance the overhanging crusts.

"Right," she drawled. She grabbed two bottles of beer between the fingers of her right hand and tipped her chin at the drawer where she kept some paper napkins. "After you get that plate to the table *without* dropping your food on my floor, go grab some napkins," she said as she moved their drinks and her plate on the table.

"Yes, ma'am," he teased.

She rolled her eyes. "So to what do I owe the pleasure of your company this evening?" she asked as she sat down at her usual spot and kicked the chair opposite her out for Oliver.

"A guy can't just decide to visit his favorite sister for no reason?"

She laughed. "I'm your only sister, and I know you better than that. If it was the weekend, sure, but you don't like to miss your CrossFit unless you have to, so there has to be a reason you drove down here in the middle of the week. What's up, Olls?"

He waved her off with the stack of napkins that he tossed onto the table between their spots. "We'll get there. I want to hear about what Sheridan had to say that was more important than answering a call from your brother, first," he said as he took his seat.

"Oh you do, do you?" She rolled her eyes at the way he folded half a piece of his pizza into his mouth and picked up a slice of her own. "We were just confirming plans for this weekend."

Once he'd finished chewing and had swallowed, he asked, "What are you guys doing?"

Parker shrugged. "I honestly don't have a clue. Sheridan's planning the whole thing. All I know is that I'm supposed to wear clothes that are good for walking around in and be ready to be picked up at one."

He hummed interestedly. "That kinda sounds like a date."

"It's not a date," she protested, albeit a little weakly, because the only thing keeping it from being a date was the fact that neither of them were calling it one. And, even though there were a million and one reasons why it was a good thing that it wasn't, she still wished that it was a real date. But she'd never tell him that. Would never confess that she spent far more time than she should thinking about Sheridan and trying to come up with witty things to send her to make her smile. But it didn't matter. Because even if she was ready to say fuck-all to the risks associated with moving this thing between them past friendship, Sheridan wasn't—and she would never dream of trying to push her into something she wasn't ready for. Whatever happened between them would happen at Sheridan's pace, not hers. Knowing that did very little to dissuade her heart from wishing, though. "I just *really* like her."

"I can tell." He smiled. "So we should hurry up and knock out the rest of Marquis' list so you can take the brakes off and do something about that. Which is actually why I drove down today. I've been looking into the remaining books on the list, and there's a Blake in Brooklyn that should be a pretty easy grab."

She could have pointed out that an even easier approach would be to forget the list altogether and call it a day, but instead she asked, "You really want to go for another one?"

"Yeah," he scoffed, looking at her like she was crazy for even asking. "It's easy money, Park."

"But why bother?" she pressed as she set her pizza back onto her plate. "We made enough on the Paris heist to pay off all your medical bills and shit from your accident last year and still leave you a decent chunk to stash away to rebuild your safety net," she said as she crossed her legs and picked up her beer. "There's really no reason for us to risk it."

"It's a million bucks. There's no reason to not risk it," Oliver argued, waving the crust of the slice he was holding for emphasis. "Not that there's a real risk here. The job would be a walk in the park."

"You might not have anything besides your own ass to risk," Parker pointed out, "but I do. You can't sit there and talk to me about Sheridan and not realize that stealing a book in fucking Brooklyn is a very big risk to me. And her. If something happened and we got caught, it'd come back and bite her in the ass."

"But we won't get caught."

"You don't know that."

"Do you want me to call Rick to see if he can help me with the job instead?"

Parker shook her head. "We've been over this already. Of course I don't want you calling Rick."

"So you're going to help me then?" He cocked his head pleadingly. "I know this makes things with Sheridan complicated for you, but I don't ever want to be in a position like I was last year again. It was one thing to be at the mercy of the system when I was a kid and didn't have any control over my situation, but I'm not a kid anymore and I can control this. We can control this."

She sighed. "Ollie…"

"I swear to you that there's no legitimate risk here. The guy lives in a brownstone in a quiet neighborhood that's still close enough to downtown Brooklyn that a little extra foot traffic won't be noticed. And the alarm system is a fucking dinosaur, but maybe he thinks that it doesn't matter because it's monitored by a home security firm."

"And that *doesn't* matter?"

Oliver scoffed and shook his head. "Their network is so porous that I'm surprised some random fifth grader somewhere hasn't cracked it and set off a bunch of alarms for shits and giggles. It's not a problem."

She pinched the bridge of her nose and shook her head. This whole thing was reckless, but if one more job would make him feel secure, she could at least help make sure he didn't get caught. "So what are you thinking?"

He smiled. "Really?"

She shrugged. "I guess so. But you better have a good fucking plan, Olls."

"You're the best." He clapped his hands. "From what I've been able to dig up, Gunn, the guy who owns the Blake, is a bigwig trader on Wall Street, so it'd be easiest to do it during the day when the market's open."

That made sense, but only if the house was empty during the day. "Is he married? Have any kids?"

"Nope." Oliver took a huge bite of pizza. When he was done chewing, he asked, "Want to go down there after dinner and check it out?"

Not especially, but since she'd already agreed to help, she nodded. "Sure." Maybe he was right, and the best course of action would be to get it all done as quickly as possible. Like pulling off a Band-Aid, or something. "What's your work schedule looking like?"

Oliver grinned. "I've got a contract I gotta deliver by next Friday, but nothing else due in the near future. I'm thinking that, ideally, we could hit this one a week from Monday? If you're cool with going that fast, you'll have to cruise the area a couple times next week during the time the market's open to get a feel for the neighborhood—see if there are any neighbors having work done on their places that we might be able to use as cover, what the road and foot traffic patterns are like, stuff like that. You know, the usual shit. I can pull street camera locations from the NYPD database so we know where to avoid and stuff, and it shouldn't be too hard to get access to the brownstone's blueprints from the housing commission."

"Transportation?"

"I'll use one of my fake IDs to rent a car somewhere between Boston and here to use. That way, even if the plate does get picked up and ran for some reason, it'll come back a dead end."

She nodded. "So, assuming location looks good and you lock down everything you need with the security system...we just have the logistics to worry about. Do we want to try to pull a switcheroo again this time? I mean, the fewer similarities between the cases, the better—right?"

"Well, yeah. But, at the same time..." He sighed and reached for his beer. "I don't know. I kinda like the idea of having a twin ready to slip in for the target book. I mean, if the book we're grabbing is just on a shelf and not sitting out in some glass case like a museum or something, it could buy us a little time before it's reported missing."

"Yeah. But is that chance of a delay in reporting worth the risk overtly connecting the two jobs?"

Oliver took a sip of his beer and shrugged as he set the bottle on the table. "I think the potential for a delay in the book being reported balances that risk. I mean, have you heard anything about the books from Dumas' place being reported yet?"

"Well, no," she shook her head. "But it's not like I'm the one they'd be calling about it, anyway. None of the books on Marquis' list are insured by my firm, remember?"

"I just thought maybe Sheridan would say something?"

"Yeah, because FBI agents totally go around talking about their open cases," Parker scoffed.

"She told you about Marquis."

"That was a throwaway comment that she made because she'd been tired. I'm actually trying quite hard to keep her work away from whatever the hell's going on with us right now."

"Okay, okay," he conceded, lifting his hands in front of himself. "Sorry."

She shook her head as she took a bite of her pizza and chewed thoughtfully as she considered the job at hand. "I guess," she began after she'd swallowed, "provided I can actually find one in the next week and a half or so, that it wouldn't hurt to bring a doppelgänger with us."

"And then we can just decide what would be best when we're in there," he agreed. "I think that sounds good. Yeah?"

"Yeah," she sighed. "Will you be heading out first thing in the morning?"

"Probably when you're at yoga," he confirmed. "I have a meeting in downtown Boston tomorrow at eleven."

"You're going to actually wake up before dawn?" The joke sounded forced even to her own ears, but she was grateful for the opportunity to think about something that had nothing to do with how stupid she was being, or how much she was risking by choosing to keep helping her brother.

He laughed and threw a napkin at her. "Shut up and eat, Parker. We got shit to do. I told Gregory that I'd check out his water heater when we were done eating, and then we'll head over to Brooklyn."

MJ Duncan

TWENTY-TWO

"So, what's next?" Parker asked, her smile wide and happy as they made their way toward the exit.

Sheridan ducked her head in thanks as she slipped through the door Parker held for her onto the sidewalk outside the Whitney Museum of American Art. She'd agonized all week over what they should do after she'd foolishly offered to plan the day for them, and she was more than a little relieved that Parker seemed to have enjoyed their first stop. She slowed her pace so Parker could catch up and turned away from the river and toward the High Line that would lead them to their next destination. "It's a surprise," she teased, swaying ever so slightly in her path to bump shoulders with Parker. "What'd you think of the museum?"

"It was cool." Parker pulled her mirrored aviators from her head and slipped them over her eyes. She grinned and leaned over to bump Sheridan's shoulder. "Although, I have to admit that never in a million years would I have guessed you'd take me there. If anything, I'd have guessed you'd pick the Cloisters or something."

Sheridan smiled. She'd actually considered the satellite Met museum on the northwestern side of the island in Fort Tryon Park. But, while she was pretty sure Parker would enjoy the Middle Ages art displayed there, she thought the Whitney, with its focus on twentieth- and twenty-first-century America art, would be something more up her alley. "Just because I prefer the classics doesn't mean I can't appreciate the more modern stuff. It was actually rather interesting to see so much American art from the past half-century."

"It was," Parker agreed easily. "What was your favorite piece?"

Sheridan bobbed her head from side-to-side and considered the pieces they'd seen that stood out to her the most. "You mean besides the broken urinal sculpture thing?"

Parker laughed. "Yeah, besides that. That was too modern and out there, even for me."

"Good to know," Sheridan drawled. She laughed as she danced away from the playful elbow Parker threw at her. "I liked the impressionist-inspired paintings. How about you?"

"I don't know," Parker murmured, her lips pressing into a thoughtful line. "I quite liked the O'Keeffes. My first real recovery for Cabot and Carmichael was her painting *Shelton with Sunspots*, that'd been stolen from this lovely gentleman who'd inherited it from his mother, so seeing so much of her work on display like that was pretty cool."

"How is your work going? Any new high profile claims to track down?"

"Nope. I have a feeling I'm heading into a bit of a lull. It's okay, though. That's kinda how things tend to happen for me, so I'm used to planning for it. Those last two more than padded my bank account, so I'll be okay dinking and dunking with the smaller claims that never seem to dry up for a while until something bigger comes in."

Sheridan nodded. She didn't know exactly how much Parker had made on those recoveries, of course, but knowing about what each piece was worth was more than enough to tell her that Parker could probably take the rest of the year off and be perfectly fine. "That's good."

Parker grinned, and then screwed up her face as she covered a yawn with her right hand. "Ugh." She shook her head. "I'm sorry."

"Am I boring you, Ms. Ravenscroft?"

"Hardly. I honestly don't think it's possible for me to be bored by anything you do."

Sheridan's stomach fluttered at the warmth in Parker's tone as she glanced her way, the slight tilt of her head a silent assurance that she truly meant it. It was at once wonderful and amazing and terrifying because she knew, as her eyes traced the shape of Parker's smile, that she wanted Parker to look at her like that every day for the rest of her life.

Her heart leapt into her throat when Parker's hand brushed lightly over her wrist, tracing the crease of the bend down into the hollow of her palm, and she swallowed thickly to try to force it back where it belonged as she rasped, "What?"

Parker stopped in the shadow of the High Line and pushed her glasses up onto her head. "Was that okay, what I just said? Was it too much?"

"It wasn't too much." She shook her head. "It was kind of perfect, honestly."

"Okay…" Parker murmured.

The world seemed to stop as Parker watched her with something dangerously close to open affection, and she licked her lips as she reached for Parker's hand and threaded their fingers together. Parker's eyes crinkled with her smile as she looked down at their hands, and Sheridan couldn't help but ask, "Okay?"

Parker nodded. "It's perfect."

And, oh, the way Parker looked at her then, her expression so soft and vulnerable, sent her pulse tripping over itself as warmth spread through her chest, making her feel like she was floating on air. "Okay."

"Very okay." Parker gave her hand a squeeze and tilted her head toward the elevator that would take them up to the walkway overhead. "Shall we?"

Sheridan nodded. "Of course." A thrill rippled down her spine when Parker didn't drop her hand as they stepped into the elevator, and she chewed her lower lip as she tried to find an avenue of conversation that would lead them back to the easy banter they'd been enjoying earlier. "Did you go to your yoga class today?"

"Yeah. Which is why I was yawning, probably." Parker squeezed her hand. "Sculpt was pretty brutal this morning."

Sheridan nodded understandingly. Parker had told her what her typical sculpt class entailed, and just listening to it made her arms tired and her legs sore. "Please tell me you at least sleep in on the weekend."

"Oh yeah. Totally. Class is at six thirty on Saturdays."

"Wow. That's like wasting half the day…" Sheridan teased as the elevator stopped and the doors opened, and she turned left to head north toward their next destination as they stepped onto the platform. "You okay to walk a bit? I think it's a little more than a mile to the restaurant…"

Parker nodded and looked around interestedly. "Yeah. I haven't been up here since it first opened."

"I think the last time I came up here was last summer?" Sheridan waved at the two sculptures that anchored the southernmost end of the High Line. "You want to go have a closer look?"

Parker smiled. "Do you?"

"That's not what I asked," Sheridan pointed out with a laugh.

"And yet, it is exactly what I asked," Parker retorted. She laughed softly when Sheridan arched a brow and shrugged, and shook her head as she turned her back on the sculptures. "You've had to suffer through enough modern art for the day, and that thing that looks like a nose is a little creepy," she said as she gave Sheridan's hand a little tug to follow.

"You're not wrong, there," Sheridan agreed as she took a couple quick steps to catch up. She smiled when Parker swung their hands between them and sighed happily as she looked over at her. "Thank you, for coming with me today."

"Thank you for inviting me," Parker replied softly, pulling her closer to her side so their arms bumped lightly together.

Heist

She held her breath as Parker's head tilted ever so slightly toward her before pulling away, and she let it go softly when Parker looked away. She'd half-thought Parker was leaning in for a kiss and, truth be told, part of her was a little disappointed she didn't. But, she had to admit that this—just walking with Parker and holding her hand—was pretty amazing, and she smiled as she stole a glance at their hands as the back of Parker's knuckles brushed against her thigh.

An easy silence settled between them as they walked, the kind of quiet that was comforting and accepting in a way that sometimes even the most precisely chosen words failed to convey. It was almost as if somebody had hit mute on the city below and the crowd around them, leaving her only aware of the security of Parker's touch, the occasional electric brush of Parker's knuckles against her thigh, and the warmth of the sun shining down on them. It was wonderful, and she was more than a little disappointed when she saw the 26th Street exit up ahead.

"This is us," she murmured as she tugged Parker toward the stairs.

Parker's stomach growled loudly, and she laughed in embarrassment. "Sorry."

"You're fine," Sheridan assured her. "Food is just up ahead."

"Well, clearly I need it, so..." Parker muttered, shaking her head.

Sheridan smiled and nodded as they started down the stairs to get back to street level. They had to go up a block to 27th before turning back toward the river, but in what seemed like no time at all, she was regretfully dropping Parker's hand so she could pull open the door to the hotel atop which sat the restaurant she'd decided on for dinner. It was more than a little ridiculous how strongly she felt the loss of Parker's touch, but she forced herself to ignore it as she gave a small bow and gallantly murmured, "After you, my dear."

"Now who's being all chivalrous?" Parker asked, her gaze shy and her smile utterly charmed as she brushed past Sheridan.

"Well, I can't let you have all the fun, can I?" Sheridan countered as they made their way across the checkerboard marble tiled foyer to the elevator that'd take them to the roof.

"Wait…" Parker pointed at the plaque beside the elevator. "We're going to Gentry Green?"

Sheridan smiled nervously. The rooftop bar and grill was considered to be among the best in the city, and if it weren't for the fact that Ivy knew one of the investors for the restaurant, she would have never been able to get them a table on a Saturday night. She'd thought it would be the perfect place to end their afternoon together, but the indescribable expression on Parker's face had her wondering if she'd been wrong. "That was my plan, yes. Is it not okay?" she asked hesitantly.

"Of course it's fine." Parker grinned. "Jess wouldn't shut up about this place after the guy she was dating last summer brought her here. I just can't believe you managed to get a reservation."

"Well, Ivy kind of helped with that one," Sheridan admitted with a little shrug that she hoped hid the rush of relief that surged through her as she realized she hadn't screwed up. And, if she'd had any lingering doubts to that fact, they were roundly silenced when Parker's hand slipped back into her own as they stepped into the elevator.

As they were lifted into the air, Parker asked, "How did you even know when to make a reservation for?"

"I didn't. I just kinda gave them a block of time when I thought we'd get here…" Sheridan laughed softly at the incredulous look Parker shot her and shrugged. "The investor that Ivy knows pulled some strings for us so we'd have a table whenever we got here. I mean, it also helps that it's barely five and we're before the real dinner rush, so…" Her voice trailed off as Parker just gaped at her. "What?"

Parker shook her head as the elevator stopped at the roof and the doors slid open to reveal the hidden garden of an oasis that was Gentry Green. "You put so much effort into planning all of this," she said, her voice soft and awed as they exited the car.

Sheridan smiled and caressed the back of Parker's hand with her thumb. "I just wanted you to have a good time."

"You are too much, Sheridan Sloan," Parker murmured, her gaze as soft as her voice was rough.

It was a decidedly wonderful combination that sent a pleasant shiver tumbling down Sheridan's spine, but before she could respond, a new voice interrupted, "Welcome to Gentry Green. Do you ladies have a reservation?"

Sheridan startled in surprise at the interruption. She'd been so focused on Parker that she hadn't realized the woman was even there. The soft ripple of laughter that spilled from Parker's lips told her that she wasn't the only one who'd been caught unaware, and she cleared her throat softly as she looked at the woman and nodded. "Yes. Under Sloan."

The woman scanned the list in front of her and nodded as she quickly gathered a couple of menus. "If you'll follow me, please..."

Sheridan smiled at Parker as she regretfully pulled her hand away so they could navigate between the tables that filled the rooftop restaurant, and took a deep breath as she turned to follow the hostess to their table.

The restaurant was packed despite the fact that it was still early, and she was surprised when the hostess led them all the way across the dining area to an intimate two-person table surrounded by waist-high planters overflowing with greenery on the far side that overlooked the Hudson River. "Will this be okay?"

"It's perfect," Parker replied as she eased past the hostess to pull a chair for her. "Ms. Sloan..."

Sheridan rolled her eyes as she felt herself begin to blush and shook her head as she obligingly took the seat Parker held for her. "Thank you."

The smile on the hostess' face said that she found the exchange utterly adorable, which only made her blush harder, and she waited until Parker had taken the seat opposite her to hand them their menus. "Your server's name is Dan, and he'll be with you ladies shortly."

"I've never been here before, but Ivy said they have a pretty decent number of vegetarian dishes," Sheridan shared as she opened her menu.

"Good. Because I'm starving," Parker half-groaned, and shook her head wryly as her stomach growled loudly for emphasis.

Sheridan laughed, grateful for the levity Parker's ravenous stomach provided. While she'd enjoying the quiet moment they'd been sharing before the hostess interrupted them, she couldn't help but be relieved that it was over as well. The push and pull inside her was both confusing and more than a little frightening, her heart wanting to take the risk and leap into something that she wasn't at all sure she was ready for, but Parker seemed to understand as she just smiled at her before directing her attention to the menu in her hands.

Parker kept up a steady stream of idle chatter as she perused the menu, somehow effortlessly coaxing her back from the edge of the panic she'd been so close to slipping into, and by the time their appetizers were set on the table, they had regained the easy flow of conversation they'd enjoyed all afternoon.

She couldn't help but marvel at Parker as she watched her animatedly recount something that'd happened earlier that week at work as she ate, her smile so open and unguarded as she gestured with her hands as she spoke. Parker was a vision, full of confidence and joyful laughter that she couldn't help but echo as time slipped around them in a blur of changing plates and clanging silverware. Everything about the meal was exactly as wonderful as she had hoped it would be, and she laughed when she swiped the bill from beneath Parker's hand so she could settle the tab herself.

"Let me chip in, at least," Parker protested.

"Nope." Sheridan pulled her credit card from her wallet and slipped it into the leather billfold. "I asked you out, I'm paying."

"Then when can I take you out?" Parker asked.

"I don't know." Sheridan grinned. "When can you?"

Parker laughed and held her hands up in an *I don't know* type gesture. "Tomorrow? Next weekend? I don't care when, so long as I don't have to wait too long to do it. What works best for you?"

"Seriously?" Sheridan asked as their server swooped by the collect the bill and her card.

Parker nodded. "Completely."

"I wish I could do something tomorrow, but I kinda promised I'd help Ivy with something at her place to pay her back for helping me with this." Sheridan waved a hand at the restaurant around them with a wry smile. Why Ivy thought having her, of all people, help paint her and Rachel's new place in Brooklyn was a mystery, but an afternoon spent covered in paint was a price she'd been more than willing to pay in exchange for the reservation. And, in the grand scheme of things, maybe it was better this way. They were supposed to be taking it slow, after all, and spending an entire weekend together was anything but that. "But I don't have anything going on next weekend…"

"Okay." Parker grinned. "Next weekend it is, then. We'll figure out what day works best during the week?"

Sheridan nodded, distracted from the conversation as their server slipped the billfold back onto the table beside her elbow. She flipped open the folder and quickly calculated an appropriate tip before scribbling her name across the bottom of the slip. "That sounds perfect," she agreed as she slipped her card back into her wallet.

"Now I just gotta figure out how to top what you did today," Parker muttered she pushed her chair away from the table and got to her feet.

"I'm sure you'll come up with something."

Parker smiled and motioned with a small wave of her hand for Sheridan to take the lead. "I'm glad one of us is confident about that."

The soft press of Parker's fingers on the small of her back as she led them back through the crowded patio to the elevator made her smile. The gentle care Parker treated her with was so unlike anything she had ever experienced before, and she found herself leaning back into the touch after she'd pressed her thumb to the button to call the elevator. She smiled when Parker's hand drifted to curl lightly around her hip, and she sighed in disappointment when the doors in front of them opened and Parker's hand fell away.

"Today was perfect, Sheridan," Parker murmured as the doors closed behind them. They were the only ones in the car, and she smiled shyly as she dared to reach for her hand. "Honestly perfect. Thank you."

The earnestness in Parker's voice made her blush, and she bit her lip as she forced herself to not look away as she replied softly, "I thought so too."

"I'm glad." Parker squeezed her hand as the elevator stopped at the main floor. "How are you planning on getting home from here?"

Sheridan shrugged. Honestly, she hadn't given too much thought to it. "Probably the subway."

"To the subway it is, then," Parker drawled as she led them from the elevator.

They strolled along the sidewalk in companionable silence toward the 23rd Street station, and she was surprised when Parker seemed prepared to follow her all the way to her train. "Parker?"

"You went out of your way to pick me up this afternoon when I could have met you down here, so I'm going to go out of my way and walk you home," Parker declared with a look that dared Sheridan to try to challenge her on it.

"You really don't have to do that," Sheridan protested weakly anyway.

"I know. But I want to. Will you let me see you all the way home?"

Parker's smile was hopeful, utterly charming, and impossible to resist, and Sheridan huffed a little laugh as she nodded. "I would like that."

Parker grinned like she'd just been given the world. "Good."

The subway was a predictable crowded mess given the fact that it was still early on a Saturday night, and Sheridan let out a sigh of relief when they eventually made their way out of the maze and into the shadows that surrounded the Chambers Street station.

Parker held out her hand once they reached the, blessedly, less packed street. "Milady?"

"You take this chivalry thing seriously, don't you?" Sheridan teased as she immediately laced their fingers together.

"Just with you," Parker murmured as she turned toward her loft.

Sheridan smiled as she allowed Parker to lead the way, just enjoying these last few minutes they had together. It only took a handful of minutes to cover the quarter mile between her apartment and the station, and her heart sank just a little when they ambled to a stop in front of her building. She smiled at Parker as she turned to pull her into a light hug. After the day they'd had, it seemed like the only appropriate way to say goodbye, and her eyes fluttered shut as she murmured into Parker's shoulder, "Thank you for walking me home."

"Oh, Sheridan," Parker whispered, the gentle words followed by the briefest brush of lips against her cheek. Parker's smile was as soft as the look in her eyes when she pulled away, and Sheridan's stomach flipped at the sight of it. "Believe me, it was my pleasure."

She was suddenly incredibly sorry that she wasn't going to see her again until the following weekend. "Text me when you get home to let me know you made it back okay?"

Parker nodded. "Of course."

The heavy bob of Parker's throat as she pulled away told Sheridan that she was just as reticent to say goodbye, but there was also no denying the fact that, unless she invited Parker upstairs, the day had reached its inevitable end. "Goodnight, Parker."

Parker's lips twitched with a small smile, and nodded. "Goodnight, Sheridan."

twenty-three

Parker glanced at the people around her as she adjusted her stance to accommodate the shift in the subway car's acceleration as it pulled to a stop at Eastern Parkway in Brooklyn. The stop was a few miles from the brownstone they were going to be pillaging, but it was a busy enough station that she could disappear easily into the crowd. Invisibility was key pulling a job like this in the middle of the day so, knowing that the city was rife with security cameras, she had decided to wear a shoulder-length, auburn wig to cover her hair and a Yankees cap to hide most of her face. It wasn't a foolproof means of avoiding having her image captured, but it was the best she could do without drawing too much attention to herself.

And, so long as they didn't screw up, it should be more than enough to keep her identity a secret. There was no doubt in her mind that Sheridan's team would eventually be called in to investigate the heist, and she and Ollie had spent pretty much the entire day before going over their plan again and again until even the most minute detail was burned into both their brains.

She allowed the crowd streaming up the stairs toward the street to carry her forward, and when the signal changed she jogged across Eastern Parkway toward the office building opposite the museum. She tapped the Bluetooth earpiece in her right ear and murmured, "Call

Ollie." The call was picked up half a ring later, and she said, "Hey, Olls. I'm here."

"I see you. I'm about half a block south of your location. White panel van."

She turned her head toward the south and nodded when she saw the van. "On my way," she muttered before she tapped the Bluetooth again to deactivate it.

Her black jeans and white blouse blended well enough with the crowd on the sidewalk that she didn't garner a second look from anyone she passed, and she nodded to herself when she saw the logo on the side panel. She had taken pictures of a van that was identical to this one when she'd been running surveillance on Gunn's place the week before. Oliver had hacked his way into the company's system and learned that Gunn's regular day was Thursday, but there were enough incidents over the last few months of random visits on other days that the sight of the van in front of his place shouldn't raise too many eyebrows. The trick had been figuring out where they could acquire a van to borrow for a few hours, and he had headed out before dawn that morning to look at the half-dozen or so locations where cleaning teams were to be dispatched that day to see which would be the best van to borrow for a few hours.

"So where did you end up finding this one?" Parker asked as she climbed into the passenger seat. She gave Oliver a once-over as she tucked her backpack between her feet and closed the door after herself. He was dressed similarly to herself in dark jeans, white shirt, and a cap—the standard uniform for the employees of the cleaning company they were impersonating—though his was for the Mariners.

"A building not far from here, actually." Oliver winked and, as he pulled away from the curb, added, "The crew that's assigned this van is working on a place that must be an absolute disaster. The company's internal scheduling showed a team of four cleaners are slated to spend the entire day there."

"Damn. Is the GPS on this thing disabled?"

"You wound me by even asking. Besides slipping a bug into the city's camera system that will corrupt every camera in every one of the boroughs for the day, making them randomly shut down for an hour or two before they come back on like nothing had happened, I also went into the company's tracking system to show that this lovely vehicle of theirs is still parked where I borrowed it. From a tech standpoint, I've made sure that we are more than covered for this."

"Oh, good," she teased. "I was worried about you being able to find something to keep busy this morning."

"Yeah, well, I did promise you that this job would be risk-free, so I figured it'd be best to cover all the bases." He laughed as he reached behind himself and grabbed a white work shirt that had the cleaning company's logo embroidered on the left breast. "Your uniform, my dear," he drawled as he tossed it at her.

Since she had a white tank on under her blouse anyway, she just slipped the blouse off and the pulled on the work shirt instead. "Thanks. I called to double-check that Gunn is at his office thirty seconds before the trading bell rang so his secretary wouldn't try to put me through to him, and he's definitely on the other side of the river for the day."

"Sounds good."

"Yep." Her phone buzzed in her pocket, and she sighed as she pulled it out to check the screen. She'd told Jess she had a doctor's appointment and wouldn't be in until after lunch, but it wasn't unheard of for Jess to send her updates if something big happened. The message wasn't from her assistant, however, and she smiled as she opened her messaging app.

Muscles that I didn't even know I had are *still* sore…

Even though she'd been seriously concerned that she wouldn't be able to plan a day as perfect as the one Sheridan had for them, she'd been pleasantly surprised by how well Saturday had gone. They had spent a few hours climbing at Brooklyn Boulders before going to dinner at a nearby cafe, and they'd wrapped up the evening with a leisurely walk along the trails of Prospect Park. She had been beyond bummed when she'd had to turn down Sheridan's offer to do something the following day because she'd already had plans with Oliver to run through everything for the job they were about the pull; but the lingering hug they'd shared after she once again walked Sheridan to the door of her building and the lightest brush of soft, soft lips against her cheek assured her that Sheridan understood.

Her smile widened as she reread the message two more times, her eyes tracing the curve of each letter before she replied, *I'm sorry. If it makes you feel better, that huge blister on my palm popped this morning.*

"Tell Sheridan I say hi," Oliver teased lightly.

"How do you know it's her?" Parker challenged with a smirk. "Maybe it's Jess, or somebody from work."

"With those actual fucking heart eyes you've got on right now, I don't think so, Ravenscroft," Oliver laughed.

Glad to know I'm not the only one still feeling the effects of three hours at that climbing gym...

"Whatever, Dobrev," Parker shot back as she began typing her reply. *You're absolutely not.* "You're just jealous."

"I absolutely am," he agreed easily.

Her screen flashed alive again. *Ivy and Rachel are going to be having a few people over to their new place next week for the Fourth, and I was wondering if you'd like to go with me?*

Parker sighed as a pleasant flutter rippled through her chest, and then swallowed thickly as she looked out the windshield of the van she was riding in en route to a job she knew Sheridan wouldn't understand. The utter dichotomy of her life smacked into her in that moment, and she hated it. Hated the way her feelings for Sheridan threw such a dark shadow over the decisions she was making here with Ollie. She wasn't so deluded to think that what they were doing was in any way "right" but, before Sheridan, she'd never felt such a heart-sinking level of guilt about it, either. Until Sheridan, all of this was just something she did because her brother had asked for her help and she didn't think very much about it at all.

"ETA?" she asked Oliver softly.

"Ten? Depends on traffic. Is everything okay?"

"Yeah." She pursed her lips as her attention drifted back to the screen in her hand. "Sheridan invited me to a Fourth of July party at her colleague's place next week."

Some of the guilt she was feeling must have crept into her tone, because he asked, "Do you not want to go?"

"Oh, I do. Which is what makes the whole thing so weird, you know? I mean, here we are, on our way to steal another book from Marquis' list, and the woman I'm kind-of-not-really-dating just so happens to be one of the actual fucking FBI agents who will be the ones investigating this heist when it eventually gets reported has just invited me to a party that's being thrown by someone else on her team."

"Christ, Parker…"

She shook her head. "Do you really feel like you need this job?" she asked softly.

Oliver stretched his arms out against the steering wheel as he pulled to a stop at a red light. He sucked his lower lip between his teeth as he stared out the windshield, and his expression turned pinched and apologetic as he nodded. "I do. I'm sorry, but I do."

"Okay," she sighed, resigned to putting his needs before her own one more time. "Then let's do it quick and clean."

He gave her a shy smile and, with a small tip of his head, murmured, "Thank you, Parker."

"Yeah." She looked back down at her phone.

"What are you going to tell her?"

Parker closed her eyes and leaned her head back against the headrest. There were only two options—try to find a way to decline the invitation without hurting Sheridan's feelings, or go with her to the party—and for as much as she knew the first option was the wisest course, she couldn't summon the strength necessary to go that route. Not when just thinking about it made her heart hurt. She licked her lips as she woke up her phone, and shook her head as she stared at Sheridan's last message for a long moment, letting the weight of her choice settle heavily on her heart before she replied, *I'd love to.*

She cringed when little ellipses appeared in the message field as soon as she'd hit send. Sheridan must have been waiting on her response while she had her little moral breakdown, but couldn't help but smile when two words appeared in a pale gray bubble. *I'm glad.*

More ellipses popped up, but she forced herself to ignore them. She could only handle one bad decision at a time, and the one she'd made to help Oliver demanded her attention at the moment. Later, when this was done and Oliver was off to wherever to deliver the book to Marquis, she could focus on Sheridan and let herself enjoy the way that particular bad decision made her feel so goddamn happy.

She blew out a soft breath as she pulled the Bluetooth earpiece paired to her phone from her right ear and tucked it and her phone into her backpack. Bluetooth technology was nice and all, but she trusted the encryption of their radio system a million times more than she trusted her wireless carrier. "Do you have the radio earpieces?"

Oliver waved a hand at the back of the van. "In my case." He hummed softly as he drove through a light that was more red than yellow and added, "Should be there in less than five. I slipped a bug into NYPD's camera system for the area that should take them at least the rest of the morning to get rid of, so we don't have to worry about getting picked up on camera."

Parker nodded and turned to set her backpack behind her seat before she unclipped her seatbelt so she could climb into the back of the van to start getting ready. Oliver's titanium briefcase was tucked behind his seat, and she pulled it onto her lap as she settled onto the floor of the van to get ready. His laptop was nestled inside along with the two custom made radio earpieces they'd be using, and she glanced through the front windshield as she opened the case for the earpiece labeled with a P. She recognized the awnings of the corner store that was two blocks from Gunn's place, and took a deep breath to steady herself as she slipped the flesh-colored earpiece into her right ear.

"Here." She tapped his shoulder to get his attention and, when his right hand appeared between the seats, handed him his earpiece.

"Thanks," he murmured as he took it from her and slipped it into his ear.

After she powered up the laptop so it would be ready for him as soon as they got to Gunn's place, she pulled her leather gloves from her backpack and slipped them on. She stuck the few lock picking tools she'd need for the standard deadbolt on the door into her right back pocket, and then she pulled a late twentieth-century reproduction of Blake's *The Four Zoas* from her bag, wrapped it carefully in a couple of cleaning cloths, and tucked it into a bag that looked like the ones the cleaning crews carried. It was probably an eighty percent match in appearance to the first edition copy *The First Book of Urizen* that they would be relocating to Marquis' collection, but it was the best she could find on short notice.

She looked up as she felt the van pull to the right and then stop, and shuffled toward the rear of the cargo area as Oliver climbed back with her to grab the case that held his open laptop.

"Thanks for getting this up," he muttered as he quickly entered his passcode and unlocked the computer. A flurry of keystrokes later, he grinned and pushed it over to the side of the cargo area. "Alarm is taken care of. We're good to go."

"You sure you don't need to stay in the van with that?" She quadruple-checked as he pulled on his gloves. They had gone over this more times than she could count back at her place the day before, but she still felt like she needed to ask because it was a major departure from how they usually worked.

He shook his head as he pushed open the rear doors of the van, and once his feet hit the pavement, she handed him the bag of cleaning supplies that held the replacement book. "The alarm system is seriously awful, and I can monitor everything from my phone. The cleaning company never sends only one person to a job, so we need to both go in for appearances' sake. Besides," he added as he moved out of the way so she could climb out of the van, "this way we can split up and find it faster."

"I like the sound of that," she murmured as she picked up a bag of cleaning supplies that was identical to Oliver's.

Even though Oliver had disrupted the camera feeds along the street, she kept her head down as she eased past him in case any of Gunn's neighbors were paying attention to them. Her shoulders tensed at the sound of the van's heavy metal doors slamming shut behind her, but she didn't otherwise react as she made her way toward Gunn's front door. She would much rather go through the back, but this was all about appearances, and the cleaning crew would have no reason to not use the front door. She set the bag she was carrying on the ground and deftly slipped the lock pick tools from her back pocket as she edged closer to the door, using her body to hide what she was doing as she disengaged the deadbolt in less than three seconds.

"Faster than using a key," Oliver observed with a hint of pride in his voice from behind her.

She smiled in spite of the situation and nodded as she pushed the door open. Her eyes immediately drifted to the silent alarm panel on the wall beside the entrance to the formal living room, and she was relieved to see that it was properly disarmed.

"Oh, have ye a little faith," he teased as he used the heel of his shoe to push the door closed.

She rolled her eyes and looked around the foyer, translating what she'd memorized from the blueprints Oliver had accessed for them to the physical building they were now standing in. The stairs straight ahead of them led to the upper levels of the home, and through the doorway to their left was the living room. Beyond that, she knew from the plans they'd studied, was the dining room and kitchen—two rooms she was willing to bet didn't have the book they were looking for. "You take the main floor, I'll take the second, and we'll meet on the third if we don't find it?" she repeated the plan they'd come up with the day before.

He nodded and waved her toward the stairs. "Yep. Go."

She took a deep breath and then jogged up the stairs to the second floor, which had three bedrooms that, from their dimensions on the blueprints they'd studied, she was willing to bet were guest rooms. She ignored the massive black-and-white gallery-style prints that hung on the pale gray walls as she hurried along the hallway, wanting nothing more than to get out of the house as quickly as possible. There was nothing more nerve-wracking than pulling a job like this in broad daylight, and though she both understood and agreed with the timing of the plan, it did very little to calm her nerves.

The three rooms on the second floor were, in fact, all guest rooms furnished with identical dark wood furniture and deep crimson bedding, and she sighed as she thumbed on her mic as hustled back to the stairs to head up to the third floor. "Nothing on the second floor."

"Still going through the bookshelves in the living room," Oliver reported.

The third floor was more open than the one below, with high ceilings and skylights spanning the length of the unit. The master bedroom faced the top of the stairs, and a quick look through the door revealed that it was decorated in hues of black and gray that screamed bachelor, and she shook her head as she made her way to the room at the other end of the hall. They'd agreed, after studying the blueprints, that it was the best possible location for a library, and she couldn't help but grin when she got close enough to see light wood bookshelves through the open doorway.

She looked around interestedly as she entered the room to get her bearings. There was a window seat stretched between the shelves that framed the window, and there was a comfortable-looking tufted leather loveseat in the middle of the room that was set at an angle so that it was still possible to maneuver around it to get to the shelves.

"Nothing in the living room," Oliver's voice reported.

Parker nodded. "Kinda figured as much. Library's on the third floor, street-side."

"See anything?"

"Not yet," she told him as she looked around the room. There were two sections of shelves that had glass doors covering them, and as she started to make her way toward them to see if what she needed was inside, she noticed a glass box on the shelf two sections over from the doors.

From what they'd been able to find out about Gunn's collection, *The First Book of Urizen* was easily the most valuable book he owned, and she hummed under her breath as she made her way over to the case that was nearly identical to those used in museums to see if it held what she thought it did.

She grinned as she looked through the lid of the case to see a rather gruesome illustration of three bodies with snakes wrapped around them, cast in hues of blood-red crimson and tarnished yellow, being lowered, or thrown, into a field of tall grass, and nodded to herself as she reported through the comm, "I got it. Third floor library."

"Almost there."

Parker quickly changed her latex gloves for white cotton and then opened the lid of the case. She carefully lifted the book from its angled display perch, and pressed the edge of her thumb to the page as a bookmark so she could check the cover to make sure the book in her hands was the one they wanted. She wasn't too worried about it, of course—the manner in which the book was displayed was pretty much a dead-giveaway that it was authentic—but there was no harm in performing her due-diligence.

"Is that it?" Oliver asked as he strode into the office.

She looked over at him and nodded as she flipped the book open to the spot she'd been marking with her thumb. "Yep. But the book was displayed with its pages open to this illustration, however"—she smiled at the way he grimaced when he saw the picture—"so the replacement isn't going to do us any good."

He shrugged and set the bag he'd been carrying onto the sofa. "So we don't leave a doppelgänger." He reached into the bag and pulled out the replacement volume they'd brought with them. "You want the bag that this one's in?"

"I didn't bring a spare, so yeah. It doesn't matter anymore that it stays sterile," she said, mentally groaning at the thought of all the time she'd wasted making sure that every page of the book was clean of anything that could be traced.

"Whatcha going to do with it?" he asked as he slipped the book free and handed her the bag.

She shrugged. "I can sell it to a rare bookstore. I won't go back to where I found it, but there are a handful of places not far from here that specialize in this kind of stuff," she said as she eased the rare first edition she'd been holding into the polyethylene bag. Once it was secured, she took the cloths Oliver handed her and wrapped them around the book before stacking it and its useless replacement back into the bag on the sofa. "We're done."

"Sweet," Oliver cheered as he shouldered the bag. He made his way to the front window to look down on the street to check that everything was good for their exit, and looked back at her with a grin. "Street looks clear. Let's get the fuck outta here."

Parker rolled her eyes as she followed him down the hall toward the stairs. She grabbed the bag she'd carried inside from the floor of the foyer before making her way to the door, and she waited for Oliver to signal that he was ready before she pulled it open. She locked the door just as quickly as she'd unlocked it, and with a muttered, "Done," followed Oliver down the stairs and to the back of the van.

She tossed her bag toward the back of the front seats before clambering inside, and took the one Oliver offered her much more carefully. She moved out of the way as he climbed in after her, and once the doors of the van were shut, pushed his briefcase toward him so he could reset whatever security systems he'd deactivated when they arrived.

"Good," he reported half a minute later, and he grinned as he powered off the laptop and closed the lid. "You want to do the earpieces?" he asked as he pushed the briefcase toward her.

She nodded and held out her hand for the plastic piece he deposited in her palm two seconds later. "Get us out of here, Olls."

"Yes, ma'am." He grinned and made his way to the front of the van to climb into the driver's seat and, before she could count to six, they were pulling away from the curb.

After she finished securing their earpieces in the case, she closed the lid and shoved it toward the back of the front seats. "Doing the book now," she reported as she reached into her backpack to retrieve the book transport case that she had used in Paris. Once she'd transferred the Blake into the case and inflated the protective tubes around it, she closed the lid and set it on top of Oliver's briefcase. She shrugged out of her white shirt and tucked it into her backpack—there was no way she was leaving anything behind that could hold DNA to bring the investigation back to her—and then, with her gloves still on, used the cleaning supplies from Oliver's bag to give the back of the van a thorough wipe-down.

She had just finished when Oliver pulled into the parking structure he'd originally borrowed the van from, and she pursed her lips as she looked out the windshield. "Cameras down here?"

"I stuck them on a loop before I got here this morning," Oliver reported, his tone smug as he waved his hands in front of himself like a magician to show they were empty. "Nothing to see here, folks."

She chuckled. "Smooth."

"You know it," he shot back as he whipped the van into an empty space.

"Is this where you got it from?"

He shrugged. "I think it might have been down two more spaces, but this is close enough. Nobody remembers exactly where they leave their cars in places like this, they just remember the general area and look for something familiar." He killed the ignition and made a grabby motion with his hand. "Hit me with the cleaning rags."

She tossed him a tub of disinfecting wipes and then made her way to the back of the van to push the doors open. Everything they might have touched got a thorough wipe-down, and she sighed as she tossed the final wipe into the bag of supplies and grabbed her backpack. She pulled off her wig and shoved it into the largest compartment, then slapped the Yankees cap back on her head. She arched a brow at him as he moved the case with the Blake into a black backpack he'd brought with him for transporting the rare book. He shouldered his pack as she did the same, and then reached for his briefcase as she gathered the bags of cleaning supplies and discarded clothes.

"You got my door?" she asked Oliver as she removed her gloves and tucked them into the side pocket of her backpack.

"Yep. We are ghosts, my dear." He winked and held out a hand. "High five."

She rolled her eyes even as she obligingly slapped his palm and then looked around the parking structure with a skeptical eye. "Where's your rental?"

"Right over there," he said, pointing at a perfectly nondescript black Chevy Malibu.

"When are you taking the book to Marquis?" she asked as they made their way toward the car. They'd agreed that since his freelance work allowed him more freedom to travel, that he'd handle the exchanges from now on so she wouldn't raise too many eyebrows by requesting time off from work.

"Tonight," he shared as he pulled the car keys from his pocket to pop the trunk. He set the briefcase and backpack inside and slammed the lid shut. "That woman has connections, Park. She arranged for a charter through a shell company to take me from White Plains to some exclusive-as-fuck-no-flight-plan-needed airfield outside Montreal where she'll meet me. So after I drop you off, I'll head Upstate and just hang out until my ride gets there," he walked through the plan again. "After the exchange I'll head back to the US, this time landing in Providence, and then I'll rent another car and drive back to Boston."

She nodded as she got into the car. It was a lot of steps to take, but with the surveillance Sheridan's boss had on Marquis, it was better to be safe than sorry. "Sounds good," she said when he climbed behind the wheel. "Keep me updated?"

He grinned and snapped off a quick salute. "Of course."

TWENTY-FOUR

"You'd think that since it's eleven o'clock on a Wednesday that traffic would actually fucking move," Kelly muttered as he laid on the horn at a particularly feisty cab driver who cut them off. "Dumbass, we're on a fucking bridge," he continued his rant. "Where the fuck do you expect to go?"

Sheridan was sitting shotgun, doing a bit of research on her phone as he drove, and she couldn't resist teasing, "Road rage much?"

"Yes!" He slammed the heel of his hand against the steering wheel. "What have you found out about our missing book?"

They had gotten a call from a detective in the Eighty-Fourth Precinct earlier that morning requesting their help looking into a rare book that had been reported stolen the day before in Brooklyn. From what the detective had told them about the case, the lack of a replacement book left behind at the scene suggested the reported theft was executed by someone other than the thieves who pulled the Paris heist, but Bartz didn't want them taking any chances. So, since she and Kelly had established a rapport with Guillard and Herault on the Matisse case, and since they were the team investigating the rare book heist in Paris, they'd been assigned this investigation in case they ended up needing to work together.

She shrugged and lifted her phone a little closer to her eyes so she could read up on the missing Blake on Wikipedia. It wasn't the most academic of sources, but for now it covered all the basics that she needed. "There are only eight copies of the book in the world. Last time one was traded publicly was in ninety-nine, when it sold at auction for two-point-five mil," she reported. "The illustrations in those eight known surviving copies are from Blake's own plates, which undoubtedly has helped drive the price up, and they're creepy as hell."

Kelly laughed. "Is that your professional opinion?"

"Yeah." She looked out the windshield. They were finally nearing the end of the bridge. "About how much longer until we get there?"

"No fucking clue," he muttered as he slammed his palm into the horn again.

"Okay. Seriously. Do you need me to drive?"

"I'm fine."

"If you say so," she drawled as she looked back at her phone. A banner alert popped up at the top of her screen, half-blocking a photo of one of Blake's illustrations, and she smiled when she saw it was a text alert from Parker.

Am going to be meeting with a client down in your neck of the woods here in a bit. Do you have time to maybe sneak out for lunch?

"I wish," she breathed, shaking her head. *Unfortunately, Kel and I aren't in the office right now, and there's no telling when we'll be back. Rain check?* She hated having to say no—the last thing she wanted was for Parker to think that she didn't want to spend a stolen hour in the middle of the week with her—but before she could travel too far down that particular rabbit hole, Parker's reply popped up on her screen.

Of course. Good luck with whatever you're doing, then.

"How's Parker?"

Sheridan rolled her eyes. "She's fine. She's going to be meeting with a client somewhere on the southern end of the island somewhere and wanted to know if I could meet her for lunch," she explained before he could bug her about it. *Thanks. Want me to call you later?*

Ellipses popped up in a gray bubble almost immediately, and she drummed her fingers on the back of her phone as she waited for

Parker's response. *Short of being graced with your company, I'd love nothing more. Be safe, Sheridan. I'll talk to you later.* There was no ignoring the pleasant little flutter in her chest at that sweet sign-off, and she sighed as she closed out the message app.

"Everything okay?"

"Yeah." Sheridan nodded. "She's just…" She let the sentence hang as she tried to find the right word to finish it before deciding on, "Perfect."

"Sure seems like it," he agreed. "I'm looking forward to hanging out with her at Ivy's thing next week. And"—he reached over to poke her in the knee—"before you start threatening me to be on my best behavior, you should know that Ivy already did that and she's like a bazillion times scarier than you are, so you have nothing to worry about."

She laughed. "Good."

"Thought you'd like that," he replied as they pulled to a stop at a red light.

"In five hundred feet," the GPS chirped, "turn right."

Kelly nodded as he leaned over to check the GPS screen in the dash. "We're not far, now. You want to call Detective Dearborn and let her know we're almost there?"

"I can do that," she agreed as she snagged the Post-it with the detective's cell number on it from the cup holder between their seats. The detective answered on the first ring, and Sheridan looked out the window at the charming streets of Brooklyn as she said, "Detective Dearborn? This is Sheridan Sloan, we spoke earlier on the phone. My partner and I are nearly at the scene, and we wanted to see if you'd be there to meet us."

"We're already here with Mr. Gunn," Dearborn replied.

"Excellent." Sheridan grabbed the oh-shit handle above her door as Kelly took a corner a little too fast, and rolled her eyes as the GPS announced their destination was on their right. "We just turned onto Gunn's street, so we'll be there shortly."

"See you soon," Dearborn signed off.

"So what do you think the odds are we'll find a parking spot close to—hey!" Kelly interrupted himself with a triumphant whoop as he pulled past an opening just large enough for their sedan. "Looks like the parking gods are in our favor today!"

Sheridan chuckled and began gathering her things as he backed into the space. "Let's just hope the investigative gods are in our favor on this case, too," she said as he threw the car into park and she opened her door. "I really hope this thing doesn't end up being tied to Guillard's case."

"Dude, me too," he agreed as he climbed out of the car and slammed his door.

She shoved her hands into her pockets as they made their way down the block to Gunn's house, her eyes sweeping back and forth over picturesque stoops and parked cars, looking for anything that might help them in the investigation. Unfortunately, the block was strictly residential. Businesses usually had security cameras facing the street they could access, but with parallel rows of well-tended brownstones lining the street, odds were good that the only street cameras they'd be able to use were at the ends of the block—a good couple hundred feet in either direction from Gunn's brownstone. Not totally useless, but they weren't going to get a good picture from them, either.

As they neared Gunn's place, the front door opened to reveal a striking woman with cropped light brown hair and chiseled cheekbones who looked to be in her mid-thirties. She wore a black suit and a white dress shirt that was buttoned nearly to the collar, and Sheridan lifted a hand in greeting as she guessed, "Detective Dearborn?"

The woman nodded, a small smile tugging at her lips as she stepped onto the front stoop. "Agents Sloan and Innes. I wish I could say it's a pleasure, but…"

"Yeah, we get that a lot," Kelly assured her with a grin. "So, what do you got?"

Dearborn cleared her throat. "Not a lot, to be honest. Mister Gunn called dispatch yesterday afternoon around four to report the theft, which he says had to've happened either Monday or Tuesday because he remembers seeing the book in his study Sunday. We came out, ran the usual due diligence—prints, photos, canvasing the neighborhood, what have you—but didn't get much. A neighbor, Ms. Betty Cuthbertson"—she pointed toward the houses across the street from where they stood—"said she saw a van from the cleaning company Gunn uses parked out here Monday morning, but he says he didn't schedule them to come in that day."

"Somebody from the cleaning company come back to make the grab?" Kelly wondered.

Dearborn shrugged. "I called his alarm company and had them pull up the logs for the last week to see if the alarm was disarmed during the day when Mr. Gunn wasn't home, but their system didn't show anything unusual, so I doubt it. The cleaners would have the alarm code, but the system would have shown if it was used or not." She held up a hand to ward off further questions as she added, "The company is cooperating with our investigation, and they're going to have every employee who'd ever worked at Gunn's at their office later this afternoon so we can question them if you'd like to sit-in."

"That sounds perfect, thanks," Sheridan said. "Did one of the other neighbors around here arrange to have that company service their house?"

"Not that we found," Dearborn said. "We went door-to-door last night when more people would be home from work and managed to speak to a good portion of the homeowners on the block, but nobody claimed to have used the agency. I'm having the cleaning company look into the GPS trackers on their vans to see which one was out here Monday—maybe that'll give us a lead."

"Anything from the street cameras?" Sheridan asked.

Dearborn shook her head. "Our tech guys are still going through the footage, but there is some kind of bug in the system that's affecting the cameras, so it's slow-going. So far they haven't found anything."

"Prints in the house?" Kelly asked.

Dearborn sighed. "Only Gunn's. The place was clean."

"Are you sure it was really stolen, and that this isn't some insurance fraud case?" Sheridan couldn't help asking.

"I'm pretty sure that he's on-the-level with this, but who knows." Dearborn shrugged. "I'm sure you guys have more experience in picking up those kinds of vibes, so I'll let you see what you think."

"Who insured the book?" Sheridan asked, idly wondering if Gunn was the client Parker was going to meet.

"Arthaus Incorporated."

She thought she'd covered her disappointment well but, judging by the way Kelly chuckled quietly beside her, some of it must have shown. She elbowed him in the ribs as she followed Dearborn inside the house. "Where was the book before it was taken?"

"Third floor library," a new voice answered.

Sheridan plastered a professionally polite smile on her face as she turned toward the voice. Two men were making their way into the foyer from the attached living room, and it wasn't hard to figure out who was Dearborn's partner, and who was Walter Gunn.

"Sam Nix," the very cop-looking cop introduced himself with a little wave. He was just under six feet tall, with sharp black eyes and a crew cut.

Kelly nodded. "Kelly Innes."

"Sheridan Sloan." Sheridan looked at the man to Nix's right and offered him a small smile. Gunn was shorter than her by a handful of inches, with dark brown hair, tired eyes, and a day's worth of stubble shading his jaw. "Mr. Gunn?"

"That's me," he agreed as he offered them his hand.

"I'm Agent Sloan," she introduced herself as she shook his hand before waving at Kelly, "and this is my partner, Agent Innes."

"Pleased to meet you," Gunn mumbled robotically. "You want to see the library?"

Kelly nodded. "Please."

Gunn waved at them as he turned and started for the stairs. "Follow me."

"Who's your home security company?" Kelly asked as they climbed.

"Iron Gate," Gunn answered without looking back. "I have their information as well as my insurance company's contact numbers on a piece of paper downstairs for you."

"That'll be great, thanks," Sheridan said as she cleared the final step at the second floor.

She looked through the open doorways as they made their way along the hall toward the stairs at the other end, paying more attention to the gallery prints on the wall than the rather generic guest rooms they passed. The black and white landscapes were interesting, with an unusual enough composition to catch the eye, and though she wanted to ask him about them, there was something in the set of Gunn's shoulders that suggested he wouldn't appreciate the inquiry.

They climbed to the third floor in silence, and she glanced briefly through the door to the master bedroom at the top of the stairs as she turned to follow Gunn down the hall toward what had to be the library he had mentioned downstairs.

"It was in there," Gunn said, waving a hand at an empty display case as they filed into the room. Dearborn and Nix stayed by the door, hands in their pockets as they watched Sheridan and Kelly inspect the room.

The case was set on a shelf just below eye-level, at a height meant to be seen, and Sheridan looked at Dearborn as she asked, just to be sure that the scene had been fully processed, "Do we need gloves?"

Dearborn shook her head. "You're fine."

"The case wasn't wired?" Kelly asked as he followed Sheridan across the room.

"No. I didn't want to have to disarm an alarm system every time I wanted to take it out and read it," Gunn answered. "I thought the house alarm would be enough."

"Do you have other rare books?" Sheridan asked, gesturing toward the glass doors that covered a handful of shelves to her left.

"Nothing nearly as valuable as the Blake," Gunn replied as he leaned against the arm of the loveseat in the corner of the room. "A couple first-edition Joyce novels, a Faulkner, a few Hemingway titles, and a random collection of first edition twentieth-century novels from your typical British icons. It's a respectable collection, but nothing especially noteworthy."

"Who knew you had the Blake?" Sheridan asked as she leaned in closer to inspect the empty display case. There was nothing particularly special about the display—it was a simple glass case with a standard piano hinge along the back of the lid—and she shook her head as she glanced over her shoulder at Kelly, whose tight smile said he had reached the same conclusion she had.

They weren't going to get anything useful from the scene.

"Friends, family," Gunn answered her question. "I mean, it's been in my family for generations, and I inherited it when my grandmother passed away three years ago. It's not like it was a secret or anything."

Sheridan nodded. "Were you approached by anyone interested on buying it from you?"

He shook his head and then paused as a thoughtful expression dawned on his face. "Actually, I was. A German lawyer called me maybe…oh, nine months ago? I don't remember when, exactly, but I told him that I wasn't interested in selling and that was it."

"Did he ever contact you again?" Kelly asked.

"No. And nobody else has, either," Gunn said. "Honestly, I'd forgotten all about that call until you just asked about it. Do you think it's important?" he asked hopefully.

"That's hard to say right now," Kelly answered.

"Do you remember the lawyer's name?" Sheridan asked as Gunn's expression fell.

Gunn sighed. "I'm sorry. No. I had no reason to remember it because I have no interest in selling the book."

"Awesome," Kelly muttered.

Sheridan pursed her lips and made a mental note to ask Bartz about possibly trying to subpoena Gunn's phone records to try and see if they couldn't find the number of the German attorney in them somewhere. "Okay. Well, thank you for letting us have a look around, Mr. Gunn. We'll be in touch if we find anything, or have any further questions."

Kelly pulled a business card from his wallet and offered it to the man. "This is my card, in case you think of anything else or just need to get ahold of us."

"Thank you," Gunn murmured as he took the card and palmed it. He heaved a heavy sigh and then turned toward the door.

Sheridan shared a look with Kelly and the detectives that said they'd talk more outside, before they fell into line to follow Gunn back to the main floor.

"Let me get that information for you," Gunn said as he left them standing in the foyer, and when he returned, he offered it to her with a tired smile. "Hope this helps."

"Me too," she said as she took the sheet of paper from him. A quick glance showed two names and phone numbers, and she sighed as she folded it and slipped it into her blazer pocket. "Thanks."

"We'll be in touch," Nix promised Gunn as they reached the foyer.

Gunn just nodded as he opened the door. "Thank you."

Kelly led them down the stairs to the street, and they wandered a few dozen yards away from Gunn's door before huddling up. "So..." he began.

"I'm going to go out on a limb here and say that it's not fraud," Sheridan spoke up with a shrug. Gunn just seemed too genuinely upset about the loss to be faking it, in her opinion. "You said there were no suspicious prints?"

"Nope. The only prints we found belonged to him," Dearborn said.

"Great," Kelly muttered.

Sheridan sighed and ran a hand through her hair as she looked up and down the street. If nothing came back from the street cams or the GPS on the cleaning company's vans, they had exactly nothing to go on. "When can we expect your files?"

"We sent them over not two minutes after we got off the phone with Director Bartz," Dearborn reported. "You should have them now. You'll keep us in the loop?"

Sheridan nodded as she pulled one of her business cards from her coat pocket. "Here's my card. Will you text me the address for the interviews later?"

Dearborn and Nix nodded. "Yeah."

"All right, then," Kelly said, offering the detectives a hand. "I guess we'll see you guys in a few hours, then. Thanks for your help here."

"Thanks," Sheridan echoed as she, too, shook the detectives' hands.

They parted ways at that, and she waited until they were safely out of ear range before she asked Kelly, "So, since you know it's the first thing Bartz is gonna ask when we get back—do you think it's connected to the Dumas case?"

"I don't know." He shook his head. "The fact that our thief here didn't use a replacement book makes me think no, but the complete lack of any kind of evidence makes me think yes. You know?"

"Yeah. But with no evidence..."

He groaned. "I know. Let's go see what Bartz wants us to do about this. I have a feeling we'll be back our here later tonight after we interview the cleaners, going door-to-door to see if anyone suddenly remembers seeing anything when we flash our badges."

Sheridan sighed and nodded. It didn't happen often, but every once in a while they came across somebody who, for whatever reason, didn't want to help out the local police but who were motivated to speak up when they were approached by a federal agent. "Yeah. I have a feeling you're right, there."

twenty-five

"Knock, knock."

Parker looked up at Jess, who was smirking at her from her office doorway. "What are you doing here on a Saturday? Don't you have something better you could be doing?"

"I do, in fact." Jess shrugged as she ambled into her office and dropped into one of the charcoal-colored upholstered chairs facing her desk. She crossed her legs as she settled into the seat and arched a brow challengingly. "But I accidentally left my favorite lipstick in my desk drawer and, since I've got a date tonight, I thought I'd come by and pick it up. What's your excuse?"

"Work…" Parker motioned at the open file on her desk for the collector's wristwatch that'd been reported missing earlier in the week. It was a lie, of course. The claim was straightforward and, while worth a respectable twenty-five hundred dollar reward, it wasn't necessarily worth putting in the time on the weekend. The circle of collectors that would be interested in a 1954 Vacheron Constantin Chronometre Royal was small, and she was just waiting for a hit on the handful of feelers she'd set loose once she took the case. She didn't expect it to take much more than a week or two for her to locate the watch, which put it near the bottom of her list of cases requiring her attention. The real reason she had ended up in her office on a Saturday afternoon was that Sheridan had called earlier to say she had to work and couldn't meet her for their planned afternoon together, and she could think of nothing else to do with her time.

"Liar."

Parker did her best to seem earnest as she shook her head. "Sorry to disappoint you, Jess, but…"

"Weren't you supposed to go up to The Cloisters today with Sheridan? Wasn't that why you were studying up on all that Medieval European art yesterday?"

"Should have never asked you to pull that book from research for me." Parker sank back into her seat in defeat and shrugged. "I was, yes. But she had to cancel because of work."

"Must be something damn important to cancel…"

"I honestly don't have a clue. Sheridan didn't tell me what they're doing." She had an idea, of course, but she hoped against hope that the case keeping Sheridan so busy this week wasn't the Blake she and Oliver had helped relocate to Evie Marquis' private collection. "Whatever it is, we're not the ones holding the policy on it. We haven't gotten any claims worthy of the FBI's attention this week."

"You should call her."

"She's working," Parker reminded her with a little laugh.

"Yeah." Jess gave her a look that clearly said she thought she was being dense. "On a Saturday. When she could have been hanging out with your fine ass. You should give her a call and offer to bring her coffee or something."

Parker sighed and shook her head. What Jess was suggesting sounded amazing, but… "I sent her a text earlier that she still hasn't responded to."

Jess rolled her eyes. "Stop pouting and just call the girl, Ravenscroft."

"I'll think about it," she stalled.

"Don't think. Do." Jess slapped her hands on the arms of her chair and pushed herself to her feet. "Or do not. Whatever. I'm not fucking

Yoda. Are you going to be in on Monday, or are you taking the week off because of the holiday?"

"I'm planning on being here unless I need to go somewhere else for a recovery."

"I'll bring you a coffee from that place down the street, then." Jess sighed and dragged a hand through her hair. "See you Monday, Park."

"Bye, Jess." Parker shook her head as she watched her assistant saunter back out of her office and, after a brief stop at her desk, disappear toward the elevators.

Her eyes drifted to her phone as Jess' suggestion of calling Sheridan bounced back and forth in her mind, taunting her with the possibility of at least being able to talk to her for a minute or two, and she sighed in defeat as she reached for her phone. She tried to tell herself it was because she didn't want to deal with listening to Jess bug her about it on Monday, but the truth was that she'd been staring at the phone for the last hour, wishing it would ring. "May as well just give it a try and see what happens, right?" she asked herself as she pulled up Sheridan's number.

She honestly expected the call to ring through to voicemail, so she was surprised when Sheridan actually answered on the second ring with a tired-sounding, *"Hey, you."*

"Hey, yourself," Parker replied in a sympathetic tone. "How you doing?"

Sheridan blew out a loud breath that reverberated with frustration, and Parker imagined she'd probably be running a hand through her hair as she shrugged. *"I'm doing."*

"Am I interrupting?"

"I wouldn't have answered if you were," Sheridan said, though not unkindly. *"We're just spinning our wheels, chasing ghosts. You know, the usual."*

"Sounds exciting," Parker teased lightly, wanting nothing more than to hear some semblance of a smile creep into Sheridan's voice.

"Believe me, it's anything but exciting. Honestly, hearing your voice is the highlight of this too-long day. I'm so sorry I had to cancel on you. I was really looking forward to spending the day together."

"It's not a big deal," Parker assured her gently. She spun her chair so she could look out her window at the sun-kissed city below. It would have been a great day to wander The Cloisters and the gardens around the museum. "All that Medieval art made it this long, it'll still be around whenever we get up there to see it."

"Yeah…" Sheridan sighed.

"You guys going to be working late?"

"I don't know …" Sheridan's voice trailed off into a yawn.

Parker closed her eyes and sighed. She hated hearing Sheridan so worn down. And, even more than that, hated the idea that she might be part of the reason for it. "Can I bring you a coffee or something?"

"God, you're sweet, but you don't have to do that."

"I know I don't." Parker got to her feet and grabbed her backpack. "But I want to. Let me?" she asked softly as she headed for the door.

It took Sheridan long enough to reply that she was beginning to think that the answer was going to be no, and she couldn't keep from grinning when Sheridan said, *"What did I ever do to deserve you? Coffee would be wonderful. Thank you."*

"I'll be there as soon as I can," she promised.

"See you soon," Sheridan replied softly before disconnecting the call.

Thirty two-minutes after they'd said their goodbyes, Parker strode through the glass double doors on the twenty-seventh floor of the Federal Building and into the Art Crimes bullpen. The level of unease she had felt on her last visit had nothing on the leaden feeling of apprehension that settled in her stomach now that she'd helped Ollie steal the Blake right from under Sheridan's nose, but she forced herself to ignore it. If bringing Sheridan a cup of coffee from the nearby Starbucks made her smile, then it was certainly worth the guilt she was suffering now.

Kelly was the one to notice her arrival first, and he greeted her with a plaintive, "Please tell me you brought me coffee too?"

She smiled apologetically. "I'm sorry. I didn't know you wanted any." She should have asked, but she'd been so focused on Sheridan that the idea of Kelly being stuck at work too never even entered her thoughts.

"It's because I'm a dude, isn't it?" he challenged with a playful pout.

Parker laughed. "I can assure you that's not the case."

"Whatever," he muttered, his lips quirked in a playful grin as he waved her off. He leaned back in his chair and, in a scene similar to the last time she visited, yelled, "Yo, Sloan! You have a visitor!"

Parker looked around the office, waiting for the tide of gawkers to descend on her like before, but the only person to come striding into the bullpen was Sheridan. "Hey, you," she greeted Sheridan with a smile as she offered her the large caramel macchiato she'd picked up for her. "Coffee, as promised."

"You are an angel," Sheridan murmured as she reached for the cup.

"An angel who forgets you're not the only one spending their weekend at the office," Kelly piped up. He laughed at the glare Sheridan gave him and held his hands up in surrender. "Yeah, yeah. I know. Behave or Ivy kicks my ass. We've been going at this thing for hours and we can both use a break, so I'm gonna go get myself a cup of coffee that's not from the break room. You ladies behave yourselves while I'm gone," he warned, wagging a playful finger at them as he grabbed his coat and made his way toward the elevators.

"What's the thing with Ivy kicking his ass if he doesn't behave?" Parker asked with a laugh. "Is that different from the other ass-kickings she's given him?"

"It actually is, but it's a long story." Sheridan smiled as she motioned toward hers and Kelly's desks. "You want to sit down?"

"Sure." Parker rubbed her hands over the thighs of her jeans as she made herself comfortable in the chair Kelly had just abandoned and looked around the bullpen. "Nobody else working?"

Sheridan shook her head as she pulled her chair close enough that her foot brushed against Parker's leg when she crossed her legs. "It's just Kel and I working this one for the time being. Bartz was in earlier, but he had a family thing he had to go to, so it's just the two of us left in here now."

Parker nodded as she pulled her water bottle from her backpack. She'd debated getting herself an iced coffee, but decided against the caffeine because it'd keep her up all night. "I got you a caramel macchiato—was that right?"

"It's perfect," Sheridan assured her. "Seriously, Parker, thank you."

"It's my pleasure." Parker smiled at the way Sheridan's eyes fluttered shut and her lips curled into a soft smile as she sipped at her drink. Sheridan was so very beautiful that her chest felt tight as she stared at her, making it hard for her heart to beat properly. A problem that was instantly enviable when Sheridan's eyes opened to look at her and her heart stopped beating altogether. Questions flashed across navy blue eyes that seemed to bore into her very soul, replaced with what she swore was shy understanding half a heartbeat later and, god, it was all she could do to not lean over and kiss her.

"Parker?" Sheridan asked softly, her pulse jumping in her throat as she met and held her gaze.

The way Sheridan's eyes dipped to her mouth when she licked her lips didn't escape her attention, and she mentally groaned as she forced herself to keep her ass in her seat and her hands to herself. "It's nothing," she whispered. She shook her head and cleared her throat softly. "I'm just really glad I came down here."

Sheridan smiled. "I am, too." She sighed and crossed her legs as she took a sip of her coffee. "How's your day been?"

"Pretty typical. Went to yoga this morning, and then I went into the office to get some work done." Parker laughed at the way Sheridan rolled her eyes. "What?"

"You could have gone to the museum without me, you know." Sheridan shook her head. "You didn't have to waste your Saturday working just because I am."

"I can do lots of things without you," Parker agreed. She lifted her right shoulder in a small shrug and, because she figured that, in this, she could allow herself to be honest, added, "But I'd rather not."

"Oh, Parker," Sheridan whispered. Sheridan's smile softened as they stared at each other, the truths they'd been dancing around since that night in Paris conveyed perfectly in the silence of the moment.

After what felt like forever spent staring into Sheridan's eyes, Parker cleared her throat softly and looked away. They were in Sheridan's office and Kelly could be back any minute, and now was not the time for these kinds of truths to be shared. "So, yeah," she continued in a stronger voice, hoping it would help guide their conversation to less dangerous topics, "Jess stopped by the office while I was working to pick up something she'd forgotten in her desk right before I called you this afternoon, channeled her inner Yoda to give me a hard time about calling you, and now I'm here."

Sheridan chuckled. "Yoda, huh?"

"Many skills, my assistant has," Parker confirmed with a small shake of her head.

"Yeah, well," Sheridan murmured as she lifted her cup to her lips and took a small sip. "Remind me to send your assistant flowers Monday as a thank you for using the Force to send you down here today."

"Oh god, that'd go straight to her head," Parker laughed. "Please don't. I'll never hear the end of it."

"Never hear the end of what?" Kelly asked as he ambled back into the unit with a takeaway cup from the nearby Starbucks.

"How are you back already?" Sheridan gaped at him.

Parker lifted her hand to her mouth to hide her smile.

"Why? Did I interrupt something good?" Kelly looked between them, waggling his eyebrows suggestively.

"Afraid not, Agent Innes," Parker said, winking at Sheridan as she pushed herself up from his chair. "Call me later? When things are less crazy?"

"Things are always crazy," Kelly scoffed.

"But I will call you anyway," Sheridan interjected, shooting him a dirty look as she got to her feet. "And I'll walk you to the elevator."

"You don't have to do that," Parker murmured as Sheridan's fingertips grazed the small of her back.

"I know." Sheridan smirked. "But I want to. Let me?"

Parker chuckled softly as she recognized that Sheridan was using her words from earlier against her, and tipped her head in a small nod. "Okay." She pointedly avoided looking at Kelly as she allowed Sheridan to guide her toward the exit. Once the heavy glass door had closed behind them, she sighed and turned to look at Sheridan. All the truths they'd been avoiding shone brightly in Sheridan's eyes, and she tilted her head to the side as she just managed to stop herself from leaning in to kiss her.

"Thank you," Sheridan whispered as she pulled her into a light hug.

"Thank you, Sheridan," Parker breathed as she wrapped her arms around Sheridan's waist and held her close. She closed her eyes as she leaned her cheek against the side of Sheridan's head, and took a slow, deep breath as she felt Sheridan melt into her. A soft sigh slipped from her lips when she felt Sheridan's hold loosen in preparation to pull away, and she blinked her eyes open as she let her hands fall back to her sides. She couldn't help but smile when she saw the small, happy smile that curled Sheridan's lips, and she shook her head as she reached out to tuck a wild curl behind Sheridan's ear. Her smile widened as she watched Sheridan's eyes flutter shut at the way her fingers grazed her cheek, and she shook her head as she forced herself to take a step back so she wouldn't be tempted to cradle that soft, soft cheek in her hand and guide their lips together. "Call me later?"

Sheridan's throat bobbed as she nodded. "I will," she whispered huskily as the elevator chimed and the doors began to slide open.

Parker took a deep breath and let it go in a rush. "I can't wait."

TWENTY-SIX

Dusk was falling on Brooklyn, casting a blanket of shadows over the brick facades of the modest row houses that lined Ivy and Rachel's block as Sheridan stepped onto the front stoop. Either end of the street was blocked with sawhorses decorated with red, white, and blue balloons, keeping the street clear of vehicles as the neighborhood enjoyed a good old-fashioned block party for the Fourth. Kids on bikes and skateboards raced up and down the street with abandon, while adults gathered around every possible tailgating game imaginable. The night was lit by porch lights and streetlights, the air was filled with loud conversations and laughter, and the soundtrack to it all was a jumble of songs pouring through windows that were thrown open despite the humidity, the conflicting beats blending to create an enjoyable melody of their own.

Sheridan smiled as she sat on the stoop, letting her legs stretch down the stairs as she leaned back on her hands, more than content to watch everything happening around her. All of her worries about having Parker spend the afternoon with her colleagues and friends had ended up being for naught, as Ivy's threats had more than done the job of keeping the oftentimes uncontrollable group perfectly well-behaved, and the day had been as wonderful as she had hoped it would be.

"I'm glad you guys came," Rachel drawled, startling Sheridan from her thoughts as she sat beside her on the stoop. She motioned toward the street where Kelly, Parker, and Ivy were gathered around one half of the cornhole set in front of their house. "She's amazing."

Sheridan nodded as she let gaze travel over Parker's tanned, defined arms and long, long legs. "She certainly is…" Her voice trailed off as she watched Kelly's red bean bag sail gracefully through the air before hitting the angled board twenty feet away and sliding through the hole near the top. "Whoa."

"Yeah," Rachel agreed with a laugh.

"Boom!" Kelly yelled, throwing his hands in the air victoriously as he turned to taunt Parker as Ivy, the judge for this round of their game, laughed beside her. "Beat that, Ravenscroft!"

"So, do I want to know what they're doing?" Rachel asked.

Sheridan shrugged. She'd been inside helping Rachel with the dishes so she hadn't been privy to whatever agreements the group had come to, but judging by the way Kelly kept his foot on the exact spot of pavement he'd been standing when he took his shot until Parker was standing at the same spot, it wasn't too difficult to figure out what they were doing. "Looks like they're playing H-O-R-S-E."

"Of course they are," Rachel chuckled. "Because cornhole isn't difficult enough on its own after an afternoon of drinking. Whose idea was it?"

"I honestly don't know," Sheridan replied with a little laugh as she tracked the slow arc of Parker's arm as she practiced her shot. "It could've been any of them," she added as the blue bean bag left Parker's hand and glided through the air. She bit her lip as she tracked the progress of the bean bag, and laughed when it dropped right through the middle of the hole.

"Nothing but net, baby!" Parker crowed. She made a little show of flexing her arms as she teased, "You ready to lose, Innes?"

Kelly laughed and shrugged. "Pretty much always, honestly. Whatcha got planned, Parker?"

Sheridan held her breath when Parker looked at her, and then completely forgot how to breathe as a slow, easy smile curled Parker's lips.

"You've got it so bad," Rachel teased in a quiet voice. "And I can't blame you in the least because goddamn, Sloan, the way that woman looks at you…"

Sheridan blushed, but could not tear her gaze away from Parker, who was now headed her way.

"I've got an idea," Parker called over her shoulder as she hopped up onto the sidewalk.

Rachel chuckled and gave her a little pat on the knee. "I'm gonna go by Ivy and leave you two alone."

"You don't have to…" Sheridan started to protest, but her voice trailed off as Rachel skipped down the stairs, clearly ignoring her.

"Beat him fast, Ravenscroft," Rachel told Parker as they passed each other at the foot of the stoop. "We've got some time still before the fireworks, but if I had to help Ivy carry that damn fire pit up to the roof for this thing, we're gonna fucking use it."

"I will do my best," Parker assured Rachel, her attention never wavering from Sheridan.

There was a warmth in Parker's gaze that was hypnotic, her pale, pale eyes dark even in the yellow halo of light that spilled around them, and Sheridan bit her lip as she watched Parker's thigh flex as she knelt in front of her.

"Hey, you," Parker murmured.

"Hey, yourself," Sheridan replied just as gently as she sat up. A light breeze stirred the air, sending Parker's hair into her eyes, and she smiled as she dared reach up and brush it back behind her ear. The softness of Parker's cheek was only trumped by the soft, oh so soft sigh that tumbled from her lips as she slowly caressed the line of her jaw. The world fell away as she stared into Parker's eyes, aware of nothing but the naked affection staring back at her and the heavy beat of Parker's pulse beneath her fingertips as her touch drifted to the hollow beneath her jaw.

Parker's eyes grew darker the longer her touch lingered, the stutter of her breath a ragged plea that she was helpless to resist. Her eyes darted ever so briefly to Parker's mouth, and she whimpered as she watched Parker's tongue slide over those pale pink lips she so longed to taste.

"Come on, you two! Stop with the eye-sex and just…" Kelly's voice trailed off into an *umpf* of surprise. "Christ, Ivy! Sorry, okay?"

Sheridan blinked as her hand fell back to her lap at the interruption, embarrassment spreading in hot waves over her cheeks as her eyes dropped to the stair beside Parker's knee. "I'm so sorry."

"God, Sheridan," Parker breathed, her voice soft and her touch gentle as she lifted her chin to look at her. "Please don't apologize for that…"

"It's just…" Her voice trailed off in a sigh.

"It's very much that," Parker agreed, her eyes softening with understanding. "How about I go finish thoroughly embarrassing your partner, and then we can just go hang out by that fire pit Rachel was telling me about until it's time for the fireworks. Does that sound good?"

Sheridan nodded, and her pulse stumbled over itself at the way Parker smiled at her in return, like she had just given her everything in the world she could have ever wanted.

"Good." Parker's eyes danced over her face one last time before, with a heavy sigh, she pushed herself to standing and glanced at the trio in the street that was very obviously looking anywhere other than at them. "It's a good thing Ollie isn't here. He'd be just as bad as they are."

"I'd like to meet him." Sheridan chuckled at the look of surprise Parker shot her and shrugged. "Maybe not with those guys there the first time, but…" Her voice trailed off as Parker stared at her so intently that it wasn't hard to tell that she was trying to decide if she was being honest about wanting to meet her brother. Which was ridiculous, because how could she not want to meet someone who was so important to her? "I don't know, maybe someday?"

"Yeah. Someday," Parker repeated, tipping her head in a small nod. She blew out a loud breath and, with what looked like it took a herculean amount of effort, turned away from her and back toward the street. "Okay. Innes, you ready to lose?"

"Bring it," Kelly taunted.

Sheridan shook her head as she watched Parker walk up to the curb and stare at the target board that was increasingly difficult to make out as deeper shadows enveloped the street. Parker took two long steps backwards and stared at the target one last time before she turned her back to it.

"Backwards? Seriously?" Kelly asked incredulously. "Twenty bucks says you miss by at least five feet."

"You're on, Innes," Parker drawled, the sly smirk that tugged at her lips unmistakable. She honestly thought she was going to make it.

Sheridan shook her head. It was a fool's bet, there was no way in hell Parker would be able to make that shot, but she couldn't look away as Parker took a deep breath and, with a dip of her legs to aid her throw, hurled the bean bag over her shoulder. A hollow-sounding thud followed a couple seconds later, and she strained her eyes to try to see how close Parker had gotten with her throw.

"No way!" Ivy yelled. "She freakin' made it!"

Parker lifted her hands in the air and turned toward her with a smile so bright it could have lit the entire block. "You want to have a try, Innes? Or do you submit?" she called over her shoulder.

Kelly laughed. "I don't know how the hell you did it, but yeah. I give up. You win, Parker."

Parker nodded as she stared at Sheridan. "Yeah, I do."

"All right! Fire pit time!" Ivy declared with an authoritative clap of her hands. "Let's go!"

Sheridan scrambled to her feet and moved out of the way so Ivy could lead the group up to the roof, and she wasn't at all surprised when Parker stopped beside her. Once everyone else had traipsed inside and it was just the two of them left on the porch, she looked at Parker and murmured, "I can't believe you made that shot."

Parker laughed. "Me neither," she admitted with a little shrug. "Must be my lucky night." She placed a light hand over the small of Sheridan's back and added, "Come on. If we don't get up there soon, you know Kelly's gonna have something to say about it."

Sheridan rolled her eyes as she turned toward the front door. "He's gonna say something anyway, I'm sure. But you're right."

The hand on her back drifted to her hand, long fingers wrapping around her palm and pulling her up short. "Are you okay?"

"Yeah." Hating the look of unease on Parker's face, Sheridan lifted her free hand to cradle her cheek. Her stomach flipped at the way Parker leaned into the touch. Her eyes fluttered as she leaned in, the audible hitch of Parker's breath the final push she needed to do what she'd almost done earlier and brush the lightest of kisses over her lips. "I'm great," she whispered as she pulled away. She chewed her lip anxiously as she waited for Parker's reaction to what she'd just done and, when the silence seemed to stretch forever but was probably only a second or two, asked hesitantly, "You?"

Parker huffed a laugh and looked at her like she was crazy for even needing to ask. "The most beautiful woman I know just kissed me. I'd say I'm having a damn good night right now."

Sheridan blushed. "You're—"

"Serious," Parker interrupted, an arched eyebrow daring her to challenge her. She wrapped her hands around Sheridan's hips, holding her close, the touch gentle enough that she could pull away if she needed to. Her expression softened to what could only be described as hopeful as her head tilted to the right and the left side of her mouth quirked in a shy smile. "I know we're taking things slow, and if you need more time, I will totally understand, but after that kiss…" She sighed and shook her head. "I just gotta ask—can I take you out on a date?"

A slow smile curled Sheridan's lips as she nodded. "I'd like that."

Sheridan laughed when the hands on her hips pulled her into a hug, and sighed happily as Parker's lips brushed over her cheek to whisper in her ear, "Thank you."

"Thank you," Sheridan murmured. For as much as she'd love nothing more than to stay right where they were for the rest of the night, there were people upstairs waiting on them, and she pulled away from Parker's embrace with a soft sigh and a regretful smile. "They're gonna say something if we don't get up there soon."

"Let them." Parker grinned and took her hand. "Come on, Sloan. Let's go watch some fireworks."

Sheridan followed Parker up the stairs to the rooftop deck, and although she was prepared to respond with a flippant "fuck you" to any comment her friends might throw their way, she was surprised when they were instead greeted with three pleased smiles as the conversation they were having continued without missing a beat.

"Drinks are in the cooler," Ivy offered, waving toward the cooler at the back of the deck with her beer bottle.

Sheridan was so thrown by the utter lack of reaction their late arrival garnered that it took her a moment to regroup, and thank god Parker recovered faster than she did because otherwise everyone would be unable to ignore how awkward she was.

"You want anything?" Parker asked softly.

She shrugged. "Sure. If you do."

Parker gave her hand a squeeze. "Okay. Go find us a seat and I'll be there in a sec."

She nodded and, with a deep breath steeling her nerves, let go of Parker's hand as they moved in opposite directions. Ivy and Rachel had set up three small outdoor sofas in a U-shape around the square slate fire pit that crackled red and orange and gold in the night, and she took a deep breath as she sat down on the end of the empty sofa closest to her partner.

Ivy was talking about how hard it'd been to find a fire pit that both she and Rachel agreed on, and Sheridan just smiled at her as Kelly leaned over to ask softly, "Everything good?"

She nodded, her eyes immediately searching for the source of everything that was good in her life at the moment, and smiled when Parker's gaze met her own. "Everything's perfect."

"Good." He bumped her knee with his condensation-covered beer bottle and laughed when she squeaked in surprise and quickly wiped away the wetness.

"Do I need to crack heads over here?" Parker called out teasingly as she sat down on the sofa beside Sheridan and offered her a beer.

"Nah. We're cool," Kelly assured her.

"Anyway," Ivy spoke up, shooting the group a playfully reproachful glare. "Like I was saying…"

Sheridan laughed and sank back in the sofa beside Parker. A flutter of happiness rippled in her chest when Parker leaned back in a way that let their shoulders touch, and she tried to hide the smile that little touch elicited from her by taking a long drink from her beer. Judging by the way Rachel's eyes twinkled and Ivy's lips curled in a smirk as they pointedly didn't say anything about it, she failed miserably, but the warm weight of Parker's shoulder against her own made it hard to care about their amusement.

It was amazing how easily the five of them fell into conversation, and they all looked up in surprise at the first loud boom from the river.

"Fireworks," Kelly cheered as he jumped to his feet and hurried toward the front edge of the rooftop deck that looked out toward the river.

Sheridan laughed as Parker leaned forward to set her empty bottle beside hers on the fire pit surround before pulling her to her feet, and she put up no resistance when Parker led her over to the edge of the roof as well. Their view to the river was anything but unobstructed, but the house was close enough to barges that they could still see every flash of color that exploded in the sky.

She smiled as Parker's arms wrapped around her waist from behind as the show picked up steam, and sighed as she relaxed back into her.

"Is this okay?" Parker asked softly against her ear.

She nodded and, after a quick glance at their companions to make sure they weren't looking their way, dared to lift her chin and capture Parker's lips in a slow, sweet kiss. "It's perfect," she assured her as she pulled away.

Parker grinned and, after a brief moment of hesitation, darted forward to kiss her again. "Yes, you are."

twenty-seven

Parker checked the time on her phone as she exited the subway station closest to her house and groaned. She should have known better than to meet Sheridan for a quick brunch at a romantic little bistro a few blocks south of the park, but with the rest of her weekend already booked and the memory of what it'd felt like to kiss Sheridan so fresh in her mind, she'd been literally unable to turn down the invitation. Not when the odds were good that she wouldn't get the opportunity to spend any quality time with her until their date the following Saturday.

Though, if she were being honest, it wasn't the brunch itself that made her late enough now that she was just barely resisting the urge to break into a jog. No, that was the fault of her complete inability to tear herself away from Sheridan's company.

Even though they'd traded frequent texts and spent too many hours late at night on the phone, there had been a shadow of uncertainty dimming Sheridan's smile when they first met up on the sidewalk in front of the bistro that broke her heart. It killed her that Sheridan thought she might've changed her mind about them when she wanted nothing more than shout the news from the rooftop. So, despite the fact that they'd yet to discuss how comfortable the other was with public displays of affection—holding hands was often written off as just gals being pals, after all—she'd done the only thing she could think of to chase that hesitancy away. She smiled as she remembered the way Sheridan had gasped in surprise when she leaned in and, in the middle of a busy midtown sidewalk, kissed her softly, lingering far too-briefly in the caress before she pulled back to nuzzle her cheek and whisper hello.

She'd never witnessed anything as incredible as the way Sheridan blossomed in that moment, happiness and an oh-so-fragile hope dawning across her face as she took her hand and walked through the door she'd pulled open for her. And watching the way that hope had taken root in the near-permanent smile that had crinkled the corners of her eyes and the carefree sound of her laughter that flowed more and more freely as the minutes ticked by had been so utterly enchanting that she didn't have the willpower to make herself say goodbye.

So, yeah. If she'd actually left the bistro when she'd needed to instead of lingering for another half an hour because she was weak and Sheridan's smile was a siren's call she was unable and unwilling to even try to resist, she would have been home in plenty of time for Oliver's arrival. But she couldn't find it in herself to care too much about her tardiness. Not when it meant that she'd gotten to spend those extra stolen minutes with Sheridan, holding hands beneath the table like a couple of teenagers as the world swept around them in a blur.

Parker shook her head when she spotted the nose of Oliver's Prius poking around the corner of at the edge of Riverside and 107th, and broke into a little jog to cover the remaining distance to her front door. "Of course you're on time today," she muttered, scowling at the little bit of Oliver's car she could still see as she slid her key into the lock.

The sound of the Yankee's announcer blared from the surround speakers in the den, and she immediately made her way toward the cozy television room off the larger formal living room. She could not care less about baseball—no matter how many times Gregory tried to convince her of its merits—but Oliver had played shortstop through college, and she knew Gregory loved having somebody to watch the game with who appreciated it as much as he did. She grinned when she got close enough to the den to see Oliver and Gregory on the sofa that faced the television, their sock-clad feet propped on the antique mahogany coffee table in front of them. Oliver's duffel and laptop bag were stacked next to his shoes on the floor beside the sofa, and from the half-full glasses of water on the table, it was clear that he'd been there for a while.

"Well, that makes sense," Parker murmured under her breath when she spotted the box score in the upper left corner of the screen as she ambled into the room. Gregory's Yankees were playing Oliver's Mariners, which meant they were probably going to want to watch the entire game together to see whose team came out on top. She honestly wouldn't have been surprised if Oliver had driven down a little early so he'd be here in time for the first pitch.

"Wish I'd known they were playing," she drawled as she propped herself on the arm of the sofa next to her brother, "I wouldn't have rushed home."

"Well, would you look who finally showed up," Oliver teased as he smiled up at her. "How was brunch?"

She rolled her eyes. "Wonderful, until I couldn't ignore the time any longer and had to say goodbye to come back here to meet your stupid ass so we can figure out what we're going to do for Tina's birthday. And," she added, shooting Gregory a playful glare, "thanks so much for telling him that."

Gregory shrugged unrepentantly. "Love you too, kiddo," he quipped as he picked up his glass of water and took a sip. "How's Sheridan?"

"Have you met her?" Oliver asked, turning away from her to look at Gregory. When Gregory smirked and nodded, he whined, "No fair. I've been stuck listening to her fawn over Sheridan for *years* and you get to meet her first?"

"Oh, believe me, Ollie, Sheridan Sloan definitely worth fawning over," Gregory told him, his eyes twinkling with amusement as he winked at her.

"Oh my god," she muttered, shaking her head. "Do you two want me to leave so you can gossip about her?"

"Aww, come on, Parker, where'd be the fun in that?" Oliver sassed with a grin.

Gregory chuckled, and Parker sighed as she pointed a warning finger at him. "Please do not egg him on."

"Psht, like I need egging on," Oliver scoffed. "So, was this like a little date? Did you get a goodbye kiss?"

"In a way," she allowed with a grin, rather looking forward to their reaction to the bombshell she hadn't shared with either of them yet. "And, as a matter of fact, I did get a very sweet kiss goodbye from her."

"What?" Oliver and Gregory gasped in perfect unison, the baseball game on television forgotten as they turned to gape at her.

Parker laughed and shook her head. "Nope. That's all you're getting. I'm gonna go upstairs and do some laundry. You two have fun watching your game. Gregory, if you've got any projects to put him to work on, please feel free to torture the boy."

"Hey!" Oliver protested with a laugh.

"Don't worry, Ollie," Gregory said, chuckling as he patted his leg. "Everything around this old place is working just fine since you got the water heater all fixed last time you were down."

The crack of a bat making contact with a ball snapped through the speakers, and they all looked at the screen as the announcer shared, in a clearly disappointed tone, "And that's another home run for Judge, this time a grand slam that puts the Yankees up six to one in the top of the second."

"That's my boy!" Gregory cheered, smacking Oliver on the arm as he pointed at the screen.

Oliver groaned and shook his head. "Yep, it's definitely one of those years again..." His voice trailed off into a sigh.

Parker gave him a sympathetic smile. "You coming up with me, or you gonna sit and watch the rest of this beat-down?"

"I don't know." Oliver pursed his lips and frowned at the television, which was now playing a commercial for boner pills because the Mariners were already making a pitching change. She didn't know much about baseball, but even she knew that it wasn't good if the starting pitcher was pulled in the second inning.

"Go work on your plans for your foster mom's birthday surprise," Gregory said, tipping his head at Parker. He smirked and added, "I'll just cheer extra-loud when we score so you have an idea of how bad you're losing."

"You know, shit like that is the reason kids stick their parents in awful nursing homes," Oliver told him with a disgruntled huff.

Gregory affectionately patted Oliver's cheek and winked at Parker. "Guess it's a good thing she's the one who's got power of attorney for me if I should become incapacitated, huh?"

"I see how it is," Oliver sighed dramatically. "You love her more."

"I love you the same," Gregory insisted with a laugh. "She's just here and you're all the way up in Boston."

"And, besides, you're going live forever, Gregory, so it doesn't matter," Parker told him. She'd been touched when he had asked her if she would be willing to take on that role, as he was concerned about granting it to any of his friends who were all his age or older and he didn't have any children to bestow the burden upon, and she had been quick to assure him that she would do it. She dreaded the day she would have to make decisions on his behalf, but she would never trust a lawyer to decide what was best for him.

"Of course I am," Gregory agreed easily. "Are you sticking around for the night, Ollie?"

"That's the plan," Oliver confirmed as he pushed himself to his feet.

"Good. I'm gonna take you two out to dinner tonight, then. If I make a reservation at Lincoln Square for seven o'clock, would that work for you guys?"

Parker smiled and, not needing to see what Oliver thought, nodded. "Seven sounds wonderful, Gregory." If she couldn't spend the night with Sheridan, Oliver and Gregory were, without a doubt, her best next option.

"Can I borrow a sport coat?" Oliver asked. "I didn't bring anything that dressy, but I've got jeans and a polo in my bag that could go with a black jacket and look fancy enough for that place."

"Of course. Guess it's a good thing we're the same size, huh?" Gregory grinned. "Although, those muscles of yours will fill out the sleeves a lot more than these noodles of mine."

Oliver chuckled. "You're ridiculous."

Gregory's eyes twinkled with amusement as he waved at the door. "Go on, you two. I'll see you later."

Parker gave him a little wave before she turned to leave, and she wasn't surprised when Oliver caught up to her a few seconds later. "You could've stayed and watched the game. I wouldn't have minded."

"Hell yeah! That's another one!" Gregory yelled.

Oliver shook his head. "I'm pretty sure that this is one game I'd much rather not watch play out, thanks." He smirked and bumped her in the back of the leg with his duffle bag. "So, things between you and Sheridan are going good, huh?"

"They are. I'm actually taking her out next Saturday on a date."

"Nice," he cheered softly as they started up the stairs. "Do you have an idea for what you're gonna do yet?"

"No idea," she admitted with a shrug. "It's gotta be romantic as hell, though. I want to sweep her off her feet."

"Always a solid plan when a beautiful woman is involved," Oliver agreed, tossing his duffel toward the guest room he always stayed in as they rounded the landing and started climbing toward her personal front door.

She sighed softly and nodded. She never bothered to lock her door unless Gregory was having company, so she pushed it open and called,

"Close that after you, huh?" over her shoulder as she strode inside. "Are you hungry?"

"Nah, I stopped at a little diner in Hartford and put down a massive plate of pancakes," he shared, patting his belly. "I'm good."

"Okay." Parker veered away from the kitchen and made herself comfortable on her sofa. "So, what are you thinking for Tina's birthday?"

"Well, when I called back there on Thursday, Brett asked if we'd be able to make to the little party he's throwing her. I didn't want to commit on your behalf, so I told him I'd talk to you about it and we'd get back to him."

"Even if I couldn't go for some reason, that's no reason you couldn't."

"I know. But it'd be weird being there without you. And, besides, I got looking at it and it would be a perfect opportunity to knock off another title from Marquis' list."

Parker ran a hand through her hair and looked at him incredulously. "Really, Ollie?"

"What? The comic is in Seattle and we'd already be out there, so it'd be a case of two-birds-one-stone."

She shook he head. "Did Marquis have a problem with the Blake or something?"

He frowned. "No. She was pleased as punch to get it, honestly. Looked like a kid on Christmas morning as she flipped through it. Wasn't even grossed out by the creepy-as-fuck pictures. I couldn't give her the grand walk-through like you did in Paris, but she seemed trust that it was authentic."

"So that's three million in the Luxembourg account, now," Parker pointed out, hoping that he'd see where she was coming from.

"It is," he agreed, nodding. "One and a half each."

"I don't need or want the money, Ollie." She shook her head. "I'd much rather just be done with this whole thing."

"But swiping the comic would be a walk in the park."

Despite the fact that she wasn't at all keen on the idea of stealing another title from Marquis' list, Parker muttered, "It still boggles my mind that she has a comic book on that damn list. I mean, every other title is, like, a literary classic in some form and then she's all…hey, and by the way, I want Superman."

Oliver chuckled. "It's probably for her son. Anyway, Langley lives in Queen Anne Hill, which isn't that far from Brett and Tina's."

"Oliver…" Parker sighed.

"It'd be nothing to drive over there and do the job. And," he added, holding up a hand to silence the protest he could see she was about to make, "I went digging through his email to see if I could find anything that might make the job easier. He and his family are leaving for Hawaii the Wednesday before Tina's birthday, so the house will be empty."

She shook her head. "We don't need to do this Ollie. It's reckless."

"It's not." He huffed a breath and the couch beside her dipped and then lifted as he pushed himself to his feet. "I'll override his security system, we go in at night through the back alley that those houses all have, and we're in and out before you can blink. We can do this."

She blinked her eyes open to look at him. "It's not our ability that I'm questioning."

"Come on, Parker. We're going to be there anyway…"

She sighed and pushed herself to her feet. She held up a warning finger to silence any argument he'd be tempted to make, and made her way over to the French doors that overlooked the rooftop patio. Storm clouds would have been a much more appropriate backdrop for the maelstrom nature of her thoughts at the moment than the bright sun that shone in the clear blue sky, and she sighed. "Ollie…"

"You don't have to do anything besides help me out that night. If I knew how to pick locks, I would just go without you, but we both know that I'm nowhere near as good at that shit as you are."

She grit her teeth. She could tell from his tone that he wasn't going to let the issue drop, but she still pointed out, "This is a monumentally stupid idea." He just stared at her, his smile grim and his eyes pleading, reminding her of the time when they were eleven and he'd begged her to help him run away from an abusive foster. He was going to do this with or without her help, and she shook her head as she muttered, "Fine."

He whooped and then a moment later she was swept off the floor in a spinning bear hug. "You're the best, Parker."

She closed her eyes and sighed. She wasn't, but she was trying. And failing, it seemed, but she really was trying. "I'm not cancelling my date with Sheridan for next weekend, so I'm not flying out there until next Sunday at the earliest."

"That's fine," he agreed quickly. "Tina's birthday isn't until Thursday and her party isn't until Saturday, so that'd leave plenty of time to do this other stuff."

"Are we surprising Tina at the party, or does Brett think we're going to stay with them?" Staying with the Johanns would mean a couple nights of couch-surfing for the both of them, but they'd done it before.

"All he said was that the party was a surprise. I think they'd be fine with us riding their sofas for however long we're there, but I'd be more comfortable in a hotel. There's that Hampton Inn a few miles from the house we could get a room at. But if you'd rather stay with them…"

"I'm fine at the Hampton. But since we're going out there early, if Brett isn't intending we be a surprise, I think it'd be nice to spend a little extra time visiting. We haven't been back since last Thanksgiving."

"Yeah, I know. It just seems like we're in the way there sometimes."

"I know. But they like when we visit and god knows we owe them at least that after everything they did for us."

"Yeah, yeah," he sighed and lifted his computer onto his lap. "Okay. So, you want to fly direct, yes?"

"Duh."

"So a four-hour layover in Minneapolis it is, then," he sassed.

She shook her head and gave his shoulder a little shove. She hated that he was so cavalier about all of this, but he'd always been a little shortsighted when it came to anything that didn't affect him directly. "Fuck you."

He reached out and shoved her back as he scrolled through whatever screen he was looking at. "Whatever. Okay, so we can both get a flight that lands there at a quarter till eleven. Sound good?"

"Yeah. Just let me get my card for ya."

"I got it." He waved her off.

"You sure?"

"Yeah. You're doing this to help me even though I know that you'd rather not, the least I can do is pick up the cost of your ticket."

"Olls..."

"Seriously, Parker, I got this part." He leaned over to bump their shoulders together. "Enough about this, though. You finally got to kiss Sheridan Sloan, huh? How was it?"

She smiled. "Better than I'd ever dreamed it might be."

TWENTY-EIGHT

Sheridan shook her head as the small carry on suitcase beside her desk fell over for what seemed like the tenth time since she and Kelly had returned to the office to push through some paperwork that would wrap up their side of the investigation to the case they'd been working in Denver since Sunday afternoon. A Lakota Sioux war shield had been stolen from the Denver museum, but the Native American art world was a small one, and it didn't take them long to trace the piece to a private collector in Vail. The man didn't at all appreciate having the considerable weight of the FBI raining down on his head, but the shield was back where it belonged and the museum was in the process of updating their security practices to keep a theft like that from happening again.

It was a much-needed win in what seemed like a string of never-ending losses so far as their cases had been going recently, and she sighed as she scribbled her name on the final page of the report and flipped the case file shut. "Done."

"Now if only we scrape together some idea of what the fuck happened with that Blake," Kelly said.

"Right?" She blew out a loud breath and raked a hand through her hair as she looked at the file for the missing Blake that was in the front tier of her organizer on her desk. They had checked the GPS for every single one of the vans owned by the cleaning company that Gunn's neighbor said she saw outside his house, but they all showed that the vans had never left the places they were supposed to be. Add in the fact that the street cameras were so buggy that day that even their best tech guys couldn't make anything out of the static, and they had nothing. And then, as if that complete bust wasn't enough, the only number with a German area code that they could find in Gunn's phone records for the lawyer he said had contacted him was literally a dead-end, as in nothing but a dial-tone an no idea who'd set the account up in the first place. Until something new popped up, she had no idea where else they should try looking next. "Maybe we should try a Ouija Board or something..."

"Seriously," he muttered through a yawn.

"Stop," she warned through a yawn of her own. "Goddamn it, Innes."

He laughed. "Sorry."

"No you're not." She groaned and rocked back in her chair so she was looking at the drop-tile ceiling overhead.

"Um, Sloan..." Kelly chuckled.

She shook her head. They were technically done for the day, and she just needed a couple minutes to recharge her batteries. He'd been talking pretty much nonstop since they met in the lobby of their hotel that morning, and if she didn't get some kind of peace and quiet soon, she was going to scream. "Just give me a minute before you start up again, okay?"

"But..."

"One minute," she insisted.

She smiled when he muttered, "All right, lady. You're the boss."

Papers rustled on Kelly's desk, and she wondered what in the hell he was doing now because they literally had nothing more to do for the day. She sighed and, without bothering to look at him, said, "Dude. Just go home."

"Well, I could, but I was thinking maybe we could get some dinner first?" a new voice answered, a smile evident in its tone.

Sheridan gasped in surprise and hurriedly sat up in her chair to smile at Parker, who was standing on the other side of her desk with her backpack hanging off her left shoulder and a takeaway cup of coffee in her right hand. They'd been sporadically texting whenever she had time over the last few days, but Parker hadn't said anything about trying to stop by. "Hey!"

"Your message earlier said you were coming back to the office for a bit after you landed," Parker explained, ducking her head shyly. "And since I was in the neighborhood closing out a case, I thought I'd pop by and see if you'd like to go to dinner?" She held out the coffee cup. "Also, I come bearing gifts."

"And she even brought me one this time!" Kelly piped up, smiling at Parker as he rocked back in his chair with his coffee clasped in his hand.

"Well, you seemed so upset last time when I didn't, I figured why not," Parker sassed as she winked at him. "Seriously though"—Parker looked back at her—"I know you've been out of town and are probably exhausted, but my client that I'd been meeting with lives only a few blocks away from here, so I just thought—"

"Parker," Sheridan laughed, interrupting her adorable rambling. "I would love to go to dinner with you."

"We're going to dinner?" Ivy asked as she and Rachel strode through the glass doors of the unit.

Before Sheridan could say anything, Parker shook her head and said, "I was thinking it'd be just me and Sheridan this time."

"Ugh, fine." Ivy rolled her eyes dramatically. "Be like that."

"I will, thanks," Parker retorted. "But, you know, I'm sure Kelly would play the third-wheel for you and Rachel if you'd like."

"No thanks." He held up a hand. "Kelly is tired of being the third-wheel."

"Now that," Ivy declared triumphantly as she pointed at him, "is what I want to hear. Innes, we have someone we want you to meet."

Kelly's eyes went comically wide, and he shook his head. "Oh no…"

"Oh, yes," Rachel chimed in. She laughed at the mildly terrified look he was giving her. "She's an actress currently starring in a little musical on Off-Off, and you two would be perfect together."

"You're not kidding, are you?" he asked.

"Not. At. All." Ivy smirked. "In fact, I'm sure we can score some tickets to her show tonight if you want to go check her out…"

"Sheridan…" Kelly whined. "Help?"

Sheridan shook her head as she looked at her watch. "Sorry, man. It's five o'clock, we've been working pretty much nonstop for four days, and I'm going to dinner with Parker. You're on your own."

"But we're partners!"

She chuckled as she stood and slipped her arms into her blazer. "Yes, we are," she said as she tossed her phone into her purse and slipped it over her shoulder. "Which is why"—she braced a hand on the edge of her desk as she leaned down to pick up her toppled suitcase—"I'm going to be nice and give you my coffee so you're extra-caffeinated, and I will see you in the morning."

Seeing that he wasn't getting anywhere with her, Kelly changed tactics. "Parker. My buddy. My pal…"

Sheridan smiled as she wrapped her hand around Parker's wrist and pulled her toward the door. "Parker is busy tonight, Kel. Sorry."

"Parker likes the sound of that," Parker quipped as she allowed herself to be ushered toward the exit. "Sorry, man. But, I mean, come on. How bad can it be? Go see the show, and if you think she's cute, let them hook you up."

"Yeah!" Ivy and Rachel chorused.

Kelly groaned as his shoulders dropped in defeat, and Sheridan paused a few feet from the door to see what he was going to say. "Fine," he sighed, sounding like he was agreeing to hours of torture. "I'm too tired to argue. We can go see the girl in the play, but you can't get pissed if I fall asleep in the theatre."

"Deal!" Ivy cheered.

"Good boy, Kel," Sheridan called out as Parker pulled open the door to the unit and waved her through. She flashed her a small smile of thanks as she called over her shoulder, "Can't wait to hear how it goes!"

"Not that all of that wasn't amusing, but is he gonna be okay?" Parker asked softly once the door to the unit closed behind them.

Sheridan nodded and pressed her thumb to the call button. "He'll be fine." She blinked twice as she finally *really* looked at Parker, and smiled as she drank in the sight of the black pinstripe slacks and matching waistcoat she wore. The sleeves of her baby blue dress shirt were rolled to just above her elbows, and the top three buttons at her neck were left open, showing an absolutely delicious amount of skin and the barest hint of pale blue satin that was just a shade lighter than her shirt. "You look, wow…"

Parker huffed a little laugh and ran a light finger over the back of her hand that was wrapped around the handle of her suitcase. "You look pretty wow yourself, there, Sloan."

She rolled her eyes. "Yeah right. I'm wearing the same suit I wore yesterday, my hair's a disaster because of the cabin pressure or whatever it is with planes that just messes with—"

"You're beautiful," Parker interrupted, her smile soft and her expression earnest.

Sheridan smiled as Parker took her free hand and threaded their fingers together. The hold was discreetly hidden between their bodies from prying eyes that were no doubt watching their every move, and she sighed as her heart fluttered in her chest at the open affection in Parker's gaze. She'd missed her these last few days, but she had been so busy working that she hadn't had much time to dwell on it. There was no mistaking the feeling of wholeness that settled inside her as she looked at Parker now, though, and she wondered how in the world she'd survived without it. "Thank you," she breathed.

Parker's smile was the very definition of joy as she tipped her head and murmured, "Always."

The distinctive *ding* of the elevator arriving shattered the moment that was, truthfully, far too intimate to be happening in a twenty-seventh floor elevator lobby at Federal Plaza, and Sheridan cleared her throat softly as she finally tore herself away from Parker's smoldering gaze.

"Let's get out of here, Ravenscroft," she muttered, not at all surprised by the unfinished edge that crept into her voice. Honestly, she was surprised she didn't always sound like she was barely resisting the urge to kiss Parker whenever they were together.

"Your wish, my command." Parker gave a small bow and extended her arm over the gap to hold the doors for them.

Sheridan made her way to the back of the car with her bag so she'd be out of the way, and she licked her lips as she watched Parker pause just long enough to press the button for the lobby as she crossed the threshold. She was surprised by how strongly she wanted to sink into her arms and let Parker carry her all the way home, and she contented herself for the moment by leaning into her side when she joined her at the back of the car.

"Hey, you." Parker wrapped an arm around her shoulders and held her close.

"Hey." She smiled. The hold wasn't as tight and all-consuming as she craved, but it was still pretty damn perfect nonetheless. "So, what case were you working that had you down this way?"

"Just closed out a watch recovery. Nothing exciting"

Sheridan watched Parker's reflection in the polished steel doors turn to look at her, and she sighed as she lifted her eyes to meet her gaze. "Hmm?"

"Tell me the truth, please. Are you too tired to do this tonight? Would you rather just go home and rest?"

She shook her head. Just seeing Parker had her feeling energized, and the absolute last thing she wanted was to say goodbye to her just yet. "You're sweet, but no. I'm good. But we can totally just pick something up and take it back to my place if you'd rather do something low-key."

Parker's eyes danced over her face, those beautiful pale gray eyes that seemed to see everything searching for any hint of a lie in her offer. She could see the exact moment Parker was convinced that she was telling the truth, and the slow, soft smile that curled her lips as she dipped her head to touch their foreheads together was filled with so much happiness that it made her heart flutter up into her throat.

"Low-key is good," Parker murmured.

"Yes, it is," she whispered.

The elevator slowed to a stop at the main floor, and Parker gave her one last squeeze before pulling away to a more professional distance. The doors opened to reveal a lobby bustling with agents heading home for the day, the noise and commotion a reminder that all of this that she was finding with Parker was real, and she beamed at Joan as the security guard took Parker's visitor's badge.

"So, is there anything you're in the mood for?" she asked once they reached the street and turned in the direction of her loft.

"I honestly don't know much of what's down here," Parker admitted with a shrug.

Sheridan ran through her mental catalogue of places between the office and her loft where they could grab a quick dinner to-go. "Do you like Middle Eastern? There's a place on Chambers that I have an app for so we could order as we walk and wouldn't have to wait long for the food to be ready…"

"Sounds perfect."

Sheridan nodded, pulled out her phone to open the app and, after adding her usual order to the cart, handed the phone to Parker. "Here ya go. You can look through their menu and see what sounds good to you."

"Order from here a lot, huh?" Parker teased as she began scrolling through the options.

"Eh, every once in a while, I guess," she fibbed. Hell, between the crazy hours she often worked and the fact that she was completely useless in the kitchen, she probably ordered at least four meals a week from the place.

Of course, her little lie was revealed the minute they walked into the small restaurant and Marcus, the manager who she often chatted with while waiting for her food, yelled, "Sheridan's here! How's that order looking, Miguel?"

"Busted," Parker chuckled.

Of course she was. Because that was how things went for her.

"You can wait here, I'll go grab it all," Sheridan murmured, rolling her eyes as she made her way to the counter. "Thanks, for that, Marcus. Really," she drawled as she set her purse on the counter. "Way to embarrass me in front of my friend."

He smirked. "Sorry."

"No you're not."

Marcus looked over her shoulder at Parker, who was perched on the edge of a bar-height chair watching them with a fond smile. His expression softened with understanding, and he ducked his head in apology. "I'll throw in some dessert on the house."

"You don't have to do that." She shook her head. "It's fine. If I learned how to cook, I wouldn't be called out like that."

"You can't!" Marcus gasped in mock-horror. "My sales numbers would plummet!"

"I'm not here that much!" she protested with a laugh.

Marcus winked and called over his shoulder, "Throw in some cookie dough hummus and chips for our girl, huh?"

"Thank you," she murmured when he handed her a tied-off plastic bag a minute later.

"Of course." He doffed an invisible cap. "Have a good night, Sheridan."

"Good night, Marcus." She shook her head as she made her way back to where Parker was waiting. "You ready?"

"When you are," Parker agreed easily as she slipped off the chair. She hurried to hold the door for her and, once they were back on the sidewalk, offered, "You want me to carry that?"

"I got it. Thanks, though."

Parker smiled and shrugged as she adjusted the strap of her backpack on her shoulder. "Of course."

It only took them a few minutes to cover the block and change that separated her building from the restaurant, and she sighed as she finally relented and handed Parker the bag of food so she could open her front door. "You want to take that to the table and I'll grab some drinks after I put all my stuff down?"

"I can do that," Parker agreed as she made her into the loft. She'd been inside twice before, so she moved confidently through the open space, gliding past the kitchen and office to the small dining area by the windows. "I'm good with water," she added before Sheridan could ask.

"Coming right up." Sheridan tossed her purse onto the kitchen counter and pushed her suitcase up against the wall beneath the coat hooks in the foyer. She shrugged off her coat and hung it on one the hooks above her suitcase—she'd deal with unpacking it all later. Her shoulder harness was next to go and, even though it was just the two of them, she still took the time to lock the gun away in the safe on the bookshelf in her office, the habit too firmly ingrained to be skipped. She kicked her heels toward the bottom of the stairs to her lofted bedroom that hovered over the office, and stretched her toes as she padded across the cool, pale oak floors to the kitchen.

A few taps on her phone had her latest playlist streaming through the Bluetooth speaker tucked away on the shelf beside her television, the sound rich and vibrant and immersive in a way that filled her entire loft with sound despite the fact that it all originated from a single speaker. She smiled and bobbed her head as she hummed along to the first few notes of *Who Will Comfort Me?*, a feeling of all-consuming happiness settling warmly in her chest as her gaze settled on Parker, who had finished laying out their food and was relaxed in her chair watching her.

"Do you want ice?"

Parker shrugged. "Whatever."

"So helpful," she muttered as she pulled a couple glasses from the cabinet beside the fridge, her shoulders still swaying lightly with the beat of the music. Parker's soft laughter echoed through the loft, the perfect accompaniment to Melody Gardot's throaty vocals, and she smiled as she skipped the ice dispenser in the door of the fridge and just filled the glasses with water.

"Thanks," Parker murmured when she handed her one of the glasses. She looked around the loft and smiled, looking so perfectly relaxed and comfortable that it was hard to believe that this wasn't something they did every night. "Good call on just getting takeout."

"I'm glad you think so. Because I can't cook to save my life, so it's kinda my go-to."

"Yeah, I kinda figured as much when that guy recognized you the minute we walked through the door back there," Parker teased.

"Hey!" she laughed. "Be nice."

Parker smiled and reached for her hand. "I can be nice."

Her breath caught in her throat as Parker's fingers curled around the side of her own, so strong and soft at the same time, and she stared, enraptured as her hand was lifted into the air. She was helpless to contain the little sigh that escaped her when Parker's lips pressed against the back of her knuckles, and when she looked away from the sight of pale pink lips against her skin, the warmth she saw shining at her in Parker's gaze stole the air from her lungs. And then, all too soon, Parker's eyes crinkled with the smile that curled her lips and her hand was lowered back to the table.

Parker tilted her head in a most adorable manner as she asked softly, "Too much?"

God, no. If anything, it wasn't enough. But she couldn't bring herself to admit that, so she settled for a simple, "Not at all."

"Good," Parker murmured, licking her lips as her eyes dropped to Sheridan's. She swallowed thickly and forced her gaze higher, her unspoken question shining brightly in her eyes.

Sheridan answered it all too willingly as she leaned across the small space separating them. She smiled at the way Parker's lips parted in anticipation as she hovered just out of reach, and the way Parker's breath hitched when she brushed their noses together sent her pulse racing.

"God, Sheridan, please," Parker whimpered, lifting her chin entreatingly but leaving that final move for her to make.

Sheridan's eyes fluttered shut at the first touch of Parker's lips against her own, and she moaned as she opened her mouth to the nimble tongue that flicked entreatingly over her lips searching for more. The way Parker's tongue slid slowly around her own as a trembling hand wrapped around the back of her neck, urging her closer, made her stomach flip. She cradled Parker's face in her hands as she melted into the kiss, eagerly meeting every stroke and twirl and press of Parker's tongue with her own. Minutes could have turned into days for all she knew as they kissed, switching off leading and following in a dance that was so perfect it might as well have been choreographed, and she sighed when it reached its inevitable end.

"Oh, Parker," she breathed when they finally broke apart, her voice rough and trembling ever so slightly as she nuzzled her cheek and brushed a light, barely there kiss across her lips.

Parker chuckled and kissed her again. "Believe me, sweetie, I know."

Sheridan smiled and stroked her thumbs over the elegant curves of Parker's cheeks as she darted forward to steal one last kiss before forcing herself to pull away. Their food was getting cold, and she knew from the way Parker was smiling at her that she felt this too. There was no reason for them to rush. They would get there soon enough, she figured, judging by the way her pulse spiked when she watched Parker's tongue slide over her lips, but she was more than content to take their time. "Thank you for coming by my office tonight," she murmured. "I'm so glad I didn't have to wait until Saturday to see you again."

"Me too," Parker breathed as she pressed up out of her seat just enough to be able to dust the softest promise of a kiss across her lips. She sighed and shook her head as she dropped back to her seat, her smile rueful as she confessed, "I could get used to that."

"What?"

"Being able to kiss you just because I can't help myself."

Sheridan smiled as affection bloomed in her chest, and nodded. "I could get used to it, too."

twenty-nine

Parker gripped the bouquet of wildflowers in her hand tighter as she stepped off the subway so the crowd streaming onto the platform didn't knock them onto the ground. "You're sure the reservation is good?" The last thing she needed was for them to be turned away at the door.

"*Of course,*" Oliver scoffed, sounding both offended that she asked and amused by her anxiety. "*It wasn't hard at all to fit you in.*"

"And you didn't bump anyone who was celebrating something important?"

"*There weren't any notes by the name,*" Oliver assured her. "*And, just to avoid a scene, I called the man whose reservation I gave to you pretending to be from the restaurant, confirming his reservation for tomorrow night at the same time. And, before you ask, there was a legit cancellation that I slotted them into, and he thought he'd messed up in making the reservation and didn't argue the change, so everything is cool.*"

She blew out a soft breath and nodded. Hacking the reservations system for Lapis Lazuli was definitely a less-than-ethical move, but it was only a blip on the morality radar considering everything else she'd done to help him out, so she didn't feel too guilty about it. And if it meant Sheridan had an enjoyable evening, the trespass was more than worth it so far as she was concerned. What was the point of having a brother who could hack into literally anything if she didn't take

advantage of it now and then to get a kick-ass dinner reservation?
"Okay. Thanks."

"Of course. You almost at her place?"

"Couple blocks away," she confirmed, her stomach tightening with nerves. Knowing that they'd been doing a variation of this dance for the last two months or so did exactly nothing to make her any less afraid of screwing it all up.

"You got this, Parker," Oliver murmured. *"Do you want me to keep talking to distract you?"*

"Yes, please."

He laughed. *"All right. So, you all packed for the trip tomorrow?"*

"Yep, finished packing this morning." She hadn't had much choice since she needed to be at JFK no later than six the next morning to have enough time to squeak through security. They'd told Brett they were arriving Wednesday afternoon, so they had the first half of the week to nail down their plans before they got swept up in family activities with the Johanns. Tina had overheard Brett's half of their conversation the weekend before, and had insisted they come over for dinner that night. She'd sounded so excited to see them again that they hadn't been able to turn down her invitation to spend Friday with the family hiking in Wallace Falls, as well.

"Honestly, with how thrilled Tina is that we're going out there, I'm kind of feeling guilty that we haven't been back since last year."

"Yeah, me too," she agreed with a sigh. "We'll have to try to do better."

"Yeah." After a beat, he drawled, *"So, when are you gonna take Sheridan back to meet them?"*

She groaned, and ignored the confused look the guy waiting at the crosswalk next to her shot her as she asked, "Can I at least see if I survive our first real date before I start worrying about that?"

He laughed. *"You'll be fine, Park."*

"I sure hope so," she muttered, "because I just got to her building."

"Go sweep your girl off her feet, sis. I'll see you tomorrow."

"See you tomorrow." Parker blew out a loud breath and shook her head as she slipped the phone into her coat pocket. She spied a thirty-something couple exiting the elevator through the glass door as she was about to press the intercom button for Sheridan's unit to be let in, so she waited to let them get the door for her, instead. "Hey, thanks," she murmured as she slipped through the door after them. She must have looked like she belonged in the building, because they just smiled and nodded at her as they went on their way.

The idea of being cooped in an elevator for the minute or so it'd take the car to rise to Sheridan's floor was enough to make her vaguely nauseous, so she instead jogged up the stairs to the third floor, and before she could make herself too much more anxious about the night ahead, she was knocking on Sheridan's door.

It seemed like it took forever before the door opened, and then time seemed to stop completely when she saw Sheridan. Always stunning, Sheridan looked like an absolute goddess in the halter midnight blue lace dress she wore that fell to just above her knees. The cut should have been demure, but the peekaboo panel of lace that stretched from the top of Sheridan's breasts to the neckline of the dress at her throat gave it an impossibly sexy look, and she had to swallow twice before she could speak once she finally looked her in the eye. "You are absolutely beautiful."

It was an understatement to be sure, but the shy smile that tugged at Sheridan's lips told her that the compliment was appreciated.

"You too," Sheridan breathed as she ran a light finger over the lapel of Parker's unbuttoned charcoal gray suit jacket, her gaze dropping from the coat to the flawless expanse of skin exposed by the open buttons of Parker's starched white shirt before landing on the tailored waistcoat that was buttoned to just beneath her breasts.

Parker swallowed thickly as she watched Sheridan's eyes darken as her hand fell away, delighting in the light flush that pinked her cheeks. She hadn't missed the way Sheridan had always seemed enjoy the sight of her in a waistcoat, so deciding on her favorite three-piece suit had been the easiest decision she'd had to make for the evening. She cleared her throat softly and offered Sheridan the bouquet of wildflowers she had brought for her. "These are for you."

"Oh, Parker..." Sheridan's expression softened, her eyes twinkling with the shy smile that curled her lips, like she couldn't believe she had actually brought her flowers. "They're lovely."

Parker smiled as she leaned in to kiss her softly. "I'm glad you like them," she whispered against her lips. She could feel Sheridan's smile as she kissed her again and, even though they did have something of a schedule to keep to for the night, couldn't resist pulling Sheridan into her as she dipped her tongue past her lips.

The sound of Sheridan humming appreciatively as their tongues swirled lightly together sent a pleasant flutter through her chest, and she sighed happily when they finally broke apart. "Wow..."

"Tell me about it," Sheridan murmured. "Do we have time for me to put them in water?"

"Of course." Parker nodded and followed Sheridan inside. She waited on the office side of the peninsula counter as Sheridan pulled a square glass vase from a cupboard over the fridge, more than content to take advantage of the opportunity to drink in her beauty and quietly marvel at how lucky she was that Sheridan had agreed to go out with her.

Once the vase had been filled and the flowers had been arranged and they were ready to go, she took Sheridan's hand and, with a light tug, pulled her close enough to kiss her softly. "Sorry. You're just so gorgeous that I couldn't help myself," she breathed as she pulled away.

"I don't mind at all," Sheridan whispered, her dark eyes shining with happiness.

"So, you ready?"

"Do I get to know where we're going?" Sheridan asked instead as she let go of her hand so she could grab her keys from her purse.

There was no way she was going to give up the surprises she had lined up, but Parker figured a hint wouldn't hurt. "We have a six o'clock reservation at a restaurant in the Village."

"That doesn't really help," Sheridan laughed as she locked up after them.

"Well, then I guess you're just gonna have to trust me," Parker teased, unable to contain her smile when Sheridan's hand found her own again.

"I guess you're lucky I do, huh?" Sheridan squeezed her hand playfully.

"Incredibly lucky," Parker agreed as she led them toward the elevator.

It was almost comical, Parker noticed, how all her nerves from earlier had disappeared as if they'd never existed as they chatted idly on the way to the restaurant. She'd been more than a little afraid that the weight of this being a "real date" would settle on them and make things awkward, and she'd never been more happy to be wrong.

"Wait." Sheridan grabbed Parker's elbow to pull her up short, her face a mask of shock as she read the name inscribed on the brass placard mounted on the wall beside the short stairway that led to the former speakeasy-turned-upscale American bistro that occupied the lower level of the townhouse where they were going for dinner. "We're going to Lapis Lazuli?"

"You're not the only one with connections," Parker teased. Sheridan's utter shock was amusing, but the longer it lasted, the more concerned she became that she'd somehow made a mistake in her restaurant selection for the evening. "Is this okay?" she asked hesitantly, holding her breath while she waited for Sheridan's response. When Sheridan nodded, she let the breath she'd been holding go quietly as it took every ounce of strength she possessed to not sink to the ground in relief right there in the middle of the busy sidewalk.

"I'm sorry. Of course it is, Parker. I'm just..." Sheridan shook her head. "I've heard this place is amazing. And that it's all but impossible to get a reservation unless you call months in advance."

"Oh, well, like I said"—Parker offered Sheridan her arm with a playful wink—"you're not the only one with connections."

"I guess not," Sheridan murmured.

The shy smile that curled Sheridan's lips as she shyly took her arm made Parker fall just that little bit more, and she sighed as she covered Sheridan's hand on her arm with her own.

Walking up to the maître d's station was the same adrenaline-fueled rush of hope that Oliver was right that he'd covered all the bases on a job and the fear of what she would do if he hadn't, and she did her best to not let any of that show when she gave the woman her name. It was, thankfully, on the list, and she hoped she covered the surge of relief that swept through her as she smiled at Sheridan and placed a gentle hand on the small of her back to tell her that she would follow her.

She had never visited the restaurant before, had never had a reason to consider even trying to get her name on the list, but as they followed the maître d' through the small, packed main dining room, she could see why Lapis Lazuli had garnered such a sterling reputation. The pale beige walls and white tablecloths were the perfect neutral background for the bright crimson upholstered chairs and the colorful bouquets spread throughout the room, while the candles on each of the tables cast an intimate halo of golden light upon the individual tables. Beyond the main room, through a painted black Dutch door, was a much smaller garden dining area, that had a long pale gray booth that stretched along the length of the garden. Intimate two-person tables segmented the long bench into separate seating areas, and natural-colored wood chairs faced the booth. Parker made a mental note to thank Oliver for the magic he'd worked when they were shown to one of the four standalone tables tucked against the back wall of the townhouse.

Parker smiled at the look of open awe on Sheridan's face as she took in their surroundings once the hostess had left them with the promise their server would be with them shortly. And, even though it was obvious from Sheridan's expression, she had to ask, just to make sure that she had, in fact, chosen well, "So, what do you think?"

"Honestly, Parker, this is incredible."

"I'm glad," Parker murmured as she opened her menu. The restaurant had a four-course prix fixe, but what set it above the competition was the fact that all the produce was fresh from the owner's farm a couple hours from the city.

"It all looks amazing," Sheridan mused as she perused her menu. "I don't know how I'm supposed to choose…"

"From what I've heard, you can't go wrong no matter what you decide," Parker shared as she laid her menu on the table. She smiled when their server, a pretty twenty-something who looked like she was probably a student at nearby NYU, stopped at their table to run through her spiel. Sheridan had questions about a few of the different dishes on the menu, which allowed her the opportunity to give the wine list a quick perusal.

Knowing that Sheridan preferred red to white, she skipped the first few pages of the impressive list and focused on the reds. When the server had finished offering her suggestions from the tasting menu for the evening, Sheridan still looked adorably confused about what she wanted, so Parker bought her a few more minutes. "Could we get a bottle of Cuvée Marie Ragonneau, please, while we decide?"

"Of course." The server retreated with a polite smile and a small bow.

"Are you trying to get me drunk?" Sheridan teased, her dark blue eyes sparkling with amusement as she glanced from Parker to her menu and back again.

"Hardly. I've got one more trick up my sleeve for the evening. I can't have you sloshed before we get there." Parker grinned at the melodious sound of Sheridan laughter. "You just looked like you needed another minute, so I figured I'd send her on a little mission to buy you some time."

"I appreciate it," Sheridan murmured. She sighed as her eyes dropped back to her menu. "So, do I get to know what the rest of your surprises for the evening are?"

"Nope," Parker teased. She leaned back in her chair and folded her hands on her lap when their server returned with the bottle of wine she had ordered. They did the usual uncorking and tasting routine, and once she'd deemed the Pinot Noir suitable—it was incredible, and she made a mental note to look into what it would cost her to get a case for her apartment—Sheridan had decided which of the offerings she wanted to taste most, and they placed their dinner orders.

The hype around the magic the kitchen worked paled in comparison to the food presented to them with an elegant flourish, and it was but a murky shadow in comparison to the easy conversation they shared, she couldn't help but think as she scribbled her name across the bottom of the bill. A glance at her watch urged her to get moving, and she smiled at Sheridan as she placed her hands on the edge of the table and pushed her chair back.

"Ready for the next part?"

Sheridan nodded as she stood and slipped her purse over her shoulder. "Of course. Is it far from here?"

"Not too far," Parker answered vaguely. "That was a nice try, though."

Sheridan laughed. "Thanks, I guess."

Parker's stomach fluttered at the feeling of Sheridan's hand slipping into her own as they made their way inside, that light touch so perfect that she never wanted to lose it. She gave Sheridan's hand a quick squeeze as she stopped at the maître d's station to request a cab to carry them to their next destination.

It was, after all, the one part of her plan she was most proud of. Finding the tickets had been her own coup for the evening, and she was quite looking forward to seeing Sheridan's reaction when she realized where they were going.

They waited in the small alcove near the bar until the cab arrived, and she rattled off the cross streets closest to their destination instead of the place itself just to keep the subterfuge alive for as long as possible. It was clear from the slight wrinkle of Sheridan's brow that the intersection was at least mildly familiar—which it should be, anyone who lived on the island knew the general area of the theatre district—and she smiled as she took Sheridan's hand and pulled it onto her lap. "Any guesses where we're going?"

Sheridan huffed a frustrated breath and shook her head. "No idea."

"You'll love it," Parker promised. "Or, well, I hope you will," she added.

"I'm sure I will," Sheridan assured her, a gentle smile curling her lips as she leaned over and kissed her softly. She squeezed her hand as she pulled away just far enough to whisper, "Everything about this evening so far has been perfect."

Parker beamed as she ran a gentle hand over Sheridan's jaw, and tilted her head enough to touch their foreheads together as she whispered, "I'm so glad you think so."

The drive from the restaurant to the theatre was short, and she had to bite the inside of her cheek to keep from laughing as shades of recognition and confusion and building anticipation bloomed on Sheridan's face the closer they got to the theatre. They were a few blocks from the main theatre drag, so there were no familiar billboards with verdant-hued witches or masks or felines to be seen, and she pretended not to notice the confused look Sheridan gave her when the cabbie deposited them on the corner of 43rd and 6th. "Ready?" she asked as she took Sheridan's hand.

"I guess." Sheridan nodded and looked around them to try to figure out where they were headed.

"This way," Parker murmured, giving her hand a light squeeze as she led them around the corner. She kept one eye on Sheridan and one on the crowded sidewalk around them as they walked, waiting for the moment she saw the name on the marquee up ahead.

She knew the moment Sheridan saw the familiar name on the lit marquee up ahead, because her mouth fell open and she yanked her to a stop so quickly the guy who'd been following them actually ran into them.

"Sorry," he muttered, shooting them a look that was a mix of annoyance and *fucking tourists* that only a true New Yorker could manage.

Parker rolled her eyes. He could suck it for all she cared, because Sheridan's face was the most beautiful mask of joyous surprise she'd ever seen.

"Melody Gardot?" Sheridan asked softly. "Are we really going to see Melody Gardot?"

"Would you like that?" Parker asked, unable to resist teasing her. When Sheridan replied with a wide-eyed nod of breathless anticipation, she smiled and gave up the game. "Good. Because that's exactly where we're headed."

And, oh, the way Sheridan just *beamed* at her as the words sank in, like she'd just given her the one thing she'd always wanted before she pulled her in for a fierce, happy kiss was enough to convince her to try to surprise her like this every goddamn day for the rest of her life.

"How did you know?" Sheridan asked when she finally pulled away, her cheeks flushed and her eyes sparkling with joy.

Parker shrugged. "Every time you put music on, I swear like ninety percent of the time it's her."

"Most people don't even know who she is..." Sheridan murmured as she allowed Parker to lead her toward the theatre's entrance.

"Judging by how hard it was to find tickets on such short notice, I'm pretty confident that's not quite true," Parker teased, squeezing Sheridan's hand. "But I noticed she was a favorite of yours, so I kinda cheated and turned on Shazam one night to get her name, and then I spent the next week putting every song of her discography to memory."

"You're not kidding, are you?" Sheridan asked as they joined the queue to enter the theatre. When Parker just smiled and shook her head, Sheridan sighed and whispered, "Are you even real? Because, seriously, Parker..."

Parker laughed and pulled the tickets from her jacket pocket so she'd have them ready. She might have used Oliver's skills for the reservation, but she'd found these tickets all on her own and she was beyond thrilled that Sheridan seemed to like the surprise as much as she'd hoped she would. She brushed a light kiss to Sheridan's forehead as they shuffled forward in line, loving the way Sheridan had pressed into her side. Once they reached the front of the line, she handed the kid at the door their tickets, and smiled as she let Sheridan lead them to their seats. She would have loved to get Sheridan as close to the stage as possible, but she was honestly lucky to have scored two tickets together in the balcony on such short notice.

"I'm sorry we're not closer," she apologized as they took their seats. They were in the third row from the loge boxes at the front of the balcony, and she was pleased to see it meant they still had a pretty good view of the stage that was draped in black curtains for the evening.

"Please don't apologize." Sheridan smiled and shook her head as she looked from Parker to the stage and back again, everything in her demeanor making it obvious that she couldn't believe what was happening.

Parker nodded as she took Sheridan's hand into her own and lifted it to her lips to press a lingering kiss to her knuckles. "Okay..."

She held her breath as she watched Sheridan's throat bob and her tongue slide slowly over her lips, and froze when Sheridan leaned closer, her eyes dark with something much more appropriate for somewhere more private. Soft lips grazed across her cheek, the light touch sending a pleasant shiver down her spine, and her eyes damn well rolled back in her head when hot breath cascaded against her ear. "When the lights go down, I'm gonna kiss you so hard for this."

"I…" Parker cleared her throat. "Um…okay."

Whatever embarrassment she felt about that less-than-smooth response was soothed by the sound of Sheridan's low, rich laughter and the crook of her lips that conveyed just how much Sheridan enjoyed the effect she had on her.

Because they'd arrived less than half an hour before the concert was to begin, in what seemed like no time at all, every light in the entire theatre dimmed to a murky blackness that was pretty much required, given the performer. Before Parker could truly begin to relax into her seat to enjoy the show, confident fingers glided along her jaw, turning her head with the faintest amount of pressure that set her pulse absolutely racing. She gasped at the first brush of Sheridan's lips against her own, and moaned softly when the fingers on her jaw swept back to tangle in her hair as a nimble tongue slipped past her lips, circling boldly around her own as she did her best to just try to keep up.

The handful of kisses they'd shared to this point had been sweet, soft exchanges that had been gentle and perfect for the moment, so she'd been totally unprepared for a kiss like this that left her breathing hard and grinning like a fool. "Wow…"

Sheridan's eyes sparkled with the reflection of the stage lights. She blinked as she nodded slowly, and then sighed as if she lost some kind of internal battle as she leaned in and captured her lips in a gentler, lingering kiss. "Very much so," she agreed softly.

A ripple of applause around them brought them back to the moment, and Parker swallowed hard as Sheridan pulled her hand onto her lap as she turned to face the stage. The concert began once the applause had died down, rich jazz beats and the melodious sound of Gardot's voice casting a spell over the crowd that was focused on her every move.

The music was incredible, of course. Gardot truly was a genius when it came to the genre, and even though her shoulders swayed a little with her favorite songs, she could not tear her eyes away from the beautiful creature beside her. Eventually the music would end, and she wanted to burn every quirk of Sheridan's lips, every crinkle of her eyes, and every soft gasp of awe into her memory so she'd remember it forever.

Sure enough, in what seemed like only a handful of minutes since the singer first took the stage, the theatre's lights came on and the crowd filling the auditorium got to their feet, the energy of their applause a rush of adrenaline that gave her chills. Sheridan was positively beaming as she applauded, and when she looked over at her to see if she'd enjoyed the show as well, Parker could only smile and nod as she clapped, because her throat was too tight with affection to speak.

She'd had inklings of awareness before this, brief instances of murky clarity suggesting depth of her feelings, but in that moment she knew, without a shadow of a doubt, that she had fallen in love with Sheridan Sloan.

Something of the revelation must have showed in her expression, because Sheridan's wide, unhindered, happy smile softened as she leaned in to ask softly, "What?"

Parker shook her head. It was too soon to say those words, but she leaned in to capture Sheridan's lips in a tender kiss that conveyed a small measure of what she was feeling.

She did her best to keep up with their conversation as they made their way back to Sheridan's apartment, and was glad that Sheridan seemed more than content to carry the conversation for them both as their cab inched down Broadway block by block until they were finally, finally at her building.

Walking Sheridan all the way to her door had never been in question, and Parker smiled at the way Sheridan refused to let go of her hand as they made their way up to the front door of the building and then to the elevator beyond. The shy smile that curled Sheridan's lips when they got to her door sent a flutter of butterflies swooping through her stomach, and she sighed as she cradled Sheridan's face between her hands and kissed her softly. "Thank you for tonight," she murmured.

"Pretty sure I should be thanking you," Sheridan chuckled against her lips.

Parker allowed the hands on her hips to pull her forward until she was pressed against Sheridan in all the places that made her blood pound, and whimpered when Sheridan's hands dropped from her hips to her ass. The world tilted and spun as Sheridan's lips slanted against her own, claiming her mouth in a kiss even hotter than the one they'd shared at the theatre. Hours could have passed for all she cared as they traded slow, deep, sloppy kisses that, on any other night would have been foreplay to something more, and she whimpered as she forced herself to pull away when the urge to take Sheridan to bed became nearly too strong to ignore.

She was doing so much wrong, but she was determined to do this right, at least.

"Come inside," Sheridan implored huskily.

And, god, the unabashed longing in Sheridan's voice and the sensation of her fingers digging into her ass were nearly enough to make Parker forget that she had to be at the airport in less than six hours. Nearly, but not quite, and she groaned as she shifted her hips away from the thigh that had slipped between her legs.

"I want to," Parker confessed softly, her voice cracking with the force of her desire. She closed her eyes to block the disappointment that she knew would undoubtedly flash in Sheridan's gaze at her next words. "But I can't." The quiet hitch in Sheridan's breath told her just how badly her words had fallen, and she hurried to try to explain, "I don't want to make love to you for the first time and then have to leave because I've got to be at the airport before dawn to fly back to Seattle for the week. When I finally get to make love to you, Sheridan, I want to take my time. I want to spend an entire weekend in bed with you, worshipping every inch of your body again and again and again until we're too spent to even pick up a phone to order a pizza." She blinked her eyes open to see if the joke landed, and was relieved to see more understanding than disappointment shining in Sheridan's eyes. "I do want you."

"You're kinda killing me, here," Sheridan murmured.

"I'm sorry."

"God, don't be," Sheridan groaned. "I want all that too," she whispered.

"Good," Parker breathed. Her heart beat up into her throat as they silently looked at each other, and she smiled when Sheridan's lips lifted to cover her own. The kiss was gentler than before, full of warmth and understanding and the promise that someday soon they would share that moment they both so badly wanted.

THIRTY

"What are you still doing here?"

Sheridan blew out a loud breath and shrugged as she looked up at Ivy. She had no reason to still be at the office at seven on a Thursday night, but it was easier to pretend she didn't miss Parker when she was at work and she could focus on something other than those husky promises that had been whispered against her lips at the end of their date. "I could ask you the same thing…"

"Touché." Ivy grinned as she sauntered across the bullpen to lean against the edge of Sheridan's desk. "I talked my way out of going to dinner with Rachel and her mother, so I figured I'd putz around here for a bit." She peered interestedly at the scattered notes on Sheridan's desk. "Anything I can help with?"

"I'm honestly just brainstorming about those book heists," Sheridan said as she glanced at her phone, hoping to see a text alert from Parker.

The screen was tortuously black, however, and she rolled her eyes at the way Ivy chuckled knowingly under her breath. "Shut up, Moran."

"I'm just happy you two finally got it all figured out," Ivy replied breezily. "When does she get back?"

"Sunday night." Sheridan sighed. "We're planning on going to dinner Monday, but who knows if that'll happen with work and everything…"

"I'll try and take one for the team if something comes up that day," Ivy offered with a smile. "So, what's your hypothesis about the books?"

"I don't know." Sheridan ran a hand through her hair and shook her head. "There's nothing beside a gut feeling connecting the Blake to the books that were stolen in Paris, so we're working the cases independently for now. For the Blake heist, we've checked out everything we know to look at and ended up with a big, fat nothing. Every angle with the cleaning crew lead has come up blank, street cameras were buggy that week so there's no film of traffic in the area around the time of the robbery, and the lawyer that Gunn says contacted him doesn't seem to exist."

"Well that's suspicious as fuck."

"Right? It's too bad 'suspicious as fuck' isn't grounds for a warrant," Sheridan grumbled. "Though, at this point, I'd have no idea where to serve it anyway…"

Ivy nodded thoughtfully. "Any idea who set up the line for the lawyer in the first place? Seems like that could be a solid lead…"

Sheridan shook her head. "Honestly? I'd bet that the call was routed through one or more intermediaries to hide its source. We could run numbers for the rest of the year and we're not going to get anywhere near the call's point of origin."

"Damn. And nothing at the scenes?"

"God, I wish. These guys swoop in out of nowhere and disappear without a trace. It's like they're fucking Filibus or something…"

Ivy laughed and pulled Kelly's chair over to beside her desk. "Very nice lesbian nerdage there, Sloan."

Sheridan smiled. "I'm impressed you know it."

"I'm so much more than just a pretty face. And, well, I was a film studies minor and whatever. What's your excuse for knowing about an obscure, early twentieth-century lesbo-tastic silent movie?"

"Had an ex that was into that kind of stuff," Sheridan said, her tone light but conveying her disinterest in continuing that line of conversation. She was, however, pleasantly surprised that the flash of anger that usually accompanied thoughts of Claire was noticeably less sharp than it had been before. She knew it was because of Parker, and she bit her lip as she glanced at her phone again.

The fact that her teeth were clamped on her lower lip was the only reason her grin was somewhat contained when a message alert lit up her screen.

"Give me those notes to look at while you're texting your girlfriend," Ivy drawled, making a grabby motion with her hand.

"What happened to not teasing me about her?" Sheridan laughed as she handed Ivy the file for the Blake case that also had her notes about details from the theft in Paris.

"Am I teasing you? I was pretty sure that I was over here just reading your disgustingly organized notes."

"Yeah, you just go ahead and keep on doing that, then," Sheridan muttered as she rocked back in her chair to hide her phone screen as she opened Parker's message.

Ollie took this, thought you'd like it... Following the note was a picture of Parker staring off across the Sound from the upper deck of one of the famous Seattle ferries. Her hair was blown back away from her face and she had sunglasses hiding her eyes, but the small, serene smile that curled her lips made her heart ache. She wondered what had made Parker smile like that, but more than that, she just wanted to hold her in her arms again. Wanted to feel the warmth of her body and taste the sweetness of her lips. Wanted to revel in the little sounds of surrender that bubbled in Parker's throat when their kisses became deeper or her hands wandered, wanted—

...He's also calling you McDreamy now.

Sheridan laughed and shook her head as she blinked back the longing that had, only moments before, threatened to overwhelm her. She ignored the small tick of Ivy's smile before she sank in her seat and lifted the file higher to try to hide it and replied, *Well, I am quite dreamy.*

"God, you're cute," Ivy murmured.

Sheridan rolled her eyes and aimed a playful kick at Ivy's chair. "Shut up."

"Hey!" Ivy laughed as she used her feet to pull the chair back to where she'd been before the kick.

Yes, you absolutely are. She could imagine the way Parker would smile as she said that, playful and shy all at once, like she was afraid of giving away too much, too soon, and she wished she could reach through the phone and kiss her. *I miss you.*

Those three words had her stomach sinking and her throat tightening with that damn-near crippling longing again, and she half-wondered if she'd be able to find a plane ticket to Seattle because she didn't want to wait another day to see her. But, while it was a nice daydream, she forced herself to push it aside as the unrealistic wish that it was as she typed back, *I miss you, too.*

Sheridan sighed and set the phone face-up on her desk. She was pretty sure that Parker would leave the exchange at that because there was nothing else to say right now, but she also didn't want to miss another message if it came through. "So, what do you think?" she asked Ivy.

Ivy blew out a loud breath and shook her head. They're fucking Filibus, all right. Have you looked into Marquis for this?"

"Oh yeah." Sheridan leaned forward to take her notes back from Ivy. "She's made plenty of trips from her house in Nice to Paris, but that isn't exactly damning evidence of anything illegal since her business empire is based out of Paris, and she hasn't made any trips stateside that we know of since the one a couple months ago. On paper, she's clean, but I have a feeling she's involved somehow." She spread the notes over the desk and frowned. "I just can't figure out how to link her to the thefts. And, at the same time, I hate zeroing-in on her in case it's somebody else."

"Who else could it be?"

"God, your guess is as good as mine," Sheridan sighed. "But the Blake is worth at least two-point-five, and the 1865 Alice and *Don Quixote* are in that same ballpark, if not worth a little bit more, so whoever wants these books has really expensive taste."

"So, assuming expensive taste and a literary bent," Ivy mused as she picked up the list Sheridan had made of the rarest and most valuable privately held books in the world, "and that the thefts are connected and that Filibus isn't done yet, which of these do you think would be next? If we can't tie Marquis to the books that have already been stolen, maybe we can catch Filibus when they're stealing the next one. Float a cushy plea bargain in front of them, and maybe they'll give up who they're working for."

"Are we seriously calling them Filibus?"

"We are." Ivy nodded. "So..."

"God, I don't know. All of them?" Sheridan raked her hands through her hair and shrugged. "I mean, I'd go for the handwritten copy of *The Tales of Beedle the Bard* because that'd be cool, and the fact that it sold for close to four million at auction makes it valuable; but it's not exactly literary, per se."

"That would be pretty sweet to have, though," Ivy murmured. "Any idea who won the auction for that one?"

"Anonymous buyer." Sheridan shook her head. "Anyway, the big names on the list are the same ones you see on the syllabus for pretty much any literature course—Shakespeare, Chaucer, Wordsworth, Tennyson, Coleridge, Yeats, Byron, Poe, yada, yada, yada...."

"But how many of those are really high-value? Like, I need to hire me a super-thief to steal those books, valuable?"

"Like any art, there's a market value and a personal value. And since neither the Dumas, Carroll, or Blake have made even a hint of an appearance on the black market so far as I can tell, I'd wager that they're going directly to the collector who wants them."

"You're positive that Marquis hasn't been back since her last visit?"

"Yeah. Bartz still has her passport flagged. There's no way she's getting in without us knowing about it."

"Well, fuck."

"Exactly," Sheridan laughed.

"If you were our mysterious collector and had to pick from this list, what titles would you choose?"

"The Shakespeare folio would be pretty incredible. I know it's all dick jokes and whatever, but it's still Shakespeare. And I actually liked *Canterbury Tales*."

"I'd go for the Nostradamus," Ivy mused. "Or the Plato. It'd be cool to just drop their names in casual conversation, ya know? And something of Poe's would be fun to have."

"We just don't have enough information about these guys to guess where they're going to strike next."

"Have you reached out to the other teams where some of these books are just so they keep an eye out? It could be nothing, but at least by giving them a heads up, if something does go down they'd probably call to tell you about it."

"I already did," Sheridan said. "And Guillard reached out to some of her foreign contacts, too. The problem is that quite a few of the books on this list are in Britain and they've got exactly two-and-a-half agents assigned to Art Crimes."

"Which is ridiculous since like forty percent of worldwide art thefts happen in their jurisdiction."

"Tell me about it," Sheridan agreed. Art theft, while major and totaling billions of dollars each year, was considered a "victimless" crime by too many agencies because ninety-nine percent of the time nobody got hurt. It's hard to convince agencies already strapped for cash that they should care about spending their precious resources tracking down a missing Renoir or Degas or whatever when they had so many other avenues of crime that actually caused injury to worry about.

That was, after all, why recovery agents like Parker had such profitable careers.

"Filibus, Filibus, Filibus," Ivy murmured. "Where are you going to strike next?" She looked at Sheridan and grinned. "If this case of yours was bigger than just one missing book on our end at this point, so that the whole team was put on it, we'd have a pool going for what books were snatched next."

Sheridan nodded. "I'm honestly surprised Kelly hasn't started one yet, anyway."

"Slacker," Ivy chuckled. She sighed and slapped her hands on her thighs. "Right. Well, this was a fun little mental exercise, but I'm getting hungry. What do you say we go grab something to eat since our women abandoned us?"

Food sounded wonderful, and Sheridan nodded as she pushed all her notes back into the case file. "I thought you said you talked your way out of dinner with Rachel's mom?"

"Semantics." Ivy waved her question off with a laugh. "I'm thinking a big, greasy burger, fries, and a beer sounds like fucking heaven right now. How about you?"

Sheridan smiled and pulled her blazer on as she pushed herself to her feet. "Sounds good to me."

thirty-one

Parker crossed her legs as she relaxed in her chair, ignoring the bustle of the restaurant around them as she glanced discreetly at her watch. They'd finished the dessert portion of Tina's birthday dinner close to half an hour ago and should have more than been on their way already, but she didn't have the heart to say anything. Not when Tina was so obviously happy to have all of "her kids" together.

"So are you two going to come home for Thanksgiving?" Tina asked, looking hopefully at Parker and Oliver. "Gregory is, of course, more than welcome to come as well."

"Hey, and you can bring McDreamy!" Oliver teased, aiming a playful elbow at Parker's side.

Parker rolled her eyes. "Can you please stop calling her that? It was funny the first time, but it's getting old..."

"Sheridan is more than welcome, too." Tina smiled, looking like she'd love nothing more than to meet her. "The more the merrier, right Brett?"

Brett nodded. "Of course."

"I'll try to see what I can do," Parker assured them. She hadn't been planning on coming back so soon, and she had no idea if Sheridan would be willing to come with her if she did make the trip, but Thanksgiving was a much easier holiday to just fly in-and-out for than Christmas.

"Good." Tina nodded happily. She sighed and looked over at Jen and Viv, who had pulled out their phones and were scrolling through god knows what.

Parker looked at the girls, too, and smiled. They were much more well-adjusted at fifteen than her and Oliver had been, but she figured a lot of that was due to the fact that they'd been taken-in by the Johanns when they were only nine and had been formally adopted when they were eleven. There was a small part of her that envied the girls for being able to grow up in a loving, supportive home, but she was glad that she and Oliver had gotten a few years to know what it was like before they'd moved out into the world.

Brett rolled his eyes at the girls—even though Parker had caught him checking the Mariner's score on his phone earlier—and nudged Jen's chair with his foot to get her attention. "You guys ready to go home?"

"We probably should," Tina answered for the group with a sigh as she glanced at her watch. "It's getting late."

"Thank you for everything," Parker said as she got to her feet. "It was a fun."

"Yeah, it was," Oliver agreed with a smile.

"Thank you for coming out for the weekend," Tina murmured as she pulled them both into a hug. "I know you've got busy lives, but it was nice to see you two."

"We wouldn't have missed it for the world," Parker assured her as Oliver expressed a similar sentiment.

When Tina released them, Brett clapped a fatherly hand on each of their shoulders as the three of them led the pack toward their cars. "You guys are flying out tomorrow morning?" he asked as he held the restaurant's door open for them all.

"Yep," Oliver said.

"Early?"

"Ish," Parker confirmed. "Ten o'clock flight. Need to be at SeaTac by eight." Which was actually sleeping in for her, but the little extra sleep she might get would be lost to the time change flying home.

"Well, have a safe flight," Brett said as they stopped beside hers and Oliver's rental.

"We will," Oliver answered for them both as he shook Brett's hand. "Thanks for everything, Brett."

"Yeah," Parker agreed as she gave him a hug. "Thanks."

Another round of hugs with Tina and a few for Jen and Viv later they parted ways, and Parker sighed as she dropped into the passenger's seat of their rental. "That was fun, huh?"

Oliver nodded as he started the car. "It was nice to see Brett and Tina again, and Jen and Viv are good kids." He looked over at her as he shifted into reverse. "Are you seriously thinking of coming back for Thanksgiving?"

Parker shrugged. "Are you?"

"If you are, sure." He smirked. "Would you really ask McDreamy to come along if you did, though?"

"Thanks for putting that idea into Tina's head, by the way," Parker grumbled, smiling in spite of herself at the way he laughed at her response. "And, I don't know. Right now I just want to get home and see her again. It's been a long week…"

He nodded. "You okay to hit Langley's place now? Or do we need to stop and get a couple coffees to wake up?"

"You're still sure you want to do this?" she couldn't help asking.

"Parker," he groaned.

"It was worth a shot," she sighed as she glanced at the clock on the dash. It was only just after nine, but the sun had set so they would have the cover of night to hide behind, and she knew from their reconnaissance earlier that week that the massive party the Langleys' neighbor was throwing would be in full-swing by now. The party was why they had decided to wait until their last night in Seattle to pull the job, because they could be pretty much guaranteed to go undetected in the added traffic and noise. "I'm good without the coffee, unless you need one."

"Nah, I'm good."

Parker nodded and pulled her phone from her pocket as Oliver turned up the radio. It'd take them at least half an hour to get from Clyde Hill to the Queen Anne Hill neighborhood where the Langleys lived, and she figured it would be a good time to catch up on the emails she had put off looking at during the week. Most of the work emails were of the read-and-delete variety, but she gasped when she saw a message from Neal in her personal inbox that had been sent Wednesday morning.

"Everything okay?"

She hummed as she started reading, and then groaned when she saw that things were at once amazing and awful. "Neal says he found a guy in Los Angeles who knows about the Jackson Pollock I've been tracking for the last eight months."

"Well, that's good, right?"

"Yeah." She sighed. "It also means I'm not flying home tomorrow. I'm gonna have to go down to LA to talk to this guy."

"Which means you won't be meeting McDreamy for dinner tomorrow night," Oliver surmised. "That sucks, dude. I'm sorry."

She bit the inside of her cheek and shook her head. Part of her wanted to point out that his caring about her relationship with Sheridan now was more than a little ridiculous given the fact that he had talked her into helping him with the Langley job, but she really wasn't in the mood to start a fight with him right now. "Did you get flight insurance on our return tickets?"

"Yep." He nodded. "So, don't worry about that." He glanced at her phone. "When are you gonna tell Sheridan?"

Parker fiddled with her phone and shrugged. "She said she was going to dinner at Ivy and Rachel's tonight, so I'll call her tomorrow."

"You just don't want me listening-in."

"Can you honestly blame me for that?"

"Not really." He grinned when she laughed and added, "So when do I get to meet her? I mean, I should totally get to meet her before Brett and Tina."

"You're serious?"

"Yeah. Why wouldn't I be?"

"Because she's an FBI agent and you seem hell-bent on pushing through the remainder of Marquis' list?"

He huffed a breath and nodded. "I'm sorry."

Parker grit her teeth and shook her head. She'd said she would help him with this thing and now was not the time to start a fight over it. The last thing they needed was to be distracted when they got to Langley's house. "It's fine. We'll figure something out," she promised vaguely. She already felt like she was juggling too many balls that she was trying to keep track of, and at this point she was most concerned about keeping Sheridan's ball in the air so she didn't get hurt by any of this. Maybe she could introduce them after everything was settled with Marquis and Oliver showed that he really was going to join her in leaving this life of crime, but until that time came, she much preferred the two only exist in the other's periphery.

The street leading up to Langley's house was packed with cars when they arrived, and Oliver pursed his lips as he searched for a spot to park.

"There." Parker pointed at an empty spot near the entrance to the alley that serviced Langley's block."

"Fucking perfect," Oliver drawled as he angled the rental into the space. He grinned as he reached behind their seats to grab his laptop bag. "You ready?"

Parker grabbed her trusty Yankees cap from the floor where she'd tossed it earlier and nodded as she pulled it on over her hair. Combined with the black slacks and bomber jacket she had worn to dinner, it was as inconspicuous an outfit she could manage without making them stop back at the hotel to change. "As I'll ever be, I guess."

"Let's go, then," he said as he opened his car door. He'd chosen a black-on-black outfit for dinner as well, so they both managed to disappear into the shadows that filled the alley as they made their way toward Langley's dove gray Craftsman that was halfway down the hill on the right.

The noise from the party was at a level where Parker didn't doubt that any neighbors who hadn't been invited to the shindig would soon be calling the police, and she glanced at Oliver as they ducked out of the alley and into the narrow pathway beside Langley's garage where a locked gate led to the backyard. "Tell me when," she said as she grabbed the pair of gloves she'd shoved in one of the breast pockets of her jacket earlier and pulled them on.

Oliver nodded as he pulled his MacBook from his pack and quickly powered it up.

She kept an eye on the alley and an ear on the party next door as he accessed Langley's security system to shut it all down, and when he gave her the all-clear, she pulled her wallet of lock picking tools from her jacket pocket. Oliver flipped the cover of his laptop shut and slipped it back into his bag in the ten seconds it took her to pick the lock on the gate, and he pulled on the gloves she handed him as he followed her along the perimeter of the yard to the back porch. The music coming from next door was even louder on the back porch than it had been in the alley, and she shook her head as she unlocked the back door. They could have broken a goddamn window and nobody would've heard a thing.

"Okay," she muttered once they were inside the kitchen, the sound from next door still a nuisance even with the door shut behind them. "You got the first floor again?" Blueprints for the house showed an office-slash-library on the first floor, but since they were looking for a comic book, there was no telling where Langley would keep it.

"Sure." He nodded. "Remember what it looks like?"

"Yeah." She blew out a breath. "Let's go."

They split in the living room, Oliver going to the bookshelves while she started up the stairs. Parker pulled the mini-flashlight she had brought with her as she rounded the landing on the second floor, and shielded the light with her hand so it didn't shine through the uncovered windows as she made her way into the master bedroom that faced the stairs.

There was no sign of the comic in the master bedroom, and she pursed her lips as she looked out the door to the hallway and children's rooms beyond. It would be utterly irresponsible to put a two million dollar collectable where children could get it, but with no better options on this level, she made her way to the bedroom closest to the master.

A glance through the door showed crib against the far wall, and she shook her head as she moved on to the next room, which looked like it was the model room for the Pottery Barn Star Wars collection. Superman didn't exactly fit with Darth and Chewie, but she still took her time combing through the bookshelf before declaring the room a bust and moving onto the final bedroom on the floor.

The pink tutu sign with the name 'Emily' painted on it in gold script that hung on the door made her certain that this room, too, would end up being a dead-end, and she wished they'd brought their radios with them so she could check to see how Oliver was doing. It took her less than three minutes to toss Emily's room without leaving a trace of evidence that anything had been gone through, and she shook her head as she started for the stairs. If the guy was a big comic book collector, Oliver would need help going through his stash.

Assuming he'd found the stash, that is.

She eventually found Oliver in the library-slash-office, where he had pulled the drapes shut to block out the street. The lights were still off to prevent an ambient glow filtering through any uncovered windows, and he was conducting his search with his flashlight. He waved a hand at rows of plastic-sheathed comics that filled two full bookcases. "Pretty sure it's *somewhere* in here."

"Well, that's good, because there was nothing upstairs," Parker shared as she made her way over to the shelves. "Guy sure does love his comics," she said as she began slowly flipping through the comics, looking for the illustration of Superman picking up a green car that graced the cover of the comic they were looking for. "You would think he'd have the thing like framed or something so he could show it off."

"Can't look at it if it's framed. But, yeah, you'd think he'd at least have it out somewhere to show it off or something and not just..." His voice trailed off. "Hey, now," he murmured.

Parker looked up from the 1984 Catwoman she was studying and arched a brow expectantly. "Did you find it?"

He nodded and pulled a single comic from the shelf he'd been going through. He grinned as he turned it so she could see the cover. "Boom. Was with the rest of the Supermans." He looked back at the spot he'd found the comic and shook his head as he thumbed through the rest of the shelf. "I almost feel bad doing this. It looks like the guy has every single one..."

She shrugged. "Hey, I'm all for quitting right now if you are." When he scoffed and rolled his eyes because, yeah, there was no way, after having the comic in his hands that he would ever put it back, she asked, "So, do you think it's worth sticking the cheapie copy you brought in the spot?"

"Eh, not really, these things are so thin it's not going to stand out as missing or anything, but I will." He took off his backpack and pulled out the stiff folio folder he'd brought that had a comic-club reproduction of the collector's edition inside it. He pulled the worthless replica of the comic book from the folder, secured Langley's Superman in the folio, and stuck the copy on the shelf. "Guy has so many comics, it could be years before he even notices this one's gone."

Parker held up her right hand, first and middle fingers twisted together. "Fingers crossed."

The sharp squeal of a siren from the street made Parker freeze and, heart beating wildly in her chest, she crept to the window that overlooked the front lawn. There was a single cruiser parked in the middle of the crowded street, effectively blocking all traffic because of the cars parked along either curb, and two beat cops were making their way to the sidewalk on their side of the street.

"You said that you killed the alarm," she hissed.

"I did," he insisted. "Nothing we've done here should've drawn their attention."

"And yet, there are cops outside," she muttered. If the cops came up the walk toward Langley's front door, they'd have to book it out the back in a hurry, but the last thing they needed to do was draw attention to themselves until they knew where the cops were going. For a long minute the cops lingered on the sidewalk between the Langleys' house and the one next door, and she sighed with relief when they turned toward the neighbor's. "They're here for the party. Somebody must have called in a noise complaint."

"Well, that made things more exciting than I would've liked," Oliver muttered. He blew out a loud breath and sat back on his heels. "Do you think we should wait for them to leave before we bail, or do you think we should go now while everyone next door is distracted by the uniforms?" They shared a long look, and he nodded. "Right. Go now while everyone's distracted."

Parker began running her gloved hands over the edges of the comics on the shelves, making sure everything was pushed all the way in liked they had found them, and once Oliver had secured the target comic in his pack, they made their way back through the house to the kitchen and the porch beyond. The noise coming from next door had dropped considerably, and she kept an eye on the brightly lit home beyond the fence as they darted along the opposite fence line, keeping to the shadows as much as possible. Only once they were in the narrow entrance to the yard beside the detached garage did she breathe a little bit easier, and Oliver busied himself with resetting the home's alarm system while she locked the gate.

While their escape from Dumas' penthouse in Paris had been a heady, intoxicating adrenaline rush, this escape had her feeling like a ghost was chasing them back down the alley. It had been *years* since they'd had such a close call—and this one wasn't even really all that close—and she didn't like it one bit. Once they'd reached their car, she yanked her gloves off as she ducked into the passenger's seat and shoved them in her pocket, and drummed her fingers on her knees as she waited for Oliver to climb behind the wheel and get them the fuck out of there.

They both held their breath as they drove past Langley's street, not wanting to tempt the Fates to challenge them any more by drawing the police's attention, and she sighed in relief once they'd reached Mercer and were headed toward Bellevue with no sign of flashing lights in their rearview. "Can we never do that again?"

"What?" Oliver shot her a wry grin. "You didn't think that was a good time?"

"No. Not at all."

He tipped his head in a small nod. "Yeah. I hear ya." After a beat, he added, "Can't believe you asked me if I screwed up..."

Parker arched a wry brow. "Like you weren't running through a mental checklist wondering the same damn thing."

"But still!" he protested with a laugh, the gut-clenching fear from earlier clearly morphing into a giddy high of relief as they made their getaway.

"But still, what?"

"I don't know, man," he relented. He blew out a loud breath and stretched his arms against the steering wheel. "I'll pick up a burner when I get back to Boston and give Marquis a call to arrange transfer of the comic."

"How's your work schedule looking? You gonna be able to get it to her?"

He nodded. "Yeah. I've got a thing I'm developing for Liberty Mutual, but I can chip away at it on a plane easily enough depending on how she wants to do this one. I have a feeling I'll be flying to Paris for the handoff just because a comic isn't going to raise the kind of suspicion that Blake would've, but I'll see what she wants to do."

"Let me know what happens?"

"Of course. Let me know if you need help getting that Pollock back? Or, you know, getting another reservation at a kick-ass restaurant to woo the pants off McDreamy…"

Parker laughed, too relieved to have gotten away from Langley's place undetected to be bothered by the nickname. "I will."

THIRTY-TWO

"Hey!"

Sheridan smiled at Gregory, who had opened the front door just as she'd reached for her phone in her purse to call Parker and let her know she was at the door. "Hey, Gregory. How are you?"

"Hold up!" A new voice bellowed. "Is that McDreamy?"

"McDreamy?" Gregory's forehead wrinkled with confusion. "What are you talking about Ollie?" he called over his shoulder.

Sheridan shrugged as she peered over Gregory's shoulder for a glimpse of Parker's brother. Parker hadn't said anything about him coming into town this weekend and, silly nickname aside, she was looking forward to finally meeting him. "I don't know. Parker said he'd started calling me that when they were in Seattle. Maybe he was feeling inspired?"

"Maybe." Gregory winked and hollered over his shoulder, "If you want to make first pitch, you better get your butt out here, Ollie!"

"Yankees?" Sheridan guessed.

Gregory nodded. "Yep. So we'll be out of your hair all night."

She forced a small smile as her cheeks warmed with the beginning of a blush. It had been two long, long weeks of nothing but texts and phone calls when all she wanted was to kiss Parker and experience all the ways they could make good on the promises Parker had murmured against her lips at the end of their date. "Right…"

"Hey, McDreamy," a tall, muscled man with sandy blond hair and a playful smirk greeted her.

"You must be Oliver." Sheridan smiled and held out her hand. He had a nice grip, firm but not crushing, and she tipped her head as she said, "It's nice to meet you."

"You too." He smiled and tilted his head in the direction of the staircase behind him. "She's been cleaning ever since she got home, so you should probably go put her out of her misery."

"I will," she laughed. "Thank you," she added softly.

"Just keep making her smile," he replied with a little wink.

"I'll do my best," she promised.

"Okay. Good. Now that we've got that out of the way"—Gregory clapped a hand on Oliver's shoulder—"let's get going. Sheridan, you can go on up, dear."

"Thank you." She ducked her head in a small bow as they traded places, the guys moving to the porch while she took up residence in the foyer. "Have fun at the game."

"We will," Gregory and Oliver assured her in perfect unison, and she huffed an embarrassed laugh at the sly wink Gregory shot her as he pulled the door shut after them.

Any embarrassment she'd felt faded the moment she turned for the stairs, and it was all she could do to restrain herself to a measured, decorous pace instead of sprinting the two flights to Parker's studio. The first time she had visited, she had felt like a teenager walking up the stairs in this big old house to get to what was, essentially, Parker's room on the top floor, but that had faded after a few visits. It was a different living arrangement to be sure, but Gregory never seemed to impose on Parker's independence, and there was no denying that they both got something out of the other's proximity.

Parker's door at the very top of the stairs was ajar, and Sheridan smiled as she recognized the faint sound of the song Parker was listening to. She hummed along to the melody of *Worrisome Heart* as she climbed the last few steps to Parker's door, and her stomach fluttered at the idea of slipping into the apartment and somehow managing to sneak up behind Parker to surprise her with a hug and a kiss.

She eased the door open, hoping the movement wouldn't be noticed, and smiled when she saw Parker sprawled across her sofa, fast asleep. Parker looked utterly adorable with her bright purple running shorts bunched at the top of her thighs, and her gray V-neck tee that had slipped with the angle of her body so more than a hint of her black bra was visible.

"Oh, sweetie," Sheridan murmured as she carefully closed the door behind herself so it didn't make a sound. Parker had insisted she would be fine to do something tonight even though she'd landed at just after three that afternoon, and she had been too excited about the idea of finally seeing her again to even think that she might need some time to recover from her weeks on the road. She felt more than a little guilty for that, but now that she was here and Parker was so close and so very touchable, she just didn't have it in her to leave.

She set her purse on the kitchen counter and quickly divested herself of her work accessories—folding her shoulder holster and gun inside her blazer before setting the bundle on the counter beside her bag. Her heels were abandoned on the floor near the rest of her things, and she ran her hands through her hair, pushing it back away from her face and behind her ears as she padded across the room to the sitting area where Parker was sleeping.

After two weeks of nothing but text messages and late-night conversations that, more often than not ended with a whispered, heartfelt *I miss you*, there was only one way of waking Parker that seemed appropriate. She smiled as she leaned down, bracing her left hand on the back of the sofa and her right on the arm beside Parker's head, and sighed as she closed the distance between them to kiss her softly.

It didn't take long at all for Parker to wake enough to reciprocate the kiss, and the sweet, sleepy, "Hey, you," Parker murmured against her lips made her heart flutter happily in her chest. She was about to pull away when Parker's left hand found her hip and her right tangled itself in her hair, urging her closer, and she laughed as she allowed herself to be pulled onto the sofa.

"Much better," Parker hummed as Sheridan squeezed herself onto the sofa against her side, her hand on Sheridan's hip siding around to the small of her back to hold her in place as they smiled at each other.

"You think so, huh?" Sheridan nuzzled Parker's cheek and brushed a tender kiss over the corner of her lips, delighting in the fact that after what'd seemed like forever, they were together again. "I've missed you…"

"Missed you more," Parker breathed as she captured her lips in a searing kiss.

Sheridan moaned softly as Parker's tongue teased her lips with a slow lick before dipping into her mouth with an urgency not unlike the one they'd shared that night outside her front door. Her stomach fluttered when Parker groaned and shifted beneath her, Parker's legs falling open just enough to allow her left leg to slip between them as their kisses deepened, their tongues stroking languidly together in an intimate dance. She fisted the hem of Parker's tee in her left hand as she rocked against her, the slant of their mouths becoming more extreme as they surrendered to the desire they'd spent too long holding at bay.

A warm shiver rolled down her spine when Parker's hands began to wander, stroking the length of her back and lower, strong fingers digging into her ass and holding tight as she arched against her. She groaned at the feeling of Parker's thigh between her legs, and drove her hips forward to increase the delicious pressure. There was no mistaking the heat of Parker's arousal even through their clothes, and she gasped, "Oh god, Parker…"

"Is this okay?" Parker asked, moving her hands from Sheridan's ass to her hips as she waited for her answer.

Sheridan smiled, touched as she always was by the care Parker treated her with. If anything, she should be the one double-checking since she was the one pinning Parker to the sofa. This wasn't at all what she'd intended when she first leaned in to kiss her awake, but she had woken up the last two nights flushed and frustrated when her dreams ended too soon, and she wanted Parker far too much to put a stop to this now if she was willing to continue. She hummed as she dragged her lips along Parker's cheek, and brushed a kiss across her ear as she whispered, "Don't stop."

The hitch of Parker's breath and the quiet whimper that followed made Sheridan clench, and she pushed herself up enough to give Parker's hands that were gliding along her sides room to move. There was no silencing the moan that escaped her when Parker's hands reached her breasts, and her back bowed at the electric pulse that arced through her when Parker's thumbs dragged over her nipples. She gasped when it happened again, and used her chin to guide Parker's lips to a place where she could claim them, their kisses immediately deep and messy and desperate.

"Please," she husked against Parker's lips when it seemed like they'd spend eternity trapped at second base. "God, Parker, please..."

Parker's normally pale gray eyes were dark as thunderclouds when she opened them to look at her. She licked her lips twice as she seemed to search for the power to speak, and when she finally did, her voice was deliciously rough with desire. "Let me take you to bed?"

Like there existed a universe where she'd ever say no. "Yes..." Sheridan began, the rest of her words silenced with a kiss as Parker's hands dropped to her waist as she sat up beneath her.

Words were entirely unnecessary as they began shuffling their way toward Parker's bed, their kisses heated and sloppy with their focus split between the kiss and the task of getting the other naked. How they managed it was beyond her, and she sighed when the last of her clothes were pushed to the floor and Parker pulled her into her arms at the side of her bed. The feeling of Parker's skin against her own was heavenly, and she smiled at the small moan that rumbled in Parker's throat when they kissed again.

"So beautiful," Parker murmured reverently as she turned her back to the bed.

The press of Parker's thumbs against her hips and the pressure of her kiss guided her onto her the mattress, and she sighed happily when Parker stretched out on top of her. Their kisses turned tender as their legs intertwined, wandering hands languidly caressing supple curves as the urgency that'd gotten them there all but disappeared. They had all the time in the world to taste and explore and enjoy, and the fact that they only needed a kiss and a sigh and the feather-light brush of fingertips over warm skin to get on the same page sent a nearly overpowering surge of affection through her.

Never before had she been this in-tune with a lover. It was almost as if they were of one mind, one heart, one soul as they moved together. The whisper of a breath against the corner of her lips had her turning her head to the side for Parker to lavish her throat with kisses and nips, and the press of her fingertips against Parker's sides conveyed just how much she enjoyed it. The heat of Parker's mouth against her skin was delicious, setting her body alight with warmth and a feeling that with every flutter of Parker's tongue and nip of her teeth, she was closer and closer to floating away.

By the time Parker's hands curled around her inner thighs and guided them gently wider, she was gone, so lost to the sensation those wonderful hands and that talented mouth that she was aware of nothing beyond them. Her pulse beat strong and heavy between her legs as their gazes locked through the curtain of Parker's hair as kiss-swollen lips grazed her inner thigh, permission sought and immediately granted with a look and an oh-so-small tip of her head.

"You are so beautiful," Parker breathed, her eyes fluttering shut as she dipped her head to press the tenderest of kisses to sensitive skin.

Sheridan wished she had the composure to assure Parker that she felt the same way when she looked at her, but the only sound that escaped her was a breathy moan, her voice completely stolen by the sensation of Parker's tongue stroking the length of her. The first press of Parker's tongue inside her coaxed a strangled cry from her lips, and the slow, slow lick around her clit that followed made her whimper. It was as if Parker knew just where and how to touch her to drive her wild, and she grit her teeth when she felt her orgasm began to crest far too soon for her liking.

She wasn't even close to being ready for this to end.

She squeezed her eyes shut and rocked her hips down and away from Parker's mouth in an attempt to delay the inevitable, and groaned when the hands on her thighs tightened and that wonderful tongue chased after her.

"Oh, god…" she gasped when Parker's lips wrapped around her clit. Parker's answering hum of encouragement made her eyes roll back in her head, and she choked out Parker's name as she tumbled into release, her orgasm washing over her in waves as Parker's tongue fluttered encouragingly over her, helping draw it out for as long as possible.

When the final tremble eased, Sheridan smiled and ran a tender hand through Parker's hair, brushing it behind her ear before gently cradling her jaw in her fingertips. "That was amazing."

Parker smiled and pulled away from her touch just enough to float the lightest of kisses over swollen nerves. "Let me have you again?" she pleaded as she moved her right hand between her legs to let the tips of her ring and middle fingers press lightly against her.

The pressure was divine, and Sheridan swallowed thickly before forcing herself to ask, even as her hips rocked to try to pull Parker's fingers inside her, "What about you?"

Parker's eyes gentled with affection as she dipped her chin to draw a lazy circle around her clit with the tip of her tongue. "Later, sweetie. I promise," she murmured, her gaze adoring as she eased two fingers inside her.

"Oh, Parker," Sheridan groaned, shifting her grip from Parker's jaw to thread through her hair as her hips lifted off the mattress to take her deeper.

"That's it, baby…" Parker encouraged softly as she curled her fingers just so to brush over hidden ridges. "I could do this forever," she breathed as she kissed between her legs.

The combination of Parker's long, long fingers pumping inside her and that oh-so-talented tongue lapping at her clit had Sheridan racing toward ecstasy again in what seemed like no time at all. Her hips rocked desperately against Parker's mouth as her back bowed and her head fall back in supplication. She fisted her left hand around the pillow beneath her head as her breath came harder and faster, the sound rough and heavy and desperate as she spiraled higher and higher until she came with a silent scream that still left her throat utterly raw by the time it was over.

She whimpered as she sank back into the mattress, eyes closed and her body blissfully boneless as she rasped, "Parker…"

"Hmm?" Parker sounded entirely too pleased with herself as she pressed a lingering kiss to her inner thigh. She chuckled at the small whine that escaped Sheridan as she shifted away from the touch, her body too stimulated to handle the teasing, and sighed as she slowly unsheathed her fingers and dragged her lips up the length of Sheridan's body to kiss her softly. "Okay?"

Sheridan hummed at the taste of herself on Parker's tongue and nodded. "Very okay," she assured her as she lifted her head to capture her lips in a deep, lingering kiss.

"You ready to go again?" Parker murmured playfully when Sheridan's hands began to wander.

Sheridan laughed and shook her head as she used her hips to reverse their positions and flip Parker onto her back. "No." She pressed a kiss to Parker's throat and smiled at the way Parker turned her head with a whimper. She fluttered her tongue over Parker's pulse point before capturing it between her lips and sucking it into her mouth, teasing the spot with her teeth in a way that made Parker gasp and squirm beneath her. It was an absolute high to know that it was her touch that was driving Parker so crazy, and she smiled as she dusted a soft kiss over the blush of a mark that hopefully wouldn't last much longer than the night beneath Parker's jaw. "It's my turn to have you..."

Parker's grip on her hips tightened as she moaned, "Oh, yes…"

thirty-three

Parker looked up from the breakfast she was preparing when she spotted Sheridan roll out of bed at half past nine the next morning, looking beautifully spent with her tousled hair and sleepy eyes and her bare, bare skin that seemed to glow in the bright morning sunlight that streamed through the skylights overhead. She smiled as memories of the night before flooded her senses as her eyes traced the lines of Sheridan's body, the curve of her hips and the swell of her breasts, and her heart fluttered in her chest as she watched Sheridan lean down to pick up the gray T-shirt she'd been wearing the day before and pull it on. She bit her lip as she watched the soft cotton slip over Sheridan's body like a caress, dragging slowly over her nipples before falling to the tops of her thighs. Her fingers itched to slip beneath the hem of the shirt and touch the soft, soft skin she could spend an eternity worshipping, and if it weren't for the fact that Sheridan didn't look entirely awake, she probably would have put down the measuring cup in her hand and dragged her back to bed.

She knew that Sheridan didn't *do* mornings, however, so she stayed in the kitchen and pretended not to notice the goddess shuffling sleepily her way. It took all of her self-control to not laugh when she saw the quirk of Sheridan's lips when she didn't react as she neared the kitchen, but she managed to pretend to be focused on the milk she was measuring out even as every one of her senses was attuned to Sheridan's progress.

It was adorable, really, that Sheridan thought she was actually sneaking up on her, and Parker held her breath as Sheridan disappeared beyond her periphery. Would Sheridan murmur hello as she made a beeline for the coffee machine? Or would she slink behind her to capture her in a stealthy hug? Would she kiss her neck? Untie the short robe she'd pulled on and slip a hand between her legs?

God, it was all she could do to not drop the measuring cup in her hand as *that* idea flashed across her mind, and she swallowed thickly as she quickly set it on the counter. She pressed her hands to the butcher block countertop on the island to ground herself, and was almost glad that her imagination was stopped from running rampant with fantasy scenarios when Sheridan's hands curled around her waist.

"Hey, you," Sheridan murmured, her voice husky with sleep.

Parker closed her eyes as her heart leapt at the feeling of Sheridan's arms wrapping around her waist as a soft kiss was pressed her shoulder through the thin fabric of her robe. "Hey, yourself," she replied softly. "Do you want some coffee?"

"Maybe later," Sheridan deferred through a yawn.

"You sure about that?" Parker chuckled as she turned in Sheridan's embrace. Sheridan looked tired but happy as she shook her head, and she didn't even try to contain her smile as she cradled Sheridan's face in her hands. Joy, pure and bright and light filled her chest as she stroked her thumbs over the curves of her cheeks, and she sighed as she dipped her head to lay the softest of kisses to her lips. "Good morning, beautiful."

A small sound of contentment rumbled in Sheridan's throat as she lifted herself up onto the balls of her feet so they were eye-to-eye. Her smile was soft and warm as she kissed her, and her eyes sparkled with happiness as she flicked her tongue over her lips.

Parker's stomach flipped at the playful lick, and she moaned softly as she claimed Sheridan's lips in a searing kiss. The grip on her hips tightened, the kiss deepening as Sheridan pressed her back against the edge of the counter, and she grinned into the kiss as she slid her hands down Sheridan's throat to her breasts. "You look so good in my shirt," she whispered as she rubbed her hands over Sheridan's breasts, a thrill rippling through her as already stiff nipples raked across her palms. The sound of Sheridan whimpering as she arched into her hands made her stomach clench, and she groaned as she dropped her hands to the hem of the shirt.

She was pretty sure she'd never wanted anyone as badly as she wanted Sheridan in that moment.

"Parker," Sheridan groaned.

"I know, baby," Parker husked as she slipped her hands beneath the shirt to grab Sheridan's ass. She angled her right leg between Sheridan's as she pulled her closer, and moaned when warm, slick arousal coated her thigh. She rocked her thigh against Sheridan as she worked the shirt higher, and hummed when Sheridan picked up the rhythm, hips rolling in a slow, sensual grind that had her stomach swooping with every thrust and diving with every retreat. She swallowed thickly as she worked the shirt up and over Sheridan's head, and smiled as she tossed it aside. "God, you're gorgeous," she breathed.

Sheridan smiled, looking at once somehow both shy and ridiculously sexy. "You are," she murmured as she slowly untied the sash holding Parker's robe closed, every movement matched to the tempo of her hips.

Parker caressed Sheridan's hips, encouraging their slow, oh so fucking perfect grind as she watched, utterly enraptured as Sheridan dragged the backs of her fingers slowly up her stomach. She grabbed Sheridan's hips as those wonderful fingers began circling her breasts, lazily spiraling tighter and tighter until a single fingertip was tracing her nipples. She sucked in a sharp breath when Sheridan's fingers closed around them and tugged, and asked, "Should we take this back to bed?"

"Why? Here's good." Sheridan dropped a quick kiss to her lips and winked as she stopped playing with her breasts and dragged the backs of her fingers up to her shoulders to push the robe to the floor.

Parker smiled as Sheridan leaned into her, and adjusted her stance as a lean thigh pressed between her legs. "God, Sheridan..." she breathed against Sheridan's lips as she rocked against her thigh.

"Okay?" Sheridan asked softly. She touched their foreheads together and kissed her softly as her right hand wrapped lightly around Parker's left hip.

"Fucking perfect," Parker assured her as she mirrored her hold, using that soft touch on her hip to guide their movement.

And, oh, how it was.

While she might have imagined a more involved scenario, she wouldn't have traded this slow, intimate dance they'd fallen into for the world. Not when it allowed her to watch Sheridan's eyes darken to the color of the midnight sky, so deep and full of gentle affection that it made her heart feel like it was too big to fit in her chest.

Sheridan's name slipped from her lips on a sigh, and she smiled as she lifted Sheridan's chin to capture her lips in a slow, deep kiss. Their tongues swirled lightly together to the tempo of their hips, languid and unhurried as free hands roamed idly over backs and sides and shoulders, stroking, caressing, and pressing tightly when the passion of the moment became too much and another level of closeness was needed.

The problem was that they were already hip to hip and breast to breast, and there just *wasn't* a way for them to get physically closer. But it was that desperation to find a way regardless that sped the tempo of their hips as they pushed harder, as if by speed and force alone they might find what eluded them. It was primal and hungry and soft and so fucking tender all at once, and her head was abuzz with the sound of their breaths falling in synchronous ragged waves as they surged closer, closer, closer, their foreheads pressed together so hard it almost hurt as fingers dug into hips and hands pressed between shoulder blades, pulling, pulling, pulling until time seemed to stop and with a whimper and a sigh they fell as one, spiraling into euphoria.

It was the most dizzying orgasm she had ever experienced, and she squeezed her eyes shut to try to block out the world that was spinning around her. The solid press of Sheridan's body against her front and the edge of the counter behind her were the only things keeping her upright as her entire world was consumed by warmth and light and, most importantly of all, Sheridan.

Parker smiled as she blindly sought Sheridan's lips, and hummed when she found them parted and waiting. The kiss was as perfect as everything they'd just shared, and she sighed as Sheridan melted into her.

I could do this for the rest of my life.

"Take me to bed," Sheridan whispered as she curled around her.

Her throat was too tight with emotion to speak, she just kissed Sheridan softly as she took her hand. The short trip to the rumpled sheets she'd gladly never leave was slowed by the fact that they couldn't stop kissing, long and slow and deep in a way that made it impossible to walk at the same time. Eventually they managed it, however, and she smiled as she guided Sheridan back onto the bed.

God, I could so do this for the rest of my fucking life, Parker thought again, feeling like she was flying and falling all at once as she laid down on top of her, their bodies fitting together like two halves of a whole as they came together again.

THIRTY-FOUR

The auction manifest for rare books sold over the last decade at Sotheby's London house made for dry reading, but even the most interesting novel would have had a hard time keeping Sheridan's attention at the moment. Honestly, anything that wasn't Parker Ravenscroft would have had a hard time holding her attention, because the memory of how Parker had looked at her when they'd finally had to end their weekend together—tousle-haired and gorgeous, with the softest, sweetest smile curling her lips as they lingered in their goodbyes—seemed to bulldoze its way into her thoughts almost constantly.

It was annoying, but mostly because that had been the last time she'd seen Parker thanks to a claim for a Tiffany diamond choker down in Philadelphia that Parker had to go investigate, and she really just wanted to kiss her again.

The shrill ring of the phone on her desk snapped her focus back to the bustling bullpen that seemed to be in constant motion around her, and she sighed as she refocused her eyes on the manifest as she reached blindly for the handset. "Sloan."

"Agent Sloan, this is Johan Lusky with the Art Loss Register returning your call."

"Oh, yes. Thank you for calling me back." Sheridan sat back in her chair and snapped her fingers to get Kelly's attention. When he looked at her, she motioned to the phone and mouthed, "Art Loss."

Kelly rolled his chair over to beside hers and leaned over to listen through the receiver that she angled away from her ear.

"Of course. You are looking for information regarding rare book thefts, is that correct?"

"Yeah. I was wondering if anything new had been reported recently? I'm working a dead-end at the moment and am grasping at straws…"

The quiet clatter of keys trickled through the phone before Lusky said, *"Yeah. I'm not seeing anything new reported, but there's a note on the bottom of this file that I want to go ask somebody about real quick. Can you hold on a minute?"*

Kelly's expression was the exact level of *what the fuck* as hers as she replied, "Of course."

"What do you think it is?" Kelly whispered as they listened to canned elevator music on hold.

"Hopefully some kind of lead," Sheridan muttered. "It's been over a month since the Blake was stolen, and if we don't come up with something soon, Bartz is gonna yank it from us."

"Would that be a bad thing, though?" he asked, playing devil's advocate. "I mean, god knows it's been nothing but a frustrating waste of time."

"There's something there," she insisted with a small shake of her head. "I just know it. Those three books are connected somehow, and if we can find the thread that ties them together, we can break this thing wide open."

"You still there?" Lusky came back on the line.

She nodded. "I am."

"Okay. So, I asked my colleague about the note on the file, and they confirmed that they'd heard the same rumors floating around, but keep in mind that what I'm going to tell you is pure conjecture at this point."

"Okay…"

"Right. Well, there's been talk from some agents we work with about there being a shopping list out there somewhere with an indeterminate number of valuable books on it. Some say five, some say six, and others eight, but nobody knows for sure exactly how many we're talking about. The rumor is that the person paying for the goods is powerful and, obviously, incredibly wealthy, but there are any number of people who could fit that description."

"Any idea where the list originated from?"

"Not really." Lusky admitted with a heavy sigh. *"But we've heard mention of it from agents in Brussels, Barcelona, and Paris."*

She shot Kelly a surprised look. "So, any idea of what's on this list?"

"I'm sorry, no."

She sighed. Knowing there was a mysterious list out there was one thing, but it would've been nice to have something a little more substantial to work with. "All right. Thanks. Let me know if anything new is reported?"

"I'll flag the file so you'll be notified the moment something comes in."

"Perfect. Thanks so much." Sheridan shook her head as she set the receiver back into its cradle. "At least we know that there's probably a list out there somewhere that Filibus is working off of…"

"Do you think The Antiquarian is behind it all?" Kelly asked. "She's certainly powerful and mega-fucking-wealthy."

"With a well-known interest in rare books." Sheridan shrugged. "Honestly, my gut says yes because this is exactly the kind of stuff she'd be into. But she's been quiet on the rare books front lately so we could be hamstringing ourselves if we focus solely on her."

"Do you think Guillard is keeping us out of the loop on purpose?"

She threw her hands in the air and sank back in her chair. "I don't know, man. I thought we had a pretty good rapport going there, but…" She shook her head. "Hopefully it's just a case of her not wanting to pass on unsubstantiated information. Or…" she stretched that single syllable out for a few beats as a new idea came to mind. "It could be Bellet being a dick."

"That makes a lot more sense, honestly…"

"Yeah, tell me about it." She tapped her pen on the sketch of a list she'd brainstormed with Ivy the week before. "If I were a betting woman, I'd say the first edition *Canterbury Tales* that's owned by a guy outside London is on the list."

"Not the Shakespeare folio?" Kelly asked, pointing at the title that she'd circled on her notes.

"Given the literary slant of everything that has been taken so far, the Shakespeare is certainly a good bet too." She blew out a loud breath and ran her hands through her hair. "The problem is that there's no way of knowing for sure, and it'd be an absolute waste of manpower to stick agents on those two books, let alone all the others that are out there."

Kelly's computer pinged with an incoming email, and she picked up her list again as he rolled his chair back to his desk. The Chaucer and Shakespeare volumes had to be on this mysterious list, but what else?

"Um, Sheridan…."

She tossed the pages onto her desk and looked at Kelly. "Huh?"

"An agent from the Seattle field office sent an inquiry to see if a comic book qualifies as art and if it'd fall under our department's purview." He made a face. "Does it? I mean, I like comics as much as the next nerd, but they're not exactly fine art, ya know?"

"I honestly don't know. Did they say anything else?"

"Just that a Superman comic was stolen. Says the guy who owned it claims it's worth a couple million, which is why he thought he'd see if it's our thing or not."

"A couple million? For a comic book?" Sheridan arched a disbelieving brow. Surely the agent had to be pulling their leg with that one. Although, god knows she'd seen much worse than a comic valued at much, much more than that. "Did he say if they have any leads on it?"

"Nothing major. The family was on vacation when they claim it had to've been stolen, but the security system didn't go off or anything. Only police call to the neighborhood during the time they were away was for a noise disturbance at their neighbor's place for a party."

Sheridan shrugged. "I honestly don't know if it'd be our type of thing or not."

"Certainly doesn't sound like Filibus, that's for sure," Kelly added. "No matter how valuable that comic is, it isn't even close to being similar to the other books we're looking into. Want me to tell them we'll check with our supervisor to see if this is something we could help with, but to run the leads they got in the meantime?"

"Yeah. We've got enough shit we're dealing with." Sheridan sighed. It didn't seem right to totally brush them off. And if the comic really was worth two million, it probably did fall under their purview. "You know what? Just go ahead and ask them to send a copy of the file over. *Somebody* around here can take a look at it to see if we can't offer some support that way for now. I don't want to be flying out to Seattle to look at a dead end when Filibus could be targeting actual rare books elsewhere as we speak."

"You got it," Kelly said as he spun to his keyboard to relay the decision.

Sheridan drummed her fingers on the arm of her chair as she stared blankly at the papers on her desk, wishing that one page, one scribbled note, one anything would pop up and shout, *I'm the clue you're looking for!*

She blinked as movement beyond her blurred field of vision caught her attention, and gasped in surprise when she saw Parker standing in front of her desk. Parker was dressed casually in a pair of faded jeans and a tight black tee, and Sheridan smiled as she dragged her eyes over Parker's body. God, she'd missed her. Parker's amused expression turned mildly concerned the longer she stared at her without saying anything, and she shook her head as she jumped to her feet. "Hey! What are you doing here?"

Parker chuckled and shrugged as she shoved her hands into the back pockets of her jeans. "I was on my way home from Philly, so I thought I'd drop by and see if you wanted to maybe grab that dinner I had to cancel?"

"Of course I do."

Kelly laughed. "Dude, Sloan, way to play hard to get."

"Would you rather stay late and keep working the Filibus case?" she shot back.

He shuddered. "Please, no."

"Filibus?" Parker asked, her forehead wrinkling as her gaze traveled from Sheridan to Kelly and back again. "Did somebody, like, steal the actual film or something?"

"Okay, for real…" Kelly threw his hands in the air dramatically. "Is there like a test you all have to take or something? How am I the only one who needed that whole thing explained?"

"I'm sorry." Parker's confusion deepened, and it was all Sheridan could do to not laugh. "You all, who?"

"Lesbians!"

"Don't make me call HR on your ass, Innes," Ivy drawled as she and Rachel sauntered into the unit with a guy in a slightly rumpled suit and a shiny pair of handcuffs between them. "You guys cool if we steal the conference room for a bit?"

Sheridan chuckled and waved a hand toward the stairs to the upper level of the unit. "Knock yourself out. You need us for anything?"

"Nah, we got it," Rachel answered. She smiled at Parker. "Hey, lady. You guys going out?"

Parker shrugged and looked at Sheridan. "Are we?"

"We are," Sheridan confirmed with a nod. She glanced at the time on her phone and grinned. It was a quarter past five, so she was good to go. "Bright and early, Kel?"

"Yup." He nodded and shot Parker a sly grin. "So don't keep her up too late, Parker."

Parker ducked her head in a small nod. Her embarrassment was unexpected, given how she usually rolled so easily with this type of teasing, but it was also so entirely adorable that it was all Sheridan could do to not lean across her desk and kiss her.

"I will ask Ivy to kick your ass, you know," Sheridan threatened playfully as she pulled on her blazer. She smirked at the concerned look that flashed across Kelly's face as his eyes darted toward the conference room and slapped a heavy hand on his shoulder as she made her way to where Parker was watching them. "I'm kidding, Innes. I'll see you in the morning."

"Oh, thank god," he muttered.

Sheridan chuckled as she slipped a hand in the crook of Parker's arm. "You ready?"

"Sure."

"So did you recover the choker?" She asked as they made their way out of the unit.

"Not yet," Parker said as she pulled the door open for them. "But I have some good leads that I can work from here."

"I'm glad."

"Me too." Parker smiled as she followed Sheridan into the small elevator foyer outside the unit. "I'm so sorry I had to go out of town like that."

"I'm sorry too," Sheridan murmured, squeezing Parker's arm gently. "After last weekend, the last thing I wanted was to go days without seeing you again, but it's kind of part of the deal with our jobs being what they are."

"Sheridan…" Parker's voice trailed off as the doors in front of them opened to reveal an empty elevator.

Sheridan smiled at the way Parker pulled her into her arms as soon as they were tucked safely away from prying eyes, and she sighed as Parker claimed her lips in a soft, sweet kiss. She ran a tender hand over

Parker's cheek as she lingered in the caress for a few heartbeats before forcing herself to pull away. "Cameras everywhere in here," she murmured as she brushed her thumb over the small frown that tugged at the corner of Parker's lips.

"Right. Sorry," Parker breathed, her eyes darting to the telltale black bubbles in the corners of the elevator's ceiling. "I've just missed—"

"Shh." She pressed a finger to Parker's lips. And, yeah, that was definitely a bad idea because it only made her want to kiss Parker more. "Believe me, I understand." She sighed as her hand fell to Parker's hip. They were still standing too close together to be appropriate given their location, but compared to what she'd much rather be doing, restraining herself to only standing a little too close to Parker took an almost superhuman amount of willpower.

"Would you want to just pick up dinner and take it to your place?" Parker lifted her right shoulder in a small shrug. "I mean, we can totally go out, too, but I..."

"Want to be alone?" Sheridan guessed. When Parker nodded, she gave her side a light squeeze. "I think that sounds wonderful."

"Good," Parker breathed as the elevator stopped at the lobby, and arched a wry brow as she motioned for her to go first.

She smiled and curled her hand around the crook of Parker's arm like she had upstairs as she led them out of the elevator. "Where did you park?"

"I left my bike in a garage over by your loft." Parker handed the security guard her visitor's badge as they passed the metal detectors.

"Living dangerously, huh?" she teased. Rates at the garages near her loft were insane if you didn't have a monthly contract, and even those "discounted" rates were borderline criminal.

"I prefer to think of it as being optimistic that Fate was done fucking with me for the week," Parker chuckled. She covered Sheridan's hand on her arm with her own as they exited the building, holding it in place as they turned toward her loft. After a few minutes of easy silence, she asked, "Can I ask what the whole Filibus thing was about? You never said if somebody stole the film or not…"

"As far as I know, the film is right where it belongs. Wherever that is," Sheridan added, because she honestly had no idea where the original film was kept. "We've been working a case that's left us completely stumped, and we've started calling the thieves Filibus because it seems like these guys swoop in out of nowhere and disappear the same way."

"Oh." Parker licked her lips and nodded slowly. "I see…"

"Anyway, it was just something me and Ivy came up with when we were brainstorming ideas about the case when you were in Seattle."

"So that's why Kelly reacted like that when I recognized the name," Parker surmised.

"Exactly," she chuckled. "Anyway, enough talk about work. Is anything sounding good for dinner?"

"I'm honestly not that hungry right now," Parker admitted with a shrug. "So whatever you'd like is fine."

"Want to just order a pizza later?"

"Sure. Or I can run out and pick us up something." Parker's arm flexed, squeezing her hand playfully between forearm and biceps. "I mean, between not making the lasagna I totally meant to cook for you last weekend and then canceling on you Monday night, god knows I owe you a proper meal…"

It was clear Parker meant it, but Sheridan didn't want her feeling guilty for things she wasn't at all upset about. Since Parker was squeezing her hand anyway, she used that hold to pull her close enough to whisper huskily in her ear, "While I am looking forward to trying this lasagna you keep talking about, I'm not at all sorry for how we spent last weekend." The flutter of Parker's eyelashes as a pleased smile tugged at her lips was exactly the reaction she'd been going for, and she smiled as she pressed a quick kiss to her cheek.

"God, Sheridan," Parker half-moaned, half-laughed.

"What?"

Parker took a deep breath, her eyes slipping shut for a couple heartbeats as she let it go slowly. She shook her head as she blinked her eyes open, and the gentle affection Sheridan saw staring back at her made her heart skip a beat. "I just really missed you this week," Parker murmured.

If it weren't for the fact that they had reached her building, Sheridan would have been tempted to say fuck-all to propriety, push Parker up against the closest wall, and kiss her with all the longing that'd built up inside her over the last four days. Instead, however, she just swore softly under her breath and unlocked the door to the lobby. She pulled Parker past the elevator to the stairs, and rolled her eyes at the sound of Parker's soft, knowing laughter.

"You are more than welcome to wait for the elevator," Sheridan pointed out, shooting a playful look over her shoulder at Parker, who was putting up exactly no resistance as she allowed herself to be dragged up the stairs.

"I have no idea what you're talking about," Parker replied, her expression so perfectly innocent that if it weren't for the oh-so-slight hint of a smile she couldn't quite contain, Sheridan might have believed her.

"Sure you don't," Sheridan sassed, laughter bubbling in her throat at the flirty wink Parker shot her in response.

She wasn't all that surprised to feel Parker's arms sliding around her waist when they stopped in front of her door so she could find her keys, but she was surprised by the soft breath that tickled her neck before Parker's cheek pressed against her own as she held her close. No teasing kisses, no wandering hands, it was just a sweet, simple hug that conveyed better than words ever could how much she'd been missed.

Tears stung at the backs of her eyes as affection bloomed in her chest, and she gave up trying to find her keys and instead leaned back into Parker. She let her eyes flutter shut as she threaded her fingers through Parker's on her hips, and she smiled at the soft hum of contentment that rumbled against her ear as a tender kiss landed on her cheek.

The slamming of her neighbor's door behind them reminded her that they weren't alone, and she sighed as she pulled her hands away from Parker's and resumed searching for her keys. She was heartened by the way the hold on her hips loosened but didn't fall away completely, and once they were through her front door, she hurried to set her things on the kitchen counter. She wanted to hold Parker, to take her in her arms and breathe in her scent, and she didn't want anything in the way.

"Just let me take this all off," she murmured when familiar hands found her hips not long after the front door slammed shut.

"Okay," Parker breathed, her thumbs rubbing small circles against Sheridan's sides as she hovered at enough of a distance to allow her to slip her holster from her shoulders.

Once her Glock was set quietly on the counter beside her purse, Sheridan turned and pulled Parker into her arms, a feeling of *rightness* settling in her chest as she held her properly for the first time in what seemed like forever. "God…"

"Believe me, I know," Parker whispered against her ear, her voice choked with so much emotion that Sheridan's heart clenched at the sound of it. "I've been wanting to do this from the moment I watched you walk away Sunday night," she confessed softly, as if afraid that if she were to put any real weight behind her words, she might scare her away.

As if that were even a possibility at this point.

"Come on," Sheridan murmured as she took Parker's hands and gave them a gentle tug as she began walking backwards toward the stairs to her bedroom. She smiled at the small frown that wrinkled Parker's forehead and shook her head. "I just want to change into something comfortable and hold you for a while. Is that okay?"

"Oh, Sheridan." Parker swallowed thickly and pulled her close enough to capture her lips in a slow, sweet kiss. Her gaze was molten when she pulled away, and she smiled as she brushed a feather-light kiss across Sheridan's lips. "Always."

thirty-five

"Turns out the library where the Chaucer is kept was profiled in *Architectural Digest* last year," Oliver announced by way of greeting as he barged through Parker's door, waving a rolled up magazine in the air victoriously.

Parker looked up from the duffle she'd been busy packing and rolled her eyes. "Hello to you too, Olls."

He laughed and ran to cannonball onto the bed beside where she was packing, sending her gym bag airborne for a few seconds before it flopped back onto the covers. "Hey. You and McDreamy are at the pack a bag stage already, huh?" He reached for the open flap. "Whatcha got in there, anyway?"

"Oh, well, you know…*things*." She laughed as he snatched his hand away, looking positively scandalized. "Like clean underwear. And a toothbrush. But you just go on ahead and keep that mind of yours in the gutter…"

"Hey, you're the one who was all—you know, *things*," he argued with a sassy little head wiggle.

"Because it was too easy. How was your meeting with that client this morning?" She asked as she left the bag on the bed and wandered into her closet. She still needed to grab some clothes for the next day.

"Good. It'll be a big account; the company wants their entire system safeguarded and their firewalls updated. The shit hasn't been touched since the early aughts, though, so it's gonna take some serious hours to get it all up to speed."

Parker grabbed a clean pair of shorts and a shirt, and snagged a hoodie off a hanger. "That's good," she said as she made her way back to her bed. Oliver had made himself comfortable on Sheridan's side of the bed, and she shook her head as she laid the clothes she'd pulled beside her bag. "But…I mean, can you afford to focus on just one account like that?"

"Yeah. I may need to dip into some of the Marquis money if it takes longer than I think it will, but I'll be more than good once I've finished the job. That little bio *Tech* magazine did on me that just came out has bumped my name recognition a lot. I mean, I wasn't exactly hurting for business before, you know? But I've been getting enough inquiries lately that I thought I'd see what would happen if I went into this meeting saying my hourly rate was twice what I've been charging, and these guys didn't even bat an eye—they just asked how much time I needed to get the job done."

"Nice."

"Yeah." He gave her duffle a little shove. "So what time are you going to McDreamy's?"

"Whenever I can ditch your ass," she teased.

"Rude! Did yoga not get you all nice and zen this morning?"

"I am totally nice and zen," Parker assured him as she ducked her head, pretending to focus on the clothes she was shoving into her bag so he wouldn't see the smile on her face. Sheridan had come over after work the night before, and even though she hadn't looked at the clock by the time they'd finally collapsed against each other, too tired to even think about attempting another round, it had to have been close to three. Or later. Whatever the case, there was no way she was waking up for her usual six o'clock sculpt, so she'd ended up going to an early afternoon Vinyasa class instead when Sheridan had left to go take care of a few errands. Staying in bed all weekend was fun, but they did that last weekend and real-life responsibilities like needing groceries and clean laundry just couldn't be ignored forever.

"I don't want to know."

"You really don't," she agreed as she whipped the zipper on her duffle shut.

"Ew," he laughed. "Anyway"—he slid off the bed and made his way toward the kitchen table where he'd tossed the magazine he'd been waving when he came in—"for as much as I love hearing all about your love life, I actually did find out some interesting shit about the Chaucer."

Parker combed her hands through her hair as she followed him toward the center of her apartment. "Ollie..." she groaned.

"Look at this library." He either completely missed the frustration in her tone or just decided to ignore it, because he smiled as he flipped the magazine open and spun it for her to see. "There's even a skeleton in that little alcove there." He tapped one of the smaller pictures in the spread. "How cool is that?"

She glanced at the pictures. The only word that could come close to describing the library was opulent. It was straight out of a bygone era, with light maple floors and dark oak floor-to-ceiling bookshelves. Every shelf in the entire room protected by glass doors—which would mean they could be looking at possibly having to spend hours looking for the book. The long, rectangular room was accessed by twin French doors that opened to the middle of the space, either end was anchored by a large window that overlooked the grounds, and the box beam ceiling was stained to match both the shelves and the freestanding tables that sat in either wing of the room. And, sure enough, there was definitely a skeleton hidden away in an alcove like a prop from the *Pirates of the Caribbean* ride at Disneyland. "The skeleton is definitely unusual," she conceded. "But, Olls..."

"Because everything's behind glass, it's impossible to pinpoint an area where the Chaucer is kept, but I figure that between the two of us—"

Parker shook her head as she interrupted him, "Ollie."

He blinked, his brow furrowing with confusion. "What?"

"No."

"No, what?"

"This." She waved a hand at the magazine. "I don't want to do this one."

"Parker," Oliver groaned. He shook his head and set his hands on his hips. "Come on."

"You come on, Ollie," she snapped as she mirrored his posture. "I'm tired of lying to Sheridan, okay? I'm tired of feeling guilty for wanting her when I'm running around wherever doing this shit with you. I'm tired, Ollie. Of all of it. I want my nice, easy, occasionally frustrating but entirely *legal* life back. I just want to wake up in the morning and go to class before work, and I want to be free to fall in love and build an actual goddamn life for myself without looking over my shoulder constantly. Do you get that?"

"Yeah. I get that." He held his hands out at his sides. "But Parker, we'll be in a totally different country. It's nowhere near the FBI's jurisdiction, and the only way Sheridan would get called in was if they somehow realized all the cases are connected."

"That's not the point!"

He threw his hands in the air. "Then what is the point?"

"We're better than this, Ollie."

"You are. I was," he agreed. His lips pinched into a hard line and he shook his head. "But look where being better than this got me. I don't have a job where I can just pick up a missing statue or something and bank a million bucks. It's just three more books, Parker."

She fisted her hands in her hair and wandered over to the French doors that overlooked the small rooftop patio outside.

"Please, Parker," he asked softly.

She closed her eyes and lifted her face to the ceiling as she blew out a long breath. He was being reckless and greedy and, even though it hurt her to do it, she shook her head. "No, Ollie. I'm sorry," she whispered as she turned to face him. "But no. I'm not doing this one with you. We've made enough on those other four books that you don't need the money anymore. Hell, you said it yourself, you just picked up a massive account for your *legitimate* business. Take the Marquis money to pay off your debts and tide yourself over while you do that, and forget about the rest of the books on her fucking list."

"But what if something else happens?"

She sighed. "There's always that risk, Olls. For everybody. You, me, Gregory, Sheridan, the Johanns. That's part of life, man. But you've got four million dollars in the Luxembourg account as a safety net."

"Half of that is yours."

"And I don't want it." She shook her head as his expression turned incredulous. "I never did. The only reason I agreed to this was to help you because you were too goddamn proud to let me help you last year when you got hurt. I'm serious, Ollie. I don't want anything to do with the money."

"I'm not taking your money," he insisted.

"So use it to set up a fucking scholarship for kids like us back in the system in Seattle or something," she shot back, throwing her hands in the air. "God knows they can use it more than I can."

He shook his head, utterly incredulous. "You're serious?"

"Yeah." She nodded. "I'm sorry, Ollie, but I am."

He blew out a rough breath and ran a hand through his hair as frustration and hurt flashed across his expression. "You'd really choose Sheridan over me?"

She swallowed thickly and shrugged as if the accusation in his tone wasn't the knife to her heart that it was. "You'd really choose to risk everything over me?"

"But there's no risk!" He picked up the magazine and dropped it back onto the table. "We can do this!"

"There is," she insisted, blinking back the tears that stung at her eyes. She hated the way he was looking at her, like she was betraying him by choosing her own happiness, but she couldn't back down. Couldn't take the words back and give-in like she usually did. She didn't want to have to choose between him and Sheridan, but he was forcing her hand. He was being reckless and so fucking stupid that she half-wanted to smack him upside the head for it all. She didn't want to do this. It killed her to do it, her heart was literally breaking as she stared at him, but their sporadic bits of thievery had always been a risk-versus-reward type thing, and the reward wasn't enough for her to overlook the risks any more. "You might not want to see it yet, but for me, there absolutely is, and padding that bank account in Europe a bit more isn't worth it."

He scrubbed his hands over his face and pressed the heels of his palms into his eyes as he shook his head. "Parker…"

"Just say no, Ollie," Parker pleaded, the tears she'd been trying to hold at bay finally breaking free to spill down her cheeks. "You don't have to do this."

"I'm sorry, Parker," he whispered. His hands fell to his sides, and it was all she could do to not look away when she saw his eyes glistening with tears. "But I feel like I do." He looked up at the ceiling and sighed. "I should go. Let you get over to Sheridan's."

Parker reached for his arm to stop him, but he pulled away. "Ollie, please…"

He blew out a ragged sigh and shook his head as his shoulders sank in defeat. "I know, Parker. And I guess I can't blame you for choosing her, but—"

"I don't want to choose her over you," Parker insisted, her voice breaking.

"She makes you happy. And you should always choose what makes you happy." He bit his lip and shrugged as he turned toward the door. "I'm gonna go, now. Okay?"

Fresh tears coursed down her cheeks as she nodded. "Call me later?"

"Yeah. Of course."

"I love you."

His lips curled in a pained, watery smile, and he tipped his head in a small nod. "Love you too, Park. But I'm gonna go now, okay?"

"Okay, Olls," she breathed. She didn't even bother to try to wipe away the tears that wet her cheeks as she watched the door close behind him, the quiet click of the latch more than loud enough to break her heart into a million pieces.

THIRTY-SIX

Sheridan relaxed back in her chair and crossed her legs as she watched Parker over the rim of her wineglass. Parker had been quiet since she'd arrived a few hours ago. Not distant, really, because she'd held her tighter than usual and the few kisses they'd shared had an almost desperate edge to them, like Parker was trying to assure herself that she was really there—but just...quiet. Thoughtful. Like she had too many things on her mind and was trying to sort through it all.

Which, really, god knows she could relate to that. But it was so different from how Parker usually behaved that she couldn't help but worry about what, exactly, had affected her mood so acutely. She didn't dare ask her about it though, just in case she didn't like the answer to any of the thousand and one hypothetical situations her overactive imagination had concocted while they'd cuddled on her couch watching a tiny house marathon on HGTV, but not knowing only gave her thoughts a virtual playground of lingering insecurities to explore.

She tried to reassure herself with the fact that Parker was here, with her, and that had to mean something, but her well-intentioned pep talks did very little to banish the shadow she was never good enough that crept into her thoughts. She hated that she doubted Parker and what they'd found together but, try as she might, those old coping mechanisms that had her constantly preparing for the worst were impossibly hard to ignore.

So, even though they'd relaxed all afternoon, it had been the least relaxing few hours she'd had in quite some time.

But maybe, she mused as she watched Parker twirl her fork in what remained of the angel hair pasta on her plate, it wasn't a problem that needed solving that had her so quiet, but just a good old fashioned calorie crash. God knows she'd been starving by the time the Italian food she'd ordered for dinner had arrived, and she hadn't gone to an exercise class like Parker had. Whatever the case, there was no mistaking that, after finishing off a comically large serving of eggplant parmesan, Parker was looking much more like herself. Her smile was wider, more open, and the shadow that had clouded her eyes, while still noticeable, had been mostly replaced with the warmth and affection she so loved to see.

No matter how much she had tried to convince herself all afternoon that everything was fine, she couldn't help but be relieved at the shift in Parker's demeanor. Maybe, just maybe, all her fears were unfounded.

Maybe, just maybe, everything was going to be okay.

"What are you thinking about?" Parker asked as she pushed her plate away from herself with a satisfied hum.

Sheridan shrugged and shook her head as she set her wine glass back onto the table. "You."

"Thinking about me makes you look that serious?" Parker smiled as she took her hand. "Should I be worried?"

The last thing she wanted was for Parker to worry about anything, ever, and she rolled her eyes at her own overactive mind as she assured her, "Of course not."

"Good." Parker's smile gentled as she pushed her chair away from the table and gave her hand a little tug.

The unspoken request was obvious, and Sheridan smiled as she allowed herself to be pulled from her seat onto Parker's lap. She melted into Parker as she released her hand and instead wrapped a strong arm around her waist, holding her close as soft, soft lips brushed across her cheek.

"I'm sorry I was kind of out of it when I got here earlier," Parker whispered. "I was just thinking about Ollie. I didn't mean to worry you."

Sheridan frowned. "What's wrong with your brother?"

Parker rolled her eyes. "There's nothing wrong with him except for his typical bullheadedness," she muttered. "He was in town for a meeting with a new client and stopped by my place right before I came over."

"Did his meeting not go well?" Sheridan asked as she ran a reassuring hand over Parker's arm.

"His client meeting went very well." Parker sighed and dropped a soft kiss to her lips. "We had a bit of a fight," she whispered, hurt and anger flashing in her eyes before she blinked the emotions away, "and I know we're adults and everything now, but I still worry about him." She shook her head, the gesture telling her that there was more to that partial explanation but that she wouldn't be elaborating on it. "But I'm sorry that I got so wrapped up in my own head that I made you worry."

"I wasn't—" Sheridan smiled when the remainder of her white lie was stopped by a gentle finger on her lips.

Parker's eyes crinkled as she shook her head. "I could tell by the way you kept watching me like you wanted to ask what was wrong, even though you looked afraid I might say something you didn't want to hear."

Sheridan swallowed thickly as she looked away, not wanting to confirm that Parker was right. A gentle finger under her chin lifted her eyes, and she shook her head as she whispered, "I'm sorry."

"You don't have anything to apologize for, sweetie," Parker breathed, her gaze soft as she dropped a light kiss to her lips. "I should have said something the first time I caught you looking at me like that, but I needed that little bit of time to try and get over the whole thing with Ollie, and it was so nice to just be held that I selfishly didn't. And I am so, so sorry about that. Just please know that the absolute last thing I ever want to do is make you worry about me." She touched their foreheads together and added softly, "Or doubt how much I want this." Her kiss this time was firmer—not desperate, exactly, but definitely pleading for understanding. "Or, most of all, how much I want you…"

The knot of worry that had tangled itself around Sheridan's heart fell away at the earnestness in Parker's voice, and she smiled as she leaned ducked her head and captured Parker's lips in a slow, deep kiss.

They were still good.

She was still wanted.

It was ridiculous how much she needed to hear those things when Parker had never once given her any reason to doubt it, but she was beyond grateful that Parker seemed to understand. And, more importantly, that she didn't make her feel like she was being overdramatic or needy for it.

One kiss became two, which turned into six and seven and eight, at which point the muscles in Sheridan's neck began protesting her position and she sighed as she pulled just far enough away from Parker to turn and straddle her lap.

"Hello…" Parker murmured, her voice low and unmistakably pleased at the change in position as she lifted her chin to press a smile of a kiss to her lips. "I like this."

A soft moan caught in her throat at the feeling of Parker's hands on her ass, squeezing and pulling her closer. She arched into the touch, her hips thrusting back to push into Parker's hands as her chest dropped forward, as if her heart were trying to give itself to Parker, and she lifted her hands frame Parker's smiling face as she dipped her head to whisper against her lips, "I do too."

"God, Sheridan," Parker groaned, her grip tightening as the kiss she tried to plant on her lips failed to land and she just stayed there, eyes closed, lips parted and waiting for her kiss.

Having Parker so obviously at her mercy was the most powerful aphrodisiac Sheridan had ever experienced, and she swallowed thickly as she dragged the tip of her nose along the side of Parker's, letting their breaths mingle but keeping that anticipatory heart-pounding distance between their lips, letting the desire she had for this beautiful, beautiful woman build until she couldn't hold out any longer.

A quiet whimper bubbled in the back of her throat as she finally, finally closed the distance separating them, her tongue sliding effortlessly through Parker's parted lips to swoop and swirl inside her mouth. She arched into Parker as the kiss slowed, their tongues stroking against each other in a much more deliberate dance as the emotion of the moment shifted, just by a fraction, over that oh-so-thin line that separated wanting from needing.

She still wanted to feel Parker's hands and lips upon her body, but she needed it like she needed air to breathe. It was an all-consuming fire that licked its way over her skin like the tongue of a devoted lover, and she groaned as she broke away from Parker just enough to whisper a single-word suggestion, "Bed."

"Fuck, yes," Parker gasped, her hands drifting up to grab Sheridan's hips and push her from her lap even as she captured her lips again, the kiss hot and deep and messy with barely controlled desire as they stumbled toward the stairs to her bedroom.

It was, without a doubt, the least coordinated effort possible as they refused to let go of each other. Sheridan knew she was going to have a bruise on her ass in the morning from where she fell onto the edge of one of the metal-framed stairs because she was so focused on not losing contact with Parker's lips that she missed a step, but the one Parker was going to undoubtedly have on her knee from where she crashed beside her when she followed her down was going to be worse. That they managed to make it the rest of the way to her bed was something of a miracle, and she'd never laughed so freely as she did when Parker stripped her bare and playfully shoved her back onto her bed as she hopped on one leg to kick her jeans aside.

"Finally," Parker muttered, her smile as bright as the sun as she climbed onto the bed so she was kneeling above her. She dipped her head, her bright gray eyes peeking through the fall of her hair as she brushed their lips together.

Sheridan grabbed Parker's hip as she wrapped a hand around the back of her neck, and smiled as she pulled her down on top of her. "Much better," she agreed, kissing Parker through her smile as trim hips fit perfectly between her thighs.

"You think so?" Parker asked, her eyes sparkling with joy as she rocked her hips forward.

And, oh, yes, that perfect, perfect amount of pressure was absolutely better than the pounding, aching need that she'd been suffering earlier. Sheridan flicked her tongue over Parker's lips as she dragged her nails along her side to grab her ass and pull her closer. "Don't you?"

Parker nodded as she drove her hips forward in a slow grind. "I do," she confessed, her voice rough and deep. She pulled back slowly before thrusting forward again as she implored, "What do you want, sweetie?"

"You," Sheridan moaned, her hips lifting from the bed to not lose contact with Parker.

"How do you want me, Sheridan?" Parker asked gently, pulling away so she had her full attention. "I want to make you feel good," she whispered, brushing a kiss across her lips. "Anything you want, sweetheart, it's yours. Please tell me what you'd like…"

Sheridan swallowed thickly. She'd never…this wasn't…

Her internal panic must have been obvious, because Parker dragged a kiss over her cheek to her ear. "Do you want me like this?" she asked as she rolled her hips forward. "Where I can whisper all the things you make me feel in your ear?"

Sheridan closed her eyes and groaned as she nodded because, yeah, this was very much working for her. She swore she could feel Parker's smile as she nipped at her earlobe, and she squeezed her eyes shut as she turned her head to the side. The tickle of Parker's soft laughter, so warm and adoring against her throat as she fluttered the tip of her tongue against her pulse point made her stomach clench, and she dug her nails into Parker's ass as dull teeth nipped at her skin. "Fuck..."

"Fingers too, or just this?" Parker ground their hips together as she nuzzled her throat.

Sheridan's eyes rolled back in her head. Parker had talked a little the last few times they'd slept together, but nothing like this. Soft questions about whether a touch was okay or too much was so, so much different from asking her to verbalize what she wanted. But, god, it was also such a fucking turn on, and she pressed her forehead to Parker's shoulder as she whispered, "Fingers."

Her heart leapt at the way the mattress dipped beneath her right shoulder as Parker shifted above her. Her pulse began to race as gentle fingers dragged over her shoulder, left breast, her nipple—good lord, the way that touch pulled so, so slowly at her nipple—a flat palm and five fingers spread wide against her stomach, possessive and tender all at once, over her hip...

"Okay?" Parker breathed, her lips pressing a slow line of kisses over Sheridan's jaw as her touch drifted lower, teasing soaked curls as she waited to be sure that this was what she wanted.

"Please..." Sheridan whimpered, her legs falling open wider as Parker's touch drifted inward, stroking lightly through the length of her before rubbing a slow, slow circle over her clit.

"You like this?" Parker asked as she dipped her fingers lower, sliding through swollen folds, coating her fingertips with slick heat so her fingers could glide smoothly over straining nerves.

Sheridan nodded. She'd reached her limit for how far out of her comfort zone she could stray, but thankfully Parker didn't seem to mind as she smiled and kissed her softly.

"I do too," Parker confessed.

Sheridan stared into gray eyes burning with affection as those deft, talented fingers slipped lower, and the unabashed reverence in Parker's voice when she whispered her name as she slipped two fingers inside her was almost enough to make her come on the spot.

Parker's breath fell in warm waves over her ear. "You are so beautiful."

And, oh, even if she didn't believe it herself, there was no mistaking the earnestness in Parker's voice. Sheridan squeezed her eyes shut as her entire body tightened in response, her nipples becoming almost painfully hard as she rocked her hips against Parker's hand, trying to pull her deeper. "Parker…"

"I love the way my name sounds falling from your lips like that," Parker husked, using her chin to turn her head so she could claim her lips in a bruising kiss. When the kiss broke, the weight of her forehead kept Sheridan staring into her eyes as she asked, "Do you have any idea what it does to me to be able to hear how much you want me?"

Sheridan curled her fingers into the back of Parker's neck as she moaned her name again.

"Just like that, baby," Parker encouraged, curling her fingers to drag over hidden ridges.

"God," Sheridan hissed as her eyes snapped shut at the touch and stars flashed behind her eyelids.

Parker hummed and kissed her softly, flicking her tongue over the crease of her lips and then, when she opened her mouth to her, pulled away to ask, "Did you know that I actually came when I made love to you that first time? That the feeling of you pulsing against my tongue and the sound of your voice pulled me over the edge with you?"

Sheridan whimpered as Parker's hips pressed her fingers deeper once again, and as her eyes rolled so far back in her head that she might never be able to see anything ever again.

"I'm so close right now that I probably will again," Parker confessed in a rough whisper.

Oh. God. "Fuck…"

"You feel so good," Parker continued her husky seduction, the push and pull of her hips finding a slow, perfect rhythm.

"Pretty sure that's my line," Sheridan rasped, smiling as she captured Parker's lips in a deep, deep kiss, their tongues sliding desperately together, matching the steady rhythm of Parker's fingers. She dragged her feet over the backs of Parker's thighs before cradling her hips with her knees to help herself meet each and every thrust, and groaned into the kiss when her building release begin to peak.

"That's it, baby," Parker murmured, pulling away to brush an encouraging kiss over her forehead. "God, you're so beautiful."

"Parker…"

"Just let go…" Parker smiled when she blinked her eyes open to look at her. "I've got you, Sheridan."

And oh, how she did.

Sheridan doubted Parker even had any idea how true that simple statement was. Because Parker had her completely and totally, heart and soul. Parker's name fell from her lips like a prayer when she came, and she clung to her as wave after wave crashed through her, the warmth of Parker's skin and the whispered words of encouragement against her ear the anchor she so desperately needed to keep her in this beautiful, beautiful moment. When the final tremor of her release faded and she finally relaxed beneath Parker, she shook her head and muttered a thoroughly spent, "Oh my god."

"I'll say," Parker chuckled as she nuzzled her cheek and pressed a reverent kiss to the corner of her lips.

"Did you…?"

Parker nodded, looking beautifully unabashed as she murmured, "I told you I probably would."

A small smile curled Sheridan's lips as affection, pure and strong and powerful bloomed in her chest. She licked her lips as she caressed Parker's face, tracing the curve of her cheeks and the line of her jaw, and sighed as she used that hold to guide their lips together. "Thank you," she breathed.

"For what?" Parker frowned, and god, she looked so adorable that Sheridan laughed as she kissed her again.

Sheridan shook her head, not knowing how to put into words how, for the first time in her life, Parker managed to make her feel like she was enough, just as she was. The furrow between Parker's brows deepened at her non-answer, so she sighed and offered, "Everything."

Something of what she was feeling must have shone in her eyes, because Parker's brow smoothed, confusion replaced with gentle understanding, and she nodded as she kissed her softly. "Always."

thirty-seven

The crush and the noise of the city on a Friday evening smacked into Parker the moment she stepped onto the sidewalk outside the yoga studio, and she grimaced as she took a deep breath, trying to hold onto the serenity she'd finally managed to find after three straight hours on her mat. Her shoulders were dead and her legs close to jelly but her mind, for what seemed like the first time since Oliver had walked out her door three weeks ago, had finally calmed.

She'd thought that she would feel less stressed, less guilty, less torn about everything after she'd told Oliver she was done with their life of crime but, oh, how wrong she'd been. If anything, after three weeks of being equal parts angry and frustrated and worried about her brother, her stress levels had only increased to the point that she was half-convinced she had an ulcer.

Especially since Oliver had finally broken the radio silence they'd fallen into after their fight.

His text had been short and, while it had started well, it was the second half of the message that had sent her from her office to her mat because it was the only thing she could think of that might keep her from screaming.

I miss you, Park. Can I come over when I get back from the UK so we can talk?

She'd deleted the message in a pique of anger as soon as she'd read it, but the words still tickled her subconscious, asking again and again and again what she would do if he was caught while the darker parts of her wondered what he would do if he was caught. Would he take it on the chin and keep her out of it? Or would her involvement in the whole thing somehow come out?

Even though his text had been vague on his exact location within the UK at the moment, she knew that he was in London. Because that's where the Chaucer from Marquis' list was. And, given the fact that night had fallen over Manhattan while she'd been focused only on her breathing and the alignment of her body as she moved through various asanas, there was a decent chance that he might even be trying to steal the book right at that very moment.

"Goddamn it, Ollie," she swore under her breath as she wove her way along the crowded sidewalk, the calmness she'd found within the corners of her mat ebbing away with every step she took.

She had really hoped that the peace she had found would at least last until she'd gotten home. Had hoped that the stress and the constant worrying and the fear and the anger that she'd been suffering might allow her a few minutes' reprieve. If she thought her body could take another class without completely failing her, she would turn around and go back to the studio where she could lose herself in her breath and her movement, but the effort it was taking her to simply put one foot in front of the other now was evidence enough that her body wasn't up to the task.

Which was probably a good thing, because the phone in the pocket of her mat bag began playing the Wonder Woman theme song—Sheridan's personalized ringtone. She swung her bag in front of her as she crossed the street to retrieve the phone, and glanced idly at the people around her as she answered the call and lifted the phone to her ear. "Hey. What's up?"

"Nothing much," Sheridan drawled, and Parker couldn't help but smile at the playful edge in her tone. She was still exhausted and

stressed and generally not in the best mood, but Sheridan always made her feel better—even if it was just talking on the phone. *"I was just wondering when you were going to get home."*

"How do you know I'm not home now?" Parker teased as she skipped up onto the curb.

"Oh, I don't know," Sheridan laughed. *"It could be the traffic in the background, or it could be because I actually left the office at a humane hour and I'm sitting on your couch right now with a glass of wine wondering where you are…"*

"You're…" Parker's legs, near dead only a moment before, found their fourth-wind as they picked up her pace without her even having to think about it. She was suddenly incredibly glad that she'd thought to take clean clothes with her to the studio so she could shower in the locker room there.

"Gregory let me in," Sheridan explained. *"I hope you don't mind."*

"Of course I don't mind," Parker murmured. She took a deep breath as a small measure of the serenity she'd found on her mat returned, enveloping her heart and soul like a warm, oh-so-welcome hug. "I'm a block away. I'll be there as soon as I can."

"I'll be waiting," Sheridan replied, her voice low and smooth, with just the faintest hint of husk beneath it all.

Parker smiled as she slipped her phone back into the pocket of her bag before adjusting the strap so it was cut across her chest instead of leaving the bag dangling at her side, and she shook her head as she found the energy to break into a light jog. Sheridan had been working so much lately that they'd only managed the occasional night together and, although there was a part of her that was glad that Sheridan had been spared most of her stressed-out melancholia, she also recognized that not seeing Sheridan had made those feelings worse.

She hated fighting with Ollie and the ever-present feeling of guilt that sat cold and heavy in the pit of her stomach for choosing Sheridan and herself over him and his foolishness, but she knew that she'd made the right choice. Knew with every brush of Sheridan's lips against her own that, despite the unease and the turmoil her decisions until that point were still wreaking havoc on her life, she was right where she needed to be.

"Hey, kiddo. You have a guest," Gregory greeted her as she stepped into the foyer and closed the front door behind herself. "Figured you wouldn't mind if she waited in your apartment, so I sent her on up when she got here."

"Yeah. She called," Parker assured him with a smile. "Thank you."

"Of course." Gregory doffed an imaginary cap. "Hey, I meant to ask you, what's going on with Ollie? He hasn't been around much lately."

Parker blew out a soft breath and shook her head. "He's got a couple big projects he's working on that are keeping him pretty busy."

"Ah, well, that makes sense. I was just worried about him."

"Me too, Gregory," Parker murmured. She ran a hand through her hair glanced toward the stairs.

"Go see your girl," Gregory chuckled. "She's been up there for close to an hour waiting for you, you know."

"I didn't know." Parker hefted her bag on her shoulder. "Guess I shouldn't have done that third class, huh?"

"You kids and your crazy workouts," Gregory chastised fondly. "I'm meeting Victoria at the club later, so I will see you later this weekend."

"Sounds good." Parker brushed a kiss over his cheek as she made her way toward the foot of the stairs. "Have fun with Victoria."

"Have fun with Sheridan," Gregory retorted with a playful smirk.

Parker huffed a laugh. She wasn't going near that one with a ten-foot pole. "Goodnight, Gregory."

Sure enough, her door at the top of the stairs was ajar, and she peered through the crack as she pushed it open. Her heart leapt into her throat when she spotted Sheridan on her couch, legs curled up beneath her, a glass of red in her left hand balanced on the arm of the sofa. Her right was folded over the top of a book, holding the pages in a V in front of her, and Parker idly wondered what it was she was reading as she hovered in the doorway, in no rush to shatter the serenity of the scene in front of her.

Sheridan must have felt her eyes on her, though, because she looked up a moment later with a shy smile. "You just gonna stand there all night?"

"No." Parker shook her head as she slipped into her apartment and flicked the door shut with her heel. "You just looked so beautiful that I forgot how to breathe for a moment," she continued in a somewhat hushed tone as she laid the bags with her sweaty gym clothes and her mat on the floor beside the door. The soft blush that crept over Sheridan's cheeks was utterly enchanting, and Parker smiled as she flicked her flip flops beside the bags. "I'm sorry I kept you waiting. If I'd known you weren't going to be working late tonight, I wouldn't have gone to that third class."

Sheridan shook her head, the color of her cheeks more apparent as Parker made her way across the apartment to where she was sitting. "It's fine," she insisted as she tossed the book she'd been reading onto the coffee table. "But why in the world would you do three classes in a row?"

"It was easier than thinking," Parker explained vaguely as she sat beside her on the couch.

Sheridan sighed. "Things with Ollie still not any better?"

"Yeah." Parker shook her head. She didn't want to think about her brother now, didn't want to let her tumultuous thoughts about him ruin her evening with Sheridan, who looked even more beautiful than ever and was close enough to touch. "But it will be fine. I'm sure." She sighed and leaned over to capture Sheridan's lips in a slow, sweet kiss. She smiled against Sheridan's lips once the kiss broke and she took the wine glass from her hand. "I've missed you this week," she murmured as she pulled away just enough to set the glass on the coffee table beside the Lynn Turner novel she'd been reading.

"I've missed you, too," Sheridan whispered.

Parker's eyes fluttered shut as Sheridan's hands framed her face to guide their lips together again, and she hummed softly as she opened her mouth to Sheridan's tongue and the kiss deepened. She melted into Sheridan as their tongues stroked lazily together, her stress from earlier chased away by the hint of wine on Sheridan's tongue and the subtly intoxicating scent of her perfume.

"I love you," Parker breathed against Sheridan's lips, the thought she'd been keeping to herself for weeks now slipping fee before she could catch herself.

Sheridan's eyes widened as a quiet gasp fell from her lips, and Parker held her breath as she waited for a response. She hadn't planned on doing it like this—she'd wanted to do it right, with a candlelit dinner and a dozen long stem roses and the whole nine—but it was just too much to keep to herself any longer.

"I love you, too," Sheridan breathed, the faintest hint of tears glimmering in her eyes.

Parker swore her heart was going to burst with joy at the ardor glowing in Sheridan's eyes as she leaned in to kiss her again, the caress slow and awed and perfect. Her heart swooped and dove with every stroke of Sheridan's tongue against her own and every ragged breath that crashed against her lips, and she clung to Sheridan as her head spun and her breath became light.

She was in heaven, and she never wanted the moment to end.

She blinked her eyes open when Sheridan's hands fell to her hips, long fingers curling around her sides as a gentle pressure pushed against her front, her mind too fogged from the intoxicating headiness of their kisses to make sense of the unspoken request. "Sheridan?"

"Let's take this to bed, sweetie," Sheridan whispered, her dark, dark eyes positively smoldering.

"God, yes," Parker whispered as she captured Sheridan's lips again, unwilling to lose that connection as she got to her feet, and she smiled into the kiss as Sheridan stretched to meet her, seemingly just as unwilling to let go as she was.

She held onto Sheridan's hips as the hand on her jaw and the weight of Sheridan's lips began leading her backward, trusting Sheridan to keep them safe as she instead focused the entirety of her attention on trying to convey with her kisses just how happy she was. She was so focused on kissing Sheridan that she lost track of where they were in her apartment, and she laughed when the edge of her mattress pressed into the backs of her legs a half-second before they tumbled together onto it.

"Sorry," Sheridan chuckled, pressing up onto her right hand as she used her left to sweep her hair out of her face. "I didn't mean to just fall on you like that."

Parker smiled as she reached up to run a gentle finger over the curve of Sheridan's lips. "You can fall on me any time you want," she assured her, kissing her again as she took advantage of their position to grab Sheridan's ass.

"I'll remember that..." Sheridan murmured as they shuffled all the way onto the bed until she was stretched fully out on top of her.

"Good." She winked and twisted her hips to try to switch their positions, and laughed when the move failed spectacularly.

Sheridan smiled at the attempt, her eyes shining with affection as she brushed the softest of kisses across her lips. "Nice try, Ravenscroft," she whispered. "But you're mine, right now."

Parker's laughter faded into a sigh, and she shook her head as she relaxed completely beneath her. "I'm yours for as long as you want me," she promised, her heart beating so heavily in her throat that it made her voice tremble.

"Even if it's forever?" Sheridan asked softly, the briefest shadow of insecurity flickering across her expression.

Parker nodded, a slow smile curling her lips as she lifted her head to kiss her softly. "Especially then."

The way Sheridan breathed her name in response, so quiet and awed, made her heart ache, and she moaned in surrender when soft lips claimed her own. She alternated between caressing as much of

Sheridan's body as she could reach and just holding her close as they kissed, more than content to enjoy the stomach-fluttering joy of knowing that Sheridan was hers. Her pulse sped at the first light brush of Sheridan's fingers against her stomach, stroking reverently up and down her side as their kisses deepened, dancing over her ribs before tracing the edge of her bra before slowly, almost hesitantly sliding higher. She let her right arm fall out to the side as Sheridan's hand covered her breast, squeezing lightly before a nimble thumb stroked over her nipple, coaxing a plaintive groan from her lips.

"Oh, Parker," Sheridan breathed, dragging a smile over her cheek to kiss her ear. "I want to make love to you."

"Please," Parker whispered, even as her heart promised, *Anything. Always. Forever.* She turned her head to captured Sheridan's lips in a heated kiss as the hand on her breast slipped away, dragging down her stomach to grab the hem of her shirt. She lifted herself into a half sit-up as Sheridan worked the shirt higher, and held herself there even after it had been tossed aside so Sheridan could remove her bra as well.

She grabbed Sheridan's shirt as she fell back to the bed, using her momentum to lift it up and over her head, and smiled against her lips as she flung it off the side of the bed. The rest of their clothes were quickly discarded in turns, and she hummed at the feeling of nothing but warm, warm skin against her own as she dragged her fingertips up and down Sheridan's back.

Sheridan sighed as she pulled away, using her lips to turn her head to the side. "Let me…"

Parker closed her eyes and gave herself over to the heavenly sensation of Sheridan's lips against her throat. She grabbed Sheridan's hips as dull teeth dragged over her collarbone, the line instantly soothed by a heavy tongue, and let out a shaky sigh when hot breath and a nimble tongue caressed her right nipple moments before it was sucked deep into Sheridan's mouth. Her head rolled back on the bed as every pull of Sheridan's mouth on her breast seemed to tug between her legs at the same time, and by the time Sheridan had finished teasing both her nipples to tight, throbbing points, she was a whimpering mess of desperation.

"So beautiful…" Sheridan breathed as she kissed her way down her stomach.

Parker spread her legs wider to welcome Sheridan's body as she moved lower, the erotic scrape of Sheridan's nipples over her hips enough to make her clench as a fresh wave of arousal crashed between her legs. "Please…" she begged, lifting her hips needfully toward Sheridan's mouth as she settled between her thighs.

She couldn't quite make out what Sheridan said in that half-second before an agile tongue swept lightly through the length of her, but she honestly didn't care as strong hands wrapped around her thighs, holding her open as Sheridan dove back in for more. Every lick was heaven, every little suck pure ecstasy as Sheridan made love to her with excruciating focus, touching her right where she wanted for a heartbeat shorter than she needed it, coaxing her carefully closer to the edge while keeping it expertly out of reach.

It was like Sheridan knew exactly what to do to drive her crazy and, if the low hum that vibrated against her clit was any indication, she reveled in it.

Parker fisted her hands in the sheets at her sides as she arched against Sheridan's mouth, her sighs of relief when Sheridan met her rhythm turning into strangled groans when that perfect, perfect rhythm was broken. She ached not for release, exactly, but for those infinite seconds of utter euphoria where she swore Sheridan's soul intertwined with her own.

The fingers on her thighs pressed tight enough to bruise as she struggled against their hold, trying to force the tempo her body was aching to find as Sheridan held her right there on the precipice of release without letting her fall. Her entire world shrank to the sensation of Sheridan's mouth against her and the sound of her heartbeat pounding in her ears, drowning out the half-formed pleading whimpers that spilled from her lips as she surrendered everything she was to her.

Sheridan's name spilled from her lips like a benediction when she finally came, her orgasm rolling through her in cleansing waves, and by the time the final tremor left her spent and gasping for air, Parker could do little more than reach blindly for her, hoping the touch would be enough to beckon her closer. She needed the weight of Sheridan's body, the strength of her touch and the understanding of her kiss to anchor her to earth as she drifted, and she sighed when Sheridan stretched out on top of her. "My god, that was incredible…"

Sheridan chuckled and kissed her softly. "I love you."

Parker moaned at the taste of herself that lingered on Sheridan's lips, and tangled her fingers in Sheridan's hair as she claimed her lips in a deep, lazy kiss. Sheridan's fingers pressing into her hip as their kisses lengthened, tongues sliding leisurely together as they both seemed to bask in the afterglow of her release stoked a new fire within her, and she grinned when, with a quick twist of her hips, she flipped their position.

She bit her lip as she gazed down at Sheridan, her heart feeling like it would fly right out of her chest if it could and give itself to her. "I love you," she swore, her voice thick with emotion as she dipped her head to capture Sheridan's lips in a lingering kiss.

Her pulse tripped over itself at the way Sheridan moaned her name as she dragged her lips over the edge of her jaw, and she smiled as she fluttered the tip of her tongue in the hollow at the base of her throat. "My turn," she murmured as she moved lower.

She took her time worshipping Sheridan's breasts before succumbing to the strangled moans and gentle hand in her hair that urged her to move on. She cradled Sheridan's hips in her hands and pressed a lingering kiss to her inner thigh as she eased between her legs, and looked up Sheridan's body as she ran the tip of her tongue lightly around her clit. The sight of Sheridan's head lolling back as her mouth fell open in a silent cry of pleasure made her clench, and she rubbed her thumbs in small circles over Sheridan's hips as she dragged her tongue through the length of sweetness that waited for her.

She made love to Sheridan slowly, thoroughly, as if this was her one and only opportunity to convince Sheridan that she was everything in the world to her. Worshipped her like she'd never worshipped a woman before, letting the breathy cries and pleas and gasps of pleasure guide her lips to where she was wanted, to lead her tongue to where she was needed. She would have gladly spent the rest of her life right here in the cradle of Sheridan's thighs, making her feel like she was the most cherished woman in the world, but there was no way to delay the inevitable forever. She smiled as she submitted to the hips lifting beseechingly against her mouth and took Sheridan's clit between her lips, sucking lightly at the swollen bundle even as she teased it with light flicks of her tongue.

The sound of Sheridan moaning her name as she came was the sweetest sound in the world, and Parker squeezed her eyes shut and groaned as she continued to lap lightly between Sheridan's legs, doing everything in her power to draw her pleasure out for as long as possible. When Sheridan finally fell limp before her, she dragged a long kiss up the length her body. A slow smile curled her lips as gentle fingers found the back of her neck and pulled her down into a lingering kiss, and she sighed as she tenderly caressed Sheridan's cheek with her thumb when she pulled away.

"You're so beautiful," Parker murmured as she stared adoringly into warm blue eyes the color of the sea at midnight, deep and fathomless, full of so much promise and wonder that it stole the breath from her lungs.

"You are."

Parker smiled and shook her head. "I said it first." She laughed at the way Sheridan's lips twitched with a smile as she rolled her eyes, and couldn't resist the urge to kiss her again. "I love you."

THIRTY-EIGHT

"Glad you could make it."

Sheridan rolled her eyes and flipped Kelly off as she dropped her purse onto her desk. It was still only a quarter till nine, so the workday hadn't even officially begun yet. "Whatever," she sassed through a yawn. "Ugh. Sorry."

"Late night?" he teased, waggling his eyebrows.

She shrugged. Normally she would brush a comment like that off, but her lips were still tingling from the lingering kisses she'd shared with Parker that morning before she'd had to run home to change for work and she was just so goddamn happy that she didn't want to try and hide it. Hell, she didn't know if she could, even if she'd tried. "It was," she confirmed, smirking at the way his eyes widened in surprise.

Although, honestly, her exhaustion wasn't so much the result of a late, late night as it was the combination of too little sleep over the last few days and a much earlier wake-up than she was used to that morning. How Parker found the energy to be up before dawn after the weekend they'd had was beyond her, but she couldn't think of a better way to start the day than waking up to the brush of reverent fingers gliding over her skin and the feeling of warm, soft lips against her own.

Kelly laughed and held up his hand for a high-five. "Get some!"

"Get some, what?" Ivy asked as she strolled into the bullpen with a super-sized travel mug of coffee in her hand. She looked toward the break room hopefully. "Are there donuts?"

Kelly's smile fell and his shoulders slumped as he shook his head. "No. I think we need to remedy that situation as soon as possible, though."

Ivy smirked. "Morning briefing is in thirty. If you think you can get down to the Dunkin' across the street and back before it starts, I'll totally cover for you…"

He laughed. "You're on."

Rachel grinned. "God, I love this office. Get me a maple bar?" she asked as she gave Ivy's arm a light squeeze before heading over toward their desks.

"And I'll take a Boston Cream," Ivy said as she pulled a twenty out of her bag and held it out for him. "Or, make that two. It is Monday, after all. Just go ahead and get a few dozen. Everyone's gonna lose their shit if you come back with donuts and there aren't enough for everyone."

Kelly jumped up and grabbed his coat. "Want anything, Sloan?"

"Sure. Surprise me."

He snapped up the bill and shoved it in his pocket. "You got it."

Ivy sipped at her coffee as he dashed out the door, and shook her head as she looked at Sheridan. "Your partner is something else…"

"He's *something* all right," Sheridan agreed with a laugh. She sighed and leaned back in her chair. "Good weekend?"

Sheridan bit her lip to try and contain her smile as she nodded. "It was a very good weekend."

Ivy chuckled and arched a brow. "That's quite a smile. Dare I ask what made it such a very good weekend?"

Sheridan blushed and shook her head. "I'm not telling you that."

Ivy's lips pinched into a thoughtful line as she studied her carefully, her dark eyes sparkling with playful amusement. "Were there handcuffs involved?"

"No," Sheridan spluttered in surprise. "There were no handcuffs involved."

"Bummer," Ivy drawled.

"Oh my god, Ivy," Sheridan laughed. "What's with everybody being so invested in my love life lately?"

Ivy smirked and shook her head. "I'm just teasing. You and Parker are just so cute together that it's fun to relive these oh-so-golden moments of a new relationship with you guys by proxy."

Sheridan arched a disbelieving brow. Even discounting the time they'd spent tiptoeing toward the whole actual relationship thing, they'd still been together for close to two months, now. "It's not exactly new anymore."

"Tomato, tomato," Ivy drawled, waving her off. "Compared to me and Rach, you've barely started…"

"Okay…so then what's Kelly's excuse? Because he mentioned something the other day about not seeing that girl you set him up with anymore…"

"He's a guy. That's how guys bond." Ivy shrugged. "I don't know. It's stupid, but boys are more often than not pretty stupid as a species, so…"

Sheridan laughed. "You've got a point there…" Her phone started to ring and she sighed. "Right, well, back to the salt mines for me, I guess."

"I'll save you a donut if you're still on the phone when he gets back," Ivy promised.

"Thanks," she murmured as she reached for her phone. It was too early on a Monday for her to be getting calls already, and she just prayed that she wouldn't be the one canceling hers and Parker's dinner plans that night because of a case. "Sloan."

"Good morning. This is Stan Fleming with the British Art Crimes Unit. We spoke a few weeks ago about rare books?"

Sheridan's eyes widened as she hurried to dig the Filibus file out of the stack on the corner of her desk. "Yes. Hello," she replied as she snatched a pen out of her organizer. "What can I do for you, Agent Fleming?"

"Have you any further ideas on the rare book cases? This morning I was handed a case involving a stolen Chaucer…"

She flipped the file open and quickly found the list of privately held rare books that she'd compiled. *"The Canterbury Tales?"*

"That would be the one, yes," Fleming confirmed.

She nodded as she circled the title on her list. It was reassuring to know that her hunch had been correct, but she was getting unbelievably frustrated at always being two-steps behind these guys. "When did it go missing, exactly?"

"Not sure of the exact time. It was called in this morning, at about eight our time here, however."

"How did the scene look?"

"For the most part, clean. We didn't find any prints when we dusted, but the door to the shelves where the book was kept was left ajar, which obviously drew Mr. Fox-Murray's attention. And there were two different shoe prints on the marble tile near the kitchen door. Neither of which, we've confirmed, belong to anyone with access to the house."

"Really?" Sheridan hummed, sitting up a little bit straighter.

"Yes. Our forensic team was able to identify the prints—one was for a pair of men's Nike trainers, size ten and a half, and the other was Adidas, men's size nine. Both are such popular brands, however, that the information isn't necessarily all that helpful."

Sheridan nodded thoughtfully to herself as she noted the information in her file. They might not be able to identify the thieves by their shoe prints, but now she knew that she was looking for a team of two men and, if they found them the size of the shoe prints could be used as corroborating evidence. "What about the security system? I'm assuming the home had one…"

"It has a top of the line system, but the report from the monitoring company doesn't show a breach. In fact, it doesn't show any activity on the system from the

time it'd been armed at roughly ten o'clock last night till six this morning, when it'd been deactivated."

"And yet you have two pairs of footprints and a missing book."

Fleming sighed. *"Precisely."*

Sheridan spun her pen between her fingers. "You didn't say—was there a replacement book left at the scene to take the place of the Chaucer?"

"Indeed there was," Fleming confirmed. *"Although, according to Mr. Fox-Murray, it was a poor replacement. He said he noticed the switch right away because the color of the book's cover wasn't anything close to the Chaucer. I can't recall and I don't see anything in my notes from when we spoke earlier, did your case have a replacement book left at the scene?"*

"No." She sighed. "There was a case in Paris that did though, and I'm betting they're all connected. I know you said you didn't find any prints at the scene itself, but have you dusted the book the thieves left behind for prints?"

"Our team is working on it now. There was a partial on the cover that is too smudged to be of use, but my team down in the lab is hopeful that they'll be able to find a usable print somewhere else in the book."

"Fingers crossed," she muttered as she dropped her pen onto her open file. "Can you send me whatever notes you've made on this case so far? I'm trying to compile a profile that we might be able to use to catch these guys."

"Of course. I believe I still have your follow up email from when we spoke before, so I'll be able to pull the address from that. And I'll let you know the moment we have anything new on the case here."

"Perfect."

"May I ask how you're so sure that they'll strike again? Assuming it is the same lot for all these thefts, that is."

Sheridan shook her head. That was the crux of the whole thing. Without knowing exactly what was on the list Lusky had told her about, there was no way to know for sure that the cases were connected. "I spoke with Johan Lusky from the Art Loss Register a few weeks ago, and he told me that they'd heard rumors that there was a list out there that has anywhere from five to eight rare books on it. If my hunch is right, four of those books have now been stolen—the Dumas and Carroll in Paris, the Blake here in New York, and now your missing Chaucer."

"*Brilliant... So do you have any leads on whoever's behind this?*"

"My gut is telling me that Evie Marquis is involved somehow, but I don't have anything to tie her to all this yet," she admitted with a heavy sigh. "Sorry."

"*She was also the first person who came to my mind when I got the call on this one earlier,*" he murmured wryly. "*Can you send me any notes you have that might help in my investigation?*"

"Of course. Let me know if you find anything that might help find these guys?"

"*Will do.*"

"All right. I'll send you what I've got here in a few, so keep an eye on your inbox."

"*And I shall send you my notes as well once I get them all compiled. I'm sure we'll be speaking again soon, Agent Sloan. Thank you for your help.*"

"Yeah. Of course. You too. Good luck."

"*To you, as well,*" Fleming replied kindly before the call disconnected.

Sheridan blew out a loud breath as she dropped the handset back into its cradle. "Fuck, me," she muttered as she rocked back in her chair. She raked her hands through her hair and chewed her lip as she stared absently at the file on her desk. If the low-ball reports on this mysterious shopping list of rare books was right, then they had exactly one more shot to catch Filibus before they disappeared.

"You look like you could use a donut."

She huffed a laugh as she looked up at her partner, who was standing in front of her desk with four large bakery boxes cradled in his hands. "Four dozen, Innes? That doesn't seem a little excessive? I mean, are all of us even in this morning?"

"Dude, they're donuts." Kelly gave her a look that clearly said he found exactly zero merit to her argument. "You can never have too many donuts."

"Did somebody say donuts?" Nathan chimed in from across the bullpen.

"Guys! Innes brought donuts!" Cornell yelled.

"Touch my Boston Creams and I'll kick all your asses!" Ivy hollered.

"The maple bar is mine!" Rachel shouted.

"We are so professional that I don't know how we can all stand it," Sheridan muttered, rolling her eyes as she stood to see what was in the top box in Kelly's hands. Judging by the crowd migrating their way like a pack of half-starved zombies, if she didn't pick what she wanted now, she'd be left with whatever boring glazed pastry was left after the good stuff had been picked over.

"It's the power of the donut," Kelly chuckled as he flipped the lid of the box open so she could see what was inside.

She shook her head and pulled a cake donut with pink frosting from the center of the box. "Yes, it is. And, while you were busy buying donuts, I got a call from Agent Fleming in London. The Chaucer was stolen."

"What?" He handed the boxes to Ivy, who had just gotten to his side and was looking for her requested treats. "Hold on." He snagged a couple devil's food donuts. "Okay. I'm good. Take them to the break room for me?"

"You got it." Ivy lifted the boxes over her head and called, "Follow me, my sugar-deprived minions!"

Kelly carefully set his donuts on an empty corner of his desk. "Watch those for me. I'll go grab us some paper towels or something."

"Better you than me," Sheridan murmured as she dropped back into her chair. She crossed her legs as she took a bite of her donut and hummed happily as she chewed. Sending him on a donut run really had been a good idea.

"Okay, here," Kelly said when he got close enough to float a paper towel at her. "So, James Bond called?"

"Something like that," she chuckled, and then brought him up to speed on everything Fleming had said about his case. "So, yeah. They're still looking for prints or something that we can use to identify these guys, but if we work from the assumption that the low-end estimates of how many books are on this list that's out there, we could be looking at having just one more chance to catch Filibus."

"So, no pressure or anything, huh?" He sighed and shoved half of one of his donuts into his mouth. When he finished chewing, he asked, "So if there's only one book left on this mysterious list that we're not entirely sure even exists or not, which one do you think it'll be?"

She took a bite of her donut as she grabbed her list of potential targets. Her gut said it was the Shakespeare here in the city, but it could be any of the titles on the list and they just didn't have the manpower to watch every single one. "I'd go for the Shakespeare folio, personally, but—"

"Conference room in five!" Bartz hollered, interrupting her. After a beat he added in an only marginally quieter voice, "Who brought donuts and didn't tell me?"

Kelly smiled. "Think he'd let us go talk to the owner of the Shakespeare? Just to, you know, see how it's kept, maybe warn them about the thefts so they can try and up their security?"

It was honestly the best they were going to be able to do given the fact that they had no concrete evidence to back up her hunch. "Go grab him the best donut that's left and we'll see if it's enough to butter him up…"

"And that's why you're the brains of the operation," he laughed. "I'll meet you at the stairs, Obi Wan."

"Please. It's General Organa. Now go."

He snapped off a salute with what remained of his second donut. "Yes, ma'am."

She chuckled softly under her breath as her eyes dropped to her notes. They still didn't know a lot, but they knew more than they had an hour ago and maybe, just maybe, the Chaucer was going to be the turning-point in their investigation.

thirty-nine

Parker looked up at the sound of someone knocking on her door and frowned. Jess never took the time to knock—she'd just barge in, already mid-way through whatever it was that had brought her and expecting Parker to catch up—and she didn't have any meetings on her calendar. "Come on in," she called, her voice lifting on that final syllable with her confusion.

Her confusion was instantly replaced with a smile when she saw Sheridan's head peek through her door. "Hey. Sorry to bother you at work, but…"

Parker shook her head and pushed herself to her feet. "You are more than welcome bother me whenever you'd like, Agent Sloan," she murmured as she rounded her desk. She hadn't seen Sheridan since Monday morning thanks to whatever case was keeping her so busy, and she smiled at the way her heart fluttered in her chest when she stopped in front of her. She wanted nothing more than to take Sheridan in her arms and show her just how much she'd missed her, and she took a deep breath as she tilted her head questioningly. "Can I kiss you?" she asked softly.

Sheridan glanced over her shoulder to make sure Kelly—who could be heard chatting with Jess beyond the door—wasn't about to walk in on them, and smiled as she looked back at her and nodded. "I don't know, can you?"

"Oh, I absolutely can," Parker murmured as she curled her right hand around Sheridan's jaw and guided their lips together. She sighed into the kiss when Sheridan's hands found her hips and, even though they kept the kiss brief and fairly chaste given their location and the probability that they weren't going to be alone for long, she was still completely breathless when they broke apart. "God, I love you."

"I love you, too," Sheridan whispered as she brushed a tender kiss to the corner of Parker's lips.

"I got that information on Frasier," Kelly announced as he sauntered into the room. He pulled up short when he saw them jump apart, and grinned. "Must I remind you that you are on the clock right now, Agent Sloan?"

"Damn it. Were they making out, and I missed it?" Jess smirked and leaned against Parker's open doorway. "You have visitors, Parker."

"You don't say," Parker sassed, rolling her eyes. She glared at both Jess and Kelly as Sheridan blushed and stared at the ground beside her.

Jess' smirk widened at her protective streak as she nodded. "Anyway, if you don't need anything further from me…"

"I don't," Parker assured her. "Thank you, Jess."

"How do you know we don't?" Kelly teased.

"I'll give you my number when you're leaving," Jess promised him with a wink.

Kelly grinned. "Can't wait." When Jess left to return to her desk, he added, "I like her."

Parker huffed a laugh in spite of herself and shook her head. "Really, I'm not all that surprised. I had a feeling you two would get on famously once you finally met. But I'm guessing you didn't come by just to flirt with my assistant." She arched a playful brow at Kelly, who looked wholly unaffected by the jab as he smirked and shoved his hands into his pockets. "Is there something I can do for you guys?"

Kelly shook his head and waved a hand toward Sheridan. "I was just coming to collect my partner."

"We had some questions for one of your colleagues, Brandon Summers, about a recovery he worked a couple years ago," Sheridan explained. "He needed to look through his file on the case to get us the information we needed, so I thought that since I hadn't seen you in a few days, that I'd pop in and say, hey." She smiled apologetically at Parker, and then sighed as she glanced at Kelly. "So you got it?"

"Yeah, Summers had an address for him up in the Bronx that didn't come up in any of our searches," Kelly confirmed. "We can head on up there when we're done here."

Parker's heart dropped. Kelly had said "Frasier" when he barged in on them, and she just prayed that the Frasier they were interested in wasn't Rick, who did, in fact, live in the Bronx. *Goddamn it, Ollie, if this is because of your shit…*

"Good." Sheridan nodded. She tilted her head toward the door. "Why don't you go finish flirting with Parker's assistant, and I'll meet you out there."

"Ah, right. You two probably want a little privacy to say goodbye and everything," Kelly drawled, waggling his eyebrows.

"Go away, Innes," Sheridan groaned.

Kelly laughed and tapped his watch. "You've got four minutes and then I'm coming back in to break things up," he warned as he made his way to the door. "Don't do anything I would do," he teased as he left the office, closing the door after himself.

Sheridan sighed. "I'm so sorry about him."

"At least he shut the door," Parker murmured, her voice soft with a hint of the worry that had settled in her gut. She had done so much to keep Ollie safe, and if he'd screwed it up—if he screwed this up—she would never forgive him.

"At least he did that," Sheridan agreed softly. She smiled and wrapped her arms around Parker's neck. "I've missed you this week."

"Missed you, too." Parker closed her eyes as she sank into the warmth of Sheridan's embrace, and she sighed at the feeling of gentle lips ghosting over her own. "You make everything better," she whispered against Sheridan's lips before she claimed them in a sweet, lingering kiss.

"Would you want to come over tonight after work?" Sheridan asked when the kiss finally broke.

Parker nodded as she brushed another tender kiss across Sheridan's lips. "I would love nothing more."

"Good." Sheridan smiled into their next kiss, and sighed heavily when she pulled away. "I don't trust Kelly to not come stomping back in early just to tease me about all this later. Do you still have the key I gave you?"

"Of course." Parker smoothed her hands over Sheridan's hips. "And I remember the code to your building, so I will head down your way once I'm done here. And, who knows, if you play your cards right," she murmured playfully as she stole another kiss, "maybe I'll have dinner waiting for you."

Sheridan's gaze softened. "You're too good to me."

"That's not possible," Parker countered. She ran a hand down Sheridan's arm and smiled as she took her hand. "Come on. Let's go save my assistant from your partner before he ruins her productivity for the day, and I'll see you later."

"Sounds good," Sheridan agreed with a little laugh.

Parker arched a brow when a tug on her hand pulled her up short just before she could reach for the doorknob. "Was there something else?" she teased as she turned to look at Sheridan.

Sheridan shook her head and leaned in to press their lips together one last time. "Since I'm being entirely unprofessional, I figured I may as well get one last kiss before I had to go," she murmured, grinning as she pulled away. "I love you."

"Love you, too," Parker breathed. She swallowed thickly and forced herself to let go of Sheridan's hand. "I'll see you later," she promised as she pulled the door open.

"Oh, hey, your brother's here," Sheridan observed softly. "Did you guys finally work through whatever it was you were fighting about?"

Parker shook her head. "Not yet." *And not likely soon, if he really did what I think he did,* she added silently as she stared at her brother, who was huddled with Jess, and Kelly around her assistant's desk, looking way too chummy with them for her liking at the moment. "Guess we'll see…"

Sheridan nodded. "Good luck, then. Call me if you need me?"

"Always," Parker promised. She sighed and forced a small smile as Sheridan's fingers wrapped lightly around her wrist in a reassuring hold. "I'll see you later, okay?"

Sheridan nodded and, with a gentle squeeze of Parker's wrist, let her hand fall as she strode out of Parker's office. "Ready to go, Kel?"

"Hey, McDreamy," Oliver greeted Sheridan with a smile.

Parker grit her teeth. Given what she was pretty sure he'd done, the last thing she wanted was for him to try to be all friendly with Sheridan. Which was more than a little hypocritical given everything she'd done before finally walking away from the Marquis job, but she couldn't control what she felt.

"Oliver," Sheridan replied with a tight nod as she paused beside him.

Oliver tilted his head toward Sheridan, who was clearly saying something to him in a low tone, and pursed his lips as he nodded. Though Parker couldn't hear his voice, she could read his lips when he replied to whatever it was she'd said with a simple, "I'll try," and she held her breath when he finally looked at her. She hated fighting with him, but not nearly as much as she hated the idea of losing Sheridan.

Sheridan turned to look at her once she was finished with Oliver, and she nodded at the question she could see swimming in Sheridan's eyes. She would be okay. Sheridan smiled reassuringly at her and then nodded as she tilted her head toward the elevators. "Let's go, Innes."

She sighed and shook her head as she watched Sheridan walk away. "What's up, Ollie?"

"Can we talk?"

Parker made a show of looking at her watch and then shrugged. "Yeah. But not here." She ignored him as she looked at Jess, whose expression was clearly concerned as she watched them. "Jess, I'm gonna work from home for the rest of the day."

Jess nodded as she looked between the two of them, her body angling protectively toward Parker. "Want me to forward calls to your cell?"

"Nah, I'll catch up on it all tomorrow. I always leave my Fridays light, so I'll have plenty of time in the morning." Parker forced a small smile that she hoped looked at least somewhat reassuring. "If you really need me, though, I'll have my cell on. Okay?"

"Text me later?" Jess asked, the unspoken second half of her question clear in her eyes. *Let me know that you're okay?*

"I will." Parker nodded. She glanced at her brother. "Just hang on a second and I'll grab my things, okay?"

He shoved his hands into his pockets and nodded. "Okay."

Parker sighed and turned on her heel to retreat to her office for a few minutes to gather her thoughts more than her things. She knew she wouldn't be getting much more work done in the couple hours that remained on the work day, if she got any done at all, but she still packed her bag with everything she might need in case she decided to call in and work remotely the next day. Once her bag was packed, she zipped it shut and slung it over her shoulder, and she took a deep breath as she walked out of her office. "If you finish those reports early," she told Jess as she passed her desk, "go ahead and cut out early."

"So I'm not in trouble for letting Sheridan in?" Jess teased.

"Not at all. Please feel free to do that any time. Seeing her walk through my door was the highlight of my day," Parker assured her with a tired smile. "Thank you."

"My pleasure, Park." Jess glanced at Oliver and shook her head. "I'll talk to you later?"

"Yeah. I'll reach out when I'm on my way down to Sheridan's tonight."

"Sounds good."

Parker hefted her bag higher on her shoulders and sighed as she ran a hand through her hair as she looked at Oliver. "You ready?"

"When you are," he agreed amenably as he fell into step beside her.

Parker was glad that he sensed she didn't want to talk while they were in the building. She was angry at him for continuing to push on the Marquis job and worried about him and terrified that his actions will come back to bite her in the ass with Sheridan, and she didn't trust herself to not blow up at him. At least if she lost it once they were on the street, it wouldn't be overheard by the gossip mill inside her firm.

And, sure enough, the moment they pushed through the revolving door onto 56th and turned toward Lexington, he decided to open his mouth. "What was the FBI doing in your office?"

Parker fisted the straps of her backpack and took a deep, steadying breath. Of all the things he could have opened with, a quasi-attack on Sheridan's presence in her life was the absolute wrong one. "What the fuck were you doing in London?"

He shrugged. "The Chaucer."

She blew out a soft breath. Even though she'd been pretty certain that was what he'd been doing, part of her had still hoped he'd had a more legitimate reason to leave the country. "Please tell me you didn't take Rick."

"I needed a second set of hands," Oliver replied. "Getting in and out was easy enough, but that library was fucking huge. It would have taken me forever to find the book on my own."

"Yeah, well, two gigantic mistakes there. The first was that you were greedy in trying for the Chaucer in the first place. And the second one was taking Rick with you. I don't want to know what you two did, but you need to call his ass right now and tell him to disappear before you completely fuck up my life."

"Why?"

"You two must have fucked up somehow, because Sheridan and Kelly were at my office talking to Summers about a recovery of his from a few years ago where Rick was a suspect, and they are on their way up to his apartment now. If he gets brought in…"

"Shit," Oliver swore as he pulled a cheap Samsung burner phone from his pocket. He punched in a number from memory and, a moment later, said, "You have the FBI on their way up to see you right the fuck now, so you need to grab what you can't live without and fucking bail. Do you still have those other papers? Because you're going to need a new life, man, this one is burned…"

Parker flexed her hands around the straps of her pack as she resisted the urge to grab Oliver's phone and rip Rick a new one herself. It would be cathartic to lay into the moron, but not the most effective use of their time given the urgency of the situation.

"Good." Oliver ran a hand through his hair. "Yeah, man. It was fun while it lasted. Run fast and stay safe, okay?" After a pause he nodded and added, "You too." He blew out a loud breath as he disconnected the call and slipped the phone back into his pocket. "He'll be in the wind in twenty minutes."

"He's just lucky Kelly mentioned his name in my office," Parker seethed, glaring at her brother.

"I'm sorry!" Oliver apologized quickly. "I didn't think—"

"Clearly," Parker snapped. She shook her head at the people who glanced their way as they rounded the corner at Lexington and started toward the subway station at 53rd. She lowered her voice and added, "You weren't thinking about anything but yourself."

"That's not fair."

"Seriously?" Parker scoffed. "Who else were you thinking about, then? Because it sure as shit wasn't me."

"Parker…"

She held up a hand and shook her head. She really wasn't in the mood to listen to him try to justify his reckless stupidity. "Did you at least get rid of the fucking book?"

"Yeah. I delivered it to Marquis Sunday."

"Does Rick have any idea what other titles are on her list are?"

"Please, like I'd tell him anything more than he needed to know," Oliver grumbled.

Parker bit back the retort that was on the tip of her tongue about the fact that he'd been stupid enough to take Rick with him in the first place. Now wasn't the time to beat that particular dead horse and, judging by the way Oliver's shoulders had rounded in on himself, he knew he'd made a mistake. The Starbucks she often stopped at on her way to the office was just up ahead, and she sighed as she waved toward it. She had a feeling she was going to need a little extra help to help her get through the rest of the afternoon. "Caffeine?"

"Sure."

An uneasy silence settled around them as they made their way into the coffee shop, the both of them stealing glances at the other and then looking away quickly when they realized they'd been caught. They had never stayed upset with each other for this long before, and for as much as she hated feeling like she did, she did find some measure of satisfaction in knowing she wasn't the only one that was hurting.

"I'm sorry, Parker. Okay?" Oliver murmured as he opened the door to the Starbucks for her.

"I know you are, Olls," she replied just as softly as they took up the back of the line. "But if you're going to keep pushing for that last book…"

"I'm not." He shook his head. "You were right, okay? It was reckless, and we almost got caught; and while I've certainly been acting like a moron lately, I'm not an idiot."

"Yeah, well…" She glanced at him as they shuffled forward in line.

"I deserve that." He shrugged. "I'm sorry my recklessness almost jeopardized things between you and Sheridan. I should have really listened to your reasons for walking away, but at the time all I heard was that you were choosing her over me."

"I didn't want to have to choose anyone, Olls. Can't you understand that? But you were so adamant about not stopping that you forced me to."

"I know." He nodded. "Seeing her walk out of your office just now and then everything else with Rick, I get what kind of a position I put you in and I'm sorry." He shook his head and nudged her with his elbow. "She's kinda scary, by the way. Beautiful, but scary."

"What'd she say to you?"

"That you were the best person she knows and that if I didn't fix this"—he waved a hand between them—"she would hunt me down and kick my ass. Apparently she's been taking Krav Maga lessons or something, and she'd love an excuse to put them to good use."

Parker chuckled. "God, I love her."

"Have you told her that?"

She couldn't keep from smiling as she nodded. "Yeah. I have."

"So it's serious."

Parker nodded. "Yeah. It's the most serious I've ever been."

"Good." He took a deep breath and wrapped an arm around her shoulders. "I'm happy for you, Parker," he murmured against her temple. "She's...well, except for the whole Art Crimes FBI Agent thing, pretty freaking perfect for you."

"Yeah, well, since we're *both* done with the whole illicit-career thing..." Parker arched a brow as she looked at him—he'd said before that he'd hang it all up after the Marquis job, but she wanted him to confirm that he really was done. She smiled when he huffed a breath and nodded. "I guess that won't be a blemish on her record for too much longer, huh?"

"I guess not," he confirmed as the barista waved them up to the register. Once they'd ordered and paid and moved off to the side to wait for their drinks, Oliver asked, "So, should we call our benefactor when we get back to your place and let her know we're done?"

Parker nodded. "Yeah. And then we can get on with the rest of our lives."

Gregory was still at NYU for his office hours after his seminar when they got back to the house, and Parker glanced over her shoulder at Oliver as they made their way through the marbled foyer to the stairs. "Gregory's missed you, by the way. I told him you've just been busy with work, but you may need to do some additional apologizing there."

"I'll talk to him before I head home tonight," Oliver promised. "He usually gets home before five, right?"

"Most of the time, I think," she confirmed as she pushed the door to her apartment open and walked inside. "I want to say his seminar this semester is from one-to-two forty-five, so as long as he doesn't have a line of kids waiting for help during office hours, he should be home soon."

"Cool." Oliver pulled the burner he'd used to contact Rick from his pocket. "It's close to ten in France, Marquis should still be awake."

"Good. I'm more than ready to put all this behind us."

"Yeah." He pulled his regular cell from his other pocket, laid it on the table, and opened the app he'd developed to scramble the signal of nearby phones to anyone not directly connected to the calls. "Me too, actually." He punched in the contact number he had for Marquis and, once the call started to ring through, set the phone to speaker and laid it on the table between them.

"Yes?"

Parker arched a brow in surprise. She wasn't expecting a man to answer the call. Nor was she really expecting that voice to be speaking English, although she figured that might be because the phone number on their end would be showing up as American.

"Yes, hello. Is this the American Consulate?" Oliver replied, smirking at her obvious confusion.

"I'm sorry, sir, but you must have the wrong number."

"Are you sure?" Oliver replied. "Because the guide book I bought in Paris says that this is the number."

"The fuck?" she whispered. Clearly, she should have listened-in on his calls to Marquis before, because she had never imagined they'd go anything like this.

"Hold, please."

He chuckled. "It's not like she's really going to give out her personal phone number. I give the guy who answered the phone the right code words, and then he patches me through to her."

"Like you couldn't find her personal phone number," she retorted.

"Oh, I've got it, just in case," he assured her, tapping his temple. "But I figured it was better to play by her rules so long as we weren't being hurt by them."

The phone clicked with the call being successfully transferred. *"Two calls in a week? I'm impressed. Do we need to arrange another exchange?"*

"I'm afraid not," Oliver replied, sounding appropriately apologetic. "I was actually calling to let you know that we're not going to be able to complete the acquisitions from your list."

"May I ask why? Our original agreement still holds, of course, but I am curious..."

Oliver's lips curled into a tight smile. "We've come across information that suggests the FBI might be getting closer in their investigation, and we both agree that the risks no longer outweigh the potential reward."

"I'm assuming you're referring to Ms. Ravenscroft's relationship with Agent Sloan?"

Parker's eyes widened. Marquis was known for keeping an eye on her investments, micro-managing was both her greatest strength and weakness, but she'd never imagined that oversight would stretch to what she was doing with her personal life. "That is certainly a part of the decision, yes," she spoke up.

"Ah, I was wondering if you were there. Very good. While I am obviously disappointed that this will terminate our agreement, I do wish to thank you got for your impeccable work thus far. You have more than lived up to your reputation."

"We're glad you think so," Oliver said.

Marquis chuckled. *"Yes, well, I wish the best of luck to the both of you in your future endeavors,"* she signed off, the click of the call disconnecting the most beautiful sound Parker had heard in a while. It was over.

They were done.

"Wow," Oliver breathed as he tapped the screen to make sure the call was disconnected.

"I'll say," she agreed.

"Were you aware that she was watching us that closely?"

"No. But it honestly doesn't surprise me." He pushed himself up from the table and headed to the patio. "You want to go grab your hammer?" he asked as he opened the doors.

Parker nodded and went to retrieve the little tool box she kept under the sink in case something small broke so she wouldn't need to go down to the garage to get something from Gregory's massive tool chest.

"Thanks," he said when she joined him on the patio. He grinned and added, "You want to spike the phone, or whack it?"

Destroying the phone was a no-brainer, but she hadn't expected him to find such joy in the task. "Whatever you want, Olls."

He handed her the phone. "I think I'd like to give it a whack."

"All right," she agreed. She lifted the phone over her head and chuckled it down onto the cement patio. It hit with a satisfying crack, and she arched a brow at him. "Good enough?"

"Good enough." He squatted down next to the phone and gave it a solid whack with the hammer, shattering the screen and pretty much destroying all the important bits inside. *"Au revoir,* Marquis," he grinned as he whacked it another three times for good measure.

"Pretty sure it's dead, Olls." She chuckled at the way he grinned up at her, and shook her head as she went inside to retrieve a broom and dustpan. Once the bits and pieces were swept up and thrown away, she looked around her apartment and sighed. It was over. "So, what's the plan now?"

He shrugged. "Just life, I guess. Yeah?"

"That sounds perfect, actually," she said as she offered him the dustpan. "Go throw this away?"

He nodded and took the pan. "What time are you going to Sheridan's?" he asked as he headed back inside.

"Don't know," Parker murmured as she pulled out her phone. She knew that Sheridan would want an update on how things were with her and Oliver, and she didn't want her worrying about it when she needed to be focused on her job. *Thank you for offering to kick Ollie's ass, but it's not needed. We've worked things out.* She glanced at her brother who was hunched over the trash can in her kitchen, slowly pouring the pieces of broken phone into the bin. *I will see you soon. Be safe, my love.* "I did promise to make her dinner, though."

"I like dinner."

"I'm sure you do," Parker laughed. "But maybe next time, okay? I haven't seen her since last weekend and..."

"You're gonna get naked, got it," he teased.

"No. Well, probably, but these last few weeks have been rough, and now that everything is done with Marquis I just need a night with her where I'm not worried about someone"—she gave him a pointed look as she leaned against the island—"possibly getting his ass arrested."

He held his hands up. "I'm sorry."

"I know," she said as her phone buzzed in her hand. *I'm glad you guys figured it out. I love you.*

"Heart eyes," Oliver coughed.

She pointedly ignored his comment. "Anyway, now that this is all behind us, I really would love it if the two most important people in my life could get to know each other better. I don't want to have to choose between you two anymore. So, maybe next weekend?"

He nodded. "I'd like that."

She smiled. "Me too."

FORTY

"Well, would you look at what the cat dragged in," Kelly drawled.

Sheridan looked up from the email she was composing and arched a brow in surprise when she saw Lucy Reynolds strolling through the doors of their unit. The C.I. usually stayed as far away from their building as possible so she didn't blow her cover at the art gallery where they had positioned her, so she had to have something big if she showed up unannounced instead of reaching out through their usual channels. "What's up, Luce?" she asked when the leggy brunette neared her desk.

Lucy smiled her trademark enigmatic smile and shrugged. "Not much. Just have some information for Bartz about a fence who approached the owner of the gallery about potential buyers for a Renoir that definitely shouldn't be on the market. I was on my way back to the gallery from a lunch in Two Bridges and figured I'd stop by on the way."

"Oh. Good," Sheridan murmured halfheartedly. The lead they'd gotten for Rick Frasier the week before had ended up being a complete bust because his apartment had been empty when they got there and he was still nowhere to be found, and she had hoped that Lucy might have some kind of new information that would help them out.

Lucy shrugged. "And," she drew that single syllable out for a good four beats, "I thought you'd like to know that I've finally heard something about those books you keep asking me about."

Sheridan sat up straighter. "Really?"

There was that smile again, slow and predatory, like she knew so much more than she was going to share. "I've been discreetly asking around about it all like you asked me to, and a contact of mine in Iceland called this morning to tell me about a rumor he's heard that there's only one more book on this list that's out there."

"How the hell do you know people in Iceland?" Kelly asked. When Lucy just stared at him in response, he held his hands up and murmured, "Sorry. So, your guy in Iceland…"

"Exactly. My guy in Iceland." Lucy winked and shoved her hands into the pockets of her slacks, clearly enjoying knowing something they didn't. "And, no, I'm not going to tell you who told me this. I gotta keep my sources' anonymity if I want them to keep talking to me."

"Right." Sheridan sighed. She hated not knowing where Lucy got her information, but they had made too many arrests—not to mention recoveries—off the information she'd given them over the last couple years to push her on it. "So does your mysterious source have anything else to say about it all?"

"Just that it's something big and it's here in the States somewhere," Lucy replied.

"Did they say when the thieves were going to hit it?" Kelly asked.

Lucy shrugged. "This weekend? Sometime in the next month? In a year? Who knows? He wasn't exactly reading off these guys' day planner or anything." She looked toward Bartz's office and sighed. "They did seem to think that it would be soon, though. But I've been spotted by the Boss Man, so I need to get up there before he does that annoying little finger crick thing to demand my presence. Hope that little bit helped, at least."

"Anything helps," Sheridan assured her with a smile. "Thanks."

"Of course." Lucy ran a hand through her hair as she turned toward Bartz. "Yes, yes, I know. I'm coming," she muttered under her breath as she started for the stairs.

"So who do you think her source is?" Kelly asked once she was out of earshot.

"God, I wish I knew." Sheridan shook her head. "Because she has ears everywhere that I'd love to be able to access whenever I needed to. But," she sighed, "I can't blame her for holding those cards close to her chest. It is what's keeping her on an anklet instead of in an orange jumpsuit, after all."

"Yeah, definitely can't blame her for that one. So, assuming her mysterious source's information about our mysterious list is mysteriously accurate..." He chuckled at the sardonic look she gave him. "Anyway, assuming all of that, what do you think?"

Sheridan sighed. That was a shitton of assumptions, but if all of them were on point and they had just one more shot to catch Filibus, they were going to have to make a move without having all the information. "Shakespeare's First Folio. It's big—sold for over six million at auction in 2001—and close enough that we could run a stake-out on Boyle's building without too much trouble."

"Yay, a weekend in the van," he cheered sarcastically.

"Better than not doing anything and then getting a call that it was stolen."

"God, I hate when you're all logical and professional and shit." He groaned and looked up at Bartz's office. "So should we run it by him when Lucy's done?"

She nodded. "Yeah."

"What do you think he'll say?"

"No idea." She shrugged as the door to Bartz's office opened. She bit her lip to keep from grinning at the way Lucy sauntered out of the office like she owned it while Bartz hovered in the doorway looking like he'd been bested in whatever chess match it was the two of them were playing at the moment, and looked at her partner. "Ready?"

"Fine." He slapped his hands on the arms of his chair and pushed himself to his feet. "You're doing the talking, though."

"And how is that different from any other time we've done something like this?" Sheridan retorted.

"Good point," he conceded.

They waited at the bottom of the stairs to allow Lucy to pass, and Sheridan gave her a small nod. "Thanks for the tip."

Lucy nodded. "Hope it helps," she replied as she breezed by them.

"Fingers crossed," Kelly muttered as they started up the stairs.

"Sir?" Sheridan called as she rapped her knuckles on his open door.

Bartz looked up from his computer and waved them inside. "What's up?"

"When Lucy was on her way in she told us that a contact of hers in Iceland is saying that there's one book left on the Filibus list. It's also supposedly here in the States somewhere, and her contact seems to believe that it will be taken soon. Shakespeare's First Folio fits that description to a T, and we'd like permission to arrange surveillance on Boyle's apartment on the Upper East Side."

"How long do you expect this surveillance to last?" Bartz looked between the two of them. "Because we're short-staffed around here at the moment with Moran and Wood in Germany and Nathan and Collins down in Florida. You guys would be doing the heavy lifting if you decided to do this."

"We expected nothing less," she assured him.

"Yep," Kelly echoed.

Bartz shuffled papers on his desk and, after a pause, nodded. "Okay. I'll give you through the end of the weekend to see if there's anything suspicious going on, and we'll decide from there if further action is necessary. Deal?"

Sheridan smiled. "Thank you, sir."

"Absolutely," Kelly agreed at the same time.

Bartz sighed and checked his watch as he leaned back in his chair. "After this first shift, we'll do it in eights. It's three now, Chang and

Patel will take first shift until ten, when you guys go on. Coffee and Hall will relieve you at six tomorrow morning, Chang and Patel will take the afternoon, and you guys are back on at ten. Wash, rinse, repeat through the weekend. Good?"

"Perfect." She nodded. If Filibus was going to try to get to the book on the top floor of a twenty-six story building, she had a feeling they'd be doing it at night, anyway.

"Right. Well, I recommend you two clear your schedules for the next couple days, wrap up whatever reports need to be turned in by the end of the day, and go grab a nap so you don't fall asleep in the van later."

"Well, the nap part of all that didn't sound so bad," Kelly quipped.

Bartz's lips twitched with the hint of a smile that he quickly hid behind his trademark scowl. "I'm glad you approve, Innes. Now, if you could go get Chang and Patel and send them up here, I need to give them the good news."

They nodded at the dismissal, and when they were in the hall outside Bartz's office, Sheridan muttered, "Only you could get away with a comment like that."

"It's a skill," Kelly agreed with a little laugh. "Anyway, I guess it's a good thing I only have some errands and video game playing I'll be missing out on this weekend. You sure seem eager to spend the weekend in a van with me, though, is your better half out of town for work again?"

"No, she's home," Sheridan groaned. She'd gotten so wrapped-up in what Lucy had told them that she'd completely forgotten about anything beyond the case. "And we were supposed to have her brother and Gregory over for dinner at my place tomorrow night…"

"Oh, shit. Are you gonna get in trouble for that?"

"No. She'll understand. I just know that she was looking forward to having me and her brother get to know each other. We've only talked to each other in passing so far, you know?"

"Ah, the welcome-to-the-family dinner, that's right." He smirked. "You're welcome for getting you out of it."

Sheridan rolled her eyes. She had actually been looking forward to spending some time with Oliver and getting to know him better. "Whatever," she brushed him off as she pulled her phone from her pocket. "I'm gonna go call her."

"I'm guessing you'll be doing that somewhere that isn't here?"

Sheridan huffed a wry laugh that was devoid of humor and nodded. "Yeah. The last thing I need is anyone here listening in. You guys give me enough shit as it is."

"We give shit because we care."

"If you say so." She grabbed her phone off her desk. "I'll be back in a few."

He nodded and pulled the files he needed to finish signing off on from his desk drawer. "Tell Parker I say, hey. I'll go send Chang and Patel up to Bartz."

She nodded and waved her phone in an *I will* type gesture, and sighed as she headed for the elevator. Short of commandeering an office, there were few spots in the building that afforded any kind of privacy, but there was a quiet corner in the archives that was usually deserted. She'd canceled on Parker before, but that didn't stop her heart from racing at the thought of calling Parker and telling her that she was going to have to work all weekend. She knew, of course, that she didn't have a choice. That this was the job, and weekends were never guaranteed, but she was so, so worried that these kinds of phone calls would eventually become too much for Parker to be willing to deal with.

She'd eventually bounced back after Claire, had found a place where she was happy being alone, but she wasn't sure she would survive losing Parker.

And that, more than anything, was what made her hands shake when she found her quiet corner in the archives and pressed her thumb to Parker's name in her contacts.

"Hey, you," Parker answered after the first ring, her voice warm and full of sunshine. *"What's up?"*

"I..." Her voice cracked and she cleared her throat. "Sorry. I...I just wanted to call and tell you that it looks like I'm going to be working this weekend."

"Oh. While I'm sorry that we'll have to reschedule with Ollie, I totally get it. Is it at least something exciting? Or can you not say?"

"One of Lucy's contacts gave us a lead on that case we were at your office for last week, and we need to follow it."

"That's good, though. Right?"

"Yeah, I guess. We're just going to be sitting in a van all weekend watching this woman's building on the Upper East Side in case the guys we're chasing move on it."

"Really?" Parker drawled. *"Well, that's awesome. I hope you get 'em."*

"You're not mad?" she asked softly.

"No, Sheridan," Parker murmured. *"I know that this is going to happen. And I know that there are going to be times I'll be the one making this kind of call to you. We don't have typical nine-to-fives, and this is just part of it, sweetie. I'm not going to stop loving you because you may occasionally need to put your job first, and even on the days when I have to put mine first, you'll still be the most important part of my life, okay?"*

Sheridan licked her lips and wiped at her eyes that were stinging with tears of relief because Parker had said exactly the words she'd needed to hear. "Okay," she whispered, the slight crack of her voice between syllables betraying her attempt to sound assured.

"Oh, babe," Parker sighed. *"I'm sorry. I didn't mean to make you cry. I was just trying to make you feel better about the whole thing."*

"No, what you said was perfect," she insisted, her voice thick with emotion. "I just...really wish I could kiss you right now."

"I do, too," Parker breathed. There was a murmur of someone talking in the background, and then Parker said, *"But Ollie just showed up, so I guess we're gonna have to save that for another day. Are you going to be okay?"*

"Yeah." She nodded. "Thank you for understanding."

"Always, Sheridan. I love you."

She wiped at her cheeks and nodded. "I love you too, Parker. I'll call when I can, okay?"

"I can't wait. Go catch some bad guys, Agent Sloan. I'll be here waiting for you when you're done."

"Bye…"

"Goodbye, sweetheart."

She swallowed thickly as she pocketed her phone, and shook her head at herself as she went in search of a bathroom mirror to make sure she didn't look like a total disaster when she went back upstairs. Had she known she'd end up a blubbering mess, she'd have brought her purse with her, but she was glad to see, when she was able to check her reflection, that except for a little puffiness around her eyes, she didn't look like her girlfriend had turned her to complete mush.

"Everything okay?" Kelly asked gently when she got back to her desk.

She nodded. "Yeah."

He studied her carefully for a moment and, when he seemed assured that she really was okay, grinned. "Good. Then let's go catch some bad guys!"

She laughed. "You sound like Parker."

He shrugged and buffed his nails on his shoulder. "You say that like it's a bad thing…"

"Not at all." She shook her head. "It's pretty much the best thing in the world as far as I'm concerned."

forty-one

Parker had been staring out the doors overlooking her patio as she talked to Sheridan, but she turned toward at her front door when a cautious knock rapped against the wood. She smiled at the sight of her brother's head peeking through the cracked door and beckoned him inside. "But Ollie just showed up, so I guess we're gonna have to save that for another day," she reported as she turned back to the windows for privacy. "You gonna be okay?"

"Yeah. Thank you for understanding."

Her heart broke at that, because there was no way she could have ever fallen in love with Sheridan without understanding and accepting that this was part of it. She swallowed thickly as she assured her gently, "Always, Sheridan. I love you."

"I love you too, Parker. I'll call when I can, okay?"

She smiled and nodded. "I can't wait. Go catch some bad guys, Agent Sloan. I'll be here waiting for you when you're done."

"Bye..."

"Goodbye, sweetheart."

"Everything okay with Sheridan?" Oliver asked when she turned back to where he had pulled out a chair at the kitchen table.

"Yeah." She shrugged. "She was just calling to tell me that she was going to be working this weekend."

"That sucks. Did she say why?"

"She did, in fact." Parker nodded as she pulled out the chair next to him. "Turns out dear ol' Lucy gave them some intel that something important on the Upper East Side here in Manhattan was going to be stolen soon, so she's going to be staking out the woman's building."

Oliver gaped at her in shock. "How the hell did Lucy hear about the Shakespeare?"

"Fuck if I know," she muttered. "But it's too much of a coincidence that Lucy's contacts are telling her about a job like that here in the city for it to be anything other than that Folio. Somebody, somewhere, must have talked. Do you think Marquis found somebody else to make a move on the Shakespeare this quickly?"

"Hell if I know." He shook his head. "I mean, it's the only thing that makes sense, unless it's some kind of twisted one-upmanship where Smythe is trying to grab it just to fuck with her for the whole Matisse thing."

"Do you really think Smythe would know Marquis was involved in that, though?"

Oliver shrugged. "If the gossip about those two is even *partially* true, I'd bet Marquis made sure Smythe knew she was involved."

"Goddamn."

"Right?" He laughed. "But if it was somebody on Marquis' payroll who let that shit slip, I wouldn't want to be within a ten-mile radius of them when she figures it out. Because impeccable manners and whatever aside, that woman is dangerous."

"Just makes me even more glad that we're done with her, to be honest," Parker muttered.

"Speaking of…" He leaned his elbows onto the table. "What do you want me to do with your half of the money from all this?"

"Ollie…" She sighed. "I wasn't kidding when I said I don't want anything to do with the money from this mess."

"But it's two million dollars."

"Exactly. It's two million reminders of all the ways I lied to Sheridan, and I don't want anything to do with any of it. I…" She ran a hand through her hair and shrugged. "I really love her, Olls. More than I thought I could ever love anyone, to be honest. And I'm never going to lie to her again."

"I get it." He rolled his hands to the side in a *now what?* kind of gesture. "So do you want me to set up a scholarship for kids in the system back in Seattle with your half?"

"I think that would be great. Yeah. Is there a way for you to do it anonymously?"

"Oh yeah. If you want, instead of doing it straight off the money where it'll eventually run out, I can set it up so it's attached to an investment portfolio so that way the money is drawn from the profits on the portfolio so it should—theoretically, assuming it doesn't get eaten in a market crash—be able to run forever."

A lifetime, or more, of good coming out of her lies wouldn't come close to absolving her of her sins, but the idea of helping god knows how many kids like her and Ollie made her smile. "Yeah." She nodded. "Do that."

"Okay." He smiled. "You're a good person, Parker Ravenscroft. You know that, right?"

"I'm trying to be. Anyway"—she shrugged—"it looks like you drove all the way down here for nothing. With Sheridan working, we're going to have to reschedule our dinner."

He shrugged. "It's not a biggie. Baseball is done until the spring, so I can come down whenever. Honestly, I was half-thinking of moving down here sooner or later, anyway."

Parker's eyes widened as she sat up straighter. "Really?"

Oliver laughed. "Really. With everything that's happened lately, I've realized that I would much rather be closer to you—and Gregory and, once I win her over with my amazing personality, Sheridan." He sighed. "I love Boston, but since we're like, actual adults now and everything, it makes more sense to be closer to family."

"I'd like that," she murmured.

"Me too." He smirked and kicked her foot under the table. "So, when will you be getting the ol' U-Haul? Aren't you guys like way past the whole second date thing?"

"And just like that, the nice little moment we were having was shattered," she drawled.

He grinned. "I'm just saying, this is a pretty sweet apartment and if I'm going to be moving down here anyway…"

She laughed. "How do you know Sheridan wouldn't move here?"

He shook his head. "This place is awesome and all, but I'm pretty sure you guys would want a little more privacy. Besides, I thought you mentioned one time that she owns her place?"

"She does," Parker conceded. Truthfully, she'd kind of figured that once they did take that next step, she'd be the one packing her bags for that very reason. And when they did finally reach that point, she could think of no better person to take her apartment than her brother. "If Sheridan and I move-in together, I'm sure Gregory would love to have you here."

"I just want to make sure one of us is here to look after him." Oliver shrugged, his expression turning serious. "He's starting to get up there and everything and…"

"He's family, and we need to take care of him," she finished for him. "Yeah. I feel the same way too." She glanced out the window. "Since Sheridan's going to be busy, maybe we can take him out to dinner tomorrow night or something. Just the three of us, you know?"

"Yeah. That'd be nice." He smiled. "I've missed you guys."

She nodded. "I've missed you, too, Olls. And I know Gregory feels the same way."

"You're not going to start crying on me, are you?" he teased.

She laughed and took a playful swing at his arm. "Whatever, Dobrev."

He laughed and took the hit with a playfully dramatic grimace. "Anyway, what do you say we go see what Sheridan's team has cooked up over at Boyle's place."

"You're not serious…"

"It'll be fun! Come on, how often do you get to know exactly where the FBI is running surveillance so you can check it out? Besides, what else are we gonna do? I mean, we do have the whole rest of the day to kill…"

She shrugged. Beyond the day, she had the whole weekend to kill, too. And she learned the hard way that her body could only do so many chaturangas before she wouldn't be able to lift her arms anymore. "Promise me that you're really done with the whole stealing shit thing? That, from now on, you're just going to focus on using your computer skills for good, rather than evil?"

He held up his right hand like he was swearing an oath. "I'm done, Parker. I promise. I just want to go have some fun."

"Staking out an FBI stake out is fun?"

"We can go climbing at Boulders afterwards," he offered with a grin. "Maybe stop and pick up a pizza on the way back?"

Okay, that actually did sound like fun. She couldn't help but smile at him in return, a feeling of lightness warming her chest as she looked at him. Finally, after what felt like a lifetime of lies and worry and guilt and stress, she had her brother back. "All right," she conceded with a small tip of her head. "Fine. But if Sheridan sees us…"

"She won't!"

"I'm just saying, you better have a good story ready for her if she does."

"Please. All you'd have to do was say that we were on our way to The Met so you could show me something artsy and that you just wanted to stop by and say hi."

"That's the flimsiest excuse I've ever heard," she pointed out with a little laugh. "And, besides that, she would kill me for interrupting her at work."

"No she wouldn't."

"And how do you know that?"

He grinned. "Because she loves you."

Parker couldn't contain her smile as her heart did somersaults in her chest and she murmured, "Lucky me."

FORTY-TWO

Sheridan scrubbed her hands over her face as she and Kelly waited for the elevator that would take them up to the lobby of the Federal Building and groaned. They'd spent the last ten hours in the van staring at Justine Boyle's building where exactly nothing interesting had happened for the fourth night in a row, and all she really wanted was to go home and sleep. But, because Bartz had a thing about nobody missing his Monday morning briefing—even agents who were out of town were expected to join in on the phone—that wasn't going to happen anytime soon.

"So tired," Kelly muttered as he shuffled into the elevator. He slapped at the button for the lobby and groaned as he leaned against the side wall. "What are the odds we get to go to sleep after this?"

She yawned and crossed her fingers.

"Yeah, that's what I thought," he sighed as he pulled his phone from his pocket.

A small smile quirked his lips as he responded to whatever text he'd received, which made her even more aware of the fact that Parker hadn't texted her yet that morning. Which, considering the fact that it was almost nine, was odd. She almost always got some kind of good morning message from Parker when they didn't see each other before work.

After they made it through the security line and were in the elevator on their way up to the twenty-seventh floor, she pulled her phone from her purse to send Parker a little note. *Good morning, my love. Heading into the office for Bartz's Monday briefing and then hopefully home to sleep. Hope you have a good day. Will try to call later. I miss you.* She sighed as she dropped the phone into the front pocket of her blazer, and rolled her head to try to loosen the tightness that had settled in her neck overnight as the elevator slowed at their floor.

Hopefully she'd be able to see Parker later, but for now she needed to try to focus on work.

She grunted her thanks to Kelly as she walked through the door he held open for her, and smiled when he echoed the sentiment as he followed her into the bullpen. That small, tired smile fell when she noticed Bartz standing at the railing outside his office. He'd clearly been waiting for them, as the moment he saw he had her attention, he crooked two fingers at them and motioned toward the conference room.

"But I just want to sleep," Kelly whined as they trudged toward the stairs.

"Tell me about it," she muttered through another yawn.

"We should've stopped for coffee."

"Tell me about it," she repeated.

He chuckled and slowed down so she could enter the conference room ahead of him. "What's up, boss?" he asked as he pulled a chair away from the conference table and dropped heavily into it.

Sheridan kept her eyes on their boss as she lowered herself into the chair next to him with only moderately more grace.

"We'll get to that when everyone else gets here." Bartz waved him off as he took his seat at the head of the table. "How'd it go?"

Kelly motioned for her to take that one, and she sat up a little straighter as she reported, "Facial recognition software on our cameras didn't pick up anything, and we didn't see anything suspicious from the street or the building's internal security footage that they allowed us to access. No alarms were triggered during the four nights we were watching the building…" Her voice trailed off and she shook her head as she stifled a yawn with the back of her hand. "Sorry. All-in-all, sir, I'd call the operation a complete bust."

Bartz sighed and nodded sympathetically. "I don't like it at all, but it happens, I'm afraid." He shrugged. "Unfortunately, though, we can't afford to continue to spend the unit's time or manpower on the surveillance of a hypothetical target."

"Yes, sir," Sheridan murmured. Really, she wasn't surprised. If anything, she'd been more surprised when he had agreed to the short surveillance operation in the first place.

"The minute we hear something about the Folio or anything else being targeted specifically, I'll reauthorize the entire investigation, but for now we have too many other fires to try to put out to focus on a single book that may or may not ever be stolen."

"Yes, sir," Kelly muttered.

Sheridan looked back at the open door when someone knocked on the frame, and was relieved to see Raj Patel hovering in the doorway. She was beyond tired, their Filibus investigation had effectively been shelved, and she really just wanted this stupid meeting to be over with so she could hopefully go home and sleep and hopefully see Parker later that night.

"Can we come in?" Patel motioned toward Holly Chang, who was standing behind him.

"Yeah. Let's get this started." Bartz waved them inside. "Would one of you guys set up the conference call so our teams in the field can call in to join?"

Chang nodded. "On it."

"How was the night shift?" Patel asked as he pulled out a chair across the table from Kelly.

"So exciting I can hardly keep my eyes open," Kelly drawled.

"I'm sorry, guys," Patel murmured.

"Yeah, thanks." Sheridan nodded.

"We brought coffee," a new voice announced.

Sheridan practically swooned as she spun her chair toward the new arrivals. Both Hall and Coffee were holding cardboard takeaway trays from the nearby Starbucks, and she gratefully took the drink Hall handed her. A glance at the lid told her it was one of her usuals, and she smiled as she lifted it to her lips. "I love you."

Kelly laughed. "What about Parker?"

"She isn't bringing me coffee right now, so…" She shrugged as she sipped at her drink. "You guys are saints," she told Hall and Coffee, who grinned and nodded their thanks in response.

Bartz rolled his eyes. "Okay, can we focus? Because three new cases came in this morning that we need to go over."

Coffee and Hall hurried to take their seats as the speaker in the middle of the table crackled to life.

"Good morning from Germany, my fellow super-do-gooders," Ivy greeted the group.

"It's a balmy eighty-one degrees and sunny here in Florida," Collins chimed in.

"Okay. Great." Bartz sighed. "Now, can we focus?" When he was answered with attentive silence, he continued, "As I was saying, we picked up three new cases this morning, but before we get to that, Moran and Wood—how's your investigation going?"

"Good," Rachel answered. *"We have a possible suspect under surveillance, and will be bringing him in for questioning at the local precinct later this afternoon."*

"Okay. Collins?"

"Feels like a little bit of a case of the tail wagging the dog, but the C.I. down here knows a guy who might have a lead for us, so we're gonna go meet with him as soon as we're done here," Collins answered.

"Sounds good. Keep me posted. Consider yourselves done here," Bartz dismissed them. "Moran, Wood, that goes for you, too. I expect some kind of report as to how your interrogation went."

"Yes, sir," all four agents in the field chirruped as on before a series of clicks sounded from the speaker before it fell silent.

"Now, for you all," Bartz said, looking at the agents assembled around the conference table. "Sloan, Innes, a Cezanne landscape—*View of Auvers-sur-Oise*—was called-in to the Twentieth this morning." He slid a file across the table toward them.

Sheridan bit back a groan as she scooped up the file and opened it. So much for sleep.

"But," Bartz continued without missing a beat, "since you were running surveillance all night and you both look like you're dead on your feet, I want you to go home and grab a few hours of sleep before you go and interview Mister De Luca."

"Thank you, sir," Kelly yawned.

Sheridan smiled. Lord knows she was just as excited about that particular order. She shook her head as she scanned the details sent over to them from the detective who'd taken the call over in the Twentieth Precinct. "Do we know who the painting is insured through?"

Bartz nodded. "Cabot and Carmichael."

"Excellent," Sheridan murmured as Kelly smirked and nudged her foot under the table.

Bartz shook his head. "I'm assigning this one to you two because you're our resident expert in this kind of thing, and I'm imagining we'll be working quite closely with the insurance company on this case since the painting was taken from the apartment of an Italian diplomat. We're going to need to show that we're doing everything in our power to catch the thief responsible and recover the painting."

"Got it," Sheridan assured him. Her fingers itched to send a text to Parker to ask if she had picked up the Cezanne case yet, but she knew better than to pull her phone out in the middle of Bartz's meeting.

"Now, the rest of you are going to need to pack your bags." Bartz slid manila file folders toward each of the remaining two teams at the table. "Chang, Patel, you're off to Columbia, South Carolina."

"My old stomping grounds," Chang murmured as she grabbed the file.

"Which is exactly why that one is yours," Bartz replied. "The South Carolina Sword of State has gone missing."

"Cool," Patel whispered as he leaned over to read the file over his partner's shoulder.

Bartz rolled his eyes. "Coffee, Hall, I'm sending you two to Minneapolis to look into a missing *Joie de Vivre* sculpture by Richard MacDonald. It was reported missing from a small art gallery, and local police have requested our help."

"No problem, boss," Coffee drawled as he left the folder sitting on the table in front of him.

Bartz nodded and clapped his hands twice. "All right. Get out of here. Sloan, Innes, call in after you meet with Mr. De Luca to let me know how it went, and I'll see you two tomorrow morning."

"Will do," Kelly answered for them as he jumped to his feet.

"Thank you, sir." Sheridan nodded as she followed suit. The Twentieth Precinct was on the Upper West Side, so even if Parker didn't have the case, maybe she'd just go over to her place after interviewing De Luca and wait for her there until she was done with work.

She was the last of the field agents out of the conference room, and she swore when Kelly stopped abruptly in front of her. "The fuck, Innes?"

He shook his head and waved a hand toward their desks, and her mouth fell open in shock. Parker was lounging casually in her desk chair like it was her own, with a wide smile on her face and what had to be at least two dozen red roses wrapped in cellophane sitting on the desk beside her.

"Go on, Sloan," Kelly laughed as he stepped out of the way so she could hurry down the short flight of stairs to the main floor.

Parker's smile widened as Sheridan approached her desk, and Sheridan shook her head as she asked, "What are you doing here?"

"Can't a girl just bring her girl flowers at work for no reason?" Parker teased, her eyes sparkling with joy and just a hint of mischief. She was clearly pleased that she'd succeeded in surprising her.

"If she doesn't want 'em, I'll take 'em," Kelly piped up playfully.

"I want them." Sheridan scowled at him over her shoulder. She rolled her eyes when he just laughed and held his hands up in front of himself.

"What time do you want me to pick you up to go over to De Luca's?" Kelly asked.

"He's in meetings until three," Parker offered, "so I'd recommend after that."

"So you got the case..." Sheridan murmured.

"I did." Parker winked. "And I have an appointment to meet with Mr. De Luca at four this afternoon to go over his claim if you'd like to go with me to speak with him then."

"I'm guessing I'm just gonna meet you two over there?" Kelly asked.

Sheridan smiled when Parker just shrugged and arched a questioning brow at her. "Yeah," she said. "We'll meet you over there at four. You want the file so you know where we're going?" she offered him the folder she was still holding.

"Just text me the address," Kelly said, pushing the file back at her. "Try and get some sleep," he added, waggling his eyebrows.

"Shut up," Sheridan muttered.

Parker laughed. "I'll make sure she gets some sleep, Kel. Don't worry."

"With you on the case?" he replied, holding his fist out to bump knuckles with her. "No worries needed, my friend. See you two this afternoon!"

Sheridan rolled her eyes as she watched him join their colleagues at the doors to the unit, and sighed as she looked back at Parker. "So, you gonna give those to me, or...?"

"Eh, something like that," Parker chuckled, gathering the flowers and presenting them to her with a small flourish. "I'd kiss you right now, but that'll have to wait until we're out of here."

She looked around the empty office and smiled as she shook her head. "Come here," she whispered as she placed a quick, soft kiss to Parker's lips. "I missed you."

"Missed you more," Parker murmured as she pulled away. She licked her lips and smiled as she sighed, her entire body relaxing with the breath. "Since your partner's hightailed it out of here, I'm guessing you've got a few hours to yourself before this afternoon?"

She nodded. "Yeah, Bartz has very kindly allowed us a few hours to try to catch up on our sleep."

"And cuddle?" Parker asked hopefully.

She smiled. "Don't you have to work?"

"Not when I haven't seen you since last week, no." Parker shook her head. "So, cuddling? Yes or no?"

"Like you ever need to ask," Sheridan chuckled. "Yes, Parker. The answer will always be yes."

"God, I hope so," Parker breathed. She rocked forward like she was going to try to steal another kiss, but pulled back at the last second and bit her lip as she smiled. "Later."

"Soon," Sheridan couldn't help but correct.

"Soon," Parker agreed with a small tip of her head. "So"—she offered Sheridan her arm—"where to, Agent Sloan?"

"How about my place for now since it's closer, and then we'll stay at yours tonight?" Sheridan asked as she slipped her hand into the crook of Parker's arm.

Parker placed her free hand on Sheridan's on her arm and gave it a small squeeze. "I like how you think, Sloan."

forty-three

Seven years later…

"Hey," Parker greeted her brother as she opened the front door and waved him inside. "No backup this time?" she couldn't resist teasing. For the first few years of the boys' life, he'd always bring someone with him to help manage the chaos whenever they asked him to babysit. Which, granted, she couldn't blame him for because wrangling two incredibly active toddlers had been *exhausting*.

Oliver chuckled as he shrugged off his coat and hung it on an open hook on the rack in the foyer. "Funny, Park." He rolled his eyes and added, "Besides, Jess' mom decided to stay until Monday so Kelly got them tickets to the theatre or something so *they* can take advantage of having a built-in babysitter for another weekend, Rachel's way too pregnant for me to even think of calling them, and Gregory is still out of town at his conference, so…"

Parker laughed and nudged him with her elbow as they started down the hall toward the family room. "Well, the boys are very excited about getting to spend some time with you."

"And I bet you and Sheridan are excited for a night out," he teased.

"Oh, we absolutely are." Parker smiled. It was their sixth wedding anniversary, and she was very much looking forward to spending some quality time with her wife. "I mean, don't get me wrong, we love these little monsters…" Her voice trailed off as she pulled up short in the doorway of the family room to take in the destruction that had occurred in the two minutes it'd taken her to answer the door. The tower of LEGOs that the boys had been working on had been demolished, littering the rug and hardwood floor with little multi-colored pieces of plastic—and she wondered, not for the first time, how the pieces managed to go fucking *everywhere* when the table had a lip around the edges that was supposed to keep the things confined—and her four-year-old twins were now doing their best Spiderman impression on the built-in bookshelves that surrounded the television. "Matthew Oliver, Gregory Brett, get your butts down from there right this minute!"

"You got middle-named," Oliver laughed as the boys dropped to the floor.

"Not helping, Olls," Parker grumbled.

"Uncle Ollie!" the boys chorused as they scampered toward their uncle, dark hair flopping into their eyes, seemingly unaffected by the tiny pieces of plastic death that had to have dug into their bare feet as they ran over them.

"Hold on, misters," Parker stepped in front of Oliver before the boys could use his legs as tackling dummies. Which, on any other occasion, she'd be all for, but there was the matter of little toes five shelves up on the bookcases to be addressed. She tugged the legs of her slacks higher to make it easier to move as she knelt in front of the boys, and had to bite her lip to keep from smiling at the adorably apologetic looks they gave her. "Are we supposed to climb the bookcases?"

"No," they mumbled.

"But, Mom—" Matthew started to argue, his brown eyes flashing with defiance—and he looked so very much like Oliver in that moment that Parker couldn't help but shoot a glare at her brother over her shoulder as she lifted a finger to silence her son's protest.

"Don't you 'but Mom' me, buddy," she warned as she turned back at the boys. "You know the rules." She looked at Gregory, whose dark blue eyes were a perfect match to his mother's and were filled with so much remorse that she decided to skip the well-intended lecture she knew she should give them. She shook her head and held out her arms. "Come here," she murmured, smiling as the boys crashed into her. "We'll pretend this time didn't happen," she said as she squeezed them tight, "but if your mother or I ever catch you up there again, you'll lose all climbing club privileges for four weeks. We climb at the gym, not at home. Got it?"

"Got it," the boys echoed, sounding relieved.

"Good." She gave them one last squeeze before she let them go. They swarmed past her to get to Oliver, their earlier excitement back in full force now that they weren't in trouble anymore, and she shook her head as she pushed herself to her feet and smoothed out her slacks.

"Go find your wife," Oliver said as he wrapped an arm around each boy and swung them up over his shoulders, where they writhed and kicked and squealed with laughter. "I'll keep these guys occupied down here so you're not interrupted."

"Please don't break my house or my children," she warned with a smile as she slipped past him.

"Hey! It was just that one time!"

"With the ridiculously expensive crystal chandelier Phyllis gave us," Parker pointed out.

"In my defense, I had no idea Matty could hit the Wiffle Ball that hard," Oliver argued.

Parker shook her head. "Don't break my house or my children," she repeated, wagging a warning finger at him for good measure.

"Okay!" Oliver sighed and shot the twins a mischievous grin. "Your mom is tough, guys."

"Mommy's tougher," Matthew informed him seriously.

Parker laughed. He wasn't wrong. Out of the two of them, Sheridan was definitely the one not to trifle with. "Speaking of

Mommy, I'm going to go see what's taking her so long," she announced to the group. "Everybody, be good."

"Yes, Mom," Oliver intoned with a long-suffering sigh that made the boys giggle.

She shook her head and, as she pushed past him, muttered, "Please remember which one of you is the adult."

"That'd be Greggy, right?" Oliver quipped as Matthew nodded seriously beside him.

"Right," she muttered. The older the boys got, the more Matty started to take after his uncle. She was going to have to keep a close eye on him when he became a teenager to make sure he didn't adopt any of the less-than-legal inclinations Oliver had given up for good after the Marquis job. "Greg, you're in charge," she called over her shoulder as she made her way down the hall toward the stairs, smiling at the sound of the boys' laughter behind her.

As she often did, she looked at the framed family photographs staggered along the stair wall as she climbed toward their third-floor master suite, loving the reminders of her happiest memories from the last seven years. The picture of their first kiss after they'd been pronounced partners for life that perfectly captured the moment—Gregory standing in front of them with his hands clasped at his waist as he watched them kiss, Sheridan's tears of joy and her own beaming smile as she kissed her wife for the first time and Oliver and Kelly cheered. The candid of them that the captain of the *Veritas* had taken of them cuddling on the trampoline of the private catamaran they'd chartered for their honeymoon. Her carrying Sheridan bridal style over the threshold of the townhouse on the day they'd moved in, eager to begin their family that'd become a reality nine months later. The boys on the day they were born. Oliver sitting on the couch in the living room on the day they'd brought them home with a boy cradled in each arm, smiling down at them like he'd finally, finally discovered his place in the world.

The last seven years had been as close to perfect as it was possible for life to be, and on this very special day, where they celebrated their marriage and the life they'd created together, she couldn't help but marvel at just how blessed she was.

"It's just me," she announced, not wanting to startle Sheridan as she eased the door to their bedroom open. Her mouth fell open as she spied Sheridan standing in front of the full-length standing mirror across the room putting her jewelry on, looking utterly breathtaking with her hair pulled up in a loose twist and a smooth line of skin visible from the nape of her neck to the dimples at the base of her spine that was interrupted only by the strap of her bra and the thinnest hint of satin beneath them thanks to the zipper that ran the entire length of her midnight blue dress.

Sheridan smiled at her in the mirror, clearly pleased by her reaction, and she shook her head as she took a deep breath and stepped fully into the room.

"My god, you're beautiful," she breathed as she closed the door after herself.

"Thank you," Sheridan murmured.

"Seriously, babe. Thank you." Parker made her way across the room slowly, her pace slow enough to allow herself the space of these heartbeats to burn the image of Sheridan in that moment into her memory forever. "This dress is incredible," she murmured as she stood behind her and, heart fluttering in her throat, wrapped her arms around her waist and pressed a light kiss to the sensitive hollow beneath her ear.

"I'm glad you like it." Sheridan relaxed into the embrace with a happy sigh. "I take it Ollie's downstairs with the boys?"

"Mmm," Parker hummed as she dragged her lips over the hinge of Sheridan's jaw. "He is."

"If you keep doing that," Sheridan warned as Parker nipped at her earlobe, "we're never going to make our reservation."

Parker chuckled as she brushed a kiss over her ear. "Do you want me to stop?" she asked, letting her breath fall in hot, teasing waves over Sheridan's ear.

"God, I don't even know," Sheridan whispered with a little groan.

And, oh, even after all these years, that edge of surrender in Sheridan's voice still made her knees weak, and Parker's eyes fluttered shut as an oh-so-pleasant shiver tumbled down her spine. She sighed as she pressed her lips to the curve where Sheridan's neck and shoulder met, and breathed in deep the intoxicating scent of Sheridan's perfume.

How in the world did she ever get so lucky?

"I love you," Parker swore, her voice trembling as she dragged her nose along the line of Sheridan's throat. She smiled when Sheridan's head turned and soft lips captured her own, and whimpered softly when Sheridan spun in her embrace. "You are so beautiful," she whispered against Sheridan's lips as she smoothed her hands up and down her sides, letting her fingertips dip beyond the flaps of Sheridan's open dress to trace reverent lines along the length of her back.

"Less talking, more touching," Sheridan murmured against her lips when her fingers met at the tight V where the zipper held the two halves of her dress together. She smiled as she said it, and Parker groaned as she grabbed two handfuls of Sheridan's ass and lifted her up onto her toes.

"I can do that," Parker promised as she wasted no time peeling the dress from Sheridan's shoulders and letting it fall to the floor. Her throat went dry at the sight of sheer lingerie and thigh-highs, and she swore softly at the knowledge that, when this far-too-brief tryst was over, she'd have to spend the remainder of the night knowing exactly what was waiting for her beneath Sheridan's dress.

They were turned so they were half-facing the mirror Sheridan had been looking into when she'd walked into the room, and she stole a glance at their reflection as she pressed a kiss to the line of Sheridan's collarbone. Dark blue eyes met hers in the mirror, and she smiled as she kissed the swell of Sheridan's right breast.

"Parker…"

The combination of Sheridan's hand around the back of her neck and the throaty timbre of her voice made Parker's pulse race, and she held Sheridan's gaze in the mirror as she moved lower, taking sheer fabric and a half-erect nipple between her lips and teasing it with her tongue until it swelled to a tight point. Passion swirled in Sheridan's eyes as she began to sink slowly to her knees, pressing a line of kisses along the length of her abdomen.

"Okay?" she breathed as she settled onto her knees in front of her, fingertips hooked lightly in the thin band of fabric that held her panties in place.

Sheridan smiled and nodded, and Parker laid a wet kiss to the point of her hip as she eased the fabric down her legs, sinking down to her heels so she could help her step out of them. Parker dragged the flats of her hands up the backs of Sheridan's legs as she pushed back up to her knees, and she sighed at the feeling of Sheridan's fingers combing through her hair as she guided her legs open wider.

"God, baby, please…" Sheridan moaned as Parker nuzzled the scar that cut a faint line low on her belly, just above soft curls.

Parker palmed Sheridan's ass as she and shifted just enough to be able to dip her tongue between her legs, and she groaned at the taste of the slick warmth that waited for her. They didn't have time to linger, not if they were to avoid a year's worth of teasing from Oliver and still make their dinner reservation. Later, when the moon hung high in the sky and they were alone, she would take her time and worship Sheridan until she was literally begging for release, but for now they needed to be quick, and she caressed Sheridan's ass as she sucked her clit between her lips.

"So good," Sheridan whimpered.

"Yes, you are," Parker took the time to whisper before she returned to her task, dipping her chin between Sheridan's leg and teasing her toward the edge of ecstasy with light flicks of her tongue, heavy licks, and long, slow sucks. She'd only been at it for less than five minutes when the hand in her hair tightened and Sheridan's hips ground desperately against her mouth, and she hummed around Sheridan's clit encouragingly.

"Oh, fuck," Sheridan groaned.

"That's it, baby," Parker murmured as she redoubled her efforts, and she smiled against slick, soft folds as Sheridan tensed above her, the hand in her hair gripping with a positively delicious amount of force for the space of two heartbeats before relaxing with the first wave of Sheridan's release.

A gentle hand around the hinge of her jaw coaxed her to her feet when Sheridan's climax eased to a series of gentle aftershocks, and she smiled as she wrapped her arms around smooth, smooth hips, caressing soft skin as she claimed her lips in a deep, lingering kiss.

"My god, Parker," Sheridan breathed when the kiss reached its inevitable end.

Parker captured her lips again, pouring all the love she felt for her into the kiss. "I love you."

"I love you."

A loud crash downstairs made them freeze, and Parker groaned as she turned to look at their closed bedroom door. "What do you think that was?"

Sheridan laughed and shook her head. "With those three, who knows." She sighed as she knelt down to pick up her underwear. "But we should probably go check it out," she said as she pulled her panties back into place.

"Whatever it was, we can replace it," Parker argued, only half-jokingly as she pulled Sheridan back into her arms. "Or, Ollie can. His firm is making him more money than he knows what to do with, so he can afford it." She smiled as gentle hands framed her face and pulled her into a kiss that was slow and sweet and had her all but swooning by the time it ended.

"But then we might lose our babysitter," Sheridan pointed out. She laughed at the way Parker pouted in response, and shook her head. "Help me into my dress?"

"I'm much better at helping you out of it, but fine," Parker grumbled playfully as she scooped up Sheridan's dress and it unfurled it between them with a snap to try to erase any wrinkles that had settled in the fabric while it'd been puddled on the floor. "Your dress, my love," she murmured as she held it out for Sheridan to step into. She shook her head as she pulled it up to Sheridan's shoulders, and sighed as she motioned for her to turn around. "Does this zipper come completely undone, or is it partly for show?" she asked, catching Sheridan's eye in the mirror and winking at her.

"It can be completely unzipped," Sheridan shared with a smile. She laughed with Parker's hands froze just below the line of her bra, and shook her head. "Not now, sweetie. We have god knows what kind of disaster waiting for us downstairs, and a reservation at a restaurant *without* crayons on the table or cups with lids to get to."

"Later?" Parker asked playfully as she finished zipping the dress and smoothed her hands along Sheridan's sides to grab her hips.

"God, yes," Sheridan murmured, her eyes dark and stormy as she turned and captured Parker's lips in a deep, probing kiss. "Now, come on." She dragged her thumb over Parker's lips before she pulled away and grabbed her heels from the bed where she'd left them. "Let's go check on the boys so we can get out of here."

Parker fixed her hair in the mirror as Sheridan slipped on her heels, and she sighed as she held out her hand for Sheridan to take. Her heart fluttered into her throat at the feeling of Sheridan's fingers slipping between her own, and she took a deep breath as she pulled their bedroom door open.

Downstairs, Oliver and the boys were engaged in an epic lightsaber battle, complete with a coffee table tipped onto its side as a shield, LEGO landmines embedded in the carpet, and an armchair that was flipped onto its back—which was probably the source of the crash from earlier. Oliver was standing in the middle of the room as the twins flanked him, lightsabers at the ready, eyes sparkling with laughter and grins on their faces, and Parker shook her head as she took it all in.

It was pure insanity come to life, and yet, it was absolutely perfect at the same time.

Sheridan must have thought so too, because Parker felt the hold on her hand tighten as Sheridan's shoulders shook with quiet laughter beside her, and she called out, "Boys!" When they all froze and looked at her, she added in a more normal tone, "Oliver I expect this room to be spotless when we come home. Boys, you need to help. Money for pizza is in the kitchen, and because I know there's no way you'll be done with your shenanigans by their usual bedtime"—she arched a brow at Oliver and shook her head when he just blinked innocently at her in response—"they are to be in bed by nine o'clock at the latest."

"Got it," Oliver assured her with a roguish grin and a salute. "We can do that, right guys?"

The twins nodded.

"Come give us a hug and a kiss," Parker said, holding her arms out. The boys hustled to oblige, and her heart filled with so much love she thought it might burst as she and Sheridan hugged their boys together.

"We'll be back after you're in bed," Sheridan told them as she pressed a kiss to each of their cheeks, "so we'll see you in the morning, okay?"

"Okay, Mommy," Greg agreed sweetly.

"Have fun on your date," Matty added.

"We will," Parker promised as she kissed each of their foreheads in turn. "Now, go kick Uncle Ollie's butt," she instructed with a little laugh as she let them go.

"You're as bad as they are," Sheridan chuckled as they watched the boys swarm their uncle.

"We'll be fine," Oliver assured them with a grin as he deftly avoided the twins' attack. "Have fun. Enjoy your night out. Everything here will be spic and span when you get back."

"It better be," Sheridan sassed with a wink.

Parker laughed. "Bye, boys. Love you."

"Love you, too, Mom," they chorused as they danced in circles around Oliver with their lightsabers held in front of themselves, poised to attack.

"Let's get out of here," Sheridan murmured as she tugged Parker toward the front door.

Parker lingered for a moment to enjoy the sight of her three favorite boys playing together and shook her head as she followed Sheridan down the hall.

"They'll be fine," Sheridan assured her as she handed her her coat.

"Oh, I know." Parker smiled as she slipped her arms into the coat and then helped Sheridan into hers. "I just…" She shook her head again and shrugged. "You, them, Ollie…this is better than a dream, and I just can't believe how lucky I am to have you all."

Sheridan's smile softened, and she licked her lips as she leaned in to capture Parker's in a sweet kiss. "I love you. Happy anniversary, sweetheart," she whispered as she pulled away.

"I love you, too." Parker smiled and opened the front door. "Happy anniversary, Sheridan."

MJ Duncan

acknowledgements

As always, my most humble and profound thanks go to all of you, my readers, for continuing to take the time to actually sit down and read something that I wrote. Being able to do what I love every day is truly a gift, and I can't thank you all enough for your support.

I must also thank my lovely, amazing, wonderful readers for all their help during the writing process for this story. Thanks to Jade, for the much-needed chapter-by-chapter feedback that kept my Muse fed and happy and willing to work on this instead of getting distracted with newer, shinier ideas. Thanks also go out to Lou for not only finding time in your ridiculously busy schedule to read this, but also for the blatant honesty that I both love and hate to receive. As always, your observations and suggestions were painfully on-point, and this story— flawed as it might still be—is better because of them. So thank you.

Made in the USA
Middletown, DE
27 July 2020